A Bridge to Elne

Novel of a French Family's Struggle Against the Nazi Occupation

by
L. E. Indianer

Bloomington, IN Milton Keynes, UK

authorHOUSE™

AuthorHouse™
1663 Liberty Drive, Suite 200
Bloomington, IN 47403
www.authorhouse.com
Phone: 1-800-839-8640

AuthorHouse™ UK Ltd.
500 Avebury Boulevard
Central Milton Keynes, MK9 2BE
www.authorhouse.co.uk
Phone: 08001974150

First published by AuthorHouse 4/20/2007

ISBN: 1-4259-2945-1 (sc)
ISBN: 1-4259-2944-3 (dj)

Library of Congress Control Number: 2006903491

Printed in the United States of America
Bloomington, Indiana

This book is printed on acid-free paper.

PROLOGUE

In June 1940, the German war machine invaded France and occupied the northern half of the country, leaving the southern Unoccupied Zone in the hands of their puppet regime, known as the *Vichy* government. Although this is a work of fiction, it is based on historical fact, chronologically correct, and is the story of two actual families living in France during the War.

The author has taken liberties to alter the events and activities of the Courty and Pontier families; however, many of the occurrences are exactly as they happened between 1942 and 1944.

DEDICATION

This novel is dedicated to these families, the French *Résistance* and *Maquis*, as well as to all the French and Europeans who had to endure Nazi occupation, and even greater hardships during World War II.

SOUTHERN FRANCE

Provence

ROCHEMAURE

MONTÉLIMAR

ABBAYE de SÉNANQUE

GORDES

CHÂTEAUNEUF de GADAGNE

AIX-en-PROVENCE

AVIGNON

MORIÈRES

ARLES

MARSEILLE

MÉDITERRANÉE

MAP BY RIV

CARCASSONNE

Roussillon

PERPIGNAN

ELNE

FOIX

PYRENEES MTS.

ANDORRA

SPAIN

1

As the six men walked through the forest, all they could hear was the crushing of leaves under their feet. It was shortly after midnight… they had been walking for more than an hour. Their truck had been left in a friend's garage in a northern suburb of Marseille; if all went well, one of their group would pick it up a few days after their mission.

They had every action of the assignment planned down to the last detail. Realizing that things could always go wrong, they rehearsed over and over again. There were contingencies for almost any problem, and each man knew precisely what he had to do. They functioned like a well-trained commando unit, although only one of them had ever served in the military. Except for the two who were hunters, the others had never previously held a weapon.

Their leader, Dr. Marcel Pontier, was a dentist, whose office was in the center of Marseille. He and his men were bound together by a shared hatred for the *Vichy*, Frenchmen who were Nazi collaborators and now controlled Provence, and the rest of southern France.

All had been recruited by *La Résistance*, of the French underground, to become members of the *Maquis*, a secret civilian army supporting the

Free French. Their small cell had been operating since December 1941. Their backgrounds differed: François was a butcher and Marcel's chief lieutenant, whose truck they had used that night; Lucien was a dock worker; Aristide, a tailor; Leon, a carpenter; and Georges, a civil servant. Georges had been an invaluable source for information, as he worked as a radio operator in the downtown *Vichy* headquarters. Marcel took extra precautions not to blow his cover.

As they walked through the forest, Marcel could see the highway where they would set their ambush. *I hope this is not the night we have to kill someone*, he thought. *I don't know if I have the stomach for it.* He gathered the men around him and went over last-minute instructions. First, they would move some large rocks onto the road, to slow down the one expected truck coming up the hill. He and Aristide would find cover on the opposite side of the road, and François and Georges would do the same on this side.

"Lucien, I want you to go down the highway about 150 meters, behind that clump of trees on the left side," Marcel said, as he pointed down the hill. "Signal us when you see the vehicle approaching, and keep the rear of the truck covered after we've made contact. Remember, we abort the mission if there's more than one vehicle. Understood?"

Everyone nodded and began the tasks at hand. Within short order, enough rocks were in place, Lucien was down the hill, and the men had found safe hiding places. Marcel had calculated that they had another hour to go before the truck arrived, if it arrived at all...one was never sure of the information they received, and on many occasions the time was wasted.

Forty minutes later, Lucien signaled by waving his rifle back and forth. *Twenty minutes early...that's different*, Marcel thought. As the truck passed Lucien's position and approached the rocks, it slowed down, then came to a stop.

It wasn't unusual to have landslides in these hills. As hoped, two men got out of the cab, one with a rifle over his shoulder. They began removing the rocks from the road in front of their headlights.

Marcel's men pulled the wool masks over their faces and approached the vehicle from both sides, behind the lights, rifles pointing at the driver and his assistant. Marcel startled the two men when he yelled, "Get your hands up in the air, and slowly drop that rifle on the ground!"

"What's the meaning of this?" asked the driver. "You're hijacking a truck full of office furniture and supplies? Who are you, anyway?"

"We're with *La Résistance*," answered Marcel, "and if you don't do as I say, we'll be forced to shoot you." The rifle was laid down and the men put their hands up. "You realize that you're aiding the *Vichy*, don't you? That's why you're carrying a rifle, huh?"

"No, *Monsieur*," said the man with the rifle. "I carry this to guard against thieves on the highway. We don't know who ordered these things. Here, look at our manifest." He reached into his coat pocket, pulled out an 8 X 10 piece of paper, and handed it to Marcel.

Marcel took it and then handed it to Aristide. "See what this says."

Aristide looked it over and gave it back to Marcel. "The address is 45 on the Rue Honnorat, and it's going to a *Monsieur* LeBlanc. Ring any bells?"

"Hmm, 45 on the Rue," Marcel mumbled. "Oh yes, I know exactly where it's going. The *Vichy* has its accounting and auditing offices in that building…on the ground floor, I believe. I'm not sure what's on the floors above that."

François moved forward, pointing his rifle at the two men. "We ought to shoot them as traitors, for doing business with the enemy."

"Gentlemen, please," the driver said, pleading. "I can assure you, we are not traitors. We hate the Germans and *Vichy* as much as you do. We work for a trucking company in Lyon, just delivering furniture. That's how we make our living."

"What time were you supposed to be in Marseille to deliver this cargo?" Marcel asked.

"At 8:00 in the morning. We were told that's when the office opens."

"Consider yourselves lucky that I'm in a charitable mood," Marcel said, as he signaled Lucien forward to check the back of the truck. "We're going to make that delivery for you. Just forget about your truck."

Lucien jumped off the back of the truck, after checking the interior. "Everything looks O.K. inside," he said. "What are we going to do with these two?"

The driver spread out his arms. "Please, *Monsieur*, I plead with you. Don't harm us. We're both married with children, and must get back to Lyon with our truck."

"I don't give a shit about your truck," Marcel said angrily. "We're not gonna shoot you, unless you do something stupid. Don't worry about your boss…if he's any kind of Frenchman he'll know that he sacrificed his goddamn truck, and what's in it, for *Le Combat*, the struggle." He cocked his head and pointed toward Lucien. "This man is gonna keep you here for the next few hours, and then let you go. If you start walking north toward the next village, I'm sure you'll be able to hitch a ride in the morning back to Lyon."

Lucien motioned the two men to start moving down the hill, and into the woods. The driver looked over his shoulder, and with his right hand saluted Marcel, *"Merci, Monsieur, merci."* Marcel tipped his hat, in response.

Without prompting, the assemblage got into the truck. Marcel drove with François in the front cab. Aristide, Leon, and Georges rode in back with the office furniture. It would take them 25 minutes to get to the Rue Honnorat, just enough time to rig the back with explosives.

They came through Marseille on the Cours Belsunce, past the Place Victor Hugo. Marcel took this route to avoid being seen near any of the main *Vichy* headquarters, which were farther south near the Vieux Port, the harbor of the city. When he reached the Rue Honnorat, he turned left until he found number 45.

François jumped out of the cab and directed Marcel over the curb, and as close to the building as possible. A few moments later, the three men in the back leaped out. Leon held up the fingers of his hand to indicate that the fuse had been set for five minutes. Without any words being spoken, the five men set out quickly in different directions. François, who had a car parked on the next street, took all the guns with him. He wrapped them in a large blanket, and would later hide them in a secret panel behind the racks of meat in his butcher shop.

As planned, Marcel headed for his office on the Boulevard Charles Nedelec, which was four, short blocks away. He had told his wife, Angelina, that he had a meeting out of town and would not be home that evening. Just as he reached his building, a large explosion rocked the city. He hurried up the stairs to his office on the second floor, and with his hands shaking, unlocked the door. He flopped down on the reception room sofa and realized that he was sweating profusely, even though it was just the end of April. As he closed his eyes, he heard the ear-piercing sirens. *The mission has been a complete success…everything has gone according to plan. Now if I can just stop shaking, maybe I can get some rest.*

2

The sun coming through the drapes awoke Marcel from a deep sleep. He knew that he had to get up before his secretary and dental assistant arrived. He always kept a change of clothes in his office for such occasions. After shaving and washing up as best he could, he put on the fresh clothes. He looked at himself in the mirror. He didn't appear to be too disheveled. He was a good looking man for 38, with dark hair and dark eyes. His medium height and build suited him.

At precisely 8:30, his staff arrived and prepared the office for their first patient. He could overhear the girls talking about the bombing and all the police on the streets asking questions. The smell from the fire still lingered in the air. Marcel came out of his private office and joined in the discussion.

"*Bonjour*," he greeted them with a big smile.

"*Bonjour*, doctor," they both replied. "What do you think about the explosion last night?" one of them asked.

He shrugged his shoulders, "I wish I could say. Do either of you know what actually happened? The whole area around Honnorat was blocked off this morning."

"I asked one of the *Vichy* police officers about it," Annette, his assistant, replied, "and he said that some terrorists had bombed one of the government offices in the middle of the night."

"Ah," Marcel laughed. "Now they're calling *La Résistance* terrorists, are they? Serves them right for siding with the Nazis."

"Some of the buildings around there were slightly damaged also," Margo, his receptionist, chirped in, "but the government building was totally demolished. I don't know if anyone was hurt or not, but I doubt if anyone was living there."

The bell in the reception room went off, and they began with their first patient. Since he had had only a few hours of sleep, Marcel tried to control his yawning throughout the day. It wasn't easy. Fortunately, his last patient at 4:00 called and canceled her appointment.

Marcel was free to leave. He gathered up his clothes from last night's foray, put them in a small satchel, walked out the back stairs to the basement where his car was parked, and drove home.

Five-year-old Babette was helping her mother fold clothes. She was a very prissy little girl, with long dark hair, who loved to constantly play house with her dolls. Angelina, eight months pregnant, was more than glad to have her help. With three active children, and one on the way, there was a lot to do around the house. It seemed to be never ending, but she enjoyed her family more than anything else, and was the happiest when they were all together. The thing that scared her was the war raging through Europe, and all the uncertainties their future held.

Angelina had long ago given up her job as a pharmacist. She and Marcel had met while they were attending the University. He was immediately attracted to this dark-complexioned, five foot six-inch beauty who lived in the Roussillon-Catalonia region of France, near the border of Spain. She had an infectious smile that lit up a room. It took her awhile to feel the same way about Marcel, because she found him to be too unpredictable, very opinionated, and sometimes very distant in his thoughts. He pursued her for three years, until she finally consented to marry him after he finished dental school. Now, she couldn't think about living without him.

They had gotten married in 1931, and the following year their first son Raymond was born. This was followed by Jean-Pierre, J.P., the next year. Marcel's dental practice flourished, and five years after he opened they were able to buy this beautiful house on the Rue Paradis. There was a park across the street where the children could run and play, and it was ideal for strolling a newborn.

Life had been good for the Pontier family, until Hitler and Mussolini began rattling their sabers. When Germany invaded Poland on September 1, 1939, they knew that it was just a matter of time before France was involved. Nine months later, the Nazis had taken over the northern half of France, leaving the southern half of the country to be run by their puppet regime, the *Vichy*, who were in many ways worse than their masters.

Marcel was vehement when he spoke about these French traitors. His family, including the two older boys, as well as many of Marcel and Angelina's close friends, grew to hate them almost as much as he did. Of course, they didn't discuss these matters around Babette for fear of scaring her, plus the fact that she probably wouldn't have understood anyway.

One thing Marcel vowed never to do was to let anyone know, especially his family, that he had first become involved in the Underground Press and was now a member of *La Résistance* and the *Maquis*. This could put them in extreme danger, plus compromise the work of the movement. Everyone recruited by the *Maquis* was screened thoroughly and took an oath of silence, as Marcel had done. They reverted to practiced hand signals when on a mission, speaking as little as possible and never using anyone's name. Within their six-man cell, only Marcel and François were allowed to make contact with the other four men. Last names of their compatriots were never discussed. The same held true with the men and women who ranked above Marcel, whom he alone met on occasion to receive orders. He didn't know their real names, and was contacted in a variety of different ways to prevent enemy intelligence from determining a pattern.

Nothing is flawless in life, and on occasion there would be a foul-up somewhere in the organization. Innocent people would die. Members in *La Résistance* would be caught, tortured, sent to Nazi labor camps, or executed, or simply be killed in the line of duty. The men and women involved with the underground movement felt that the risks were worth the gains. Disrupting and sabotaging the enemy's ability to communicate, govern, and control the populace, was a contribution that made them all proud to be Frenchmen. They would do what they had to, to make life miserable for the *Vichy* here in the south and the Nazis in the north. Their main fear was that their families could be punished for their acts against the existing regime, even though they knew nothing about what was going on. This is why they were so cautious and so protective.

Marcel pulled the car into his garage, got out with his dirty laundry and put it in the wash basin. He entered the house through the kitchen and found Angelina and Babette in the dining room. There were clothes all over the table. Babette ran to him and he picked her up and held her tight. "How's my little princess, today?"

"Fine, Papa. I'm helping *Maman* get everything nice and clean."

"I can see that. You're doing a very nice job." He walked over to Angelina, bent down and gave her a big kiss. "Hello, darling. How are you feeling?"

"Alright, for a fat lady." She got up and hugged him. "How was your meeting last night? You're home early."

"The meeting went well. Not very exciting, though." *If she only knew*, he thought. "My last patient canceled, so I came home early to help you with dinner."

"*You're* going to help me with dinner!?" she exclaimed. "That's something you haven't done for a long time. I could use the help, though…I'm feeling a little achy today."

"Wasn't I a big help, *Maman*?" Babette asked.

"You were my biggest helper today, Babette." She kissed her on the back of her head, and rubbed her back. "I don't know what I would have done without you."

Marcel set Babette down, and then put his arm around his wife. They walked to the kitchen together and just held each other for a few moments. "So what do you want me to make tonight?" he asked.

She looked in the icebox and shook her head. "Food is really getting scarce around town, Marcel. It's almost impossible to get meat anymore."

He thought of François, and said, "Darling, things are not going to get any better for quite a while, so we all have to accept this and make some sacrifices. I do have a patient of mine, who is a butcher on the other side of town. I'll call him and see what I can do, O.K.?"

"Oh, I don't know, Marcel. I've been using *Monsieur* Shapiro ever since we got married, and he does need the business. A lot of people have stopped going there since the *Vichy* goon squads began harassing him, with all those anti-Semitic signs they've painted on his window."

She sadly moved her head from side to side, "And whenever he can, he puts away a little extra for us, although it's not nearly enough."

"Alright, why don't you keep going to Max and just let me know what extras you need. I'll see if I can get what you want. Alright?"

Angelina nodded and pulled out some chicken from the icebox. "*Monsieur* Shapiro saved this for me this morning. He's such a nice man...it's a shame they're picking on him just because he's Jewish!"

"Things will probably get worse...there's some strange and terrible stories I've been hearing." He led her over to the kitchen table. "*Cherie*, why don't you sit and let me prepare this?" She pulled out a chair and sat down. Marcel put the chicken on a wooden board, and began cutting it up into sections. He rinsed all the pieces off, put them in a baking dish with a little water, and then added some salt and other spices. He cut up some carrots and potatoes, laid them inside the dish, put on the lid, and stuck it into the oven to simmer at a low temperature. He wanted to eat early, because he could barely keep his eyes open.

He came around the table and began rubbing her shoulders and neck. "Ooh, that feels so good...don't stop."

"Good enough to come back to the bedroom with me?" he joked.

"Don't you ever think about anything else? Look what you've done to me...I'm as big as a cow. This is it, Marcel...no more children!" He bent down and kissed the back of her neck. She sighed, "Ooh, that does feel good, though. Maybe later..."

Just then the door opened in the front of the house. J.P. and Raymond came running in. "*Maman, Maman*, where are you?" Raymond shouted. "J.P. got into another fight!" Babette pointed toward the kitchen. The boys ran there and were surprised to see their father, also.

There was blood on J.P.'s shirt, from his nose bleeding, and a large bruise on his cheek. Angelina stood up and shook her head, "Are you hurt badly? You've got to stop fighting all the time, do you hear me?"

"I'm alright, *Maman*."

"Let me take a look at him," Marcel said, coming around the table. He turned J.P.'s head from side to side, and felt his nose. "No broken bones...he's O.K." He rubbed the hair on J.P.'s head. "So, what were you fighting about?"

"You know Claude DuPay...that bully kid in the sixth grade I told you about?" J.P. said excitedly. Marcel nodded. "Well, he was mouthing off on how great Hitler was, and started calling some of my Jewish friends these terrible names.

Then he started pushing Estephan Libo...Jesus, that was a mistake!"

"Watch your mouth, Jean-Pierre," Angelina scolded.

"Sorry, *Maman*, but you should 'of seen how hard Estephan hit him. It knocked him down and then he jumped on top of him, hitting him some more."

"That's when one of Claude's friends jumped on top of Estephan," piped in Raymond, "and started hitting him from the back. And J.P. pulled......"

"Yeah, I pulled them off and one of them turned around and hit me in the face. That's when I beat the crap out of him...the little Nazi bastard!"

"Jean-Pierre!" Angelina shouted, as Marcel and Raymond chuckled. "Didn't I just tell you to watch your language? I'm going to have to wash your mouth out with soap."

J.P., knowing how to sweet-talk his mother, came over and hugged her. He had her good looks, plus the strong features of his father, and with his curly, dark hair and athletic build, already had the girls eyeing him. Although only eight and a half years old, he was taller than ten year old Raymond, who was much lighter complexioned, smaller in build, and couldn't care less about sports. Raymond spent most of his time reading, listening to music, or playing chess.

With his big brown eyes, J.P. looked up at his mother and sighed, "But *Maman*, I don't know what else to call these guys, and you always told me to describe everything the best I could."

"You still don't need to use naughty words. You speak to him, Marcel."

"Your mother is right, J.P.," Marcel said, as he winked at him. "So, what else was said, boys?"

"They said that the Jews caused the bombing this morning and were going to pay for it," Raymond said. "Is that true, Papa?"

"No, I'm sure it's not true, Raymond. These boys don't know what they're talking about, and are nothing more than what J.P. called them," Marcel replied. "If *Maman* wasn't here now, I'd have a few more choice words about these people."

"Tell us what you'd call 'em, Papa," J.P. laughed.

Angelina held her lips tight and shook her head. "O.K. boys, that's enough! Go upstairs and clean up for dinner. Your father is very tired and we're going to eat earlier." They gathered up their books and walked back toward the dining room. "Tell your sister to get ready, too."

After she heard the children running up the stairs to their rooms, Angelina sat down, while Marcel got the kitchen table ready for dinner. "Who do you think was responsible for blowing up that building, Marcel?"

He took his time putting the dishes and silverware around the table, and then casually answered, "Probably *La Résistance*, I would imagine."

"But they never did anything this big before, have they? And why that place on the Rue Honnorat?"

"I'm not sure why, but it might be an office that the *Vichy* are using," he said nonchalantly. "The girls in the office said that the blast was really huge. I suppose that these kinds of things will start escalating as the war goes on…especially now that the Americans are involved."

"Do you think that we're in any danger of being bombed by the Allies, here in Marseille?"

"No, of course not. The Allies are only bombing targets controlled by the Germans, not the *Vichy*. And as long as they stay in northern France, we should be fine." He opened the door of the pantry and brought out a bottle of table wine. He found the wine opener and uncorked the bottle. "I don't want you worrying about this, all right? You need to take care of yourself and the new baby."

"Well, I do worry, *Cherie*. *Monsieur* Shapiro told me that he's heard from his relatives in other parts of France. They said that the *Vichy* have begun rationing food and sending as much as they can north to the Germans. I'd hate to think that our kids wouldn't have enough to eat."

"Every time I hear what these traitors are doing, I want to scream!" he almost shouted. "If things get too bad, we may have to consider something I've been thinking about for the last six months."

"For the last six months? What is it you haven't told me…what do we have to consider?"

"Well," he paused, "it's just what you're saying…about the food… about the dangers." He came over, sat down next to her, and held her hands. *I hate this fucking war, but I've got to be strong for them.* "Listen, darling, I want what's best for you and the children. If things get worse, well, maybe after the baby comes, we should think about you and the kids moving to Elne, and living with your parents and Paulette until the war is over."

"But…"

"It will be much safer on the farm, and everyone will have plenty to eat. Besides, who knows what can happen in a major city like Marseille, especially if the Germans decide to come down here. There won't be any chance of that in Elne, and you know that your family would love to have you."

"Yes, I know, but I wouldn't want to go without you. What would you do? When would we see you?"

"I would see you on weekends, or whenever I could. I can take care of myself and would be a lot less worried if you were there. Remember, I have to stay here and make a living for us. There would be nothing for me in that small village. You'd have to go without me."

She didn't speak, and he could tell that she was saddened by this thought. He leaned over and took her in his arms. "Dear," he whispered in her ear, "let's not get upset about something that may never happen." She nodded into his shoulder. "We'll just take it one day at a time and see how things go."

They heard the three children coming down the stairs. Marcel got up to check the food in the oven. Babette skipped into the kitchen and sat down next to her mother, followed by the boys pushing and shoving each other, before they too sat down. Raymond said the prayer before dinner, and the family enjoyed their evening meal together, all of them a little more quiet than usual.

3

For the next week, sirens could be heard throughout the days and into the nights, as the *Vichy* police scoured the city in search of the "terrorists" who destroyed the building. This was the largest act of defiance that *La Résistance* in Provence had mustered. Many men and women were brought into headquarters for questioning, some even tortured, but as yet none of the local *Maquis* were among them.

Marcel called a meeting of his group four days after the bombing. They met in the woods, north of the city, so that each person could get there by a different route. He especially wanted to reinforce the tight-lipped policy that they were taught. Any slip of the tongue could mean certain imprisonment, if not worse, and possibly bring them all down.

Suggesting that their clandestine activities be put on hold, at least until the current crises passed, Marcel informed them that a much bigger target was in store in the near future. For security reasons, he wouldn't relate the information he had received from his *Maquis* contact until the proper time, which they knew was standard procedure. When the group dispersed and headed out of the woods, he held Georges back and they walked even further north, not saying anything until Marcel was sure that everyone was out of sight.

"Georges, have you been able to detect any changes in the Nazi communications with your headquarters?" Marcel asked. "Anything that might be of interest…something to be passed on?"

He thought for a moment before answering. "The volumes of calls have definitely increased, considerably. But the only thing I've picked up on the radio, is that the fuckin' Nazis are pissed over the bombing. They're pushing their goons to find the culprits." He paused, and then continued, "Everyone has been running around the place in a panic when these calls come in from Germany and Paris. I'll tell you, Number One," as he always referred to Marcel, "it's beautiful, really beautiful!"

"Well, we're definitely making an impact, but this is only the beginning for those bastards." They walked a little further, and seeming not to be that interested, Marcel offhandedly asked, "How do all these calls get to you, here in Marseille? Are there some relay stations nearby?"

"There are two that I know of," he replied. "The one that controls the calls coming from Paris, is somewhere between Aix and Avignon." He shook his head, put his hand up to his mouth, and looked down at the ground. "I'm not quite sure about the relay station for the calls coming from Germany; although, whenever there's a breakdown with the lines, I've heard some people in the office mentioning the little town of Riez, northeast of here. That may be it…I'm not quite sure."

"Hmm, well keep your eyes and ears open for any more details on these two places, but," he pointed his finger at Georges, "don't go out of your way, or seem too obvious in asking any questions about them. We can't risk that…understood?"

"Understood, Number One. I *do* know that both are supposedly very well guarded, especially the one between Avignon and Aix."

"Good, I'll keep that in mind."

They walked over a small hill, Marcel shook Georges hand and they parted, one going east and the other west. Marcel had the information he wanted, something he could pass on to the people above.

Marcel met someone he knew as Florette, his *Maquis* contact, three days later in his office, on the Boulevard Charles Nedelec. She came in at 4:30, under the pretense of being a new patient. He did a cursory exam, and since it was so near to closing time, he told Annette and Margo that they could leave for the day, while he finished up.

"This was very bold of you," he said, "to want to meet in my office."

"I thought it would be a good idea to establish you as my dentist," Florette, a tall, stocky woman in her thirties, and wearing her wispy hair in a bun, declared. She wasn't that attractive, but she had a certain presence about her that put people at ease, and at the same time demanded respect. "That way, I have an excuse to come here for dental appointments without arousing any suspicion. Is there any chance of a problem with the office girls?"

"No. None whatsoever. They don't suspect a thing, and besides that, they hate the *Vichy*."

"We can't be too careful, Marcel, because things are getting tight. Since the bombing last week…which you did a brilliant job on, by the way…the bastards have spies all over the region trying to bring the net over us."

"Yes, so I've heard. But, I'm beginning to see that we have a big advantage over them, and one that we should keep exploiting."

"Oh? What's that?"

"Well, we know the targets we want to hit, and the times we want to hit them. So, they have to keep guessing, keep wondering what'll be next. This puts the pressure more on them than us."

"Good point. And by mixing up our targets, there won't be a pattern they can lock on to." She smiled, "I'll tell you, Marcel, you've got a good mind for this sort of thing, and it's not going unnoticed by the leaders of the *Maquis*."

"I'm not looking to win any medals, Florette, only to get my country back." He gritted his teeth, shook his head, and slowly said, "I've hated the Germans ever since I can remember, and I'll do whatever it takes to get rid of them, and their *Vichy* puppets."

"But like I said before, be careful and don't take any unnecessary risks. We have to keep this thing coordinated and work through a chain of command."

"Believe me, Florette, I concur 100%. Although, sometimes I can't help but verbally vent my anger. I know that we can't just blow them up with one big bomb. It takes time…it takes planning."

"No one in the organization is doing a better job than you, Marcel, and we're relying on you for input and leadership." She got up from where she was sitting, and looked out the window. Without turning around, she asked, "So, have you gotten any information from that operative of yours, that works at *Vichy* Headquarters?"

Marcel knew that the small talk was over and she was now down to business. He related what Georges had divulged to him and what he had asked Georges to find out in a discreet way.

"Good," she said simply. "But I don't think we can risk his asking any questions, regardless of how discreet he is. He's too valuable, so pull him off…we'll get our intelligence people to look into the locations."

"Fine. I'll contact him as soon as possible."

She turned around and extended her hand to Marcel. "I'll make another appointment here, as soon as I get the necessary information. In the meantime, just lay low for awhile. This next mission may turn out to be the biggest blow that we can deliver to these pigs, and it's going to take some extensive planning."

They shook hands and she headed for the door. "By the way," she asked, "exactly what should I tell your receptionist is wrong with my teeth, when I call for the appointment?"

Marcel laughed, "I'll tell Margo, in the morning, that you're going to need some extensive dental work, and you'll be calling back within the next month." He opened the door for her, adding, "I'll be looking forward to your visit. Sounds like a mission of top priority."

"All the way from the top."

"DeGaule?"

"DeGaule." She walked out the door. *"Au revoir."*

"Au revoir," he said, feeling elated at the prospects ahead.

4

The winter of 1942 had been brutally cold in Poland. Now that spring was here, Johann assumed the temperatures would have risen considerably, instead of the few degrees they actually did. He had spent the last six months rebuilding the bridges and rail lines that had been destroyed by the *Luftwaffe* when Germany had invaded Poland in September 1939, and again by the Russian bombs after Germany invaded that country in June 1941.

Troop movements along these routes to Russia were enormous. Pressure was put on Johann, and his staff of fifty enlisted men, to complete as much as they could. They were given hundreds of Polish and Jewish prisoners to do the back-breaking work. Many of these men died of exposure and starvation, but there were always hundreds more to take their place. Johann couldn't stomach the inhumane treatment of these people, but as a German engineering officer he couldn't question his orders. He immersed himself in his work day and night, closing his eyes to what was actually happening.

On the day he had graduated from the Berlin College of Architecture in 1936, Johann I. Weller was drafted into the German army, sent to

Officer's Training School, and then commissioned as a *leutnant* in the *Wehrmacht*. Even though this was not the job he was trained for, he accepted the fact that this was wartime and he had to do his part. Designing beautiful buildings could wait until the war ended, although he didn't have a good feeling about the outcome, now that the Americans were involved. Rumors of the death camps being built here in Poland were appalling to him. Thankfully he had no part in their construction, especially if the stories were true. He was not a Nazi. He detested their whole ideology and thought the *Füehrer* a maniac, but he was smart enough to keep his thoughts to himself. Not that he was a coward…it was a matter of survival.

Johann grew up in a very cultural environment, in a small city north of Munich called Schwanndorf. His parents were both professional musicians, liberal, and worldly. His childhood was filled with art, music, and literature. Friends of the family, coming through their home, were of the intellectual community and many of them were Jews. He feared now for the safety of his parents and their friends, because Nazi Germany didn't tolerate any free thinking, and hatred for Jews was widespread.

Since the war began, he was exposed to an entirely different side of life, and this year had been the hardest of all his thirty-three years. He was tall, slender, with sandy hair…an almost statuesque poster-boy for the German army. Before starting his graduate work in Berlin, in 1933, he and Anna Bern were married in a small Lutheran church near her home in Heidelberg. Both had attended the University there, the oldest in Germany. She also was tall and beautiful, with blonde hair and bright blue eyes. She and Johann couldn't have been happier, and after several years of trying, she finally got pregnant in the spring of 1941, almost one year ago.

Before his leaving for Poland, they had found a small apartment outside of Munich, where he was helping the *Luftwaffe* construct a new airfield. A month after he was reassigned, Johann got word from his parents that Anna had contracted tuberculosis. They were having trouble getting medical care for her, because all the hospitals were filled to capacity with wounded soldiers coming back from the eastern front. As hard as he tried, he could not get an emergency leave for another four weeks, but by then it was too late. Anna Bern Weller, and her unborn baby, died two weeks after his parents first notified him. Because of the contagious nature of the illness, she was buried immediately. Now, there was no reason to take his leave and go back to Munich. He was devastated, and wished that they had been killed together in their apartment by one of the Allied bombing raids.

His depression lasted for several months. He came out of it by totally focusing on his work, and praying to be reassigned away from this horrible place. The daily routine he developed for himself consisted of an early-morning inspection of the sites he was working on, and a daily staff meeting with a few of his sergeants supervising the work. The remainder of the day was spent in his mobile trailer working on blueprints and civil engineering drawings, with the aid of his First Sergeant, Hermann Koch.

Hermann had been with him for the last three years and Johann trusted him implicitly. A short, pudgy, dark-haired man of forty, Hermann was always jovial and had helped Johann overcome his troubles, more than anything else. He had been in the army for nineteen years, and seven years ago had married a farm girl he grew up with. They now had two daughters and he could not have been prouder.

Johann had gotten up a little early that morning, unable to sleep with the reoccurring nightmares of the war. He was sitting at his drafting table when Hermann opened the trailer door. He was carrying a stack of letters that he had just picked up from the weekly mail wagon.

"*Guten Morgen, Leutnant,*" Hermann said excitedly. "It looks like you received some important mail from the War Department."

"*Morgen*, Hermann," Johann said, as he looked up from his work. "Let me see it." Hermann handed him the stack. There were a couple of letters from his mother, one from his father, another from a friend he hadn't heard from in a while, probably a letter of condolence, and two official looking, large envelopes from Berlin. He kept these last ones in his hand and laid the others on the table.

He opened the first one, jerked his head back, and smiled. "Well, look Hermann," he said loudly, "I have been promoted. You will now have to call me, *Hauptmann.*" He pulled out the new, captain's epaulettes for his uniform from the bottom of the envelope, and then showed them to his sergeant. "What do you think?"

"Congratulations, *mein Hauptmann.* You deserve to be promoted, more so than some of those idiots out there that are leading us."

Johann laughed, "You better watch your language, sergeant. You could be sent to Russia for that remark." He opened the next envelope, took out the letter, and began reading. "O.K., let us see what we have here."

"Maybe I got a promotion too," Hermann joked.

"Oh, my God!" Johann exclaimed. "It is better than a promotion."

"What is it? Don't keep me in suspense."

"Our whole engineering brigade is going back to Germany for a few months...let me see...Wittenberg...for some special training, and being reassigned from there...they do not say where. I think Wittenberg is along the Elbe River. And look at this," he pointed at the next paragraph, "we will each get a one week furlough, before having to report to camp."

"Oh, that is marvelous, *Hauptmann*! Yes, yes, much better than a promotion. So when do we leave?"

"Not until we complete our current assignments, which are those two small bridges east of here, and a few miles of those railroad repairs, leading to who knows where." He shook his head, "Probably to those concentration camps we've heard about."

"I'm sure those stories are exaggerated. We couldn't be doing those horrible things."

"I hope you are right." He paused, "But anyway, I think we will have plenty of time to finish what we have to do. They want us to report to camp no later than 7 July, which means that we will try to leave here around 25 June. That might even give us a couple extra days at home."

"Ah, that would be fantastic." Hermann walked over to a cabinet and pulled out a bottle. "Sir, how about some schnapps? This calls for a toast."

"It is kind of early, but this is a special occasion…right? Pour us a couple, Hermann."

He did so, in two small metal cups. They made two toasts, one "to going home", and the other "to the end of this fucking war."

What I would have given to have Anna, and our new baby, waiting for me when I arrived back home, Johann thought. *Life could have been so beautiful for us, but that part of my life will no longer exist. Now, I will have to concentrate on keeping my parents healthy and safe.*

5

It had been three weeks since Marcel had first seen Florette in his office. Now he was on his way to meet her at the *Abbaye de Senanque*, in the Vaucluse area of Provence. She had sent a message the week before, through a contact, saying she needed to see him in Vaucluse, rather than meeting again in Marseille. Since he only worked in the morning on Wednesdays, Marcel was able to reschedule his patients for other times that week.

The drive through the countryside was pleasant. He always enjoyed seeing and taking pictures of the historic sights, especially if the lighting was right. As usual, he brought his Lumiere Eljy, 35mm camera. Halfway out of Marseille, though, he had the feeling that another car was following him. He pulled over near a busy market, and let it go by. He watched as the car continued for another two blocks, and then turned to the left. He never saw it again, as he left the city. *Maybe I'm becoming paranoid*, he thought as he drove along, but he had had a similar feeling just a couple days before, when walking to and from a restaurant for lunch.

He was now an hour-and-a-half into his drive, when he passed the ancient dwellings known as *bories*. These domed, limestone slabs, with walls up to four feet thick, dated back to 3500 B.C., and they never ceased to amaze him. People still lived in them up until the 1890's. He went past them, stopped, and took a picture from a new vantage point.

Just a little farther on, he approached the valley that separated the road from the hilltop village of Gordes, which spills down in terraces from a 16th century Renaissance château. He rolled the window down on the passenger's side, and snapped another picture, even though he had dozens of similar ones of this impressive sight. For the first time in weeks, he was feeling relaxed and not thinking about the war. The countryside did that for him. With all its tranquil beauty, it was hard to believe that a war was actually going on.

One-half hour later, he approached the gates of the 12th century Abbey and drove in. The structure itself was surrounded by a sea of lavender. He spotted two monks walking through the fields, and made a mental note to buy a bouquet of lavender from them after his meeting. Angelina would like that, because it always gave the house such a wonderful perfumed scent.

He parked his car in back of the church, so it wouldn't be visible from the road. He looked at his watch and saw that he was about ten minutes early. There were no other vehicles in sight, and Marcel assumed that Florette had not yet arrived. He went around to the front of the church and walked into the vestibule, when he spotted her sitting under a glass window. They made eye contact, and she motioned him to sit next to her. There was no one else in the sanctuary, so he didn't bother with the formalities of kneeling and crossing himself. He wasn't that religious and besides, this was a business meeting. He knew that Angelina would not have approved…she thought of him as a hopeless case, when it came to religion.

"*Bonjour*, Florette. *Comment allez-vous?*"

"Good morning, Marcel. I am well, thank you," she said, as she got right down to business. "To begin with, we have found the location of the relay station going to Paris, which is the more important one. The other one northeast of you, has yet to be found, but we will," she added, with an air of confidence.

"That sounds like good news. Is *that* one where my man thought it was?"

"Well, sort of. It's right outside a small town called Morieres. Are you familiar with it?"

"Yes, I remember driving through there on the way to Avignon."

"Correct. Actually, it's five kilometers east. As you pass the town, going toward Avignon, the first dirt road you come to, make a right turn; then go about one-half kilometer through the forest. When you reach the clearing, you'll be able to spot a low building in the distance, with a tower in back of it...probably another kilometer. There are a lot of wires coming down from the top of the tower, almost like a maypole."

"Do you want me to have a look at it today?"

"Precisely. I'll drive into Morieres with you and wait near your car. You'll proceed on foot to the dirt road, and then make your way to the clearing to survey the target. We haven't gotten close enough to determine how protected the station is, or how best to plan our attack."

"Are you inferring that another *Maquis* group will be involved with this mission?" he asked.

"Marcel, you and your men will be leading the mission...that's why you're here today. Depending on what intelligence information you find, we may have to bring in one or more groups to successfully complete the operation." She paused for a moment, and then continued. "As I told you in Marseille, we have a lot of faith in your judgment and want you to take on more leadership. This is the biggest test you'll have."

"I see," he said, as he folded his arms and looked straight ahead at the crucifix on the wall.

As he collected his thoughts, she waited for him to speak again. A monk, in a brown robe, walked in from a side door carrying freshly cut lavender, and arranged the flowers in an urn, sitting on the altar. They both sat there quietly watching him perform his task, and after a few minutes he walked out of the same side door.

Marcel then stood up, looked down at Florette, and simply said, "Let's go."

The half-hour drive to Morieres was uneventful. Marcel's old Citroën smelled wonderful, with the bouquet of lavender lying on the back seat. He mentioned to Florette that he thought he was being followed on two occasions, but he couldn't be sure. She advised him to go about his normal routine, and not to confront the people following him…that would only bring on more suspicion.

She saw his camera on the floor of the car and asked, "Do you develop your own film?"

"Yes, I have a small darkroom in my basement," he replied. "It's sort of a hobby of mine."

"Well, good…it might be of help to us if you took some pictures of this facility, provided you can get in close enough without being seen."

"All right, I'll do my best."

They arrived in the small town, and Marcel parked the car on one of the side streets. Florette jumped out immediately, walked toward the main street, and disappeared into an antique shop. Marcel walked in the opposite direction. He turned left at the next street, and began walking parallel to the main highway toward the forest, which he assumed he would eventually hit. He wanted to survey the area a little more thoroughly, to see if he could go through the woods and avoid going on an open dirt road.

After a few blocks, the street ended into another one perpendicular to it, with a row of houses in each direction. He turned right, across from the houses, and almost instantly saw the forest through an opening. He spotted a little vacant lot further down and crossed the street. He walked through the lot, down an embankment, jumped over a small stream and entered the woods. Rather than continuing to walk directly toward the dirt road, he set out at an angle that would take him towards the clearing.

Twenty minutes later, he spotted the clearing and the dirt road. He realized that he was at least ½ kilometer past the beginning of the clearing, and only had another ½ kilometer to go. To verify this, he moved slowly toward the road. Then, coming within fifty meters of it, he saw the tower and part of the relay station on the other side, even closer than he expected.

He pulled out his camera, took a picture of what he was observing, then started making his way back into the forest. Shortly thereafter, he heard a truck coming up the road from the main highway and hid behind a bush. When the truck was in plain view, he snapped a photo. The red lettering on the side of it proclaimed, "COURTEAUX FOOD SUPPLIERS---AVIGNON".

He moved a little further back, and then started running parallel to the road until he was finally looking directly at the entrance of the relay station. The truck was still at the gate house, where a guard apparently was checking the driver's papers. He could see now that the compound was completely surrounded by a tall fence. He snapped another picture, got on the ground, and began crawling forward to get a better view. He stopped behind a large clump of trees, got on his knees, and waited for a few moments to catch his breath.

He could hear voices across the road, and knew immediately that they weren't speaking French. He slowly peeked around the tree, and was surprised at what he saw. There was another building on the other side of the entrance. It was larger than the gate house, which had been blocked by the food truck that had now entered the compound. Three armed, German soldiers leaned against that building, smoking and engaged in conversation, while another sat in an armored personnel carrier (APC) parked next to it. Another German soldier he presumed to be the guard, came out of the gate house and motioned for two of the men to go toward the relay station.

At that moment, Marcel stood up and snapped another picture. The guard, and the other men, all looked across the road in unison and began pointing in his direction. "*Was ist das?*" he heard them say. He quickly dropped to his knees behind the tree and froze, sure that he was about to be caught. He was sweating profusely and breathing rapidly, knowing he couldn't stand up and run. The heavy footsteps of two, or three, of the soldiers were approaching the edge of the woods, not twenty-five meters from where he knelt. Hearing their boots crushing the dead leaves, he crossed himself, knowing that this was the end. A second later, as if by some miracle, a large jack rabbit ran past him toward the soldiers, crossing the road to the other side.

He didn't let his breath out, until he heard the men laughing and saying, "*Ein kaninchen, ein kaninchen…*ha, ha, ha, haaa." They turned around and began walking back to the compound, still repeating these words and laughing. He assumed this to mean "rabbit", but he wasn't laughing about it…he felt sick to his stomach and felt like throwing up. Fortunately, he had only eaten an apple for breakfast and had a cup of coffee.

Trying to calm his nerves, he sat on the ground for another ten minutes surveying the land behind him. There was a high, grassy knoll several meters to his left, and very dense woods behind that. He made a mental picture of that, definitely not wanting to risk another photo.

Slowly, he began to crawl into the deeper forest. He finally stood and looked back at the compound. There were two search lights on each of the four corners that he had not noticed before. They would surely illuminate the whole area at night. The clearing on the back side was less than one hundred meters from the forest. He estimated the station, itself, to be about seventy-five meters from the front gate. Feeling that he was safely out of earshot, he couldn't resist taking one more picture of this whole scene, and did so.

On his walk back to Morieres, he kept thinking, *how could I be so stupid? I came so close to losing everything, because of this damn camera. I've got to be more careful in the future. I could have jeopardized my whole family.* Trying to calm down, he took deep breaths and let them out slowly, as he continued to walk through the woods.

6

Marcel got into his car and started the engine. Within ten seconds, Florette appeared from nowhere, and hopped in the other side.

"Circle back to the highway and go east, toward Châteauneuf de Gadagne," she said. "There's a safe house I want to show you before you go home. It should only be about four kilometers from here."

When they were on the highway, she gazed over at him and remarked, "You seem a little shaken. Tell me what happened."

He very carefully told her what he had seen, and his almost fatal encounter with the Germans. It was her, now, that looked unsettled, something Marcel had never seen in their previous meetings. He could tell that Florette felt as if a ton of bricks had fallen from the sky. As a very methodical person, he saw that this disrupted her thoughtfully laid out plans, and those of the whole *Maquis* organization. It was their hope that the Germans would never come into the southern Unoccupied Zone…that the War would be over, before that would ever happen. Putting up with the *Vichy* was one thing…dealing with the Germans was a whole different game.

She gave out a long sigh before she spoke, and then it was in a very soft voice. "Well, it's not like our intelligence people didn't warn us of the possibility of this happening." She shrugged her shoulders and let out a deep breath. "But, the reality of the damned Nazis being here is still hard to fathom." She paused again, and then asked, "Marcel, do you think the soldiers are in the pictures you took? It could be very important to us."

"I'm pretty sure that they're in at least one of the pictures. I won't know until after I develop them."

"Can you make enlargements of these prints…let's say up to 8 X 10, or better yet, 11 X 14?"

"I don't have the paper for 11 X 14's…it's too hard to find. With my enlarger, the 8 X 10's won't be a problem."

"Good. Make about four or five copies. I need to pass this on as soon as possible, so I'll contact you within a few days for a pickup."

"Fine," he said. "I'll start working on it tonight. By the way," he added, "what kind of intelligence information are you receiving?"

"It's very vague, to say the least. But, there is one report we've received from the Brits that states a strong possibility for the Germans to start moving a few troops down south in key areas, and then in larger numbers before the end of the year. I believe what you saw today is a good indication of that."

"What do you think their reasoning is for doing this? Isn't the *Vichy* doing their job?"

"Oh, it's not that at all," her voice sounding more energetic. "The *Vichy* have nothing to do with it. The Germans have a strong impression that the Americans are planning to land troops in North Africa, to aid the Allies. *That* would eventually open up the southern part of France, for an invasion of Europe from the Mediterranean."

"Wow," he gasped. "When you think about it, it makes a lot of sense, doesn't it? Do you foresee this now affecting our mission at the relay station?"

"Possibly, we'll have to see." She leaned forward, looking out the front window. "Stop here," she ordered. Marcel pulled over to the side. She pointed across the highway to a group of identification signs, with arrows all pointing down a narrow road to the left. "That's the place we're looking for. Let's wait here a minute so we can talk. After we see the safe house, I'll be leaving you."

"All right." He knew better than to ask where, or how she would be going.

"Now, let me get this straight. There's one main, double-fenced gate, which opens inward to the compound. Immediately inside the gate are two wooden buildings: a small, guard house on the left, and a larger building on the right, possibly a barracks, with four windows."

He nodded.

"You were able to see one armored personnel carrier, but no other vehicles, and there was a machine gun mounted on the APC. The five soldiers you saw were all carrying semi-automatic rifles, as far as you could tell. You never saw any soldiers near the station, itself, which was about seventy-five meters from the gate. The station was an elongated building with two front entrances on each corner, and one in the middle…maybe eight windows in total. The radio tower sits in the center of the compound, between the station and the gate, and is mounted on a concrete slab about three feet high."

He nodded again.

"Did I forget anything?"

He thought for a few seconds, and said, "Only two things: the narrow clearing behind the back fence and the search lights surrounding the place."

"Ah, yes, the lights and back fence. How deep is that clearing again, between the woods and the fence?"

"About one hundred meters. I couldn't see if there was anything, or anyone, behind the relay station, though." He paused, and then another thought came to him. "One other thing I forgot to tell you, originally. There's a grassy knoll in the woods, across from the front gate. It could be useful to set up cover for our men going in. It's about thirty meters from the road, and maybe another twelve meters to the gate." He paused for a few seconds. "This is where I was positioned."

"Going in? How would you propose to do that, if you were planning the mission?"

"Hmm," he thought for a moment. "You know, I'm no military genius, but I think that the element of surprise is essential."

"I agree, from what you've told me." She rubbed her chin, "Yes, they definitely have the advantage of the enclosure, and the clearings surrounding it. Plus they have that APC, and the men are well armed."

"Five that we know of. We would have to assume that there are more in the barracks...let's say another four or five...and of course, we have no idea how many are in the station." They looked at each other and nodded.

"Oh, wait a minute," he continued. "I just remembered...there was smoke coming out of a stack, in the center of the station. It's definitely not for heat, so that must be the kitchen and mess hall area. Figure a couple cooks, and at the most, two or three radio operators in the other half."

"Let's see," she looked at her hand, and counted on her fingers, "that would add up to about fifteen soldiers in the compound. It may be too much for us to handle." She glanced over to Marcel, "So, any ideas?"

"Only one, and this may sound crazy."

"I'm open to anything, so go ahead. We've got to keep the pressure up, regardless of the risks."

"A Trojan horse," he said simply.

"What kind of horse?"

"A Trojan horse…you know, like the Greeks used to defeat Troy, in 1100 B.C." Marcel laughed. "Well, not exactly this type of horse, but…remember the food truck I mentioned, originally?"

"Yes. The one from Avignon?"

He nodded. "You'd have to check out those Courteaux people… whether they're *Vichy* connected, or whatever their arrangements are with the Germans. They're obviously supplying them with food. Their truck would be a perfect way for us to get a lot of our people into the compound. The guards never even bothered to open the back to see what was in it, so they must have been doing business for awhile, and trusted them."

Florette was gaining new-found respect for the way Marcel logically interpreted information, and handled himself. Today, he had crossed over to the upper echelon of the *Maquis.*

He concluded, by recommending that at least twenty people be placed in strategic locations in the forest surrounding the compound.

"I appreciate your input on this, Marcel. We'll take everything under advisement and then get back to you. It's going to take a considerable amount of planning…more than I ever anticipated."

She pointed across the road, "Do you see the second sign from the top?"

"Do you mean the one that says *Le Clos des Saumanes?*"

"Yes, that's the safe house we'll be using, when the time comes. Quite a funny name isn't it…'A walled property to breed donkeys?' Let's cross over and go down that road. It's the first place we come to, on the right."

He crossed the highway and followed the dirt road 1500 meters until he came to a terracotta villa. It had a five-foot wall on three sides, of the same yellowish-beige color. The large wooden gate was open, and Florette motioned for Marcel to drive in. It was a charming, three-storied stucco home, with a large, brick courtyard…plenty of space for several cars.

Across from the front door, in the courtyard, was a small chapel made of native stones, the mortar between them quite visible. The windows were all stained glass, and a two foot, brass cross was perched atop the arched entrance. Marcel thought that it looked rather like a large, child's playhouse.

As they got out of the car, he grabbed his camera to take a picture of the chapel, but Florette put up her hand in protest. "Better not do that," she said. "You never know who might get hold of your film, and trace it back to here. We need this place, more than you can imagine."

He put the camera back in the car and walked with her towards the house. "You're right…I never thought of that."

Before they could reach the front door, a middle-aged man with gray hair, opened it. "Welcome, welcome," he said, smiling. He gave Florette a kiss on both cheeks. "It is so good to see you again, and this," he gestured to Marcel, "must be the young man you told me about." He shook his hand. "My name is Philippe… and you are Marcel, I presume. Come in, please. I was just preparing tea, or would you prefer wine from our vineyard?"

"Tea would be fine, Philippe," Florette answered. "Where is your wife?"

"Beth won't be back for another week. She went to Bordeaux to visit her mother, who hasn't been feeling too well."

They followed him into the foyer, where the stairway leading to the bedrooms began. Then they went through a small, cozy sitting area to the right, which had a small fireplace and radio; it continued through an archway into a very large kitchen and eating area. Florette and Marcel sat down at the long, wooden table, while Philippe poured the tea for each of them.

Marcel felt instantly very comfortable with this warm, intelligent Frenchman. "Tell me, Philippe," Marcel began, "what is the history behind this villa? It's lovely."

"Oh, *merci Monsieur*. Actually, it was bought by a priest, by the name of Abbè Mottet, in 1840. He was the Archbishop of the Saint Sulpice Church, in Paris. It was built originally as a *Bastide*, or provincial manor, in the late 1700's. Then the priest added the tower, the terrace, and the chapel to give it a more of a Tuscan look."

"My wife would love this place," Marcel said.

"Please bring her any time and be our guest."

"That would be very nice, *merci*. It will have to wait until after the War, though, and then I'll be sure to take you up on your offer."

"It would be our pleasure," he replied, as he directed his attention to Florette.

"Let me explain Philippe's role with *La Résistance*," Florette began. "Before the War, he was the editor of the newspaper in Avignon. He…"

"Of course," Marcel interrupted, "Philippe Lambert. I've read many of your editorials." He reached across the table and shook Philippe's hand again. "It's an honor to meet you, *Monsieur*. I can understand why you're no longer with the paper."

They all laughed, and Florette continued. "Yes, Philippe has been strongly anti-Nazi from the beginning of that movement. He naturally had to give up his position in 1940. The *Vichy* forced him to retire here to his vineyards, with the promise that he wouldn't cause trouble. Fortunately for us, he was able to supply some old printing presses, and other equipment for our underground newspaper, before he left his job."

"I wish I could have done more," he added, "because those bastards are going to destroy Europe. Furnishing this safe house is another way I can be of help."

"And a big help it is too, Philippe," she covered her hand over his. "We've used this house several times already, and it's been ideal for hiding our people for a few days. You and your wife have been more than perfect hosts, and will surely be honored when this war is over."

"You're most kind, but the honor is mine to serve France."

She turned to Marcel, and said, "This is why I wanted you to see the villa, and the two of you to meet. You know, of course, that no one should know, or be told of this place until the proper time."

"Yes, of course," Marcel replied.

After they finished their tea, and some friendly conversation, Florette stood, and said, "I think that we've taken up enough of Philippe's time." Marcel stood. She shook his hand, and said, "I'll be in touch soon. Have a safe journey home."

The men exchanged their goodbyes. Marcel told Philippe how much he enjoyed meeting him, and looked forward to the next time. He walked out to his car alone, leaving the two of them in the house.

He got back to the main highway and headed southeast. For the next hour and a half, he reflected on his extraordinary day. Things were changing so quickly that it was not a question of if, but when he would move his family to Elne, Angelina's parent's home. He was now convinced that they would be safer there, especially if the Germans came into the Unoccupied Zone.

He had another hour to drive, and was now coming into Aix-en-Provence, an international students' town that he always admired. The university was founded in 1409, and the city reeked of charm. As he was driving down the *Cours* Mirabeau, the grandest of Aix's boulevards, he got the feeling again that he was being followed, this time by a police car. He was approaching the city limits, when the car pulled up beside him, and the officer motioned him to pull over. He did so, but not before shoving his camera underneath the seat.

The officer got out of his car and approached Marcel on the driver's side. "*Monsieur*, would you step out of your car please," he said matter-of-factly.

Marcel did as he was told. "Have I done something wrong, officer?"

Ignoring the question, he said, "Let me see your driver's license."

Remembering that he shouldn't be confrontational, Marcel handed it to him without asking any further questions.

The officer looked at the license, opened a small notebook, flipped a few pages, and studied it for a moment. "You are *Monsieur* Pontier, from Marseille?"

"That's correct. I am Doctor Pontier."

He handed the license back to Marcel, and then continued his questions. "Why are you here in Aix, and where else have you been today?"

"Well, officer," he tried to sound as calm as possible, even though his anxiety was rising, "I had the day off, and sometimes I like to drive in the countryside, just to get my mind off the office." Glancing into the car, he saw the flowers, and added, "I did stop at the *Abbaye de Senanque* to buy some lavender for my wife," he pointed to them, "but other than that, there was no special place I went."

The officer looked inside the car, and then demanded, "Open your trunk."

Marcel took his key and unlocked it, hoping there was nothing incriminating on the inside. What the officer found was a deflated soccer ball and some old dental posters, which Marcel had drawn for a lecture he had given months before.

Without another word, the officer closed the trunk, made some notes in his book, and simply said, "You're free to go." He got back into his car, made a U-turn and drove back into Aix.

Marcel waited until the police car was out of sight, walked into the bushes, and relieved himself. He returned to his car and leaned against it for several minutes, waiting for the cramping in his stomach to go away. He didn't know whether he could take any more excitement in one day.

He got back into his car and headed south. One thing he was almost sure of…this was no random stop. *It would have been interesting, he thought, to see what was in that notebook. I'm going to move my family out of Marseille as soon as possible, after the baby is born. I can't risk the consequences, if something should happen to me.*

7

It was a beautiful, spring day in Elne, and Paulette was taking her lunch hour in the courtyard of city hall, where she worked. She enjoyed sitting in the sun, after going through a long, dreary winter. The Pyrenees, the mountain chain that forms a natural barrier between France and Spain, were only twenty miles away and she could see the snow-capped peaks in the distance. She ate the bread and cheese that she had brought with her that morning, wishing that she could share a bottle of wine with someone, and spend the rest of the afternoon just sitting here.

Normally, she would walk home and eat with her mother and father, Elizabeth and Paul Courty. Elizabeth always prepared a large, hot meal for lunch and a much smaller meal for dinner. Today though, she didn't have the time…she and the mayor, Jean Astruc, for whom she worked as an administrative assistant, were preparing a new quarterly budget. The regional *Vichy* government office based in Perpignan was getting more demanding on local government officials.

They expected them to account more often for normal, everyday programs and expenditures. They were slowly implementing new taxes on the people, and more controls on their lives. The mayor, who

Paulette always saw as an easy-going and efficient public servant, was becoming irritable and run down from the stress.

He was in his office, standing over his desk, when Paulette walked in. He thanked God everyday that he had her. He could always rely on this dark-complexioned, thirty-two year old attractive woman, who normally wore her hair pulled back in a bun. She was thin and stood straight, with her shoulders back, and seemed taller to him than her 5' 4". He greatly admired her for her strength, both physically and mentally, and didn't know how he could handle this office without her. He wanted to increase her salary, because she had been working with him for almost a year, but she understood the budget crunch he was under.

"Well, let's get back to work, Paulette," the mayor said. "We certainly don't want to keep the little, pencil-pushing idiots in Perpignan waiting on this report, do we?"

His huge chest heaved with laughter, and Paulette was happy to see this large man lighten-up a bit. *He was almost sixty years old, ready for retirement and certainly didn't need another war in his life. He should be home playing with his grandchildren*, she thought. "No, we wouldn't want to do that," she smirked. "But, I've thought of a way that we could take away from Peter to pay Paul."

She handed him the proposal, which she had worked on for the last two days. He took it and looked it over for a few minutes. She continued when he was through, "You see, by eliminating a few of the unnecessary pork projects, we can retain what's really important for community services and running this office properly."

"Brilliant, brilliant," he said excitedly. "All right, Paulette, let's put all the numbers together, and get a proposal typed up. This shouldn't take us more than a couple of hours."

"O.K., then you'll have to promise me to relax for a little while. We'll go out to the courtyard, take that bottle of wine you have stashed in your desk, and enjoy the remainder of the day in the sun."

"You've got a deal," he grinned at her. "I need a little relaxation."

They worked diligently for the next few hours…he had been interrupted several times by phone calls and teletypes from the Perpignan office. "A bunch of incompetents running that place," he told her.

When they had finished, they went downstairs, into the courtyard; he brought the wine and two glasses, while she brought the bread and cheese, left over from lunch. They sat across from each other on a stone bench and table, looking out over the houses in the town center, and beyond that, the farms in the valley, where they grew mostly fruit and some vegetables. Elne was the big orchard of the county.

It had turned a little bit cooler than a few hours before when Paulette had her lunch, but neither one of them was complaining. They were both just enjoying the beauty of their ancient town on this perfectly, clear day…clear enough to see the Mediterranean Sea, four kilometers away…that is, if they climbed the tower. *Perhaps I'll do that later*, she thought. It was always a thrill to get to the top of that magnificent 10th century Romanesque Cathedral, because the view was incredible in all directions. The Pyrenees were looming in the distance west of them, and the spring waters, melting from the winter snow, ran into the River Tech at the base of the mountains. You could see where the river originated, traveled through Elne and beyond, and where it dumped into the sea.

Tomorrow, Friday, would be a lively market day in the town square, a reflection of Elne's 1000-year-old agricultural tradition. Even that would be watched closely by the *Vichy* agents, who would want to take their cut.

"*Monsieur* Mayor, do you think it would be all right to come in at 12:00 tomorrow?" Paulette asked. "I'd like to take my mother to the market in the morning, and I've got some personal things that I have to take care of."

"Of course," he gestured with both hands. "I won't submit this proposal until late morning, or early afternoon, so they'll think we spent all night working on it," he laughed. "Hell, I may even wait until Monday morning, so why don't you take the whole day off. You have it coming."

"Oh, that would be wonderful," she replied. "I won't be rushed, and I can spend more time helping my parents around the vineyards."

"How is Paul's *Vin Doux Naturel* coming in?"

"Oh, it's been an amazing season for the grapes, so far. Last year's crop was a little too sweet, but judging from their early taste, this could be a banner year."

They clicked their glasses together, and he said, "Here's to great, French wine. I'll be looking forward to the tasting."

"You and your wife will be our honored guests in the fall." She raised her glass, and clicked his again. She stood, came around the table, and kissed him on both cheeks. "Rest up over the weekend. Things will get better eventually."

She walked off toward the cobblestone street, turned, and waved to him. *It was a shame,* he thought, *that her fiancé had been killed two years before, and she was still unmarried at thirty-two. Someone someday would fall in love with her, because she was just too good a catch to stay single.*

As she walked along the narrow cobblestone streets, Paulette thought about the pending three-day weekend ahead, how relaxing it was going to be, and the chance to spend some quality time with her parents, Paul, 64, and Elizabeth, 56. They were in fairly good health, but as they were getting up there in age, she had noticed that they were not able, or it was simply harder for them to do certain tasks. Where in the past, Paul, a stocky, tall man, had spent twelve hours a day in the fields, that time now had been cut down to six, or less, including a longer lunch and an hour mid-day nap. Elizabeth, a small, thin woman, was still a bundle of energy; however, her arthritis was becoming more of a problem, and Paulette had observed that it was making it more difficult for her to move as fast, or to lift heavier objects. Getting older was something Paulette was not looking forward to.

It wasn't long before Paulette was walking through the ancient Roman archway that once made up the entrance to the walled, inner city. Their home lay inside the walls, at No. 21 Rue Catalonia, named after the region of France where Elne was located. The pie-shaped, five acre farm and vineyard, was behind their four-storied, stucco home that was outside the walls. A private door, built inside the thick wall, gave them access to their farm.

The entrance door, off the street, led immediately to a staircase leading up to the first floor of the house. Another door, off the inside entrance, opened to the barn and loft. A ladder led up to the loft. Once there, another small ladder built along the back wall, led to a trap door inside one of the first floor bedrooms. Also on the first floor were a combination kitchen and living room, a separate paneled dining room, and a staircase leading to the four other bedrooms on the top two floors. Off the living room area, were two glassed, French doors that opened to a large balcony that had a wonderful view of the northern plains, and to the south, a glimpse of the Pyrenees.

Before crossing the street to her house, Paulette stopped at the flower market to buy some pink tulips. Most French families worshipped fresh flowers, especially after the long winter. Even though the climate in Elne was quite temperate compared to Paris and other cities in the North, it nevertheless could occasionally get down to freezing.

Elizabeth was sitting on the balcony having her afternoon tea, when she heard the front door open. She leaned over the edge, just in time to see the back of Paulette's head. She sat back down and waited for her to come up the stairs.

"I'm out here, darling," she shouted. "Pour yourself some tea and come sit with me. I have some interesting news for you."

Paulette walked through the open glass doors, onto the balcony. She gave her mother a quick kiss and sat down next to her, in a deep-slanted, wooden chair. "So, *Maman*, what's the news?"

"First tell me about your day. Didn't you care for any tea? I boiled up a fresh pot."

"No, *Maman*, I just finished a bottle of wine with the Mayor."

"In the middle of the day? You should be ashamed of yourself!"

"Well, it was a special occasion, for a project we completed ahead of schedule." She then proceeded to tell her what a nice day she had, and the one day-off bonus her boss had given her. "This will give us a chance to do some early morning shopping at the market."

"Oh, that will be wonderful," Elizabeth said excitedly. "I'll be able to store up on some things I need for the next few weeks."

"For the next few weeks?" Paulette asked quizzically. "Why do you need so much?" She moved forward in her chair to hear the answer.

"Well, that's the news I wanted to tell you." She took a sip of her tea. "Angelina called me this morning, and told me that Marcel was bringing her and the children to stay for awhile."

"You mean that she's already traveling with the new baby? Madeline is only two weeks old."

"They won't be coming for at least two more weeks, so the baby will be a month old."

"So, what's the big news? They always come for a month or so in the summer."

"They'll be staying for much longer than a month." She paused, as she could see that Paulette was squinting at her, wanting more information. "When I asked Angelina why, all she would say was Marcel would explain everything when they got here."

"There's nothing going on between the two of them, is there?"

"That's the first thing I asked, but Angelina laughed and assured me that there were no problems, and everyone was happy and healthy."

"Sounds awfully vague, but I'm sure Marcel has a good reason to do this, because he hates staying in Marseille by himself. Hmm," she shook her head, "I'm dying to know what it is."

"You ask too many questions, Paulette. If she wanted us to know something, then she would have told me."

"I suppose you're right, but I know it's something important…I just know it." She got up and looked out at the old city. "Anyway, I can't wait to see the new baby and the other children. It will be wonderful having them all here."

"Having who here?" Paul asked, as he walked onto the balcony.

Paulette turned around when she heard her father's voice. She always thought him to be a very handsome man, and she noticed that he was now starting to get a little gray at the temples. She walked toward him, saying, "The Pontier clan is coming, Papa." She gave him a kiss on both cheeks.

"Ah, yes…*Maman* told me that at lunch," he said. "You're home early today. Is everything O.K.?"

"Everything's fine, Papa." She once again related the day's events. "Mayor Astruc can't wait until the wine tasting. Do you still think it will be better than last season?"

"Oh, without a doubt! The grapes already have a much drier taste. And if not," he gave a hearty laugh, "we'll drink it all ourselves."

49

"You'd love that, wouldn't you," Elizabeth said sarcastically..."you old goat. Did you get the presser running?"

"It's like brand new, dear," he said. "It took me over an hour to repair one of the gears, and now it's working like a dream." Their small winery was on the opposite end of the vineyard, toward the River Tech. "Tomorrow," he continued, "I'll start cleaning out the barrels."

"I'll be glad to help you Papa, after *Maman* and I go shopping in the morning," Paulette offered.

He put his arm around her, and she rested her head on his shoulder. "Yes, that would be nice...just like old times, huh, when you and Angelina used to help us on the weekends, before the two of you went away to college?"

"I remember when you got the two of them drunk, Papa," Elizabeth added. "And they were only teenagers! What was Angelina, sixteen, and Paulette, maybe thirteen?"

Paulette chuckled, "I'll never forget that day, because I was so sick, I swore that I would never drink wine again."

"We did get carried away, didn't we?" Paul asked.

"All I remember is that after the grapes were pressed, we kept sampling the new wine, while we were trying to transfer it to the barrels for storage. And you," Paulette said, pointing to Paul, "kept making all these crazy toasts to everyone, and anything you could think of...old King Louis, the wine harvest, the Perpignan soccer team...it just went on and on."

They all laughed, with Paul laughing the loudest. Elizabeth got up and took her empty glass into the kitchen, where she began making a salad, with the ingredients picked from her garden that morning. Paul and Paulette remained on the balcony, discussing the world situation, something they did on almost a daily basis. They both agreed that the war would soon take a turn in favor of the Allies, and all they needed to do, was to sit here in peaceful Elne, and wait it out.

8

Marcel and Angelina began discussing the move to Elne shortly after the birth of their second daughter, Madeline. Angelina wasn't thoroughly convinced that this was the right thing to do, but Marcel couldn't tell her of his activities with the *Maquis* and the potential problems that might occur. He had fears for his family, and himself, if anything should go wrong.

It was now the middle of June, 1942. Madeline was a strong and healthy two week-old, and Angelina was almost back to her normal weight. It had been a month since that eventful day in northern Provence. Marcel had not engaged in any covert activity since then, other than to send Florette, via a messenger, the developed pictures of the relay station and its surroundings, three weeks before. He was pleased that they had come out much better than he had anticipated.

He had received a message from Florette one week ago, saying, "The flowers are blooming", which meant that the plans for the attack on the relay station were almost complete. He made no reply, as he didn't feel it necessary at this time, to let her, or anyone else know of his plans to move his family in the near future. At his persistent urging, though, Angelina finally called her parents in Elne, and told her mother to expect them within the next couple of weeks or so.

A few days later, Marcel was in his office, finishing a procedure on his last morning patient, when his receptionist, Margo, interrupted him.

"Doctor, there are two gentlemen in the waiting room who insist on seeing you. I told them that you were with a patient, but…"

Just then the two men walked into the exam room, both dressed in black suits and ties. Marcel knew immediately that they weren't French and a cold chill went through him. He could feel his heart beating rapidly, but tried to stay calm. The taller of the two, said in a thick German accent, "Dr. Pontier, we need to speak to you at once. We will give you three minutes to complete what you are doing and then you will come with us."

This wasn't a question…it was an order. "Yes, of course," Marcel replied in a business-like tone. "Why don't you have a seat in the waiting room, and I'll be right with you?"

"No, we prefer to wait right here," said the taller one again, "so please be quick about it."

"As you wish." Marcel turned back to the patient in the chair, who seemed startled by this whole scene, and began rinsing out her mouth. "*Madame* Chanfrau, I'm sorry for this inconvenience, but there is absolutely nothing to be alarmed about." He could hear himself saying this more for his benefit, than for her's. He turned to his assistant and said, "Annette, please schedule *Madame* for another appointment, some time this week. Also, help Margo reschedule our afternoon patients."

Margo escorted the befuddled patient into the reception area, and closed the door. Marcel took off his clinic coat, hung it in the closet, and took out his suit jacket. Before putting it on, he looked at the two Germans, and asked, in a more belligerent tone than he had wanted, "I didn't want to get into this discussion in front of my patient, but may I now ask…who *are* you, and what do you want?"

Unfazed by this, the shorter man reached into his pocket, withdrew an identification card with a large swastika at the top, his picture on the side, and flashed it at Marcel. "We are with the *Gestapo*, but I'm sure you knew that already, didn't you?" he said with a smirk on his face. "*Und*, you are in no position to ask anything, *Herr* Doctor. If you cooperate with us, you'll have nothing to fear."

The phrase, "with the *Gestapo*", were probably the most dreaded words Marcel could have imagined, and he could almost feel his face turning pale. He continued trying to appear unruffled, because he thought this was the best approach to take. "Cooperate? I have no earthly idea what you could possibly want with me. As you can see, I'm just a dentist. If there is someone in your office with a dental emergency, it would be much better to see him here, where I have my equipment."

Seeming to completely ignore him, the shorter one motioned for Marcel to sit in a chair near the window. "Just sit down. We will check your office before we take you with us."

Marcel sat down, with his jacket over his lap. They both began going through his desk drawers, discarding everything on the floor after they looked at it.

The taller man started taking the books off the shelves and shaking them, to see if anything fell out. After completing these tasks, they looked through the drawers containing the dental instruments. Finding nothing, they opened the closet, found two large boxes on the top shelf, and dumped them on the ground. It was nothing more than miscellaneous junk. Marcel was relieved that he had taken home the work clothes, and boots, that he wore when he went on *Maquis* business. When they came to the filing cabinet, they tried pulling open the two sliding drawers, but they were locked.

"Open this!" the shorter one commanded. Marcel took the key ring out of his pocket, and unlocked the top of the cabinet. They took their time going through the alphabetized files, which were mostly personal documents, contracts, and lectures. All of this material was thrown on the floor, also, and by the time they were through searching the office, Marcel thought a tornado had hit it.

"All right, Doctor, you will come with us," said the taller one, as he opened the door to the reception room, and motioned Marcel to lead the way.

"And just where are you taking me?"

"We are going to our headquarters, and please, no more questions!" the shorter one growled. "We will do the asking from now on. Do you understand?"

Marcel sighed and nodded. He walked out into the reception area, only to see his office staff huddled together behind the counter. To try and alleviate their obvious fears, he attempted to act as normal as possible. "Have you contacted any of the patients, yet?"

"No, Doctor," Annette said. "We'll get started on it right away."

"Good," Marcel said. "And do me a favor…please straighten up my office, as best you can."

"Would you like me to call your wife?" Margo asked.

"No, that won't be necessary. There's no need to worry her over nothing, especially now with the new baby," he added, thinking, *this will evoke some sympathy from these two Nazi bastards.*

Obviously it didn't, because each took one of his arms and nudged him toward the door. "Enough time wasted," said the shorter one, "let us go now!"

They walked down the stairs and out to the curb, where a very large, bald man stood against a black, four-door Mercedes Benz. The man opened the rear door, and Marcel was pushed toward the middle of the rear seat. He was flanked on each side by the two goons. The shorter man said something in German to the bald man driving, and then they were on their way.

Sitting between these two intimidators made Marcel realize that he had to come up with a definite plan on how to deal with their expected questions. With the *Gestapo* now involved, he knew that he was in serious trouble. Any indication of weakness on his part, could put his whole family in danger, and surely lead to his imprisonment, or execution. *But first they would have to prove whatever charges they had, or maybe not.* He had heard how the *Gestapo* operated, and he thought it best to deny everything, and simply take his chances.

Within a few minutes, they had arrived at the Vieux Port area, and the *Vichy* Headquarters building. Marcel felt a weakness coming over his whole body, and used all of his remaining energy to get out of the car. He caught himself before his knees buckled, hoping they didn't see this, and gathered up enough strength to walk normally into the building.

The two agents brought Marcel to a small room in the basement, and he could sense a marked change in their attitude. Where before they were almost civil, now their demeanor was arrogant and belligerent. They both grabbed his arms and heaved him through the door, onto a cold, slab floor. There were no windows, only two upright chairs, and a single light bulb in the center of a seven-foot ceiling.

"You will wait in here until we are ready to talk to you," the taller one said very slowly. "I would suggest you cooperate, or you *will* regret it."

"I can't imagine why I'm here," Marcel said directly to the taller one, "and what information I can possibly offer you."

"Silence...silence you French *schwein!*" screamed the shorter one, as he slapped Marcel across the face, with the back of his leather-gloved hand. "You will only speak when we ask you to speak!"

Marcel could taste the blood in his mouth, but held his ground, seeming to ignore the demand by the shorter one. "I need to use the men's room, if that wouldn't be too much trouble?"

"Shit in your pants, for all we care," said the taller one, as they walked out, slammed the door, and locked it.

Marcel sat down, feeling completely dejected. "Fucking bastards," he said to himself. "One day I'll get even…one day."

He sat there for three hours before the two agents, now accompanied by the bald driver, returned to the room. Marcel had been holding in his urge to pee, until his stomach and teeth ached.

Sitting down in the chair across from him, the shorter one began the interrogation, while the two other men stood on either side of Marcel's chair. "So, Doctor, I hope you have had time to think about cooperating with us? Bruno," indicating the bald man, "loves to beat up on people who don't answer our questions."

Marcel remained silent, knowing anything he said wouldn't help.

"We have reason to believe," the shorter man continued, "that you are a part of *La Résistance* movement," Marcel shook his head, "…that you ran the Underground press," Marcel shook his head again, "…and that you were involved in the bombing on the Rue Honnorat. Is this not true, *Herr* Doctor?"

Marcel leaned forward in his chair and shook his head, as he spoke very slowly and preciously, "No…no…and no. I've never been involved in any of those things."

Without warning, Bruno's elbow hit him on the back of his shoulder blade, and Marcel gave out a loud groan. He reached back with his left hand to rub his sore shoulder, but the shorter one pushed him against the back of the chair.

"You recently were reported to be seen out of the city, many miles from here. Exactly, what were you doing?"

"I was enjoying the countryside, on my day off, that's all. I stopped to get some flowers for my wife, and then came home." He rubbed his shoulder, which was aching terribly. "Is that a crime, now?"

"You are very clever, are you not?"

"No, I'm not clever...I'm just telling the truth, and don't know why you're questioning me. What kind of proof do you have of any of this?"

The shorter one slapped him again on the other side of his face. "You do not seem to understand...I am the one asking the questions, not you, *schwein*. Once more, tell me of your involvement with *La Résistance*."

"I...have...no...involvement in anything. You can beat me all you want, but I can't tell you something I don't know."

The shorter one motioned to the taller one, to get Marcel on his feet. He grabbed him under the arms and lifted him up off the chair. "Maybe this will help refresh your memory," and nodded to Bruno.

Bruno hit him with an uppercut into the stomach, with such force that Marcel could feel all the wind knocked out of him. He fell to the ground, doubled over in pain, unable to catch his breath. To make matters more humiliating, he could feel himself urinating uncontrollably down his leg.

On seeing this, Bruno pointed and said, "Look at this French fag, peeing in his pants and all over the floor."

The three of them were laughing, and thoroughly enjoying their day's work. "You're right, Bruno," the taller one said. "All the French are fags, and should be dressed in ballet skirts. They are so dainty that they can not possibly fight a war. Yes, we should recommend to Berlin that all Frenchmen wear tutus, just like the filthy Jews have to wear the yellow stars."

Marcel was happy that they were amusing themselves, because for the next few minutes they joked about the effeminate French, and this gave him a chance to breathe again. *I can't think of anyone I have hated more in my entire life, than these three assholes*, and this just reconfirmed his commitment to *Le Combat*. He finally couldn't help himself from coughing, and began spitting up blood.

"Ah, King Louis is coming back to life," said the shorter one. "Look at the mess you've made on the floor, you disgusting *schwein*." He kicked Marcel in the hamstring of his left leg. "Get up and sit on that chair. There is someone I want you to meet again."

Marcel managed to get on his knees and work his way up to the chair. His whole upper body ached and he took short breaths to keep himself from fainting. He finally sat in the chair, waiting for the next blows to come. Instead, they all left the room, and a woman came in with a bucket of water and a mop, and began cleaning the floor around him. She looked at him with a very sad expression, but didn't say a word. He could tell that she was just a poor washer woman, trying to eke out a living, and he actually felt sorrier for her than himself.

A few minutes later, the three of them entered again, escorting a man who looked vaguely familiar. He couldn't place where he had seen him before, but it became apparent who he was very quickly.

"Stand up," the shorter one ordered Marcel, who slowly raised his body off the chair. He then turned to the man who was being held by the arms, by the taller one and Bruno, and asked him, "Do you recognize this man who commandeered your truck?"

Of course, Marcel thought to himself, *this is the truck driver that we let go that night. Maybe he was Vichy after all.*

The man looked hard at Marcel, but then shrugged his shoulders and said, "Like I told you before, it was dark and they all had on wool masks. I really couldn't see them that well."

The shorter one looked back at Marcel, and ordered him, "Tell him your name and what city you come from!"

Marcel found that he was so hoarse from the beating, he could hardly speak. When he slowly got out the words, he knew that this was not his regular, deep voice, and this would be to his advantage. "I am…Doctor…Marcel…Pontier. I live…here in Marseille."

"No, no," the truck driver shook his head after a few moments, "I'm certain that I never heard that voice before; furthermore, the size and build of the man I saw that night was much different. He was much taller than I am…and much heavier." He shook his head again, "No, without even seeing his face, I would swear that this was neither him, nor anyone else that night. They were all very large men."

Marcel breathed a sigh of relief, but showed no emotion, because he knew that the three *Gestapo* goons could come to any warped conclusion that they wanted. The shorter one looked disgusted, and waved his hand toward the door. The other two escorted the truck driver out, as the shorter one turned to Marcel and said, "I still think you are the guilty one. And yes…very clever. I know that we will meet again." He was about to leave, when he faced Marcel again, and said, "I do not want our French subjects to see you like that, and think that you've been mistreated, so take off all your clothes and leave them here, by the door. They will be cleaned for you, and then you can leave. You can be assured that the next time we meet, I will probably shoot you." He walked out and slammed the door.

Marcel was dumbfounded…one minute he thought he might die, and the next minute they were letting him go. *They were just intimidating me*, he speculated, *because they have no real proof…and that brings up another question, who, or what, made them seek me out to begin with? I'll have to seriously think about that, but for now I've bought some time, and that's all that matters. I know that the truck driver did a good job of acting…I spared his life, and he just returned the favor.*

He started taking off his clothes, when the washer woman walked in with a bowl of hot water, some soap, a wash cloth, and a large towel. She laid them on the floor and left. He continued until all his clothes were off. He put them in a pile near the door, picked up the stuff that she had brought, and put it on the chair opposite his. He sat down, with his back to the door, and began soaping up the wash cloth, when she walked back in and took his clothes.

He wanted to laugh out loud, because this was all too surreal; but, there was always the possibility they might be watching him, so he started soaping himself down, especially where he had peed down his leg. He used the wash cloth to rinse himself off, but there really wasn't enough water. It would have to do for now.

It was another half hour before the woman came in and laid his pressed clothes on the floor, near the door. She looked at him before leaving, and sadly said, "I'm so sorry, *Monsieur.*"

Marcel quickly dressed and began following the route up the stairs, toward the front entrance. He passed one of the offices, the door of which was ajar, and caught the eye of one of his *Maquis* men, Georges, the radio operator who worked in this building. Georges was startled at seeing Marcel, but looked away quickly. Marcel continued to walk out the entrance and onto the street, toward his office. He would talk to Georges later, and explain what had happened to him. Maybe Georges had heard something in his office, as to why he was singled out for this interrogation.

Right now, Marcel had other things to think about. Plus his body ached like hell. One thing was certain…his mind was more focused than ever. Although he had never shot, or killed the enemy on his missions for *La Résistance*, there was no doubt now that he would ever hesitate to do so, given the opportunity. *They made a big mistake in roughing me up and they are going to pay the price.*

He made a decision not to tell Angelina anything that happened today. It would only worry her, and she would resist the move to Elne even more. He had to insist that they pack the children up and leave as quietly as possible, in the next couple of days. After ten minutes, he reached his office, got his car from the underground garage, and drove home slowly. He knew that from here on, his life, and that of his family, was going to take an entirely different course.

Angelina didn't seem to notice how puffy Marcel's cheeks were. He was able to go up to their bedroom immediately on arriving home, and apply cold washcloths to his face. At dinner, she said that he looked a little bit flush, but he assured her that he was probably catching a little cold, and nothing more was said.

When he broached the subject of leaving in a couple of days, there was no argument, but rather an agreement on her part that this would be a good time to go. "I'll begin packing myself and the children tomorrow, darling," she said cheerfully.

He was relieved that there were no questions, and other than going to bed much earlier than he usually did, Marcel acted as normal as he could. It took him awhile to fall asleep because there was no comfortable position. He awoke in the middle of the night coughing, which sent a pain through his ribs. He also had a terrible taste in his mouth. He went to the bathroom and spit up blood, after which urinating produced the same result. *The blows I received probably affected my kidneys,* he thought, *so I'll try drinking a lot of fluids for awhile.*

For the next two days, Marcel went to work as usual, keeping an eye out for anyone following him. He spotted no one and hoped that the *Gestapo* had given up on him, although he knew deep down, that this was probably wishful thinking.

The girls in his office accepted his explanation, "that it was all a big mistake", and were more than pleased when he told them that he was giving them a month's vacation with pay, instead of the normal two weeks. Not mentioning where he was going, he informed them that he would be leaving in a couple of days. They were to stay on until all the patients were cancelled, and told that they would be rescheduled at a later time. They were more skeptical about this unusual procedure, but wisely said nothing, because they had complete faith in Dr. Pontier.

Marcel came home at 4:30 on the last day of work. He drove his car to the back of his house through a wooded, vacant lot that he owned on the street behind his. The boys helped him with the luggage, toys, and baby paraphernalia. This all had to be repacked, and reconfigured, to fit into the trunk and the floors of the car.

Even though there was a certain amount of whining and crying, many things had to be left behind, for lack of space.

At 7:30, after they had their dinner, and went to the bathroom, they locked the house and got into the car. Marcel had purposely left a light on in the living room, knowing that none of them would be coming back to their home for quite a long time. This would give the appearance that the family was still in the house, if even for a few days until the light bulb blew out. He backed up the Citroën through the wooded lot, and onto the other street. He felt relieved that there were no unfamiliar vehicles in sight, and proceeded to take the most circuitous route through the city as he could.

Just before entering the highway which would take them west toward Elne, a police motorcycle pulled up alongside them. Thinking fast, Marcel said to his family, "Let's all sing *'Frere Jacques'*", and they all began singing. The police officer looked over at them, smiled, and drove on.

Marcel turned on to the highway, and settled in for a drive that would take at least six or seven hours. When they finished singing their last "ding, dong, ding", Marcel began giving the children his routine speech for this long trip, "Now, you know the rules…"

"No fighting or bothering our sister," Raymond and J.P. said in unison.

"Very good, boys," Angelina said, while feeding baby Madeline in her lap. "You have your father's talk down exactly."

Everyone was feeling good, and Marcel was especially happy that he had his whole family together. They were safe for the time being. *In these times, nothing was ever, forever*, he thought. Once they were settled in Elne, he would go into the hills with the *Maquis*. There was no way he could return to Marseille, until the War was over. Yes, things were definitely going to be different.

9

By the time he arrived in Wittenberg, on the Elbe River in Germany, Johann was exhausted, more mentally than physically. After his engineering brigade had finished their projects in Poland, he had barely six days to spend with his parents in Schwandorf. He was shocked to see the devastation caused by the Allied bombing in this part of Germany. He had to report to headquarters in Berlin for one day after leaving Poland, and it was even worse there. *How the Nazis could have been so stupid and greedy*, he thought. *Was this the beginning of the end?*

He hadn't been home for almost a year-and-a-half and had no idea how badly his parents were struggling. Except for some cash that they had always kept in a safe at home, most of their assets had been frozen by the German banks. His mother had to sell some of her jewelry and heirlooms, at a fraction of what they were worth. They were now living day-to-day with what they could scrape up.

"Why did you not let me know you were having such problems?" he asked them. "I get paid every month and could have sent you at least half of it. That is all I really need."

"You have enough to worry about, dear," his mother said. "After Anna died, we did not want to bother you with our problems."

"Son," his father added, "we will get by until the War is over. Besides, there is nothing to buy, except at black market prices."

"So, you will pay the black market price for what you want," Johann said emphatically. "Look at the two of you…how much weight have you lost, at least ten, or fifteen pounds each?" He took off the money belt, wrapped around his waist under his uniform, and laid it on the table. He took out 1500 Deutsch Marks and handed the money to his father. "Here, put this in the safe and use as much as you need to."

Before his father could object, Johann held up his hand and said, "I am going to be sending you about 150 DM each month, and I do not want to hear any more discussion on the matter. Believe me, this is nothing compared to what you have both done for me over the years." And that is how it was left.

Over the next week, before he left for Wittenberg, Johann helped his parents get more organized…something he had learned well in the army. For a few hours each day, he scoured the city for a food supplier he could trust. He finally found one who would sell them food staples for a reasonable price. He used whatever persuasion and influence his captain's uniform could command, even though it was not his nature to pressure people for favors. But this was wartime, and he had to look out for his family.

By the end of the week, Johann felt much better about his parent's financial situation; but, he worried for their safety, knowing that more bombers would be coming. There were long goodbyes and hugs when he got ready to leave, because no one knew when they would see each other again.

For the first time in his life he realized that the responsibility for their household, at least temporarily, had now fallen on his shoulders. The last thing he said to them was, "Promise me that you will go into a shelter, when you hear the air raid sirens."

Johann's brigade all arrived on the 7th of July, 1942, from various places, as ordered, only to find field tents set up for their living quarters. They were the first engineering group to get there and were told that the others probably wouldn't arrive for another week. It therefore became their job to build three barracks for the officers and NCOs.

There wasn't much for Johann to do, except draw up some rough plans and supervise the construction. They were on grazing land 200 meters from the river and three kilometers north of the quaint town. Images of the destruction at home still lingered in his mind. Although he liked to keep busy, he was glad to relax and not go through any special training this week...though he still had no idea why they were here; but more important, he wasn't mentally ready for anything.

It was almost like a bad dream that he couldn't shake--each morning waking up to realize that it was all true. Even after losing Anna and their unborn baby, he wasn't quite as depressed as he was now. Everything seemed to be multiplying and collapsing around him. Hermann didn't seem to get the full impact of Johann's plight, when he tried to explain it to him...his family was safe in their small farm village, and up to this point, untouched by the War.

"*Mein Hauptmann*," Hermann said thoughtfully, "we have a long way to go before the War will be over, so try to get hold of yourself and stay focused on your job. I understand how bad you feel for your parents and all the things you have told me, but it will not do any good to keep dwelling on it. Relax for a few days...enjoy the sunshine and the warm weather, and let the cards fall where they might."

It amazed Johann how philosophical one with a grade school education could get. *If Hermann had gone to college, he probably would have been a general by now*, he thought. *Hermann was probably right; nevertheless, I will have to sort things out by myself.*

It was a welcome relief to feel the warm air again. Each day Johann tried to make the most of it by not wearing his shirt, but just a pair of shorts when he was working. For this week, at least, he was the commanding officer. He allowed his men to wear whatever was comfortable, even though it wasn't regulation.

At night, when they went into town to visit one of the local beer halls, everyone wore their uniform. Since they were the only military personnel in the area, they made quite a hit with the locals, spending their money liberally. Johann had to be almost dragged by Hermann to come with them, but he finally relented after the third night.

After a few beers, he started to unwind. He enjoyed the company of his men, and they in turn respected him as their leader.

The following night, while standing at the bar, he struck up a conversation with a pretty young *fräulein*, whom he quickly realized didn't have very much to talk about. From her actions, he could tell that it wouldn't be hard to get her into bed.

"I do not know, Hermann," Johann exclaimed, after leaving the beer hall, "I must be cracking up. I have not slept with another woman since I met Anna back in college, and now I just turned down that beautiful, young body in there. What the hell is wrong with me?"

"Well," Hermann began, "it is obvious that you are looking for a lot more than just a beautiful, young body."

"Yes, but it is just sex. God knows that I should be ready for that by now."

"I am not worried about you, *Hauptmann*. You are cut from a different cloth and have higher standards than most men. One day you will find someone again and there will not be any doubts in your mind." He paused, nodded his head, and said, "Of this I am sure…you will see."

The week passed quickly. When the three other engineering brigades arrived, the construction was completed and the camp was set up properly. Johann had even added a fence around the compound, with entrances in the front and rear. He put a small kiosk at each entrance to act as a guard house.

"Exemplary job, *Hauptmann*," Major Erik von Klemper commented, as he looked over the compound. "You will be noted for this in my report to Berlin."

"Thank you, *Commandant*," Johann said, "but to be truthful, I did not know what this compound was going to be used for. I added the fences for security, which can easily be taken down, if you need to."

"No, *Hauptmann*...everything looks perfect. I am glad that you had the foresight to put a gate at the back of the compound, also. You will be hearing more about this when I brief you and the other officers later today on the training you will be going through here."

At precisely 1600 hours, Johann and the other three officers, plus the twelve NCOs, met with Major von Klemper in the officer's barracks. Johann saw the major as being a no-nonsense type person, very military, and probably not much older than himself. Indeed, von Klemper's family was a well-known name in the German military. He was a few inches shorter than Johann, dark and well built, but, having a pox-marked face made him more rugged looking than handsome.

"I am sure that everyone here is wondering why they were brought to this little town," the major began, "and for what type of training. First, let me assure you that you and your men will be doing a very important job for the Fatherland, and one not to be taken lightly.

"As you may, or may not have heard, our desert troops in North Africa, led by our glorious Field Marshall Rommel, have been having a rough time against the British. To complicate things even more, our military intelligence in Berlin has every reason to believe that the

Americans will, perhaps in the next few months, be joining in that fight. This would give the Allies overwhelming superiority in that region, one that we cannot match, simply because we cannot spare any troops or equipment from the Russian front.

"Strategically, Russia is much more important to us than the sands of Africa. Under Rommel, we can still win the battle with what we have in place. But, in the event that the British and Americans gain any kind of stronghold, there is the possibility that they may try to invade Europe from there, coming across the Mediterranean into southern France. And that is where you come in," he gestured to the men assembled.

This was the first time since the War began, that Johann had ever heard an officer, with a field command no less, even suggest that the mighty, German war machine might lose a battle, or for that matter, even be threatened. After seeing the destruction at home, he was more convinced than ever that his country was in very serious trouble. The words that the major spoke, "cannot match their superiority", stuck in Johann's brain and made him feel sick to his stomach. It was hard for him to concentrate on what the major was saying now.

"…and it is up to us to make it difficult for the Allies to land on European soil. As you can see," he said, pointing to the insignia on his uniform, "I am a *Wehrmacht* infantry officer, not an engineer like you three, or an architect as *Hauptmann* Weller. My specialty is setting up defensive measures to deter the enemy. By defensive measures, let me clarify that by saying defensive measures along waterways…rivers, lakes, canals, and most importantly, seas and oceans. That is exactly why we picked this spot along the Elbe River.

He held up a cylindrical tube. "I have here some preliminary blueprints that I want you to look over, and hopefully improve on." He opened the cylinder and passed out the drawings to the officers. "You will see that most of the deterrents are different configurations of barbed wire and spikes, mixed in with thick wood, or concrete. These could be used against soldiers themselves and anti-personnel carriers, including tanks. For the next several weeks, we will be building, experimenting, and training our men to install these devices along the beach, and in the river itself.

"All of you have been chosen because of your backgrounds and, as I said before, I would welcome any new innovations you can come up with. I might add that Rommel himself is designing some new devices, which will be used for land warfare. Some of you may have to work with these things at a later date." He paused and looked around the room. "Gentlemen, are there any questions?"

"Major, will we be building any permanent structures, such as observation towers, or pillboxes, for example?" a young lieutenant asked.

"That is always a possibility, *Leutnant*," the major answered. "The *Korps* of Engineers have definite specifications for these things, and at some time we could be ordered to build them. Right now, we are only concentrating on slowing down any type of invasion from the sea."

Another lieutenant raised his hand, and when recognized asked, "Sir, you mentioned that we would be training for some time. Does that mean that we will be going to Paris from here for a little R and R?"

Everyone laughed, including the major, who replied, "No, I am afraid that we have a war to fight, *Leutnant*. Eventually, we will be going to southern France, but before that we'll have several assignments here in Deutschland, mostly on the Rhine River. The army will be testing out what we develop, and making any adjustments they feel are necessary."

"Major von Klemper," Johann said slowly, getting over his initial shock, "you said that we will be going to the southern part of France. Does Berlin not expect the invasion to come from England, across the English Channel, or does this seem more probable?"

"*Hauptmann* Weller, I think that it is best not to speculate, or even discuss this type of information so freely, especially with the enlisted men present," the major replied, in a tone much more serious and different than the moment before. "We are all on a need-to-know basis…just soldiers following orders."

"Yes, Sir. I understand."

"Very well then. If there are no further questions…*Hauptmann* Weller, I would suggest that you get your heads together, come up with some ideas and plans to start building these devices. We will talk again at dinner this evening."

"Very well, Major. We will begin immediately."

"If you need me for anything, I will be in my communications truck checking on the supplies. They are due to arrive here early tomorrow morning." The major clicked his heels, threw out his left arm in a Nazi salute, "*Heil* Hitler!" and marched out of the barracks.

All of the men jumped up and saluted in a similar fashion. *Heil Hitler, my ass!* Johann thought to himself. He had a feeling that this maniac, Hitler, was going to destroy all of them.

For the next four weeks, they designed some new equipment, used some of it, scrapped some of it, and tested the good stuff in the water and on the beach. It amazed the junior officers how well everything fell into place. Only a month before, none of them had ever heard of the hardware they were building…*German ingenuity*, they thought…*that must be it.*

As usual, Johann immersed himself in his work, trying not to think about the past, or what lay ahead. He couldn't get close to any of the other officers, especially the major, because they all fervently believed in the thousand-year *Reich* and Aryan superiority. "They must have their heads in the sand," he told Hermann privately.

It was almost the middle of August, 1942, when they tore down the temporary camp. They packed up their gear and moved to their next assignment, the small city of Porz, between Cologne and Bonn. It lay on the east bank of the Rhine River, the most important inland waterway in Europe. Here, they would demonstrate their equipment to the military brass, get their approval, or rejection, and then train other troops to install it along the European shores. It would be three months of nightly bombing raids before they were reassigned to France.

10

Marcel was relieved to be out of Marseille. He still ached from the beating he received, and the drive to Elne didn't help. Angelina could see that he was uncomfortable, and when she asked him about it, he said, "Oh, its a little strain in my back from bending over patients all day. It will be fine after a few days rest at you parent's house."

"I wish you could stay longer, darling, but I know you have to get back to work."

If she only knew what kind of work I would be doing, she'd be very upset, he thought.

"I know the fresh air will do you good. Maybe we'll take some nice, long hikes with the children through the vineyards and into the forest. *Maman* will be happy to take care of Madeline."

"Yes, *Cherie,* that'll be very relaxing," Marcel said. All he really wanted to do is stretch out in bed for a month. He took a quick look over his shoulder and said, "I see the children are all asleep. I was beginning to wonder why it was so quiet. If we don't have to stop, we should make Elne in a couple of hours." He looked over at Angelina, and said, "How are you doing?"

"I'll be fine. I just changed Madeline, so she's good for another few hours. And the other three will probably sleep until we get there."

They arrived at the Courty's house at 2:00 A.M. They were greeted by Elizabeth, Paul, and Paulette, all waiting anxiously to see the children, especially the new baby. After some milk and crackers, they put the children to bed. Elizabeth had prepared some snacks, and for the next two hours the adults sat at the dining room table talking, eating, and enjoying an excellent, ten-year old *Bordeaux* that Paul had stored in the wine cellar.

"So, Papa," Angelina began, "soon you'll be bottling your own wine in a couple of months. Is it as good as you wrote us?"

"Aah, *magnifique*!" Paul exclaimed. "It's even better than what I thought...very smooth, with a wonderful aroma."

"As good as 1929?" Marcel asked.

"As good, if not better," Paul answered. "All of you will have to come back for the wine festival in November."

"Angelina and the children may still be here, Papa," Marcel replied, "but I'll make a point to return for the festival."

"You still haven't told us why you're staying so long, Angelina?" Paulette asked. "Is there something we should know about?"

"Why don't you tell them, Marcel?" Angelina said. "You can explain it a lot better than I can."

Marcel explained to them his concerns about the Germans possibly moving south, believing that the Allied invasion would come from the Mediterranean. "I just know that Angelina, and the children, will be much healthier and safer here on the farm with the three of you. Elne is not a strategic area like Marseille, so there's no reason to think there would be any problems here." He paused, and then added, "I hope it won't be too much of an inconvenience for all of you."

"Inconvenience?" Paulette said, "of course not. We love having them here." Paul and Elizabeth nodded their approval. "I was just so curious when we heard that you'd be staying longer than normal, I couldn't imagine what had happened. Now, we can see your concerns."

"Elne is probably the safest place in Europe, Marcel," Paul added, "and we're delighted you made this choice. Perhaps the boys can help me make the wine."

"They would love that, Paul," Elizabeth said. "But, please don't get them drunk, like you did these two," pointing at Angelina and Paulette. Everyone laughed.

The conversation continued for awhile longer, until the bottle of *Bordeaux* was gone. Never once did Marcel even hint of his plans, or his involvement in *Le Combat*, the struggle.

11

In August, the Rhine River would normally be a lovely place for residents and tourists to walk along its banks, picnic, and enjoy the beauty of one of the major waterways in Europe. Normally, also, a plethora of boats of every description, would be seen, forming an almost picture postcard on the water. But, these were not normal times in Germany. The daily, Allied bombing of the major cities, along the eastern shore, kept everyone far away. In addition, there was now a ban on privately-owned pleasure boats using the river.

The High Command of the *Wehrmacht* had chosen Porz to test these defensive, beach barriers. It was ideally suited along the Rhine to land amphibian craft, and it was a small city that would not be attractive to the bombers. Occasionally, errant bombs did fall, and when approaching aircraft were spotted, the testing stopped as quickly as possible.

The materials Johann's company used to build these ramparts were changed over and over again for strength and durability, as well as design. The depth of the water was another major factor to be considered. Further changes would have to be made once they got to their final destinations in southern France. But it became obvious to Major von Klemper and Johann alike, that the High Command was most impressed with the combinations of concrete and steel, as well as those made with railroad ties and razor wire, to fit all their needs. Their objectives were to either slow down the amphibians, or to destroy them completely, both leaving the Allied troops stranded in the water, and hence, setting them up as easy targets.

As Johann observed all the destruction around him, he knew what he and his men were doing for the war effort would probably make little difference in the long run. For the first time in history, airpower was going to make a substantial difference in the outcome of a war. Now having seen all these burned out cities, he realized that American and British airpower was far superior to anything the *Luftwaffe* could muster.

After they were in Porz for a month, Major von Klemper called a meeting with Johann, two of his lieutenants, and the non-coms. "Gentleman," he said, "although all the tests so far have met the brasses' approval, our invasion and defensive planners now want something that will go even deeper to slow down the landing, before they get anywhere near the beaches. *Hauptmann*," he said looking at his captain in charge, "it will be up to you to design a structure that will sit in water at least 15-20 feet deep, with a mine not visible from the surface."

"What time-frame are we looking at, Major?" Johann asked.

"I would like the preliminary plans in a few days, and then the final plans and models within a week or so."

"Yes, sir," Johann said. "Should we pull any of our men off their present duties?"

"No, *Hauptmann*. I want you to continue to build the underwater obstacles that have been approved. We will need as many as possible to fortify a lot of coastline along the southern and western parts of France. They will be put into mass production shortly at our factories in Frankfurt, but in the meantime, do not stop building. These will eventually be taken by rail to your assignment area."

"Where might that be, Major?" a young lieutenant asked.

"Right now, that is classified," the Major smiled. "To tell you the truth, *Leutnant*," he shrugged, "I do not really know myself." Everyone laughed, and after a few brief announcements, the meeting was adjourned.

Johann was happy that he would have a new project to keep himself busy. He hadn't heard from his parents for two weeks, and this was starting to worry him. He could just imagine what the area around Munich was like now. He had spent hours trying to call home, but was never able to get through, probably because the telephone lines were all down, or the military had them tied up. He would try to get back to Schwanndorf the first weekend he had free.

For the next ten days, Johann and his officers designed preliminary, and then final plans for the deeper-water, amphibious obstacles. To avoid transportation and installation problems, they kept the weight to a minimum with a concrete, square base five feet wide, and four feet tall, enough to anchor the device in the water. A pyramid of steel pipes would come up from this base and house a mine at its apex, strong enough to destroy a landing craft. The plan was to submerge this in thirteen feet of water so it would not be visible from the surface. "Of course, this will have to be built, tested, and more than likely refined some more," Johann told his men.

The next day, Major von Klemper informed Johann that his plans seemed feasible, but would have to be built at another location, with a few prototypes sent back to Porz for testing. If these worked as planned, they would also be sent by rail, along with the other barriers, to the French coast.

"I hate to ask you this, Major," Johann said, "but do you think it would be possible to get a weekend pass, sometime in the near future?"

"*Hauptmann*!" Von Klemper said strongly to the captain, "that would be highly unlikely at this time, unless it was an absolute emergency. You, more than anyone else, know what kind of pressure we are under to get this project completed. Why would you ask for a leave, now?"

"It is my parents, sir," Johann replied. "I haven't heard from them for almost a month, which is very unusual. I would not think of asking, if I felt this would cause a problem or delay the project. But frankly, I am quite worried. If there happens to be a down time, while we're waiting for the materials and shipments to arrive, I would appreciate your considering this request."

"We're all worried about our families back home, Johann, but unless there is a complete stoppage of work, the answer is no. The Fatherland always comes first, and since you are the key man for this whole endeavor, I cannot afford to let you go." He paused, and then said, "But, I will consider your request."

"Thank you, sir, I understand. I will continue trying to call them, and…" Johann never finished his sentence. The bomb hit their compound 75 meters from the office where they were standing. It threw both of them to the ground, as the small building collapsed around them. Johann lay on his back for almost five minutes, with the rain hitting his face, before he regained consciousness. He felt a ringing in his ears and a very warm feeling behind his left shoulder. He reached back to touch it and could feel the blood soaking his uniform.

Looking around at what was left of the room, he saw the major six feet away lying under a pile of boards. Johann slowly crawled toward him, removing the boards and debris off the major's body. Seeing a gash on the side of the major's head, he immediately yelled out, "*Sani!*", and within seconds Hermann and one of his men, who also acted as the unit's corpsman, were at their side. They had come from a building further away from the blast, which was only partially damaged. The corpsman immediately started testing the major's vital signs.

"It looks like the Major has suffered a concussion," the corpsman began, "and that cut on his head needs to be stitched. But other than that, he should be fine in a few hours." He looked over at Hermann, and said, "Sergeant, would you please get the stretcher and a couple of men to help carry the Major back to the first-aid room?"

Hermann nodded, and then pointed to Johann's back, saying to the corpsman, "Ludwig, you better take a look at the *Hauptmann*, also. He is bleeding pretty badly. How do you feel, sir?"

"I am a little sore, but I think I can walk over to the first-aid room. Just take care of the Major first."

Johann wobbled toward the outside, but had to stop abruptly when he started feeling dizzy. Hermann ran over and put Johann's arm around his shoulder, and began to carry him toward the first-aid room. "*Mein Hauptmann*, you have lost a lot of blood, so relax and let me carry you." When they got to the infirmary, Hermann ordered two of his men to take a stretcher back to get the major. He then started taking off Johann's jacket, shirt, and undershirt, all soaked with blood. Seeing a big gash in Johann's back, near his left shoulder, Hermann grabbed some gauze and tape, applied it to the wound, and slowly eased Johann face down on one of three made-up hospital beds.

Within a short period of time, the major was carried in on the stretcher and put on a makeshift, operating table, where the corpsman dressed his wound. Shortly thereafter, Major von Klemper regained consciousness for a short period of time, looked dazedly around the room, and seeing Johann lying on the bed, asked, "What has happened… where am I?"

The corpsman spoke softly near the major's ear. "Sir, an Allied bomb hit our compound. The *Hauptmann* apparently has a shrapnel wound to his back, and you have suffered a concussion. You also have an open wound to the side of your head, which I have temporarily taken care of. I do not think it is serious; however, I feel that you and the *Hauptmann* should be evacuated to a military hospital, and be looked at properly by a surgeon. I have already called for an ambulance to take you both to Frankfurt."

With his eyes half-closed, the major asked, "How much damage has been done? What about all the men, and all…?" his voice trailed off.

"Major, this is Sergeant Koch," Hermann stepped in and said. "It has been raining so much, with a lot of lightening and thunder, that no one even heard the plane that dropped the bomb. My guess is that it was returning from a bombing mission further inland, and just released it without caring what it was going to hit."

"Sergeant," the major said groggily, "what did it hit? Is anyone else hurt?"

"Yes sir, unfortunately it destroyed barracks number two and killed four of the men that we know of…we are still clearing away all the debris. There was also damage to the workshop, and one of the machinists was killed. Several of the men have minor injuries and scratches and are being taken care of in the NCO mess area." Hermann could see that the major was dozing off and he motioned to the corpsman that they should step outside and allow the two officers to rest. The ambulance would arrive shortly and take them to a hospital.

Once outside, they apprised the OD (Officer of the Day) of the status of Major von Klemper and Captain Weller. It would take some time before the compound was cleaned up, the bodies were prepared for burial, and some order was brought to the camp by the remaining officers. Hermann suggested that the corpsman should look after the other wounded men, and that he would stay here until the ambulance arrived.

Over the last few years, Hermann had grown very fond of Johann, and thought of him as a brother. He prayed that it wasn't too serious an injury, and that his recovery would be swift. The ambulance arrived an hour later and took the two men away. Hermann stared for awhile at the devastation one bomb had caused, and cursed the Nazis for all the problems they were causing the people of Germany. *After the War, I will leave the Army and work on our family's farm. I never want to be around men killing each other ever again. All I want now is peace and quiet with my Frau and girls.*

12

Marcel knew that when he left his family in Elne, he would not be returning directly to Marseille. He had made a break with his life and practice there temporarily, because he couldn't afford another run-in with the Gestapo. *They must have something on me, or why would they have picked me up and interrogated me the way they did?*

Before he left, he had swapped his Citroën for Paul's older and smaller Peugeot, on the pretense that they could use it, with four extra people there. In reality, the *Vichy* and the police could identify his car, and he needed to get rid of it. Being very cautious, he had taken extra license plates with him on leaving Marseille, and had changed the tags one afternoon, when he was by himself in Elne.

Instead of driving along the coast toward Marseille, Marcel headed northwest to Carcassonne, less than two hours away. Florette had told him of a safe-house there, frequently used by the *Maquis*. Whether he wanted to or not, he was now going to be a full-time *Maquis* operative, and would probably live in the hills with the rest of them. He was sure that the person running the safe-house would know how to get in touch with Florette, because that was his first priority. As a marked man by the *Gestapo*, he had to let her know what his status had become, and subsequently help transition him into the *Maquis* network.

He was relieved not to be going back to Marseille, and that his family was in a safe place, with plenty of money that he had given to Angelina. He didn't want the five of them to be a burden on Paul and Elizabeth, even though they would never have complained. His body felt good from the five day rest he had in Elne, and he could now concentrate on disrupting the *Vichy* puppets and their German backers--two entities he equated with the demons of hell.

It was a pleasant drive through the rolling hills, and before he knew it, he could see the city in the distance. He had always enjoyed visiting Carcassonne. The almost perfectly preserved Medieval City, still fully inhabited, towered above the Aude River and was majestically surrounded by massive, double, stone walls and more than 50 fortified guard towers. In the center was the Château Comtal, itself fortified and surrounded by a moat. *How warfare has changed,* he thought. *This was adequate protection, back in the 12th Century, but today, the German tanks and planes could turn this into rubble within an hour.*

He drove into the city through a succession of gates, drawbridges and towers. Once inside, he parked the car in a vacant area once used to tie up the horses. There was a labyrinth of narrow pedestrian streets full of shops, cafés and restaurants. He began to look for the Cadeaux Watch Shop. He found it quickly, a short block from where he parked. So as to not attract attention, he stood outside looking through the glass window, closely studying the array of clocks and antique watches, also noticing that there were customers inside. It was 11:30 in the morning, and since he had eaten only a light breakfast before leaving Elne, he walked up the narrow street searching for a restaurant that was open for lunch. He would avoid any crowds this way, and go back to the watch shop after he was finished.

The street led him to a charming square, with a bust of a general sitting on a pedestal in the center, and surrounded by flowers. No doubt, the general had defended Carcassonne at one time or another. There were several outdoor cafés in the square, and Marcel chose the Madeline Brassiere, where two, wooden-carved, fat chefs stood at the front door. He decided to eat inside, even though it was much more pleasant on the square. The fewer people he came in contact with, the better.

He was shown a table near the back wall by a rather pudgy woman in an apron. She handed him a menu. He laughed to himself, thinking that *maybe this is the fat chef's wife.* He began looking over the menu, when a middle-aged stranger approached his table.

"I would suggest the *Cassoulet, Monsieur,*" the man said. Marcel looked up, and before he could speak, the man asked, "Do you mind if I join you?" He pulled out the chair facing Marcel, and sat down. He extended his hand, which Marcel took, and continued, "I am *Monsieur* Simon Cadeaux…and you *Monsieur*?"

Marcel was stunned, and at first couldn't speak. After a few moments, he said, "I am Doctor Marcel Pontier, from Marseille."

"Ah, Marseille, a wonderful city. My wife and I loved to visit there before the War, but now traveling is much tougher, wouldn't you say?"

"Yes, extremely more difficult," Marcel said, letting Cadeaux feel him out on his own. "I've always enjoyed coming to Carcassonne, too."

"So, what brings you here on this beautiful day, Marcel? You're a long way from home."

"Well, Simon, let me ask you a question first."

"By all means…go ahead."

"How did you happen to sit down at my table, when there were plenty of free tables available?"

"Very good observation, Marcel. Actually, I saw you staring in my window, and when I walked in here to Madeline's…an excellent choice by the way…I recognized you." He paused for a moment, to see if this got any reaction from Marcel. "Were you looking for something in particular in my shop?"

Marcel was about to speak, when the pudgy lady came over to the table and kissed Simon on both cheeks. "*Bonjour,* Simon. *Comment allez-vous?*"

"Ah, *bonjour,* Madeline. *Tres bien, merci,*" Simon replied. "For starters, I think we'll have a bottle of whatever red table wine you have, and some olive oil to go with our bread." She nodded and walked away. "Now, as you were about to say, Marcel?"

Marcel laughed, and said, "So, that's Madeline? And is her husband the chef?"

Simon laughed also, and replied, "Yes he is, and how did you know that?" "Well," Marcel began, "when I saw those two carved figures outside, I surmised as much."

"Well, you guessed right. Here she comes with our wine, so we better take a look at the menu."

Madeline put the wine, and a dish of olive oil and vinegar, on the table. She took out her notepad and pencil, and asked, "Well, gentleman, what would you care to have for lunch?"

"Simon, what was that dish you recommended?" Marcel asked.

"It's a local specialty, called *Cassoulet,*" Simon replied. It's like a goose stew, with a lot of garlic. It's excellent…really, you ought to try it. In fact, I'll have that myself, Madeline."

"Sounds too good to pass up…make that two, please."

"*Merci,* gentleman. It will be about 15 minutes, so enjoy your wine."

After she left, Marcel poured each of them a glass of wine. They raised their glasses and Marcel made a toast, "*Vive la France.*" They clinked glasses and tasted their wine. Marcel leaned over the table, and in a low voice said, "I *am* looking for a particular item. Her name is Florette, and I thought you might be able to help me get in touch with her."

Simon's face remained passive at the mention of Florette's name. He played his role to the hilt, not wanting to reveal any knowledge of this person, in the event Marcel was a possible *Vichy* agent. "Is this the name of a certain type of watch or clock? I don't recall hearing of it before." He took another sip of wine. "Tell me, Marcel, why would you come all the way here to locate this item? Couldn't you have done this in Marseille?"

Marcel didn't know how fast to proceed, so he decided to plunge straight in and tell him the truth. "Simon, your name was given to me by Florette, in case I was ever in the Catalonia region, and needed help…needed a safe-house. The truth of the matter is, I can't go back to Marseille, because of a run-in I had with the *Gestapo*. I would normally make my contacts from there, but now I've got to let Florette know where I am, and then make plans accordingly. If I've come to the wrong place, then I'll have to find help somewhere else."

"This all sounds very intriguing, but I'd rather not know any more than what you've told me."

Madeline brought the small, individual, black pots of *Cassoulet* to the table, along with some more bread. "*Bon apatite*," she said, and walked away.

They both began eating their food, before Simon spoke again. "When we finish our lunch, why don't you walk around town for a few hours? It will give me time to digest the situation, and see whether or not I can find this item." Marcel nodded. "You'll find plenty to do, by browsing through the shops and visiting our beautiful Cathedral, the Basilica of Saint Nazaire. It never hurts to pray once in a while, and it's quite dark in there."

Marcel got the meaning, and said, "Thank you, I'll do that. Where do you want me to meet you?"

"Why don't you come by my shop around 4:00, and we'll talk some more?"

At exactly 1600 hours, Marcel walked into the Cadeaux Watch Shop, to the sound of a melodic chime. Simon walked through a curtain from the back of the store, and greeted Marcel warmly. "So, Marcel, did you enjoy your day in our beautiful city?"

"As a matter of fact, I enjoyed it very much. I even took another tour of the castle, and had a chance, this time, to study some of the mechanical drawings. Fascinating how they did things back in the 1200's."

"Yes, they were real craftsman back in those days," Simon replied. "We seem to be losing more and more, as time goes on." He walked past Marcel to the front door, locked it, and then put a "CLOSED" sign in the window. Then he walked back toward the rear of the store, and motioned Marcel to follow him. "Let's go upstairs and have some tea. I have a surprise for you."

Marcel followed him through the curtain, into a large room used for watch and clock repairs. There was a bathroom to the left, and two doors on the back wall.

The door in the middle led to the outside, while the one on the right led to another storage room, with an indoor staircase at the very rear of the building. Marcel had no idea there was a second story. It wasn't evident from the street side. They climbed the stairs, which opened to a small living room and kitchen, and to Marcel's amazement, Florette was sitting there pouring tea.

"*Bonjour*, Marcel," Florette said, as she stood and gave him a kiss on both cheeks.

"*Bonjour*, Florette. I never expected to see you here today. This is a surprise!"

"Well," Florette began, "after Simon contacted me, I had to come here and see for myself, if you were who you claimed to be. I couldn't be 100 % sure from the description Simon gave me, especially since you were here in Carcassonne, of all places."

"Then why did you allow me to come up here, Simon? Weren't you taking a chance?"

"I can answer that," Florette said, as she walked into an open door of a bed-room, Marcel and Simon following close behind. "Do you see that small window?

"It's not visible from the street, because it blends into the façade on the front of this building." Marcel nodded. "I could see you coming along the street, and all I had to do was flip this switch on the wall, which was ingeniously wired up by Simon.

"That, in turn, activated the bell, which was the signal for Simon to bring you up."

"As you know by now, Marcel," Simon said, "any breakdown in our network could be disastrous to a lot of people. That is why we need to be extra cautious."

"I couldn't agree with you more, and I'm sorry if this causes any extra *problèmes* for *La Résistance*." Looking at Florette, he said, "I had to get my family out of Marseille, and I hope and pray that now they're safe, so I can devote my full time and energy to helping the *Maquis*." Not that they would ask, but he didn't think it was necessary for him to tell where he took Angelina and the children.

"This is a war, Marcel," Florette said. "There will always be problems. You did the right thing by coming here, and we definitely want you to be in a leadership role with the *Maquis*. Let's sit and have some tea."

She paused, as they all sat down. "I'd like to hear all the details about your experience with the *Gestapo*."

"A lot has happened since we last met, Florette. Before that though, tell me Simon, was it just a coincidence that you came to eat at Madeline's today?"

Simon just laughed.

13

Having been in Elne for three weeks, Angelina and the children settled in quite well into her parent's home. She and the baby took one of the bedrooms on the main floor, next to the living and dining rooms, and Babette slept in the adjacent bedroom. The two boys, Raymond and Jean-Pierre, shared one of the bedrooms on the top floor, while the Courtys used two of the three bedrooms on the middle floor. Elizabeth, Paul and Paulette were elated to have all their family together. It was like old times for Angelina and Paulette, who relished these get-togethers, with this one possibly lasting a lot longer.

The children already had some friends in the village from their previous visits, so they had no complaints and loved being out in the country. Raymond kept busy by reading half the day, playing chess with a friend or his grandfather, helping Paul on the farm and taking long walks. J.P. couldn't care less about reading or playing chess. He wanted to be outside all day running around, or playing soccer and rugby. The dirtier he was by dinner time, the better. Babette loved just staying in the house helping her grandmother and mother with their daily chores, and playing dolls with her two little friends. Once a week, Paulette took Babette with her in the morning to work, where she helped around the office, and at noon, they went to the outdoor market, before going home for lunch.

"Maybe Madeline will be more like J.P.," Elizabeth said, "because Babette is just like Raymond."

"J.P. must take after his father," Paulette injected. "I've never seen anyone so active. Doesn't he ever sit down?"

"Very, rarely," Angelina slowly said. "I think he probably does take after Marcel, who finds it very hard to relax, also. Although, I do think Marcel had a very nice rest while he was here."

"He seemed to be in some type of pain," Elizabeth said, "and when I asked what was bothering him, he said it was his back; although, he seemed to be holding his sides a lot, when no one was watching. Has he seen a doctor, lately?"

"Seen a doctor?" Angelina laughed. "You must be kidding, *Maman*. I don't know if he has been for a check-up since we've been married. You know, doctors always make the worst patients. Besides, Marcel told me before we left Marseille that his back had started to bother him at the office from leaning over patients so much. I'm sure he would let me know if it were something else."

The women were all in the kitchen cooking dinner, and as they did every day, they had a glass of wine and discussed the day's events. Babette was in her room having "tea" with her dolls, and the boys were helping Paul at their winery. They would be home soon to listen to the French version of the 6:00 Nightly BBC Report from London. This was their only true source of world news, since the Germans now controlled all the radio stations in France, and produced nothing but propaganda. News of the War became the focus point at the end of the day, and everyone, including the boys, looked forward to it. Raymond and J.P. came to realize that everyone in France was affected by *Le Combat*, and they listened so intently to the family's discussion every night, that they were now taking an active part in it.

At precisely 5:50 p.m., Paul and the boys came up the stairs. They greeted everyone, went to the bathroom to wash up before listening to the BBC, and then having dinner. Elizabeth told them all to go upstairs and change their shirts, also, because they were filthy. Paul knew better than to argue with her, and the boys had already learned that whatever *Grandmere* wants them to do, they do. She had always been the disciplinarian in the family.

When they came back down the stairs, Angelina could see that her father had a noticeable limp. His left leg was always giving him problems, but she had never seen him limping. "Papa is your leg getting worse?" she asked.

"Oh," Paul said as he reached down and rubbed his leg, "my knee must be getting arthritic from the war injury. It bothers me from time to time, but I live with it."

"Well, have you seen a doctor about it?"

"Eh!" he said while shaking his head and looking up at the ceiling. "What do they know? There's nothing they can do about it anyway."

"You don't know that," Angelina countered.

"You're wasting your time talking to Papa," Pauline shrugged. "Believe me, I've tried and have gotten nowhere."

"Your Papa is just a silly old goat," Elizabeth said as she was getting a bowl out of the dining room credenza, "so don't bother trying to reason with him. He would rather just suffer with the pain."

Paul got the short-wave radio out of the closet and turned it on, so he wouldn't have to listen to the three of them talk about the solution to his problem. It usually took 10-20 seconds before one could hear the static. This was the signal in their house for everyone to be quiet, while Paul fine-tuned the radio to get the station clearly. Today, for some reason, it was taking a little longer, but finally the static disappeared, and at exactly 1800 hours, a voice was heard. Paul turned up the sound and they waited in anticipation for the latest news.

"*Bonjour France. Ici la B.B.C.* (Good afternoon, France. This is the B.B.C.)

Les Français parlent aux Français (The French speaking to the French). It is hard to imagine that our country has now been in German hands for over two years. It was a bleak day on June 14, 1940, when Paris fell and Nazis troops marched down the *Champs Elysees*, and even a darker day a week later, on June 22, when the armistice was signed.

"General Charles de Gaulle, leading the *Free France* movement from here in London, urges all French patriots to continue fighting the Germans in the north, and the *Vichy* in the south, led by the traitor Henri Philippe Petain. His collaboration with the Nazis will one day be severely punished.

"If you have not received the reports since June 5th, the United States declared war on Bulgaria, Hungary, and Romania. On the 21st of June, German troops seized Tobruk in North Africa, but less than a few weeks ago, July 2, 1942, the British halted the Germans at El Alamein."

The family all cheered, and the broadcast continued.

"The victory in Egypt, at El Alamein, was brought about by a combination of strong British resistance, and an apparent supply shortage of Rommel's troops. In a speech to Parliament yesterday, Prime Minister Winston Churchill declared to its members, 'It won't be long before Tobruk is in our hands again...'

"For us, *Le Combat* will continue, until the day when we can again celebrate our recent, national holiday, Bastille Day, July 14th, in the proper manner."

There was a long pause. Some music started playing, and the family waited for the anticipated codes to *La Résistance* to be broadcasted. Finally, after 20 seconds, the message began. "Allie will wear a hat. Zachary declares time out. An attitude will come to Hannah. Sarah will eat her piece of cake. Good luck, Cavity. Stay tuned for more news to come."

Paul turned the radio off and returned it to the closet. Everyone took their seat at the long, wooden table in the dining room. The blessing was said by Paul, and the food was passed around. "I hope they killed a lot of those Nazi bastards at El Alamein!" Paul gruffly said.

"Could the powerful, German machine have some kinks in their armor?" Paulette asked. "Supply shortages? What's that all about?"

"Hitler is probably using everything he has on the Russian front," Angelina said. "What do you think, Papa?"

"What I think," he began, between bites of chicken, "is that we can all be thankful that the Allies have won a major victory in Africa, and this just paves the way for the Americans to be there soon."

"And then we can really kill a lot of those Nazi bastards," J.P. piped in. Right, *Grandpere*?"

"J.P.!" Angelina exclaimed, "what have I told you about using naughty language like that?"

"But, *Maman*," J.P. answered, "*Grandpere* said the same thing, and he should know…he was in two wars."

Elizabeth, who was sitting next to J.P., grabbed his ear between her two fingers, and said, "Listen to me young man, you don't talk like that in my house! Do you understand?" He nodded. "*Grandpere* shouldn't be using foul language around you children, so he's not too smart either." She let go of his ear, which had now turned red, then looked over at Paul and shook her finger at him.

Paul smirked, caught J.P.'s eye, and winked at him. "Elizabeth, why are you getting so excited? They're only words, and besides, how else are you going to describe these Nazis..." he caught himself, before he said anymore to alienate her.

Everyone laughed under their breaths, except Elizabeth.

"How long do you think the War will last, *Tante* Paulette?" Raymond asked. "To take Africa, and then Europe, could take another three or four years, wouldn't you say?"

"That is very perceptive, Raymond," Paulette replied. "How did you come to that conclusion?"

Raymond thought for a moment, and then said, "Well, from all the reading I've done on the 1st World War, it would be hard to do it in less time; unless maybe the Americans could come up with some super weapons, or maybe have someone kill Hitler."

"I wish I could kill Hitler," J.P. said. "I'd teach that son-of-a..." he stopped himself just in time, as he saw his mother and grandmother looking at him. "What I mean to say, is one day I'll be fighting the Germans, and I'll show 'em what France can do."

"I think that Raymond is right," Paulette said. "The War will probably last for at least three more years, and hopefully not longer. So, J.P., I don't think you'll get a chance to kill any Germans. Let's hope not."

"I'm just thankful that you and the children came to stay with us," Elizabeth said to Angelina. "Marcel was right in bringing you here."

"I had my doubts at first," Angelina replied, "but I can see now that being here in Elne is about as far away from the War as we can get."

Babette, who had not been heard from during their dinner discussion, stood up and got into her mother's lap. "*Maman*, please don't let Raymond and J.P. go away and fight in the War. I don't want them to be away like Papa."

Angelina hugged her, and said to assure her, "Darling, you don't have to worry about your brothers. They're going to stay right here with you, and Papa will be visiting very soon."

Paul was sitting at the end of the table, rubbing his chin as in deep in thought. Elizabeth noticed this and said to him, "*Cherie*, what are you thinking about?"

He didn't speak for a moment, but then said, "It was just that last message to *La Résistance*, from the BBC. Do you think…no it couldn't be…"

14

According to the doctor, at the Reich Hospital in Frankfurt, it wasn't a minute too soon that Major von Klemper and *Hauptmann* Weller were hospitalized. Both men required surgery...Johann's being more acute and severe, in removing the shrapnel, and repairing some blood vessels that were damaged in his back. He had also lost a lot of blood and required several transfusions. The major indeed had a concussion, which necessitated a few days of bed rest. The head wound could have become severely infected, had the surgeon not removed a small piece of metal beneath the scalp.

Before the major left the hospital to return to Porz, he looked in on Johann to see how he was feeling. "I understand from the doctors that you will be here for another week or two," he said. "If you feel up to it, take a few of those days and see if you can get yourself back home, because I will need you in Porz as soon as possible."

"Thank you, Major. I hope this starts feeling better soon." He touched his back with his right hand and tried to maneuver his left shoulder. He winced at the touch, and said, "If you want to know the truth, it seems to be worse than ever."

"Yes, the doctor told me that it will take some time before it heals fully, so just do what they tell you, and I am sure you will be fine in a short period of time." He reached over the bed and shook Johann's hand. "There is a truck outside waiting to take me back. I will see you soon." He turned around and walked out the door.

Johann thought to himself that *the major was a pretty decent fellow, when he wanted to be.* He was still pretty staunch, as you would expect from a career military man, but he didn't know whether he was a Nazi, or not. He had never been that close with von Klemper to discuss his politics, nor would he ever become a good friend. Someone in Johann's position had to be very careful in whom he confided, because he was diametrically opposed to the entire Nazi doctrine.

At the end of his first post-surgical week, Johann's condition showed great improvement. He was starting to rotate his shoulder without too much effort, and his doctor said he could leave the hospital by the middle-to-end of the following week. A few days later, on one of the visits to his room, the doctor happened to mention that he had to go to Munich for a few days to operate on some big-wig general. It was only a simple hernia, but the general had requested him. He had no choice, even though he was needed here to treat a lot of patients he was already taking care of.

"There is a shortage of surgeons here already," Dr. Ritter began telling Johann, "plus the war casualties are piling in every day, and they expect me to leave all this?" Albert Ritter was a tall, thin man, a few years older than Johann. He had done his surgical residency, before the war, at Johns Hopkins in Baltimore, Maryland. His choice to return home in 1935 was not a difficult one, because his whole family lived here. He had since built a reputation in medical circles as one of the finest young surgeons in Germany. He was commissioned as a Major when he was drafted into the army in 1940.

Johann could tell he was frustrated, but he was happy there was someone he could talk to. Albert felt at ease with him, also, and the two young men found themselves chatting quite a bit. Jokingly, Johann asked him, "What would happen if you just recommended another doctor in Munich, and told them you could not come because of your workload here?"

Albert laughed, and said, "That would be like committing suicide. I would probably be sent to a labor camp or worse yet to the Russian front. Do you think, for one minute, the general gives a damn about all the patients I will be operating on over the next week? Huh, he couldn't care less."

"You are probably right. Like they say, 'rank has its privileges'." He paused a moment before saying, "Albert, you mentioned that you might be leaving in a few days. I was wondering if you thought it would be alright for me to travel with you to Munich? I have a while before I need to get back to Porz, and my shoulder is feeling a lot better."

"To see your family in Schwanndorf, right?" Johann nodded. "Let me check the shoulder before I have to go, and if everything looks alright, I would be happy to have you come with me. In fact, my corpsman and I will be traveling in an ambulance packed with supplies and equipment, so there would be a cot for you to lie down on, if you needed to." He started walking toward the door, turned around and said, "I have to make rounds now, so we will talk some more later."

This just might work out perfectly for me Johann thought. For the next few days his progress improved even more. Even though his arm was in a sling, he was able to walk around the hospital for almost two hours without getting tired. When it came time for Albert to leave, he examined Johann one more time, and told him that he would have an orderly pack his things for him. They would be leaving in an hour for Munich.

Albert's corpsman tried to avoid driving through the big cities as much as possible, but a few could not be avoided. The devastation was remarkably worse than Johann had seen previously, but Albert was not surprised to see other cities, like Frankfurt, in the same horrible condition. They talked throughout the seven hour trip, but because of their driver, never once precisely stating their own political views; however, there were enough innuendos, giving them a pretty good idea what the other was thinking and nothing further had to be said about the subject.

Before arriving in Munich, Albert asked his corpsman to bypass it and drive directly to Schwanndorf. "I do not want you to have to find transportation," Albert said. "It would be too tiring and you have had a long trip already."

"Well, thank you very much, Doctor. I hope I can repay you for all this some day."

"I will let you buy me a beer, at the end of the War. The pleasure is all mine, having met someone who thinks as I do," Albert winked at Johann, who nodded in agreement. Nothing more had to be said and both men knew that.

When they arrived in Schwanndorf, there was very little change from the last time Johann had been there. A few more buildings had been damaged and he was thrilled to see there wasn't more. The Weller apartment was in a strictly residential area and was less prone to the Allied bombings. He got out of the ambulance and thanked Albert and his corpsman again.

"Johann," Albert said, "we will wait here for you until you go inside and make sure everything is alright."

"That is very nice of you...it will just take a few minutes to go upstairs and check on them."

The corpsman grabbed Johann's bag and they went up to the second floor of the building. Johann knocked on the door, but no one answered. He had a key to the apartment and was about to put it into the lock, when the lady next door opened her door and saw the two men.

"Johann," she happily greeted him, "how good to see you."

"It is good to see you, too, *Frau* Klineschmidt. Have my parents gone out for the day? I knocked, but no one answered."

"Oh, I suppose they never got in touch with you, did they?" she asked.

Johann's mouth became dry and his stomach started feeling quezy, thinking what might have happened to them. "Are you telling me that someone took them away?"

"Oh, no!" she exclaimed, "nothing like that. They both decided that it would be better to live outside the city. They tried to call you, but didn't have any success."

Johann, relieved, said, "Did they say where they were going?"

"All they said was that they were going out to the country, and that you would figure out where they were." Johann closed his eyes, and rubbed his thumb and index finger on his forehead. "I know it sounded a little vague to me also, but I hope this makes some sense to you."

Johann thought for a moment or two, and all of a sudden he nodded up and down and said, "Uh huh, I think I have a pretty good idea where they went." He shook *Frau* Klineschmidt's hand vigorously. "Thank you very much…it was so nice to see you." He quickly motioned the corpsman to grab his bag and they began walking toward the stairs, before she got a chance to ask where his parents were.

Just as they were about to start down, she said, "Johann, I see that you have hurt your arm. I hope it is nothing serious?"

"No, *Frau* Klineschmidt, it was just a scratch. *Auf wiedersehen,*" he waved, and they walked down the stairs, and out to the car where Albert stood waiting.

"I take it that you did not have any luck. Is everything all right, Johann?" Albert inquired. "You seem fairly happy."

"My parents, I believe, have gone to an old, family summer home that my grandparents bought quite awhile ago. We have not been there in many years, but it would surely be a lot safer for them than staying here. It is to the south of here, on your way to Munich, so I hope it will not be much of an inconvenience to drop me there?"

"No, of course not. Hop in and just tell us where to go."

An hour later they arrived at a picturesque, Bavarian cottage on a beautiful lake, less than a kilometer off the main highway. The Weller's were alarmed to see an ambulance coming down the dirt road. When Johann came out of the back of the truck with his arm in a sling, they came out of the house and embraced him, asking all kinds of questions about his condition. He assured them that he was on the mend, and after introducing Dr. Ritter as his own personal physician, which got a chuckle out of Albert, he too told them that Johann was progressing well.

"Please come in, and we will have some tea and sweets," *Frau* Weller said to all the men, "I have just baked a cake."

"*Danke, Frau* Weller," Albert said, "but it is getting late and I have to be in Munich to examine a general, who I know is anxious to see me."

"He can wait a while longer," she said, not wanting to take 'no' for an answer. "You have had a long journey and need some refreshments."

They all went into the cottage, except for the corpsman who, because of protocol, excused himself saying that, "I have work to do on the truck". Hilda Weller brought the tea and cake out to him, after everyone was seated around the long, wooden table. The short visit turned into an hour, after the Wellers discovered that Albert had studied in the United States, and he discovered that they had performed there on several occasions. The three of them talked about their experiences in the States, but never glorified any of these, not wanting to show their true feelings toward the enemy, or toward the present regime in Germany. Paranoia was not uncommon in the Fatherland.

"Thank you very much *Frau* Weller, *Herr* Weller," Albert said as he stood up to leave. "I have thoroughly enjoyed our conversation and your wonderful *strudel*. I wish you both well. I'm sure that Johann will sleep a lot better, knowing that you are here in the country."

"And thank you for bringing Johann home, Doctor," *Herr* Weller said, shaking Albert's hand. "You have no idea how worried we were, since our communications have been cut off."

"As I was also," Johann said, looking at his father and mother. He laughed, saying, "If I had not been wounded, I probably would not be standing here today."

He put his arm around Albert, saying, "Of course, Albert had a lot to do with my being here, also."

"Now, as your doctor speaking, Johann," Albert said, "I want you to have a few days rest. I know that your parents will take good care of you, and I will be back to pick you up for our drive back to Frankfurt." With that, he said his goodbyes and left.

15

Marcel remained in Carcassone, with Simon Cadeaux, for two nights. Florette needed time to confer with her *Maquis* commander regarding the new status of Dr. Pontier and how he could be more effectively used in the field. When she returned to Carcassone, she and Marcel first had an extensive meeting outlining the long-term plans for disrupting the *Vichy*, and in the event the Germans did take over the southern part of France, what they would concentrate on in those regards.

"In the immediate future, though," Florette impressed on him, "we have to keep up the pressure, and the main target is the one you looked at...the German relay station in Morieres. There have been some extensive plans drawn up since we met, and we need your input before we implement this assignment."

"I've been thinking a lot more about this, also, Florette," Marcel said. "How many *Maquis* cells would you use?"

"Right now, we are figuring on four groups...one going in with the Courteaux food truck, as you had suggested...one across from the entrance to cover our truck that is going in, and one group on each side of the compound to give adequate cover, once we open fire. How does this sound to you, so far?"

Marcel picked up a piece of paper and started drawing the compound by the memory he had of it. After a few minutes, he slowly began to speak, thinking and analyzing as he did so. "Off the top of my head, I'm assuming that you consider a group as being six people." She nodded in agreement. "If that's the case, I don't think that you have enough, unless that's all the personnel you can spare."

"That would be an item we could certainly discuss, if your argument was strong enough. This would be our most ambitious project to date, to be sure, and we can't afford a failure. We always prefer to use as small a force as possible, mainly because we really don't have a huge number to begin with...much smaller than the enemy think we have. But, at the same time, we need a big success and want this planned out thoroughly, so give me your best estimate."

"Look," he said, holding up the drawing, "here's the perimeter of the German compound, and here..." he began sketching again, "are...the...two guard houses, the tower, and the long building at the rear, which we believe to be the barracks, mess hall, and the actual radio station itself." He paused and wrote some numbers corresponding to the different areas. "Let's assume that there are two soldiers in each of the guard houses...and all these numbers may be high, but I would rather be on the high side than too low. I could only see one armored personnel carrier, an APC, but there is a possibility that there may be two, and each one would have three people manning them."

Florette interrupted, "Marcel, what do each of these men do on the APC?"

"Well, you have a driver, who I would assume has some type of weapon, such as a pistol; one soldier manning a fixed, large machine gun on the top of the vehicle; and another man sitting up there also, who probably has an automatic, or a semi-automatic rifle."

"How do you know so much about these things, Marcel? I've never asked you, but were you ever in the military?"

Marcel laughed, "Yes, for a short time in the last year of the War…I had no training and was only 17 or 18 years old. I was attached to an infantry battalion in Verdun, and do you know what they had me doing?"

"No, what?" she asked, laughing herself now.

"I was a forward observer in a hot-air balloon that was tethered to the ground. Guess I was the most dispensable person in the battalion, because I was shot at so many times I'm lucky to be here now. But since then, I've always loved to read about military history, and probably picked up a few things here and there. I'm really just an amateur at this sort of thing."

"You're being too modest. I think you have a natural instinct in these matters, Marcel." She paused, "So, why don't you go ahead and continue your summation…you're touching on things we haven't considered."

He picked up his drawing, "Here at the tower, itself, I remember seeing one guard patrolling around it, and…by the way, do you have two or three sharpshooters for this operation?"

"I think we can manage that quite nicely, yes."

"Good, because we'll need them…especially to take out the guard at the radio tower, the guards at the gate, and on the APC's." He pointed at the sheet again, "I would imagine about three people in the radio shack itself, and four that work in the mess hall. So, all told, they have about 18 people working at one time, and to be on the safe side, I would presume the same amount are sleeping in the barracks. That adds up to 36 soldiers in the compound at any given moment. With your four groups of six, that's only 24 of our people going up against the infamous, German army. That may be enough with our element of surprise, but personally, I would prefer to have at least one more group behind the compound. There may be an opening, like a gate that I couldn't see, plus the soldiers in that rear building may go out the back doors, if they have them, and we would catch them cold."

"That's an excellent point," she paused and thought for a moment. "Do you think this could turn into a disaster, if the guards checked the truck at the entrance?"

"It's definitely not what we want, but at the same time, it would be more of a surprise to the Germans, than to us. We should definitely consider this in our planning and what counteractions we could make in this event. On the other hand," he chuckled, "this could be the signal for our people to begin the attack. On being discovered, the men in the truck would open fire on the Germans they encountered, instead of waiting until whatever time they were supposed to have started. So, no, I don't feel that it would be a disaster at all."

"Marcel, in the best case scenario, when the truck gets inside the compound, we feel that it should go directly to the front of the rear building, where our men could flair out from there and begin the attack inside the radio station, kitchen, and barracks. Our people on the perimeters will then open fire on anyone outside, and then enter the compound as quickly as possible."

"That sounds like a good plan, but make sure the sharpshooters kill the soldiers on the APC's immediately, because they could wreak havoc on this whole operation." He looked at his drawing again and said, "Florette, what about the guard walking around the tower?"

"All the men will be wearing white, dressed as caterers, so we want to have the driver get out of the truck and approach the guard with a plate of food, and then knife or shoot him once the firing inside the building begins. Another caterer look-alike will use the same ploy, knocking on the door of the radio station, offering food to whomever is in there, and taking them out with a silencer-pistol."

Marcel nodded his approval, "Hmm, keeping everything quiet for as long as possible, huh?"

"Yes, as long as it will work; then we will use a couple of grenades to start the attack, by throwing them into the barracks, and then come in blasting." Florette paused for a moment, looked down at the ground, and said, "Of course, this is all on paper; what can happen in the real attack may be entirely different. That's why we need the feedback from you and others."

"When do you think the attack will take place?"

"Probably within the next few weeks, or so. In the meantime, you and I will have to first meet with the key people in this operation. Then we'll relocate you in the hills near Marseille, where you can still have access to your own men whenever necessary. You'll be living with a few other members of the *Maquis* who are in similar circumstances as you, and have proven themselves to be very competent. They already know that you will be in charge, and welcome the opportunity to be part of your original unit. There are two women and one man, and each has been told only that your name is Marcel, and that you are the new district commander."

"Ah, I have a title now…just what I need for my résumé. When will we be leaving?"

"Tonight, after it gets dark." Florette stood up and stretched. "I think I'll take a little nap for a couple hours. I haven't had much sleep for the last few days." She started to walk toward the bedroom, and then turned around, "You'll be following me in your car, which we'll drop off at a safe place in Provence. You can easily get to it, if necessary, for the operations. Please make sure I'm up by 18:30, and ask Simon if he would pack us both something to eat on the road." With that, she walked into the bedroom and closed the door.

Marcel thought to himself, *the real adventure has now begun. God help us!*

16

Johann and his parents had a nice three day visit, thankful that they located each other and were together again. He was much more tired than he thought from the long trip, and was able to rest, eat well, and complete his recuperation in his grandparent's old cottage. Being out in the country did wonders for his psyche, even more so than his battle wounds. His parents had restored the old place nicely, bringing fond memories to everyone of an earlier, more peaceful time in their lives.

"I am so happy that I found you," Johann said to them, before he left with Albert and his corpsman. "My mind is relieved that here, you will be away from all the bombing. I am not sure when I will be back…I am going to be reassigned to somewhere in France within the next couple of months, and will write and let you know where." He hugged them both, "Please do not worry about me; remember, I am not in the front lines fighting anyone, and I will return as soon as I can."

"God be with you, son," Hilda said. "Take good care of yourself."

When it was time to depart, it was harder than ever to leave his mother and father. He tried to sound optimistic, but once he was deployed to France, there was no telling when he could get back here. With the communications being what they were, it was almost impossible to call them by phone, or for that matter, even send a letter. But more important, in these troubled times, one never knew from visit to visit, if this was the last season they would spend together.

It was an uneventful trip back to Frankfort. Johann and Albert promised to stay in touch, although they both knew there was a good chance they would probably not see, or hear from each other, until after the War. They had a lot in common, and friendships like these were hard to come by. It was reassuring for Johann to know that other people thought like he did about the insanity of this whole Nazi regime. Desertion was never an option for either one of them, because first and foremost, they were good and loyal Germans. They took orders from their superiors, and would keep their hopes up that things would eventually get better.

Johann had wired ahead, and when his train arrived in Porz, Hermann was there to pick him up and take him back to the camp. Things hadn't changed much since he had been taken away in the ambulance. New buildings had sprung up in place of the ones destroyed, and the activity level seemed the same.

"I can see now that I am not indispensable," Johann said to Hermann, as he surveyed the construction of the barriers. "Is everything more or less on schedule?"

"It took us several days to clean up the camp, bury the ones who were killed, and reconstruct three buildings," Hermann replied, "so, we are running a little behind schedule. The main thing is, you are back safe and sound, *Hauptmann*."

"Thank you, Hermann," he said, stretching out his arms, "I am ready to get back to work, now that I know my parents are alright." On the way from the train station, he had told him about his side trip to Schwanndorf. "Have any of the new, deeper, underwater devices been built?"

"No, *Hauptmann*…the major was waiting for you to come back and supervise their construction." Hermann paused then said, "He wanted to see you as soon as you arrive. He has been a little bit on edge lately, so I think it is best for you to report to him now."

Johann walked back to the administration building and knocked on the major's door. "Enter," came the stark reply. When Johann came into the room, Major von Klemper was leaning back in his chair, with his feet propped up on his desk, and a cold wash towel across his forehead. When he saw Johann, he stood up, smiled, and shook his hand.

"How nice to see you, *Hauptmann*…it is good to have you back. How do you feel?"

"I am doing much better, sir. I had a nice rest at my parents home for a few days," Johann told him, not wanting to hide anything, but then he changed the subject quickly. "And, how is your head feeling? I see that you were using a washrag."

"According to the doctor, I unfortunately will be suffering from headaches for awhile. I suppose that is one of the side effects of a concussion, so every day I must lie back and use this thing," holding up the rag. "Now that you have come back, you will be able to take some of the responsibilities off my shoulders…mainly, supervising the officers and men to get moving quicker."

"Sergeant Koch felt that we were running only a few days behind, considering the rebuilding and training of some new replacements… isn't this so, Major?" Johann inquired.

He rubbed his forehead, and let out a sigh, "Johann, Berlin is breathing down my back to get some of the newer prototypes tested as soon as possible. They could care less that we were bombed and lost some men. 'We are being bombed everywhere' they said. They are only interested in results, so please fire up the men, as I know you can. To be frank, their chief engineers have changed their opinion regarding the placement of the mine inside the barrier, so see what you can do about that also."

Over the next week, Johann had redesigned the deep-water barrier. He put the mine in a stabilized basket, to detonate only when struck directly by a landing craft, and, working around the clock in eight hour shifts, he had two prototypes built. Major von Klemper was well pleased, and ordered the testing to begin. The following week, using old barges similar to the Allies' landing craft, and wired for remote control, the tests began.

Everyone in the battalion was on the beach watching and waiting in anticipation, but to no avail. One of the craft went over it, with only a slight scrape. The other got hung up on the crisscrossed configuration, but no blast occurred from the mine. Two divers were sent out to survey the situation, and found that the hull of the barge was too flat, not penetrating deep enough to hit the mine and set off the explosion. The major was livid, which set off a diatribe against Johann, and his incompetent officers, in front of the whole battalion.

Johann was taken aback. He told his lieutenants, when they convened later that day, that the major was under a lot of pressure, and as a direct result of his concussion, he was suffering from severe headaches. They went back to the drawing boards and redesigned a barrier that wasn't as tightly wired together, so that a flat landing craft going over it would spread the wood apart, allowing the mine to leave its basket, and rise toward the surface.

When Johann went to tell the major of their new design, he exclaimed, "I do not give a fuck how you do it, just do it! Or, maybe you need to go home to your precious parents and have a chance to think some more, you pampered son-of-a-bitch. Now get out of my office…I am sick of you!"

Maybe it was the concussion Johann thought, but the major had definitely taken a turn for the worse. His personality had changed 180 degrees, and from then on, Johann avoided him as much as possible. The following week, with the newest barriers in place, the test was resumed; this time with completely different results… both barges were blown to smithereens. Large shouts went up from all the men in the battalion, knowing that they had produced something to help win the War, and save the Fatherland.

The major stood stone-faced, and remarked to the officers around him, "Well, it is about time. Too bad we did not have any Jews aboard those barges; it would have made this a lot more exciting." Two of the officers laughed and nodded their heads in agreement. "*Hauptmann*, write a report, with all the details of the project, to my secretary to be typed up and sent to Berlin. I want this done immediately… understood?" He didn't wait for Johann's reply, but turned on his heels and strode off to his quarters.

Johann gathered the men around him and thanked them for a job well done. He instructed his lieutenants to start producing as many of these as they could. Two days later, he and Hermann took one of them by truck down to a Frankfurt factory, where they would be massed produced.

It was early fall, and Johann could feel a little chill in the air. Going over the plans with the engineers, at the factory in Frankfurt, hadn't taken as long as he anticipated, and he decided to drop in on Dr. Albert Ritter, who was finishing up his day at the hospital. Hermann said that he would browse around town and meet Johann the next morning at the factory's mill shop.

"I am delighted to see you, Johann," Albert said. "How is your shoulder feeling? Take off your shirt and let me take a look. What brings you to Frankfurt?"

"I am doing fine, Doctor," Johann said, as he was removing his shirt. "It feels almost back to normal. I had some business here and thought I would stop by and say hello. I must return to Porz in the morning."

"Wonderful, you can stay with me tonight. I have an extra bedroom in my apartment." He examined Johann's shoulder and his range of motion. "Alright, you can put your shirt back on. Everything looks perfect, and you are free to resume your normal activities." After a brief pause, he said, "Now about tonight…"

"Yes, that sounds very nice, but you have to let me buy you dinner, that is if there are any decent restaurants still open."

"Oh, there are a few good ones left, mostly in the basements of some old houses. I was starting to tell you that I have a date tonight, but I am sure she has a friend that could come along for you."

"Well, I do not know about that, Albert. You see, I have not…"

"I know…you told me on the way to Munich about your wife, but you need to start living again and get out more. It will do you good…that is an order from your doctor."

"Alright, if you insist…I suppose I could use a night out with some good wine and a decent meal. I hope this does not interfere with your plans?"

"Of course not, Johann," he replied. "How often does one get to be with a good friend in times like these? Besides, you will see that it will be a lot of fun for both of us. Let me give you my address and the directions to the apartment…it is only a short walk from here. You can go there now and freshen up, and I will find Gretchen and tell her to bring one of her nursing friends with her."

"This sounds good, Albert. Should I wait for you at your apartment?"

"Yes, please…I have got to change out of these scrubs, so I should be home within an hour. You will find everything you need…if you want to take a bath, or just relax with a beer."

Albert wrote out the information and handed it to Johann, who had no trouble finding the well-furnished apartment. He had brought a change of clothes and decided that a nice, hot bath would do him good. He soaked for 25 minutes, followed by a short nap in the guest bedroom. It was as if the times were normal and the War was a distant memory. Albert woke him when he arrived, and he took his time getting dressed in his clean uniform. He sat in the living room sipping a beer, waiting for his friend to get ready, and enjoying the moment.

The restaurant was exactly as Albert had described…in a basement under an old building, with natural, oak tables, beer steins on little shelves, and different size cow bells hanging everywhere. Gretchen, and her friend Eva, were already seated, waiting for them to arrive, and Albert made the introductions. The nurses were both quite attractive and everyone seemed to get along like old friends throughout the evening. The *bratwurst* and *pommes frites* were the best that Johann had tasted in months, and Albert took the liberty of ordering the three bottles of wine they consumed before, during, and after their meal…starting out with a *Spätlese*, a dry white wine; then *Schillerwein*, a rosé; and after dinner, a sweet white wine, *Rheinpfalz*, which was served with *Bienenstich*, a honey-almond cake.

"You know, I could definitely get spoiled doing this every night," Johann said light-heartedly. "In fact, I think I am a little drunk."

"Good for you, my friend," Albert said, and then raised his glass for the tenth time that evening. "A toast to my good friends and to

Deutschland…may it live another thousand years, and may we all meet here to enjoy it after the War."

They clinked their glasses together, and said, "To *Deutschland*."

When the waitress brought the check to their table, Johann insisted on paying for it. "For all you have done for me, Albert, it is my pleasure. It has been a marvelous evening and I have enjoyed meeting you lovely young ladies, also," he said, as he raised his wine glass to each of them.

Eva had grown up in a small town not far from Frankfurt. Her father was a Lutheran minister and she had a very strict upbringing. She had come to Frankfurt five years earlier to attend nursing school, loved her work, but knew very little about anything else. "The evening is not over, Johann," Eva said softly, as she wrapped her arm around his neck and whispered in his ear. Her hand found his thigh and rubbed it slowly. "Why don't we all go back to Albert's and have a nightcap?"

"That sounds like a wonderful idea," Albert said, slurring his words. "Shall we go?" They all stood up and walked out the door toward the apartment.

They trudged up the stairs to his second floor flat. Once inside, Albert and Gretchen headed straight for his bedroom, without saying another word. Johann had a pretty good idea how far Eva would go, but he still felt a little awkward when they stood in the middle of the living room and began kissing.

"Would you like some *schnapps*, Eva?" he asked, trying to go slow with this nice, full-figured girl that he really felt nothing for. He was having a well-deserved, fun evening, and he could now accept that it was time to move on with his life.

"I would like something better than *schnapps*," she said, as she took his hand and led him into the guest bedroom.

They began undressing and caressing each other with a fervent desire, and once in bed, Johann was inside her, both moving in a fast rhythm. It wasn't long before he knew he couldn't hold it any longer, and let it go with a large gasp. He was exhausted, but managed to say, "Thank you, Eva, it has been a long time."

"Oh, Johann," she moaned, "that was wonderful. It has been a long time for me, too."

He lay on top of her for another minute, enjoying the intimacy of a woman beneath him, and finally rolled over on his back. She sat up, leaned over and kissed him hard on the lips, then excused herself and went to the bathroom to use the *bidet*. When she returned, he went to clean up and relieve himself, also.

She was leaning against the headboard, smoking a cigarette, when he got into bed. She offered him a drag of her cigarette, but he told her that he didn't smoke, so she put it out in the ashtray on the nightstand. He put his arm around her and she cuddled up next to him. He could feel her breasts against his chest, and thought that *these are probably the largest ones I have ever seen.* He almost laughed out loud, but caught himself in time, and let out a sigh instead. That seemed to please Eva, and she let out a sigh also. There was no doubt that both of them were content, and now were on the verge of falling asleep.

They remained in each other's arms for some time, when a loud siren woke them. They sat straight up rubbing their eyes. "Is there an air raid shelter nearby?" Johann yawned.

"Yes," Eva said, half asleep, "down the block."

Just then, Albert knocked on the door, and asked, "Are you two up?"

"Yes," Johann responded. "Do you think we better get dressed and go down to the shelter?"

"No, I never leave the apartment in one of these raids," Albert answered through the door. "I think that we are just as safe here, and furthermore, it is nothing but a pain-in-the-ass to have to go all the way down there and sit for an hour or so.

"Besides, if our time has come, so be it. I am going back to bed and will see you in the morning." With that, he walked back to his room and closed the door.

Johann and Eva didn't say anything, but rather got back under the sheets, slowly exploring each other as they hadn't before. They could hear the bombs exploding in the distance, as they made love for the second time.

In the morning, everyone said their goodbyes, and vowed to see each other again soon, and, as usual, not knowing if and when *soon* would ever come.

17

It was the last weekend in August, 1942, and the village of Elne was a month late with its annual, two-day festival to honor their local patron, *Sainte Eulalie*. They were also celebrating two other important days: June 24th, the shortest night of the year, which was called *Les Feux de la Saint Jean*, in which they would light a giant fire for Peace, Love, and Friendship; and August 15th, the Festival of *Sainte Mary*, where the statues of the Virgin Mary and Christ were carried around the village. Mayor Astruc had to combine these three holidays, because he could only get permission for one celebration from the *Vichy* government in the Roussillon-Catatonia region; therefore, all of them were bunched together, and late.

The main square was decorated with streamers, flags, and banners, which gave it a very colorful and festive atmosphere. To raise money for the church, booths were set up along the perimeter of the square to sell food prepared by all the local women. Tables and chairs were arranged like a big, outdoor café, in order for the people to sit and to eat the food they had purchased, if they didn't want to bring it home with them. It would allow them also to just have a glass of wine, while watching all the festivities. A variety of local bands, and dancers, performed throughout the day and early evening. A stage was set up along the old city walls, and many of the people wore traditional costumes. Even the police officers dressed in uniforms from the Louis XIV era, as they had always done in past years.

For the children of the village, and surrounding areas, it was like a big carnival that came to town once a year. There were booths set up for them in the fields outside the square, with games such as throwing a ball and knocking down three pins on a stand, or throwing a wooden ring on a wine bottle. As a prize, the child would get a ticket to be taken into the square and redeemed for a small sandwich, or sweet on the children's table. Sometimes, instead of food, there was a booth where they could use their ticket to have their fortunes read, or their faces painted.

Babette was excited to be with Raymond and J.P. She skipped while holding their hands, and enjoyed all these spectacular things. "Can one of you win me a prize?" she asked them. "I'll be able to get a piece of butterscotch."

"I think J.P. would do better than I would," Raymond said, as he turned to J.P. "Spend one of the coins *Maman* gave you, and see if you can knock one of those bola pins off the stand."

"Please, J.P., please," Babette pleaded. "I'll share the butterscotch with you."

"O.K., Babette," J.P. said, looking down at his little sister, "let's walk over to that booth, and I'll knock one of those pins over for you."

When they reached the booth, there was a cute girl standing there, about J.P.'s age and height. He had never seen her before. Her hair was light brown, with long curls. Over the last year he had been more conscious of girls, and he knew that he wanted to meet this one. He stood and watched, as she threw the balls at the pins, knocking them down, but not off the stand to get the ticket.

He was impressed that she didn't throw like most girls, and thought that he would try to help her out, even though she didn't seem too upset about not winning. "I think you should give her a ticket," he said out loud to the man running the booth. "She knocked down the pins. She can't help it if she's only a girl, and can't hit them any harder."

"What do you mean, only a girl!" she said indignantly. "I bet I can do anything you can do."

He was taken aback with his first rejection by the opposite sex, and didn't know what to say. Finally, he stammered, "Oh, I didn't want to be mean. I was only trying to help."

"Well, I don't need your help," she seemed to soften a little bit, now that she had gotten a good look at him. *He is kind of cute*, she thought, and in a nicer tone of voice, she smiled and said, "O.K., let's see what you can do, smarty."

J.P. smiled at her and handed the man a coin. He picked up the ball and threw it as hard as he could. The top pin went flying off the stand. He smiled at her again and she smiled back, saying, "That was nice."

"Thank you," he said, and picked up the second ball.

Babette clapped, and shouted, "Oh, J.P., you got me a ticket…you got mc a ticket."

There were two more pins sitting on the stand; J.P. threw again, hitting the neck of the pin on the right. It went down, but not off the stand. "That's alright," the girl with the curls said, "you can get the next one…just hit it lower, O.K.?"

"You can do it, J.P.," Raymond said.

Now, they are all cheering me on, J.P. thought. *Boy, I really like this girl. I bet she'll make a great friend.* He picked up the third ball, reared back and threw it dead center on the pin, which caused it to spin around on the edge of the stand. They all waited in anticipation, clapping their hands until the pin finally rolled off.

The girl smiled, and said, "You did great, J.P., especially the last one...those are the hardest to get, the ones sitting on the table."

"You both did great," the man in the booth said. He held up two tickets and turned to the girl, "I was going to give you these for knocking over the pins, before Sir Galahad, here, opened his mouth." They all laughed, as he handed them to her, and then gave J.P. the two he had earned. They thanked him and walked towards the square.

"Well," J.P. began, "now that you know my name, what's yours?"

"I'm Sylviane...Sylviane Barton."

"Hi, I'm Raymond Pontier, and this is our little sister, Babette."

"Hi, Raymond...hi Babette...how old are you?" she asked the little girl.

"I'm six years old and I'm going into the first grade," she said, as she let go of Raymond's hand and took Sylviane's instead. "How old are you?"

"I'll be nine in a couple months, and I'm going to be in fourth grade when school starts next month."

"Really, I'm going into fourth grade too," J.P. said excitedly. "I'm nine also, so I bet we'll be in the same class."

"Oh, that *will* be nice," Sylviane smiled. "How come I've never seen either of you in school before...did you just move here?"

"We're from Marseille," Raymond answered, "but this year, our father wanted the family to stay in Elne with our grandparents, because of the War."

"We come here every summer, for a month or so," J.P. added, "but I've never seen you in town, either."

"Oh, that's because we live about 2 kilometers away, and don't usually come in unless we go to church on Sunday, or my mother has to shop. Of course I come in to go to school."

They had reached the square, and one of the first booths they came to was the Courty booth, where Elizabeth, Paulette, and Angelina were selling their mince meat and apple pies. Babette ran up to Angelina, "*Maman, Grandmere*, look what J.P. won for me," she held up her prize, "two tickets for the children's table. Isn't that wonderful?"

"Yes, dear," Angelina said, "that was very nice of J.P. to do that for you. But remember what I told you about eating too many sweets… they're not good for your teeth, and Papa would not like that."

As Sylviane came up to the booth with J.P. and Raymond, she gave a big wave, and said, "*Bonjour Madame* Courty, *Bonjour Mademoiselle* Courty, how are you?" She came around the table and gave them both a big hug. Raymond and J.P. looked at each other and shrugged. "J.P. and Raymond were just telling me that they were living here in Elne with their grandparents, but I had no idea it was you."

"Yes, my sweet Sylviane," Elizabeth joked, "I have to claim them as mine."

"They're mine too," Angelina said, sticking out her hand, which Sylviane shook. "I am their mother, *Madame* Pointier."

"You just met her parents, too," Paulette added, "the Barton's. They bought two of our pies."

"Oh, yes, your father was two years behind me in school."

"*Maman*," Babette asked, "may I go get my treats now?"

"Yes, *Cherie*, if one of your brothers goes with you."

J.P. jumped right in, "Why don't you take her, Raymond?"

"Well, alright then," Raymond said. "I'll use one of the tickets to get something too." Babette grabbed his hand and they started walking toward the other side of the square. Raymond would have preferred to stay and talk to Sylviane also, but it looked like J.P. beat him to the punch.

125

"*Grandmere*, Sylviane and I are going to be in the same class," J.P. said enthusiastically. "Why haven't you and Tante Paulette ever mentioned her to me before? We could have been playing together every summer. Have you known her family for a long time?"

"We've known the Barton's for as long as I can remember, and besides, this is a small village and *Grandpere*, *Tante* Paulette, and I know just about everyone."

"I can remember when Sylviane was born, J.P.," Paulette said, "and when we went to her first communion, a couple years ago."

"We always have a wonderful time when all of you come to visit us at the farm," Sylviane said, putting her arm around Paulette. She looked at Angelina and continued, "I hope that you'll come one day soon, *Madame* Pontier," and then looking at J.P., added, "Bring your whole family, too."

J.P. turned red, and then asked her, "What kind of farm is it?"

"It's mostly a dairy farm, but we have chickens too…and a few horses."

"Horses!" J.P. exclaimed, "Do you ride them?"

"Of course, I ride all the time. Would you like to come out and ride with me someday, J.P.?"

"I've never been on a horse, except the time Papa took us to the park in Marseille. He paid a man to take us on a pony around this little ring."

Sylviane laughed, "Then I'll show you how, if you want me to? Remember, though, I'm *only* a girl!"

The adults were amused as their usually, over-confident child, Jean Pierre, got all flustered, then managed to say, "I told you that I was sorry about that. I'm sure there are *some* things you can do better than I can."

"I'm only kidding, J.P." She smiled, and then left Paulette's side, coming over to J.P. and grabbing his hand. "Let's go find Babette and Raymond and see what they got. I have these two tickets that we can use." She looked back at the three ladies, "Goodbye everyone…it was nice meeting you, *Madame* Pontier." With that, she and J.P. walked hand-in-hand across the square.

Angelina, Paulette and their mother just stood grinning, watching the two children walk away, when Angelina said, "I think that J.P. has finally met his match."

"If not that, his first love," Paulette added.

Elizabeth held her hand on her face and shook her head, "And he's only nine years old? Believe me, knowing J.P., he'll have a lot more."

J.P., Sylviane, Raymond and Babette spent the rest of the day together watching all the festivities. When dusk came, Sylviane's parents, Raphaël and Gisele, found the children sitting in the square listening to a band playing. The Barton's were charming people, and *Monsieur* Barton bought a pitcher of lemonade for everyone to share, while they all sat and listened to the music for another hour.

When it was time for the Barton's to leave, J.P. walked with them to their car, which was outside the city walls. Raymond went home with Babette, who said that, "Today was the best of my life". Although he didn't want to say so, after meeting Sylviane, J.P. was thinking the same thing, even though he didn't really understand why.

"Will you be coming tomorrow morning for the Festival of *Sainte Mary*?" J.P. asked Sylviane.

"That would be fun; may I go, Papa?"

"Yes, we can all go in the morning before church. Exactly what time does it start, J.P.?"

"I think it's at 7:30, so I'll see you all in front of the Cathedral then."

"J.P., would you like to climb with us up *Le Canigou* tomorrow afternoon for *Les Feux de la Saint Jean*?" Gisele asked, getting a big smile from her daughter. "We'll take a truck up as far as the road goes, and then climb the rest of the way, about 700 meters."

"I'll have to ask my mother, but I'm sure it will be O.K.," J.P. answered. "I've never done that before, but it sounds great. Thank you, *Madame* Barton... I'll see you in the morning." He waved, and started running back to his house. He couldn't wait to ask his mother.

The next morning, J.P. and the Barton's met at the Cathedral of Elne, and then walked behind the eight boys carrying two platforms with the statues of the Virgin Mary and Christ. The boys, all between the ages of 16 to 18, were dressed in white; those carrying the Virgin were draped with a blue sash, and those carrying Christ with a red sash.

The march took over an hour, and families throughout the village stood outside their homes to witness the annual event. Many people joined in the march along the way. By the time it returned to the Cathedral, most of the town was there to attend the morning Mass, including all of J.P's family. J.P. never liked going to church, and even when he was much younger, he began questioning his religion. Today, though, he didn't mind going, because Sylviane was sitting next to him and he felt that he wasn't making much of a sacrifice. At this point, it would have been a big decision between sitting here and playing soccer outside.

At 1:00 that afternoon, the Barton's picked up J.P. Elizabeth gave them a bottle of wine to bring to their early evening dinner on the mountain and Angelina gave J.P. a warm jacket to wear if it got cold later. Before J.P. left the house, Angelina reminded him not to use any bad language. Raphaël asked Raymond if he would like to come also, but he declined, saying that he was going to play chess with his grandfather, as he did every Sunday. J.P. couldn't have been happier, as he would have Sylviane all to himself.

The ride up *Canigou* was very bumpy, especially for J.P. and Sylviane. They were sitting across from each other, on two benches in the back of a milk truck, and thought it was all great fun. The road stopped abruptly in an open field of wildflowers; they were now at 7000 feet, and when the two youngsters climbed out the back of the truck, J.P. was astonished at how beautiful the view was.

He had never experienced anything like this before, and with Sylviane at his side, they stood there for several minutes. Pointing at the valley below, he said, "Look, you can see the whole village…there's the Monastery and the tower of the Cathedral, and…I think I can even see my house, over there on the left."

"Yes, I see it," Sylviane said. She pointed even further left, "And if you look way over there, past the River Tech is one of the barns on our dairy farm. You can't see the house, because it's behind all those trees."

"Damn, this is amazing!" J.P. exclaimed.

She hit him lightly on the arm, and laughed, "J.P., what did your mother tell you about cursing? I'll have to tell her that you've been misbehaving."

"Oh, I'm sorry. Things like that just come out, I guess. I'll have to watch myself, so your parents don't get mad at me." He paused for a minute, as they continued to look at the view; then said, "Do you want to throw around the soccer ball that I brought?"

"Sure, Papa has been teaching me to play. I could use the practice."

They walked back to the truck, where Gisele and Raphaël were getting everything packed to take up the mountain. They told the children that it would be another 10 minutes before they would all begin hiking toward the top, so they had time to play in the fields for awhile. J.P. couldn't get over how well Sylviane handled and maneuvered the ball and he commented that, "You could be on my team, any time."

When they were ready to go, everyone had a walking stick and a knapsack to carry on their trek up *Canigou*. One third of their way up the 2,100 foot climb, Raphaël stopped and said, "I have something very interesting to show everyone, so leave your knapsacks here, and follow me."

They were all curious, and did what they were told. With Raphaël guiding them, they traversed the mountain for 10 minutes and crossed over a ridge leading down to a path on the other side. They followed this for a short period, came around a sharp curve, and to their amazement was a large opening into the mountain.

Gisele was the first to speak. "What *is* this, darling? How did you find it?"

"Well, *mon Cherie*," he began, "how are all of you at keeping secrets, and I don't mean just a little secret, but one of national importance... one that could save lives?"

The three of them swore not to tell anyone, unless it was of the utmost importance, and in J.P.'s case, if it involved the life or death of someone in his family. "This really sounds serious, Raphaël," Gisele said, "but I assume it has something to do with the war...am I correct?"

"Yes, you're correct," he said, "and the only reason I'm telling you this, is because of the possible Nazi take-over of southern France, like we discussed before."

"My father told us about that, *Monsieur* Barton," J.P. said. "That's why we left Marseille and came here to be safer."

"Yes, I've met your father, Jean Pierre. Marcel is a very smart man and he was right to bring you to Elne." He paused, wanting to change the subject, rubbed his chin, and continued, "You see, in the worst case scenario, if our family, or the Courty's and Pontier's ever have to flee the country, this would be one way to do it." He pointed to the opening of the mountain, "This is a tunnel that leads through a large section of the Pyrenees, and ends up in Spain."

"Papa," Sylviane asked, "how long has it been here?"

"It was originally started by a railroad company back in the 1890's, but they felt it wouldn't be feasible because of the snow conditions in the winter. Then, during the Spanish Civil War, it was used extensively by refugees fleeing Spain. A lot of them froze to death during the cold months, because there are several parts of the mountain where the tunnel ends temporarily, and then picks up again further on, sometimes as far as a kilometer or more."

"Where did the people go that came to France?" Sylviane asked.

"Many of them settled right here in the Catalonia area, and are still here. Remember when we took you to Barcelona? What did you learn there, Sylvie?"

She thought for a moment, before it came to her. "Oh, I remember… Barcelona is in the Catalonia region of Spain and we share some common dialects."

J.P. thought to himself, *I'm going to have to start studying to keep up with this girl. It's nice that we're sharing some secrets together. I'm not going to ask him how he knows my father, because that's probably a secret too.*

"*Cherie*, you asked how I found the tunnel; actually, I learned about it when I was in high school, and took a hiking field-trip with Father Cardone…much like we're doing today. Not that many people know about this, and we wouldn't want this secret to get into the wrong hands, OK?" Everyone nodded, and then Raphaël started walking into the tunnel, motioning everyone to follow him.

As they got further into it, it became very dark, and Raphaël turned on his flashlight in the direction they were walking. It seemed to go on forever, being much bigger than they anticipated; it was about 18 feet high, 20 feet across, and solid granite. After a few minutes, Raphaël stopped and said, "We can turn back now. I just wanted everyone to get a feeling of how big and long this thing is. With the War going on, you never know when it might come in handy." With that, he led them out of the tunnel, back into the daylight. They traversed due east along the same narrow, dirt path, until they reached their knapsacks.

They continued climbing until they were 500 feet below the summit. The mountain had leveled off into a flat, mesa-like area, and it was now approaching 5:00 in the afternoon. There were several monks from the Monastery already there, setting up stones in the outline of a cross, and putting twigs and branches inside the outline. They exchanged greetings with the robed men, and then found a place a little further away to set up their blankets for the picnic dinner. With their backs to the cross, they were facing southeast and could see the Mediterranean and a large city in the distance along the coast. J.P. was informed that it was Barcelona and he was in awe. "That's the most beautiful sight I've ever seen. I can't wait to tell *Maman* and everyone about this. Wow, this is really something!"

They finished their dinner just in time for the lighting of the cross, *Les Feux de la Saint Jean*. The monks chanted and the fifty people who were there, danced in celebration of the shortest night of the year. As is the tradition of *Les Feux* that a friendship would last forever, Sylviane and J.P. held hands and jumped across the fire twice. Both felt that today's adventures were the best of their lives.

18

Marcel had followed Florette to Montelimar. It was a city on the Rhone River, in the Dauphine area just north of Provence. For a few days, they had gone over plans for the ensuing attack on the German relay station, plus some other future operations, which directly, or indirectly, affected Marcel. Most of the leaders of the *Maquis* were business people, or professionals like him, and were very well organized. Marcel felt right at home with these men and women, because all of them had a fanatical love for France and an even greater hatred for the Nazis and their *Vichy* puppet regime.

The Maquis leaders liked most of Marcel's plans, but didn't want to commit that large of a force to one small area, so they settled on 16 people, far less than the 30 that Marcel had suggested. Marcel could understand the points they made, and said, "We'll have to make do with what we have, plus use the element of surprise to our strongest advantage." The date was now set for October 1, 1942, and all the district commanders would meet at the former newspaper editor's home, *Le Clos des Saumanes*, in Châteauneuf de Gadagne, the night before. They scheduled them to come at different times of the day, so as not to arouse suspicions in town, and each commander would in turn arrange their own group rendezvous for the next day.

After their meetings concluded, Florette and Marcel left Montelimar, a city known more for their nougat candy than anything else. They drove south in Marcel's car…Florette would find a way back to wherever she was going, as she always managed to do. In the Luberon hills, 50 miles north of Marseilles, Marcel turned onto a dirt road, as Florette had directed him. At its end sat a house, its garage door open. He parked his car in the garage, grabbed his duffel bag of clothes and other items, and the two of them set off by foot up into the hills.

They walked for more than an hour through the woods, until they came to a newly-made campsite with three, small huts surrounding a circular, stone campfire. Three people, two women and one man, came out of the woods with their rifles drawn, ready to shoot.

"Claudine," Florette yelled, "It's Florette, and I've brought Marcel with me." On seeing that it was she, the three put down their guns, and greeted the arrivals. Claudine was a stunning, 31 year old woman, with reddish-brown hair and green eyes. Beside her was Olivia, 43, with short-cropped black hair, the slim body of a long-distance runner, and a pleasant smile; Denis, 48, at 5'10", who could pass for a German scholar, having thick, hyperopic glasses, wavy blond hair, and the build of a rugby player. All three were very cordial to Marcel, and by the end of the evening, an almost instant bond developed between them. They knew that they were going to be spending a lot of time together fighting this war.

Marcel was anxious to learn more about all of them, but that would come in time. He had to leave in the morning, and make his way to Marseille. While they were having dinner, prepared this evening over the open fire by Denis, he and Florette briefed them on the October 1st operation. It wasn't yet decided who in his group, now consisting of eight people, would be going on the mission.

"One thing is for sure," Marcel said to them, "everyone is going to be used in some capacity…even if it means just picking up the other members of the unit who will scatter to different destinations, after the operation." He looked around the campfire and was well pleased having these three additional people. "Don't ever be afraid to offer any constructive suggestions, if you feel it will help any mission that we're on in the future; but remember, I'll have the final say on anything we do."

Claudine didn't waste any time in speaking up, and explained herself in a very logical fashion. "Marcel, the one thing that bothers me in your plan, is the use of only one truck to bring the food into the German compound."

"Go on," Marcel said, sounding interested, although he thought he made it clear that he was talking about future operations, and not this one.

"Well, that means that the area with the most firepower, namely the APC's and the guards at the gate, will be left alone when the shooting begins. They'll be free to open fire on the other side of the compound. More than likely, more of our people will be killed that way and…"

Marcel interrupted her, "But we…"

Claudine held up the palm of her hand to stop him, "I know, we have our group across from the gate, plus the sharpshooters on the perimeter. But the people on the hill can't see what's going on, because the two guard houses block their view. And, I think that it's too much to ask of the sharpshooters, from that long a distance, to be responsible for taking out that whole group of soldiers at the gate."

Florette, spoke up, "So your suggestion is to bring in another truck at the same time, which I think would be almost impossible, since they only expect one truck."

"Plus," Marcel said, "if we did it your way, it would alert them that something was wrong, and could blow the whole mission. But, what would this other truck specifically do, once it was in the compound?"

"First of all," Claudine began, "getting it in the compound would have to be prearranged with the Germans," she moved her wrist in circles, "you know, on some rational excuse to bring in more food, or whatever you can come up with. Its sole responsibility would be to eliminate all the Germans in that area."

Marcel looked at Florette and they both nodded their heads from side to side. Marcel finally said, "Why don't you run this by the leaders, Florette, and see what they think. Actually, it all makes sense, but I know that they don't want to use any more of our people."

"They don't have to, Marcel," Claudine added. "Just take a group from one of the sides and put them in the second truck. The more we get in the compound, the better our odds. This is where 90% of the fighting is going to take place, right?"

This is one very bright, young lady, Marcel thought to himself. "You're right about that. It's like having two Trojan horses in there."

"OK, I'll see what I can do," Florette said. "Right now, I think I'm going to get some sleep." Olivia and Denis followed her, each going into a separate hut. Marcel and Claudine stayed up for another hour, talking about worldly subjects.

Marcel and Florette left early the next morning, each going in separate directions. Marcel would make his way to the northern part of Marseille, by way of the back roads. He had gotten a message to François, his chief lieutenant, to assemble the other four men in his group, and meet him at an abandoned hunting cabin. They had used this as a rendezvous point before, and because of its remoteness in the woods, Marcel had considered it to be quite safe. As always, every man knew to take a circuitous route to get to the cabin, in case he was being followed. In the event that this was happening, he would abandon his efforts to get there.

On the drive south, Marcel had plenty of time to think of all that had transpired over the last two months. He thought of the elaborate planning that had gone into the relay station operation, and how quickly, in one night, this attractive, smart lady had shot a hole in their labored endeavor. He knew she was right and kept questioning himself, over and over, on *why hadn't I thought of these things?*

He kept thinking of her as a woman, also, and how much he enjoyed their pleasant conversation, after the others had retired for the night. He realized that he shouldn't let thoughts like these even enter his mind -- number one because he was happily married, but foremost, it might interfere with his judgment as her *Maquis* commander, and get them killed. He would have to keep this relationship on a strictly professional basis.

Claudine, he had learned, was a math professor at the University in Lyon. *No wonder she was so logical*, Marcel thought. She was on the run, because of her outspoken, anti-fascist views, and was threatened by the *Vichy* on more than one occasion. She had gotten word, through a friend that she was going to be arrested for her public statements, which continued even after the warnings.

"What cowards some of my colleagues are who never speak out," she had told Marcel. He had become fond of her from that minute on. She had been married for a few years, but her husband fell into that "silent" category, and, "I just couldn't live with a man like that," she said, so they got divorced.

Enough of Claudine he thought, as he neared the meeting place. It was scheduled for 9:30 A.M., and he would be there at least 20 minutes before that. As today was a Saturday, none of the men would be working, giving him plenty of time to go over the details of the operation. As briefly as possible, he would also explain his personal situation to them. The less they knew, the better for everyone involved.

Marcel parked his car in a secluded spot, half a mile from the cabin; François arrived shortly thereafter, followed by Lucien, Aristide, Leon, and Georges, who immediately asked, "I was shocked to see you with the *Gestapo*...what in the world happened?"

Marcel told them the whole story of his interrogation and why he had to flee Marseille with his family. When asked by Aristide where they were, he simply said that they were safely out of the country, and left it at that. From now on he would be living in the hills, he told them. François would be his liaison to the rest of them, just as he had arranged this meeting; although, François was contacted this time by another *Maquis* member, sent by Florette.

"Georges, do you have any idea why I was picked up and interrogated?" Marcel asked. "Were you able to hear any information around the police station on how much or if they know anything about our operation?"

"You know, I didn't want to look like I was *that* interested," Georges said. "I didn't ask any direct questions, but just tried to listen to the office rumors that go around. Frankly, the only thing I heard that would qualify for an investigation by the *Gestapo* was the night we blew up the *Vichy* offices. Since they didn't have any clue who did that, you were picked up because there were rumors of your being involved with the Underground Press."

"So they were just picking at straws?" Marcel asked.

"Apparently so," Georges replied. "If they for one minute thought that you were guilty, they would have had you shot. I'll tell you, those three men in the *Gestapo* are not nice people. Even the local heads of the *Vichy* government are peeing in their pants when they're around them."

"Well, after we pull off this next assignment…that I'll tell all of you about in a minute…the *Gestapo* will surely be looking for me again. So," Marcel sighed, "my best option, is just to do what I've done, and learn to live in the hills…which is something that some of you may have to do in the future also. I have a feeling that things around here are going to be getting much more dangerous for everyone, so stay alert."

Marcel went over the operation, discussed the risks, and asked if anyone would rather not participate. Having no one decline, which he expected, they set up the meeting place, and time, for October 1st. He would be allowed to take one more person, and his first choice would probably be Claudine.

François had brought enough food for Marcel, and the other three living in the hills, to get by on for the next two weeks. With François' help, he loaded this into his car, and since Marcel was just outside Marseille, he decided to take a chance and drive by his home. There didn't seem to be any activity going on around the neighborhood, so he drove to the back entrance of the house and entered through an open door, which he thought was odd…*Maybe we left it open when we went to Elne.*

He walked up the steps to the kitchen, which seemed to be in order, but was shocked on entering his small, library office. Drawers had been pulled out of all the cabinets, books had been thrown all over the floors, and his desk had been ransacked. The same kind of treatment was given throughout the house, including the closets. He hurried down to the basement and checked the darkroom. All his film boxes had been opened and scattered, and any negatives he had strung up, or filed, had been taken. *I'm lucky that I gave all the pictures and negatives of the relay station to Florette*, he thought.

It was apparent that the *Gestapo* now had him on their list of fugitives. Marcel reacted quickly, and decided to leave the house the way he found it. His family was safe, and there was nothing here that couldn't be replaced. *The sooner I get out of Marseille, the better.*

On the drive north to the Luberon hills, he questioned why he had taken the chance to go back to the city, and concluded that *that was a pretty stupid thing to do.* He had even considered contacting his dental assistants. He would tell them to *temporarily close the practice until the War was over*, but it would have put them in too much danger, and he was sure they would figure it out by themselves. More than likely, the *Gestapo* had gone back to search his office, also.

When Marcel returned to the camp, Denis walked back through the woods with him to carry up all the groceries. They were all glad to get the food, because they were very low on supplies and, for two weeks, hadn't made a run into Bonnieux, a small town nearby. A sympathetic farmer there, who was a friend of Olivia's family, had given them everything they needed for a very reasonable price.

Until Denis told him that he was going to bathe, Marcel didn't realize that there was a stream running 150 feet behind the camp. Marcel grabbed his towel, soap, and a change of underwear, and followed him. It felt good to get two days grime off his body, and after redressing, the two men sat on the bank and chatted for almost an hour.

Denis was very likable and easy to get to know. He and Marcel shared a lot in common, especially their love of sports and history. He was a pathologist by profession, and worked at the hospital in Avignon, where his wife and three children lived.

"Being so close, do you ever get in to see them?" Marcel asked.

"I try to go at least once a month, if possible," he said. "It hasn't been easy on any of us, especially my wife, but we're managing. I had been in *La Résistance* for six months, and got caught stealing a bunch of medical supplies. When the hospital administrator found out, he called the *Vichy* police and had me arrested."

"Arrested!" exclaimed Marcel. "Didn't he have any sympathy for what you were doing?"

"Sympathy?" Denis laughed, "Not this guy. I heard that he had studied in Germany, and was very pro-Nazi. If I ever get the chance, I'll kill him."

"Funny you should say that," Marcel said. "I have three *Gestapo* agents who I feel the same way about, so we'll have to add your man in Avignon to our agenda." They both laughed. "So how long did you spend in jail?"

"Three weeks. One night I overpowered the guard on duty when he came into my cell. He thought I had broken my leg." In a matter-of-fact tone, he added, "I was faking of course, and wound up breaking his neck. I've been on the run with the *Maquis* ever since."

"Holy shit, Denis!" was all Marcel could say. They both sat there for awhile, lost in their own thoughts. Denis got up and motioned for Marcel to follow him back to the camp, where they could smell the dinner cooking. Tonight was Claudine's turn to prepare the meal, and as everyone discovered, she was quite a gourmet.

While eating, Olivia told Marcel that she had been a biathlete-- shooting and cross country skiing. Her regular job in the winter, when she wasn't training, was a ski instructor at Val d'Iserè, one of the leading ski resorts in the French Alps. She could have easily fled to Switzerland when the War started, but chose to stay and fight.

What a diverse trio I have here, Marcel thought.

19

The day had finally arrived, Saturday, October 3, 1942, and the adrenalin was high within the *Maquis* group. The district commanders had all met the night before at Philippe Lambert's villa, and other than a few minor changes, everything was on go. The main changes, which Marcel already knew about because his group was directly involved, were the change of date from October 1st, and the use of the two food trucks. Florette had made a special trip to Marcel's camp to inform him that Claudine's plan had been accepted, and that his group of six men, plus Claudine, would lead the assault in the trucks.

All the men from Marseille had found their way to the camp the day before, and were introduced to their three new comrades. Denis and Olivia would be driving two cars to take their group to Avignon, and then pick them up after the mission at a designated spot.

Everyone had their own thoughts on the drive to Avignon, the fortified city of the nine French Popes. Denis was hoping that he wouldn't run into his family, or any colleagues that knew him, and for this purpose he grew a full beard, which came in as a bright red. Thinking that this was a good idea, Marcel did the same, although his was black. They both found that this was one of the ways to help pass the time in the hills.

Corteaux Food Supplies was located along the Place de l'Horloge, the main square, and Denis knew exactly where it was. The courtyard was left open for them, and they drove both cars inside, and then closed the gates. It was now 7:30 A.M., and they were shown inside the building by Estephan Corteaux, the owner and a long-time member of *La Résistance.* In order to get them in the front gate of the German compound, Estephan would be the man who would drive the lead truck. He had told the Germans that he had to bring a second truck today, because of all the food they needed for *Oktoberfest*, and no questions were asked. He was risking everything to be part of this mission; furthermore, it was Estephan that was responsible for informing Florette that this unknown German compound actually existed. Security-conscious as she was, Florette had never mentioned this to Marcel. He, like Marcel, had already moved his family to an unknown destination, and after today, would take to the hills with the *Maquis*.

Estephan gave everyone white hats and long white coats, which all food employees were expected to wear. The coats would help conceal their weapons, when they stepped out of the trucks. At precisely 8:00 A.M., after briefing Estephan of the final plans, they split up into two groups and departed Avignon. In the lead truck with Estephan, were François, Aristide, and Georges; in the number two truck, were Marcel, Lucien, Claudine, and Leon, who did the driving. By this time, Marcel expected the other ten people on the mission to already be imbedded in the woods surrounding the German compound.

At 8:30 A.M., the trucks entered the outskirts of Morieres, then turned down the dirt road leading to their destination. Marcel could hear his heart beating, as his number two truck slowed, leaving a one minute gap between the vehicles. As they approached the compound, they could see Estephan's truck already in the yard, heading toward the back building. *So far, so good*, Marcel thought, and he could not see any of the *Maquis* in the woods, which he hoped was also a good sign.

Halfway to the entrance gate and guard houses, Leon stopped the truck, pretending that he had stalled. When they saw François and his group emerge from their vehicle, Leon started the truck and drove to the entrance. A guard opened the gate, and without bothering to look inside the truck, waved them in. Once inside, Marcel was relieved to see only one APC, with three soldiers aboard, and two guards...the one that let them in, and one in the other guard house. "Five Germans, total," he whispered to the others.

Leon, the carpenter, who was also a whiz with engines, purposely stalled the truck again, five feet in front of the APC. Pretending to be mad, he jumped out of the truck, cursed in French, and opened the hood to look inside. Claudine, on cue, then came out of the back door, went around the opposite side of the hood, and asked, "What's the problem?"

There was no reason for Leon to answer, because on seeing Claudine, all the soldiers perked up, and called out to her with whatever French phrases they knew. She smiled back, and knew that she had them in the palm of her hands within 10 seconds. *Smile now you bastards, because I'm about to kill you*, she thought.

Marcel and Lucien came out of the truck also, rapid-fire rifles concealed under their coats, and stood with Leon. Marcel could see that things were progressing as planned on the other side of the yard. The men had carried the boxes of food into the kitchen, and had come back inside the truck to get their weapons. Georges came out first carrying a small, covered platter and slowly walked to the radio shack. This was Marcel's cue to get things rolling at his end, and pointing to the soldiers, said to Claudine, *"Les Monsieur's...faim?* Are the gentlemen hungry?"

Claudine turned around, looking directly at the five Germans who had gathered near the APC, put her five fingers to her lips, and asked, *"Voulez-vous une entrée?"*

"Oui, oui," they all replied in unison, not knowing exactly what to expect from this gorgeous creature.

Claudine motioned for the three men in the APC to come down and join them, but they were reluctant and she didn't ask them again. She went to the back of the truck, got the small platter of appetizers, brought it back to the APC, and laid it on its fender.

Seeing what it was, the soldiers were very pleased, and said. *"Ja, Ja. Vielen dank. Sehr gut."* Two of the soldiers got down from the APC to have a taste, but the one manning the heavy machine gun stayed put. Marcel whispered to Leon and Lucien that he would take him out first.

Georges now entered the radio shack with his platter. He startled the two busy men, who were sitting with their headphones on in front of a lot of radio equipment. One of them merely waved him away, but the other, who was a lot more cautious, stood up and pulled out his Lugar, pointing it at the Frenchman. *"Was wunschen Sie,* What do you want?" he asked, and then added, *"Was ist das?* What is this?"

Georges spoke a little German, and said, *"Guten Morgan, meine Herren. Sie sind Vorspeises für Ihnen.* Good morning, sirs. They are appetizers for you."

The officer waved his Luger toward a desk sitting on the side of the room, indicating that Georges should put the platter there. Georges nodded his head, as a servant would do, and walked over to the desk. As he did so, he noticed that the officer had put his pistol back in the holster, but was still standing there watching him. With his back to the two Germans, Georges put the platter down, unbuttoned his coat, and took the wrapper off the appetizers. He then slowly removed his pistol, with the silencer, from his waistband.

This is the moment of truth, he thought, then said out loud, in German, "*Ja, das ist gut!*" He turned quickly, shooting the officer in the chest; the man looked startled, as he fell back, grasping at his chair with one hand, and his heart with the other, until he slid to the ground. The other man turned and saw his commander; he reached for his holster, but it was too late...Georges got him in the back of the head, his brains splattering on the sophisticated equipment. No one had heard anything outside this room.

Georges took the two plastic explosives out of his pocket, and shoved them between the receivers and the short wave radios, then put a fuse in each of them. They were now set to go off in approximately 20 minutes. He put his pistol back in his waistband, buttoned his coat, and walked outside as if nothing had happened. He tipped his hat, so that the *Maquis* in the yard and beyond the fence could see that the first part of the mission was accomplished, and they should now jump into action.

François waited at the entrance to the kitchen, until Georges briefly returned to the truck, hid his automatic rifle underneath his coat, and walked toward the dining room door. Aristide and Estephan were now poised to go into the barracks. As soon as these four men were in place and starting to open the three doors, Marcel only had to say one word to his group at the entrance, "Now!"

On that command, the other three took out the weapons beneath their coats, and almost simultaneous with the gunfire coming from across the compound, fired at the soldiers at close range. For everyone, except Marcel, it was like shooting ducks in a pond. When he fired his rifle at the soldier behind the machine gun, it ricocheted off the armor in front of the gun, and broke a window in the guard house. Marcel didn't have another clear shot, as the young soldier swung his large gun around and was ready to fire at the three men, when Claudine shot him with her pistol, from her side of the APC. The bullet entered the base of his skull and exited through the top of his head. Marcel looked at her, let his breath out, and nodded appreciatively.

After making sure that all the Germans were dead, they jumped into their truck to go to the other side of the compound to assist the others. As soon as Leon started the engine, a bullet came through the windshield, grazing his shoulder. Then they saw the guard, who patrolled the tower, walking swiftly toward them firing his weapon. All of a sudden, he fell to the ground, and Marcel could see a puff of smoke coming from the woods…a sharpshooter had gotten him.

Marcel looked at Leon's shoulder, and said, "It's only a flesh wound."

As he drove toward the rear building, Claudine opened a first-aid kit, pulled out a bandage and tape, and put it on the upper part of Leon's arm.

Before Marcel's group had arrived, François and Georges had opened fire in the kitchen and dining room respectively, killing the two cooks in the kitchen, and four soldiers having breakfast in the dining room. They could hear the grenade and shots going off in the attached building next to them, which Aristide and Estephan were taking care of, and all the gunfire at the front gate. They looked out the window, and saw Marcel's truck starting out across the yard. They felt it was safe now to go back to their truck, get the plastic explosives and dynamite, and start rigging these explosives to the 60 foot radio tower.

When the fighting first began, Aristide opened the door of the barracks, and threw in a grenade. When it exploded and they heard the screams, he and Estephan came in blasting their automatic, sub-machine guns, killing six right away. Then Estephan saw four more

147

soldiers in the back of the barracks. At first they were hiding behind their bunks, but then got up, grabbed their rifles, and ran down a hall, separating a private room and the showers. He cut two of them down, but the others got out through the back door. He ran toward the open door and heard rifle shots coming from a distance. Cautiously, he peeked around the corner, and saw the two men that had gotten away, laying face down in the mud. He gave a thumbs-up to his hidden comrades in the woods. In a soft voice, he said, "Well, we're finally killing these fucking Nazis, aren't we, and that's priceless."

It was the last words Estephan would ever utter. As he turned around to assist Aristide in checking the bodies in the main part of the barracks, the door to the back room had opened without him hearing it, and a German officer was standing there with a Lugar pointed at his head. The bullet hit him directly between the eyes, and Estephan fell back into the shower area with a loud thud, as his head hit the hard concrete.

Aristide looked up immediately as the single shot was fired. He yelled out, "Estephan! Noooo!"

The officer came out of his room and began firing, missing Aristide by inches, but Aristide's round of bullets cut the German in half and he fell in his own blood, as it was gushing out of his mouth. He was so furious, that he shot all the bodies again. Then he put his gun strap over his shoulder, and went back to get Estephan.

On hearing all the new gunfire, Marcel and Lucien cautiously went toward each side of the barracks, while Claudine assisted François and Georges at the tower, with Leon acting as a lookout. Marcel shouted, "Aristide...Estephan," but no one answered. He started to yell again, but just then Aristide walked out, with Estephan over his shoulder. There was blood all over both of them, and Aristide was crying. Marcel could see his man's massive head wound.

"Oh, my God," Marcel sighed. *Even though I've just met him, I think that Estephan was probably one of the most courageous people I've ever known…he obviously would do anything for France, and now he paid the ultimate price.*

Aristide laid him down in the truck and covered him with a sheet. He then joined Marcel, Lucien, and Claudine, who had now gone to gather the enemies' weapons, munitions, food and uniforms that would be used by the *Maquis*.

François and Georges completed rigging the radio tower, and set the fuses for 10 minutes. "We have only 5 minutes more, before that thing blows in the radio shack," Georges alerted everyone. The entire operation, from the time the first truck entered up to now, took just 15 minutes.

"I think we better pack up and leave now," Marcel said. "We can't take a chance on the shack blowing up sooner, so let's get going."

Everyone loaded whatever contraband they were carrying into the two trucks. With Estephan killed, François would be driving truck #1, and with Leon wounded, Marcel would drive truck #2. They left not a minute too soon, for as they were driving toward the front gate, the radio shack exploded, causing the whole building to go up in flames. The fuse had gone off 3 minutes early and debris was flying everywhere.

Before they had time to admire their accomplishments, they saw two *Vichy* police cars, with sirens blaring, coming up their escape road. Marcel yelled out his window to François, in the truck ahead of him… they would both park behind the guard house on the left. They would fight from there, but hopefully one of the Maquis units was positioned across the road, on the hill.

After parking, everyone jumped out of their trucks. They could hear gunfire coming from across the road, and the two cars screeching to a stop. Marcel ran back behind the APC, and could see the police 50 meters up the road, pinned down, but firing up the hill. He looked up at this giant, armored truck he was standing behind, and had an idea. He yelled over to the others, "Can anyone here drive this monster?"

Leon raised his hand, and said, "I can drive anything that moves, chief. I take it that you're not thinking of a long ride, are you? My arm is not up for it."

"You just have to drive it out of here and make a right turn," Marcel replied. "I'll get up there and man the machine gun, so we can help those guys up on the hill. It will be a lot more effective than their rifles." Leon nodded his approval, and ran toward the driver's cabin. Marcel climbed up in the back, and threw the dead German soldier that Claudine had killed, over the side. *That young man almost killed me*, he thought for a moment.

Leon started the engine and slowly began moving forward. Marcel sat in the gunner's chair, and checked to make sure that the safety was off and the weapon was ready to be fired.

"Be careful, Marcel," Claudine, looking concerned, yelled out.

"I'll try," he yelled back.

Leon was now parallel to the two guard houses, when he opened his door and called back to Marcel. "Hold on, because I'm gonna to gun this thing and make a sharp right turn."

"OK, I'm ready," Marcel said, as he pushed his feet against a slanted, metal plate on the floor, and braced his back against the chair.

Leon floored the gas pedal and the heavy vehicle lunged forward, but not with the speed either of them had hoped for. The front end was now clearing the guard house, and Marcel knew that once the police saw it, it would be an easy target to hit. He swung the machine gun sideways, so that he would be in a position to start firing immediately.

The first shots hit the passenger's door of the APC, as soon as it became visible…just a few more feet and Marcel would have a shot at the police. Two seconds later they were past the guard house, and Marcel squeezed the trigger with his right forefinger, but nothing happened. He could hear the whiz of bullets rushing by his head, and two pings on the armor cage below the machine gun. He checked the safety again, but that appeared fine. Leon was making the turn now and heading directly toward the police cars, who were both turned at an angle facing the compound fence. With his left hand, he swung the gun around to face over the front cabin, and before putting his hand back on the handle, his eye caught a glimpse of another safety switch on the left grip.

"Oh, shit," he yelled out, "two goddamn safeties!" He released it, and began firing. At first, the bullets were flying over the tops of the cars. He lowered the gun slightly and riddled the car in front with a flurry of gunfire. The police were hiding behind their vehicle and firing over their hoods. With a slight turn of his wrist, he caught two of them in the head and chest, the force of the bullets throwing them into the ditch behind them.

Leon had now gotten far enough down the road, where Marcel could see the back wheel and trunk of the car. He opened fire again, this time aiming at the gas tank…it exploded with such a fury that he could feel the heat 50 meters away. The remaining two police officers were killed instantly. Marcel stopped firing, and for a short period there was complete stillness and silence, as if the world had stopped. Then, as if it were orchestrated, a soft chant turned into a loud roar coming from the woods around the compound, and the small hill to the left of him. The *Maquis* came out of their hiding places, raising their arms and rifles above their heads, and shouting in triumph.

151

Marcel turned his head around and saw François, Lucien, Aristide, and Claudine running up the road toward the APC, shouting, "*Vive la France, Vive la France.*" Leon had gotten out of the truck and jumped up on the firing platform with Marcel. They put their arms around each other's shoulders and waved their fists in the air.

The celebration went on for 5 minutes, and then Marcel motioned for them to quiet down. He spoke as loudly as he could, so that everyone could hear him.

"This is has been our biggest victory, because all of you have done your jobs magnificently. Today's operation will be imprinted in your minds forever, but unfortunately, we can't celebrate too long, or share this day with our families or friends, because of who we are. As members of *La Résistance*, we must maintain our silence, for there will be many more battles to fight before France will be free from Nazi tyranny." He raised, and shook his fist in the air, "*Le Combat* will continue!"

Just then, the first blast went off from the concrete base of the radio tower, and 10 seconds later it was followed by a second explosion of the tower itself. Shrapnel was flying everywhere, as the remains of the tower tumbled over. Everyone around the area cheered, and almost spontaneously started singing *La Marseillaise*, the French national anthem:

Allons, enfants de la Patrie,
Le jour de gloire est arrive !
Contre nous de la tyrannie
L'étendard sanglant est levé…

Marcel had come down from the APC, when they began singing the second verse. He put his arm around François and Claudine, as they sang together, and when it was through, he and Claudine hugged in more than just a friendly way. He liked the feel of her body against his, and he knew by her motions, that she felt the same.

As he broke away from her, he nonchalantly said to everyone in their immediate area, "I think we better start dispersing, before we have more company. And please, don't take any unnecessary chances getting back to the camp." He waved to the people in the woods, with both hands in an outward motion, indicating that they too should start leaving to their destinations.

The seven of them went back to their two vehicles near the guard house. Their euphoria was dampened on seeing blood trickling out the back of truck #1, and on feeling the loss of Estephan. They quickly cleaned up the blood and wrapped the body in two more sheets, hoping that would contain it. Marcel decided to move the body to his truck, since Florette would be with Denis at their rendezvous point. She would know the procedure to dispose of one of their own.

When the trucks reached the main highway, Marcel went east toward Fontaine-de-Vaucluse. François headed west toward Chateaurenard to meet Olivia and an unknown *Maquis* member to take the truck. The day before the mission began, Estephan had been wise in white-washing the Corteaux Food Supply signs on each side of both trucks. They would have been too easy to spot, once the word got out to the local police.

It had taken 30 minutes until they met up with Denis, Florette, and a young Maquis member, who would be driving the truck. They were ecstatic to hear the results of the raid, but very sad when shown the body of Estephan. "There is a small cemetery we use for the *Maquis*," Florette said. "It's in a very remote area, and the family will be secure in attending the graveside service and burial." She wiped a tear from her eye, saying, "He has such a wonderful wife and children …they'll be devastated."

After Marcel briefed Florette, she gave him some supplies and food from the truck. Before leaving, she warned him, "The *Vichy* will be combing the countryside for the next few weeks, so try to keep as well hidden as possible...I'll be in touch."

By noon, all nine of Marcel's group were back at the Luberon hills camp. They shared bread and cheese and wine, and rejoiced again in their almost flawless accomplishment...killing Germans who had invaded their country.

"I still can't believe what you all did," Olivia kept saying. "It will give you tremendous satisfaction forever...even if you live to be 100."

"Like, when you won the silver medal in Shooting at the Olympics?" Denis asked.

"Oh, much better than that," she replied. "That doesn't compare to what they did today."

"You never told me you were in the Olympics, Olivia," Marcel said. "What year was it?"

"It was at the 1936 Summer Olympics, in Berlin," she responded. "I call it 'the Hitler Games'. With all the Arian bullshit he was professing, it was so evident what this maniac had in mind for the rest of Europe." She took a swig of wine, put both elbows on her knees, and gave a slight chuckle, "I think I got more pleasure in watching that American Negro man...Jesse Owens...beat all those sons-of-bitches, than I had in winning my own medal."

Olivia had captured the attention of everyone now because normally she was always so serious and never talked much. With a couple glasses of wine, she was starting to open up, and the interest in what she had to say, was evident.

"Well, did you get to see the little Austrian painter?" Leon asked. He was sitting with his shirt open. Denis had redressed his wound and a big bandage was wrapped around his upper arm and shoulder.

"Just a glimpse of the bastard, as he was leaving the stadium…after Owens won his second medal." Olivia paused for a moment, and then said, "I wish I could have shot him then; it would have saved thousands of lives that are going to be lost. But…enough about the past." She waved her hand around the group, "What you made happen today, will be the big news all over France by tomorrow, and will go down in history, so I salute you," she raised her glass.

They had been hearing sirens in the distance for the last hour, and they were right in assuming that it was related to their Morieres experience that morning. Marcel took a sip of his wine, and then stood up to address his group. "Thank you, Olivia, for those nice words, but you and Denis had a part in this also. We work as a team, and everyone has a job to do…that's how we'll stay alive."

He put his glass down, rubbed his hands together, and continued. "So…as much as I hate to break up this little party, I think it would be best to get back to reality. There's gonna be to be a massive search on, which could last indefinitely. You can hear the sirens. A lot of innocent people are going to be interrogated to find out who's behind all of this. There's no doubt that what we did is going to affect their lives; all the French can hold their heads higher now, but some will have to suffer because of it. As *Maquis* fighters, we all chose to be proactive and believed it will make a difference…that it is the right course to take; however, it can all come tumbling down, if our lips aren't sealed, and this especially is true for François, Leon, Georges, Aristide, and Lucien, because you're still in Marseille and not on the run yet.

"There's also a good chance that we'll have to give up this camp soon and move somewhere else. It's not good to stay in one place for too long, so I'll keep François informed, if the four of us here relocate."

"Marcel," François asked, "do you think that we should be making our way back to Marseille now, rather than spending the night, as was planned?"

"That would probably be wise, while you still have plenty of light in the forest," Marcel said. "It wouldn't surprise me, if they started sending small, spotter planes to look for the *Maquis*, and nine of us wouldn't be hard to locate. Also, if you're away overnight, people might get suspicious. "

"Alright," François said, speaking to the others in his group, "we'll start leaving in 30 minute intervals, starting with Lucien, and then Georges, Aristide, Leon, and I'll bring up the rear. Find your way back to wherever you parked your cars, and stay on the back roads as much as possible."

"François," Aristide asked, "should we each meet in your shop, at our regular times, or will that be different now?"

"No, nothing has changed," François replied, "but, just make sure you're not being followed. If there's any doubt in your mind, then abort and I'll find some way to contact you. Understood?" The four men nodded their heads. "OK then...why don't you start out, Lucien?"

Over the next two hours, all the men from Marseille had left. There were a lot of handshakes, hugs and a few tears shed, because this was a day that no one would ever forget.

The men and women took turns bathing in the stream, and washing the filthy clothes they had worn in the raid. Everyone was exhausted, and after dinner, Marcel went back to his hut, undressed down to his underwear, and lay down on the hard wooden floor, on top of his blanket. With his head resting on his knapsack, he was almost asleep, when he felt the floor vibrate. He looked up and saw Claudine towering above him.

At that moment, Marcel thoughts were not on the War, or his family. *God help me, but I really do want her now more than anything.*

Instinctively, he reached up and took her hand, to bring her down to him. She gently let go, took off her blouse and shorts, and knelt down beside him. She leaned over, as his arms went around her, and they kissed passionately. She put her leg between his, and he could tell that she was completely naked. He could feel her soft breasts against his chest as they held each other tightly, and himself getting hard at the same time. She let her hand slide down his stomach until she held his erection, massaging it ever so gently. He softly caressed her between her legs, and then let his mouth drop down to suck on her hard nipple.

Nothing needed to be said, as they continued to enjoy each other completely. Marcel finally lifted her on top of him and Claudine slid easily onto his rising phallus. They were in rhythm immediately and didn't stop, until they both came and together let out a long breath. They lay there for some time, until Marcel whispered, "Claudine, I want to...", but she put her finger to his lips.

"Don't say a thing, my darling," and they fell asleep in each other's arms.

20

On September 16, 1942, Major von Klemper announced to his assembled battalion that German forces had now entered Stalingrad. "Russia will be ours in six months," he proudly proclaimed to his applauding audience. Even though some of the assembled may have been skeptical, they didn't show it.

"What a croc of shit!" Johann said to Hermann, when they were back in their office. "Have those idiots not seen what is happening to our people and cities, here at home?"

"You are absolutely right, *Hauptmann*," Hermann said. "And here we are, building barriers against the invasion of Europe by the Allies, and *der Füehrer* is expanding to another front in Russia."

"And right before the Russian winter starts, to boot," Johann added. "You would think that some of those generals had a sense of history, and remembered what happened to Napoleon." He pounded his fist on the desk, "Dumb, dumb, dumb, is all I can say. You...do not...fight...a war...against the Russians during the winter, period!" He paused for a moment to collect his thoughts. "I think that they have all gone mad, Hermann; furthermore, it would not surprise me if thousands, or hundreds of thousands of our brave men die on the Eastern Front."

"Yes, *Hauptmann*, it is very sad…very sad. It destroys families all over our country." Hermann took a picture out of his wallet, and looked at it for a moment. "I cannot imagine what would happen to my wife, and my two beautiful girls, if something were to happen to me. How would they survive?"

Johann just shook his head, and said, "I do not know. I suppose we have to think positive and do the best we can, under the circumstances." Trying to make Hermann feel better, he added, "I would not worry about it…you and I are going to come out of this fine. If that bomb could not kill us, then nothing will."

Except for his almost weekly visits to Frankfort to check on the production of the barriers, Johann found himself quite bored with the routine around Porz. Every day, his men would do more testing along a 10 kilometer stretch of the river. There were different terrains, but the results always came out the same.

The one routine he did look forward to was having dinner with Albert and the two nurses, followed by a night of sex with Eva. Even though they didn't really have anything in common, she was wonderful in bed. It capped off a night of good food, rare in Germany now, and a large amount of alcohol…something he never indulged himself in before the War…a beer or two was all he could handle.

One night, Albert couldn't leave the hospital, because the casualties were mounting. Eva was doing overtime work also, but promised to meet Johann at the apartment when she got off duty. He grabbed a quick dinner, went back to Albert's for a long, hot bath and waited for Eva. When she arrived two hours later, he thought it would be nice to talk to her for awhile, just to get to know each other better without the *schnapps*, but he found her very shallow and the conversation went nowhere. They went to bed, had quick sex, and thankfully slept for the night.

In the morning, he went back to Porz to begin his routine again. Compared to the night before, he almost welcomed the boredom. There were times like this when his mind wandered to his pre-war life with Anna, and the future they had planned for their family. More and more, he appreciated her intellect and the wonderful conversations they had. *Because of this madman who wants to control the world, all of that is gone forever and will never take place again. I pray, that one day, Hitler rots in hell!*

21

During the weeks that followed the raid on the German relay station, the three *Gestapo* agents in Marseille interrogated over 100 people in the Provence area, and searched the homes of dozens more. Two men, who had nothing to do with the raid, or *La Résistance*, were tortured and then shot.

The head agent, who had interrogated Marcel, organized teams of search parties. They were made up of the *Vichy* police to look for the *Maquis* in the hills, but had no success. Marcel was correct in moving their camp every few weeks to a new location, but in the event that they were discovered, the four of them had plenty of weapons, and were ready to fight. It was exhausting for everyone to be on the move like this, but they realized that what they had achieved was having such a positive impact on the morale of the French people, that it was worth their own sacrifices. At the same time, it was an enormous embarrassment for the Germans and their *Vichy* puppets, who were now hunting them down like dogs.

For ten days after the raid, the BBC had a field day broadcasting the *Maquis'* masterful plan. Charles de Gaulle and Winston Churchill, at separate times, came on the air to congratulate their marvelous feat, and both leaders promised "to award medals for the heroics of these brave men and women, after the Nazis were defeated." Even though he didn't hear the broadcast, Marcel had no idea that their actions would elicit such reactions.

On October 24th, a prearranged date, Marcel made his way down to a safe house, on the outskirts of Marseille. There he met Florette and François. The three of them hoped to get an update from each other on what was transpiring in their particular area, and on what future plans were in store for their group.

François had related that Annette, one of Marcel's dental assistants, had been held overnight at *Vichy* headquarters, and interrogated by the *Gestapo* on the whereabouts of Dr. Pontier. According to Georges, who was in the building when she was brought there, Annette was severely beaten, but was unable to tell them anything, so they let her go.

"I'm going to kill those bastards one day," Marcel said on hearing this. "In fact, Florette, I think that the sooner we do this, the better."

"Why now, Marcel?" Florette asked. "Why not wait until things calm down, and they won't be expecting it?"

"That's just the point...they won't be expecting it now, because of all the heightened security. Furthermore, I feel that we shouldn't be put on the defensive for what we did, but rather hit them again, when they least expect it. These assholes know too much, and more innocent people are going to die, or be tortured like Annette."

He sighed, and continued, "You know, I've been planning on this for a long time, and have some ideas that Georges and I discussed a few weeks ago. He told me their daily patterns, and I think I have a way to get rid of all three of them at one time. I would recommend that we not wait until they have a chance to fully brief more *Gestapo* agents, who may be on their way here."

"Alright, what do you have in mind?" Florette asked.

Marcel laid out his plan for her and François, and as expected, she told him that it had to go through the regular channels for approval. He also briefed them on the location changes, which the four of them in the hills were making.

Marcel laughed, "Our most recent new home is in the *bories*, outside Gordes."

Florette looked at Marcel with a confused expression. "What are the *bories*?"

"There are thousands of these ancient dwellings around Provence," François explained. "They are built like beehives out of limestone slabs. I don't think that anyone has lived in them since the middle of the last century."

"They were mainly used for shelter and storage," Marcel added, "so I think they'll fit our needs very nicely for awhile. The walls are about 1.5 meters thick, so it should keep us cool in the summer and warm in the winter."

"Ah, yes," Florette said. "I think I've seen them before. Don't they date back to 2000-3000 B.C.?" Marcel nodded. "Who would have ever thought that they would be used again in the 20th century? Ah, the stories you'll be able to tell your grandchildren, Marcel."

"Yes, if I live that long," he replied. "So, tell us what else is in the works."

Florette lit up a cigarette, took a deep draw, and blew out a long trail of smoke. "North and west of Provence, there have been a few forays… nothing of the magnitude that all of you pulled off. I understand that after the War, De Gaulle and Churchill want to decorate the ones that took part in the raid. The leadership is ecstatic regarding that topic, and still hasn't stopped talking about it.

"But, as of now, they haven't come up with definite plans regarding your group, because they wanted you to lay low. After I tell them what you said, they may change their minds…we'll see. Another reason things are slow, is that within the next month, our intelligence reports indicate an imminent German takeover of our Unoccupied Zone. They obviously got the same intelligence we did, namely, that the Allies, with a large contingency of American troops, are poised to invade North Africa. So, our leadership is spending most of their time planning ahead for that eventuality."

"Well, Florette," Marcel said assuredly, "I think that even strengthens my proposal."

The meeting broke up after an hour, and they made arrangements to meet again within a week. Marcel picked up some supplies from François and Florette, and drove back to the hills. He knew that he soon had to get back to Elne to check on his family and warn them of the Germans; although, he still didn't believe that they would ever come to that part of France…but there was always that possibility.

On the drive north, he thought of how much he missed Angelina and the children, but at the same time, he didn't feel guilty about his one night affair with Claudine, although he was sure there would be more. *There's a war going on and things like this happen, especially when you're thrown together like she and I are.* He wanted to stay alive, and was not going to let something like this upset him.

22

With the completion of the beach obstacles, Johann had no excuse now to go back to Frankfurt. He spent his time assisting the *Wehrmacht* rebuild some small bridges which had been damaged or destroyed. He missed his conversations with Albert, because they had become close friends; however, he was almost happy that he didn't have to see Eva.

I doubt that anyone will ever replace Anna, he thought. *If we only knew Albert at the time she was sick, he would have gotten her the medicines she needed.* He dwelled on these thoughts to the point of making himself depressed again. Hermann could see this and tried to help, but Johann was numbing himself against everyone and everything around him. The boredom, the War, and the destruction it was causing was getting to him also.

On November 7, 1942, Major von Klemper announced to his assembled officers that the Allied forces had landed in North Africa, and that everyone here should be ready to move out the following day. They would first stop in Frankfurt to assist in the loading and securing the barriers onto the train cars, which would transport them into the northern part of France. A few men from the battalion would be staying with the train, while the remainder would be in a motorized convoy heading to the same destination.

Johann's spirits lifted, when he heard that they would be leaving Germany for a more tranquil place. The stopover in Frankfurt might give him a chance to contact Albert, whom he had not seen for over a month. Everything went off as planned, and when the battalion arrived at the factory the next day, the officers supervised the transfer of the obstacles to the open, flat-bedded, train platforms. They covered them with canvas tarps, and secured them with heavy ropes.

The whole operation took only six hours, and knowing his men needed a little R & R, Johann gave them the rest of the day and night off. The convoy would leave the next morning at 0700 hours. There were temporary enlisted men's quarters (EMQ), as well as visiting officer's quarters (VOQ) located near the factory. Johann went to the VOQ, showered, changed clothes, and then headed for Albert's flat.

Because of all the bombing, it took him a long time to find the street Albert lived on. When he did find it, the place where the apartment building had stood was now a big pile of rubble. Johann just stood there in shock, gazing for several minutes at the site, which was once a beautiful, architectural structure.

He snapped out of his trance knowing that he had to find his friend, who was more than likely on call at the Reich Hospital. It took him more than an hour to get there, and the first person he saw on the surgical wing was Gretchen, Albert's girlfriend. She put her arms around his neck and gave him a longer than usual hug. There were tears in her eyes when they parted. Looking up at him, she asked, "You haven't heard, have you, Johann?"

Seeing her this way, he felt that he already knew the answer, but asked anyway, "He is dead...right, Gretchen? He never went to the shelter, did he?"

23

Paul, Elizabeth, Paulette, Angelina, and the two boys gathered before dinner to listen to the French edition of the BBC. For some reason, there hadn't been a broadcast for several days and they were anxious to hear the war news. Usually, when this occurred, they expected something noteworthy was about to be broadcast.

"*Bonjour France. Ici la B.B.C. Les Français parlent aux Français.* Today, November 8, 1942, the Allies continued the invasion of North Africa, which had begun yesterday. With the Americans now coming ashore in massive numbers, the Allied troops are now prepared to more than double their strength against the ghastly Nazi regime. Whip out your song books, France, and start singing, 'Over There…The Yanks Are Coming'". The WW I song began playing on the radio.

They all cheered, and began whistling the song. "This is great news, Papa," Paulette said. "The Americans have always come through when we need them."

"There's still a long way to go, Paulette," Paul said, "but, this is great news."

"Papa," Angelina asked, "do you remember what Marcel said might happen, if the North African invasion took place? The Germans would probably take over *Vichy* France."

"Why would they do that?" Raymond asked.

"Because," answered Paulette, "if the Allies get a foothold in North Africa, the Nazis will assume that the Allied invasion of Europe will come across the Mediterranean and take place in southern France. Not in the north, along our western coast."

"But the Germans would never come here," J.P. said. "Papa said that they wouldn't…didn't he?"

"Well, let's hope not," Elizabeth said. "Besides, your father is in no position to know any of that."

"Hmm, I wonder," Paul mused.

"And what does that mean?" asked Elizabeth.

"Oh, nothing," he answered. "It's just that…"

He was about to speak, when the music stopped, and the BBC announcer came back on the air. "Kudos are still pouring out for that marvelous raid on October 3rd, led by the *Maquis* fighters and their leader, Cavity. It was the only known German operation going on in *Vichy* France, which shows the world that the *Vichy* are being controlled by their Nazi friends. Charles de Gaulle is still urging that people involved with the Vichy, come over to the side of the Free French. One day, *Vichy*, you'll pay dearly for your actions as traitors…just as your police did on October 3rd." There was a pause. "Harriet prepares the meal."

When the codes began, Paul turned off the radio and everyone sat down for dinner. "I thought Marcel would be coming home for the *Beaujolais* Wine Festival this month?"

"I thought so too, Papa," Angelina said. "He must be very busy."

Paul grunted, "I'm sure he is…yes, he must be *very* busy."

24

It was frustrating for the two *Gestapo* agents, plus their enforcer Bruno, not to have come up with any solid leads as to the individuals who carried out the destruction of their relay station, and the murder of so many German soldiers. They were pretty sure that Dr. Marcel Pontier was a member of *La Résistance*, but they had no proof of his involvement with this particular mission, and no clue as to his whereabouts. Searching his house twice turned up absolutely nothing, and the interrogation of his assistant and others, to within an inch of their lives, got them nowhere.

"I think that we scared him off, and he's running for his life now," Bruno said. The other two didn't believe that for one minute; however, they never mentioned Marcel's name in their reports to their superiors, because they were under enough pressure from Berlin already. They feared they would be reprimanded for not having killed Pontier when they had the chance.

Berlin was furious that "these inferior Frenchmen were able to carry out this operation against a well-armed company of superior soldiers of the Fatherland." They wanted retribution immediately…"Or we will find other positions for you three incompetents!" They knew that this was not an idle threat, and took Berlin's words very seriously.

The shorter agent suggested to the other two, "Maybe we should consider this an act of 'collective blame', as our agencies are doing around Europe, and start shooting 10 Frenchmen a week, until the perpetrators give themselves up." He thought for a moment, and then said, "But, Berlin would never go for that, because technically, we are not supposed to be here in the first place."

The sadistic, taller agent spoke up, "We have already killed two…I do not think it would make any difference, if we killed another eight of these faggots."

"Maybe not," the shorter one said, "but it is probably best to wait until our troops move down from the north, which could be any time now. They would give us support and the security we need, if the *Vichy* turned against us. For now, we will continue doing what we have been doing, and interrogate as many suspects as possible. Eventually, someone will have information we can use."

In the early morning of November 9, 1942, Marcel, Denis, Claudine, and Olivia arrived at the safe house on the outskirts of Marseille, the same one that Florette had used for their meeting two weeks prior. Marcel's proposal had been given the go-ahead on November 7th, after the *Maquis* leadership confirmed the Allied invasion of North Africa.

Since François, and the others who lived in Marseille, might be recognized during this operation, they would not be used later that afternoon; however, *La Résistance* always encouraged their members to establish alibis for their whereabouts, if in fact they were ever questioned. They would make sure that plenty of people saw them at the time the mission was taking place.

By using several maps and drawings of the target area, Marcel had gone over and over the plan a dozen times, and familiarized the three of them with the topography of Marseille. Claudine was designated as the driver for this operation …the driver whose job it was to pick up Marcel, Olivia, and Denis, immediately after the mission was accomplished. She would be driving a stolen car, with an untraceable license plate, which Florette had left for them at the safe house. Everything had to go off like clockwork, because they would be in one of the most congested areas of the city.

At 10:00 A.M., Marcel took them on a dry run, to make them more comfortable with the operation. He felt that it was especially important for Claudine to get her bearings with the streets surrounding the pickup location. There was very little traffic that time of day, and when they returned to the safe house, everyone felt a little more at ease, now having seen the area firsthand.

At 2:30 P.M., they drove to the center of Marseille in two cars. Marcel was driving the lead car, accompanied by Olivia. Claudine was driving the stolen Citroën, with Denis joining her. When they arrived at the *Vieux Port*, France's premier port, Olivia and Denis got out of their respective cars, and walked in opposite directions along the commercial docks. Marcel continued driving, with Claudine not far behind, and made a sharp left turn at *La Canebiere*, taking the car directly east of the port. After several blocks, he turned north on *Cours Belsunce* and found a parking space. He got out of his car and jumped into the Citroën. With Claudine following Marcel's instructions, she circled back to the *Rue de la Republique*, a major street that led south, back to the port.

She found a parking space, and before Marcel got out the car, he held her right hand and said, "I'll see you on the corner at 4:05…if anything goes wrong, go to plan B." He squeezed her hand a little tighter, as she leaned toward him and they kissed.

"Good luck, Marcel," she called out, as his door closed. It was now 3:30. In another five minutes, Claudine would walk across and down the street one block. She would get a better view of the café, to make sure that all three of her friends had entered safely. Until then, she sat in the car and pretended to read a newspaper.

Olivia and Denis wandered around the docks looking at the fishing boats, a common tourist attraction. Marcel, meanwhile, walked to the corner of the *Rue de la Republique*, and turned right onto the *Quai du Port*, where sat the QDP Café. People have lived here in the old town for 26 centuries, and its mixture of cultures was so varied, Alexander Dumas called it "the meeting place of the entire world". The café looked south across the harbor, where the town rises. High on top of the hill sat *Notre-Dame-de-la-Garde Basilica*.

There were two levels of outdoor seating at the QDP, one on the open sidewalk, and the other under a green awning, one step up. As planned, Marcel stepped up, and before walking through the door, he glanced to his right, seeing a "RESERVED" sign on the farthest corner table. *Perfect*, he thought. He then entered the café, walking directly back to the kitchen.

There weren't any customers, except for an elderly couple that had just walked out when he had entered. He thought he had vaguely recognized them as being former patients of his, but they showed no sign of knowing who he was…*the beard must be working*. Marcel had expected very few customers at that time of day; usually it didn't get busy until 4:30, and then stayed that way until midnight.

When he entered the kitchen through two maroon curtains, a man and woman in white aprons were there to greet him. To make sure of whom he was, the man said, "Charles de Gaulle?"

Marcel responded, "No, Napoleon Bonaparte." They shook hands, and then the man went to a storage closet, bringing out some rope. Marcel began to tie the man up behind a long metal counter, as the woman stood outside the curtains to make sure no one else was coming.

Olivia walked in shortly thereafter, came up to the woman and said simply, "Cleopatra", and was promptly shown into the kitchen, also. Marcel was almost through tying up the man, as Olivia was given a white apron and cap to put on.

He was about to help the man sit on the floor, when the man said, "*Monsieur*, please hit us in the face as hard as you can…it will look more like we put up a fight."

Marcel didn't want to hurt his hand, so he picked up an iron pan and hit him on the side of his face. The man cried out in pain, but then said, "*Merci*". He then started tying up the woman, and when it was completed, he used the back of his hand and slapped her in the face. She winced, but then just nodded as the blood ran out the corner of her mouth. They were now both sitting behind the counter. Olivia got down, put a table napkin in their mouths, and tied it to the back of their heads.

It was now 3:50, when Olivia saw a man through the window. He sat down at a table to the right of the open door. She picked up a scratch pad and pencil, and walked out to greet him. "May I take your order, *Monsieur*?"

He looked up from the newspaper he was reading, "*Oui*," said Denis, "I'll have coffee with cream."

She went back into the kitchen, and simply nodded to Marcel. She got the cup and cream ready, but waited to pour the coffee. At 4:00 sharp, with the curtain parted slightly, they saw the three *Gestapo* agents take a seat at their reserved table under the awning, two tables away from where Denis was sitting.

"I'll say this for the Germans," Marcel joked, "the bastards are punctual."

Olivia poured the coffee for Denis and took it to his table. "Here you are *Monsieur*, your coffee with cream." She turned, as if she were going back inside, pretended to just notice the agents, and then walked toward them. "Ah, *oui Messieurs*," she smiled, as she took out her pad and pencil, "May I help you?"

"*Oui, Mademoiselle*," the taller one said, "we will have three black coffees with an assortment of your pastries."

"*Merci, Monsieur*…it will only be a few moments." She turned to leave, when Bruno caught her by the arm to stop her.

"I know you from somewhere," Bruno said, "but I cannot think of where." Still holding her, he paused for a moment and asked, "Where is the other waitress that is usually here?"

"Monsieur, you are hurting my arm!" she exclaimed. He let go and as she rubbed her arm, she said, "Marie is sick today, and I'm just filling in. I'll bring your coffee and pastries in just a moment." As she turned and walked away, the three of them laughed heartily. On seeing what had transpired, Denis wanted to jump up and shoot them right then, but controlled himself and went back to reading his newspaper.

"I am sure that I have seen that *fräulein* before," Bruno said to the others.

"You have fucked so many *fräuleins*, Bruno," the shorter one said, still laughing, "that she is probably one of them." They both patted Bruno on the back and laughed some more.

Having been told what the agents usually ordered, Marcel had already prepared the coffees and pastries. He set them on a tray by the time Olivia arrived back in the kitchen. She then informed him what had happened just now.

"It's alright," Marcel said, "just stay calm and act normal. It will all be over soon enough, so continue with the plan as we rehearsed it. Try to smile…it will keep them relaxed and more off guard."

Olivia took the tray of refreshments and proceeded through the café. As soon as she came outside, Denis carefully pulled out his revolver, with the silencer attached, from the inside of his coat's breast pocket. He kept it hidden behind his newspaper. At the same time, Marcel came out of the kitchen with the same weapon concealed by a small towel, and waited just inside the entrance to the café.

Olivia was at the agent's table, about to serve them, when another elderly couple came off the sidewalk, up the step, and proceeded to go inside the café. Olivia and Denis noticed them immediately and Olivia knew that she would have to do some stalling. When they were inside, they momentarily startled Marcel, until he saw a French lapel medal on the man's jacket.

"*Bonjour Madame, Monsieur…S'il vous plait,*" Marcel said, as he motioned them to a table. They sat down, and were surprised when Marcel sat with them. He spoke to the man in a whisper, "I see from your lapel, that you were awarded the *Croix de Guerre*, for bravery in combat…so you are a true Frenchman."

"*Oui*, of course," the elderly man said. "I fought in the last War."

Marcel leaned toward them, "Then listen very carefully to what I'm saying." They nodded together. "Please don't look up, but the three men sitting outside are German *Gestapo* agents. What is about to happen is something that you don't want to see, or become involved in, if you are ever questioned." They nodded again. "So please, stand up, walk out slowly, and forget that you were ever here…*Compris?*"

"*Oui*," the elderly man said softly. "*Je comprends.*" They stood up and walked slowly out the door, arm-in-arm, turning on the sidewalk in the opposite direction from where they had come.

Marcel breathed a sigh of relief, as did Denis and Olivia on seeing the couple leave the café.

Trying to be as friendly as she could, Olivia served the coffee and pastries, "Here you are *Monsieur's…Bon appétit." This will be your last meal*, she thought.

Marcel and Denis were poised to join Olivia, when Bruno said in a loud voice, "*Ach so*, now I remember who you are…Olivia Bonnet! We were in the Berlin Olympics together." Marcel came out and walked toward Olivia, with Denis right behind him, as Bruno continued talking. "I threw the shot-put and discus, and you won a metal for what, Running?"

"No, Shooting," she said, as she reached inside her apron grabbing the handle of her pistol.

"So, why are you here, waiting on tables?" the taller one asked, ignoring Marcel and Denis, who were now standing next to Olivia.

"To kill you Nazi bastards," she said with a scowl. She raised the revolver, underneath her apron, and pulled the trigger. All that was heard was 'swoosh' from the silencer, as the bullet tore into the chest of the taller one, sending him back against his chair.

Startled, the other two sat back and reached inside their coats for their *Lugers*, but it was too late, as Denis' shot hit Bruno in the neck, which tore through his skull. Marcel fired a little high into the shoulder of the shorter one, which made him release the grip on his *Lugar*, and grab for his injured shoulder, letting out a long moan.

Marcel got closer to the *Gestapo* leader, pointing the pistol at his head. "How does it feel to be on the other side, asshole?"

"Please, I need a doctor," the shorter one pleaded, with blood gushing through his fingers, all over his leather coat.

"I *am* a doctor, you little worm," Marcel said sarcastically.

The agent squinted and looked at Marcel. "Pontier?" he asked incredulously. "Is it you under that beard? I plead with you to spare me."

"Yes, you dumb fuck, it's me. You should have killed me when you had the chance. I have no intention to spare you so that you can continue torturing more innocent Frenchmen." With that said, he took one step back and fired a shot into the man's right eye.

Marcel looked at Olivia and Denis, and commanded, "Make sure the other two are both dead…shoot them in the head. Hurry!"

When the job was complete, Denis headed immediately for the corner of the *Rue de la Republique*. Marcel and Olivia followed him 10 seconds later, after they went back inside the café's kitchen, threw their aprons and hats on the ground, and gave a victory sign to the two patriots tied up on the floor.

Claudine had gone back to her car ten minutes before, and when she spotted Denis on the corner, one-half block away, she slowly moved the car toward him. When Marcel and Olivia were by his side, she sped to them. Everyone got in the car, and they were on their way. The traffic was starting to get busier, but they had plenty of time to get back to the side street where Marcel's car was parked. By 4:30, both cars were heading north, outside the city limits of Marseille.

That night, for the second time, Marcel and Claudine made love.

25

On November 12, 1942, the armed forces of Nazi Germany entered the Unoccupied Zone of France in massive numbers, and with relatively no resistance. They secured the southern half of the country, took over the power that the *Vichy* had held, but kept them on as a puppet government to run the local districts. There was absolutely no question as to whom the ultimate power belonged.

It was early that morning when Johann's engineering battalion crossed over the border from Germany into France. It was a convoy of four trucks, two APC's, and two field cars for the officers. In two hours, they would be joining a *Wehrmacht* infantry group that was moving down from Paris. They would continue south together to Elne, a town at the foot of the Pyrenees and on the Mediterranean, which no one in their group had ever heard of.

"*Hauptmann*," Hermann, who was driving, said, "I have a very good feeling about the place we are headed for." He knew that his captain had been very down lately, and on learning of his friend's death a few nights ago, he was now even more depressed. "We will be away from any war zone, so this should give us a chance to be more at ease and get some rest."

"Yes, Hermann," Johann said, "I do have to clear my mind and get away from the bombs. This may be just what we need." He sounded better than what he actually felt, because in his mind he was continually reliving the past year and all his personal losses. He wondered if other people kept feeling the same things over and over, as he did. *I know that dwelling on the past is not healthy, and I have it much better than most; after all, I could be stuck in a ditch on the Eastern Front, and fighting the Russians.*

Johann closed his eyes, and tried to take a short nap. All he could think about was *now I am coming into a different country and having to disrupt the lives of people I do not even know, or dislike.* He finally fell asleep for an hour. When he awoke, they were driving through a small, French town with very narrow streets.

The people that he saw there, and in subsequent towns and villages, all had somber, contemptuous looks on their faces, and he could feel their hatred. To avoid their looks, he tried to keep staring straight ahead, and got better at it as the day went on. Just as dusk turned into night, his engineering group met up with the infantry. They had 150 kilometers to go, before they would reach Elne that evening.

Marcel had spent the previous night with Simon, in Carcassonne, and when he had awakened, he got word of the German invasion that morning. This was a stopover on his way to Elne. Now he could be with his family early enough, in the event the Germans did decide to occupy the old town. Except for the bigger cities, there were no reliable intelligence reports on exactly where they were going to locate themselves, and he still felt that Elne would not be one of those places.

He hadn't seen Angelina and the children for some time, and couldn't wait to be with them again, if even for a short period. There was a meeting of the *Maquis* leadership council in Montelimar, on November 14th, which he had to attend. Now that the Germans were here, there would be much to discuss about future undertakings. Every district commander was expected to supply some intelligence information on their particular area, but since their assassination of the *Gestapo* agents in Marseille, the council wouldn't expect Marcel to go back there at this point. He was counting on Florette to survey the area with François.

Although not as spectacular as the raid at Morieres, the killing of those three agents, in broad daylight, was thought to be just as symbolic to *La Résistance* movement, Simon had told him over coffee. "It was an absolute masterstroke on your part, Marcel. This will send a message that it's now 'an eye for an eye'."

"To tell you the truth, Simon," Marcel began, "I was doing it more out of revenge than anything else. Hopefully, this will erase my name from their list. I'm just glad we did this before today, because in the future it will be much harder to enter Marseille."

"There is always the possibility that the *Vichy* police now have that list…isn't that so?" Simon asked.

"I can't tell you why, but by now, all the important German files that relate to me, or any of my people, don't exist," Marcel replied, hoping that Georges had destroyed them, as he said he would.

Before Marcel left Carcassonne, Simon talked to him about the increasing number of refugees that his group was trying to get into Spain. Most of these people were Jews, or part of the intelligencia of France, Belgium, and Holland that the Underground Railroad had been hiding. "With the Germans now in the Unoccupied Zone, I expect they'll also be rounding up these people here, to be shipped to the concentration camps. We're going to have to find better ways to smuggle them over the borders, not only into Spain, but also into

Switzerland. So, if you come up with any brilliant ideas, please get back to me or Florette…at some point, I may have to be one of those escaping."

Marcel was taken aback by his last statement, but did not want to reveal that his family was in Elne, near the Spanish border, so kept his question as generic as possible. "May I ask, why you, Simon? You're not teaching, are you?"

Simon laughed in his normal, friendly way. "No, I'm not a member of the intelligencia, but I *am* Jewish and have to be realistic about what is happening in Nazi Germany…and what has already happened here in France. Those monsters have rounded up thousands of Jews around Paris and shipped them like cattle to the East."

Marcel shook his head and seemed alarmed. "I had no idea that things have gotten that bad. Simon, do you think it's safe for you to remain here in Carcassonne? You can always come into the hills with us."

"At this point, I'm not sure what to do, but I know that I have to make a decision soon. As far as the business is concerned, I have a Christian friend who could take it over, so that's no problem. At a time like this, I couldn't leave my family to face the Nazis, so it's a real dilemma." He laughed again. "You know, being French, and Jewish, is not the best combination these days."

Marcel let out a long sigh. "Don't worry…we'll figure out something. In the meantime, though, you shouldn't remain around Carcassonne for long." He paused for a moment. "After I make some inquires, and think this out, I'll come back here next week and have some options that we can decide on." As Marcel was leaving, he turned around and asked, "By the way, how many people are we talking about?"

"In my family, you mean?" Simon asked, "Or the refugees?"

"For now, just your family," Marcel answered. "I suppose that the council will have to set up a whole new network for the refugees, plus someone to take your place, which I imagine would have to be soon. I'll pass this on to Florette, in case you don't see her in the next few days."

Simon agreed. "Yes, that sounds like the wise thing to do. As far as my family goes, there would be eight of us, which includes our two grandchildren."

The two men shook hands, and Marcel left by the back door. He got in his car and headed south towards Elne. He would hide his car deep in the woods before he got there, just in case the Germans did come and he had to leave early. On the drive down he thought more about Simon's predicament, and realized *that no matter how bad things get, someone can always have it worse.* He would talk to Paul, to see if he had any ideas about crossing the Pyrenees. Paul had lived in Elne all his life and knew the area better than anyone.

There was static on the radio before Paul was able to locate the station. He wasn't sure that the BBC would be broadcasting this time of the afternoon, but thought he would try anyway.

"*Bonjour France. Ici la B.B.C. Les Français parlent aux Français.* It is confirmed that under General Montgomery, the Axis has been smashed in Egypt. Thousands of Italian and German troops have surrendered, and Rommel is racing back to Libya with the remnants of his army."

Nondescript, classical music began playing, as Angelina smiled at what had been said. "The news sounds good, doesn't it Papa?"

Paul threw up his right hand. "Eh! It will only be good when they kill all those bastards."

"Killing, killing, killing!" Elizabeth said, shaking her head from side to side. "You men are all a bunch of fools. If you let women run the world, there wouldn't be any wars."

Paul raised both hands in the air, saying, "*Mon dieux.* My God! The woman has an answer for everything." There were three beeps on the radio. "Shhh, it sounds like more news coming in."

"Under the command of General Dwight D. Eisenhower, United States Army, Navy, and Air Forces began landing on the shores of North Africa several days ago."

There was a five second pause, during which Paul got up from his chair and walked to the radio, resting one hand on the credenza, and holding his pipe in his mouth, with the other hand.

"Congratulations, to whoever was responsible for the elimination of three *Gestapo* agents in the center of Marseille. It was a bold move for these heroes of *La Résistance*." There was another pause, followed by, "Etienne and Irene build the house. The skiing will be good at Val d' Isere`. Erin and Ron move far away. Stay tuned for more news to come."

Paul turned off the radio and sat back down in his chair. "Killing *Gestapo*... now *that* is wonderful! But what were the *Gestapo* doing in Marseille in the first place? We've only heard about the Germans in that relay station raid at Morieres."

"Maybe they've already started invading the Unoccupied Zone," Angelina said."

"I think they would have announced that on the BBC," Elizabeth said.

Paulette came into the room, with a tired look on her face, and sighed, "Hello, *Maman*...Angelina." She walked over, kissed Paul on both cheeks, and affectionately asked, "How are you, Papa?"

Frowning, he said, "A little stiff, today...just can't do all the things I used to do."

Without looking up from her folding, Elizabeth said, "He still thinks he's twenty-five." She held up a shirt in front of her, folding the sleeves together, and looked at Paulette, who was walking over to sit down at the table. "So how was your day, Paulette?"

Paulette slouched down in her chair. "Oh...the same. It's frustrating to be stuck in an administrative job. Working with Mayor Astruc is all right...he's a nice man, but the *Vichy* is becoming so demanding. It's hard to believe that they're Frenchmen." She sat up and put her elbows on the table. "Lately, everyone is scared to death they'll be put in jail if they don't perform their jobs properly."

A few seconds later, J.P. came running into the house. His short gray pants and brown shirt were ruffled, from having played outside and at school, and a smudge of dirt was on his face. "*Maman...Maman,*" he shouted, out of breath.

"What is it, Jean-Pierre?" Angelina asked in her normal, calm voice. "Look at you...you're all dirty. You better get washed up for dinner."

"*Maman,* listen to me please...I think I saw Papa coming over the bridge, on the River Tech," J.P. said excitedly.

On hearing this, Raymond and Babette came from her bedroom, into the main room. In contrast to J.P., Raymond's dark, short pants and white shirt were neatly pressed, and Babette was wearing a blue frock, white blouse, black shoes, white socks, and holding one of her dolls. She stared up at Paul with a questioning look, and said, "*Grandpere*...is my Papa coming home?"

"Where were you when you saw him, J.P.?" Raymond asked.

"Down near the vineyards," J.P. said. "I could swear I saw Papa on the bridge, carrying that brown leather bag of his."

Babette walked over to Angelina and hugged her leg; then, looked up at her angelically, with a big smile. "Oh, *Maman*…Papa is coming home…I know he is."

Angelina was now getting excited and put her arms around J.P. and Babette. "Darling, let's hope that J.P. is right…it's been too long since we've seen Papa, but he did say that he would try to be here for the wine festival." She rubbed the top of Babette's head, and then looked over at her mother. "If that's Marcel, I wonder why he would be walking and not driving the car. I hope everything is all right in Marseille."

"As a dentist, I wouldn't think that Marcel could be in any real danger," Elizabeth said.

Paulette stood and walked toward the stairs. "One never knows… things are happening so fast. Excuse me for a minute…I'll be right down."

"Yes, you never know," Paul casually said. "But you're right, Angelina …why *isn't* he driving my car?"

A few minutes later, there was a knock on the door, and Marcel walked in carrying his brown leather bag. Looking every bit the country Frenchman, he had on his tweed, Herringbone sport coat and black beret. J.P. ran up and put his arms around him, while everyone else just stared in surprise at this stranger with the mustache and full, black beard. Marcel gave a roaring laugh, stroked his beard, and said, "Yes, yes, it's me under all this. Oh, it's so good to see you all!"

Raymond and Babette shouted, "Papa, Papa…it is you!" coming over to hug him also.

Marcel's heart melted, as he looked up and saw Angelina waiting patiently, with a big smile on her face. He disengaged himself from the children and embraced his wife. "Oh, *Cherie*," he whispered in her ear, "I've missed you so much."

"Darling, I've missed you more than you know," she said, as they parted after a minute.

Marcel walked over to Elizabeth, kissed her on both cheeks, and then shook hands with Paul, followed by pats on the back for each other. He spotted the baby in the corner, and picked her up from the crib. "Oh my God, what a beautiful girl you are, Madeline! And look how big you've gotten."

"I help take care of her, Papa," Babette said.

"I bet you do, Babette. You've always been such a good helper."

"One day, she and I will play with our dolls together," she said, as all the children gathered around Marcel.

"Papa," Raymond said, "I miss my school and my friends. When do you think we can move back to our home in Marseille?"

Marcel nodded his head and sighed, but J.P. jumped in and said, "I like it *here*...I can run and play in the fields, and help *Grandpere* pick the crops."

"Believe me, with the War going on, all of you are much better off here in Elne with your grandparents and *Tante* Paulette," Marcel said. "Conditions in Marseille are getting worse every day." He looked around the room. "Where is Paulette?"

"She should be down any minute now," Elizabeth said. "I better start dinner." She turned, picked up a basket filled with vegetables, walked over to the fireplace and started putting the food into a large black pot.

They all chatted for several minutes about the family, and things in general. Angelina put a bottle of red wine and two glasses on the table, and Paul poured himself and Marcel each a glass, holding it up to the light to check the color. "This is our *Vin doux naturel* from last year's crop. It seems a little sweeter that normal." They touched glasses and each took a sip.

Paulette walked down the stairs and smiled warmly when she saw Marcel. "Aahh, Marcel! I like your beard...very distinguished. How are you?" He stood, and they kissed on both cheeks. Paulette poured herself a glass of wine and sat with the men. The three of them lifted and touched their glasses together.

"I'm doing pretty well, under the circumstances," Marcel answered. "What's new at City Hall?"

"Same old thing," she sighed, "but, I want to be doing more for France." She wiped the wine off the side of her lips. "Today, I saw in a secret communiqué, that Marshal Petain has severed diplomatic relations with the United States."

"Oh, really," Marcel replied. "Now, I'm sure things are going to get much worse."

Speaking very slowly, Angelina asked, "How do you know that, Marcel?"

Marcel stood, walked to the window, looked out; then, came back to the table, and held the back of his chair with both hands. He bit his upper lip with his lower teeth and then let out a long, winded sigh. "I won't be able to tell you everything...for security reasons. I think the less you know, the safer all of you will be."

A silence filled the room, as everyone sat down at the table and looked up at Marcel in anticipation. Only Angelina remained standing, and facing Marcel at the opposite end of the table, she said, "But darling..."

Marcel held up his hand to stop her from speaking. "Let me finish, please." He paused for a few more seconds to collect his thoughts, knowing that what he was about to tell his family would be a shock to them, but at the same time, he wouldn't have to live a lie anymore. "A year after Germany invaded France, I joined *La Résistance*. I just couldn't sit still and let these *Vichy* traitors, especially politicians like Pierre Laval and his *Vichy* government, destroy our country."

Angelina looked across the table at him, with her mouth and eyes wide open. In a deliberate strong tone, she asked, "You did this without consulting me?"

In a conciliatory reply, Marcel answered, "But, darling…I didn't want to worry you. I…"

Angelina interrupted him, in an uncharacteristically harsh reply. "Marcel …I need to know what's happening! I'm here with the four children…I don't see you for long periods of time…" She paused to catch her breath, and then continued, "And now you're putting yourself in danger…what if something should happen to you?"

She shook her head, and looking disappointed, said in a lower voice, "You're not thinking of us!" She lowered her head, apparently not wanting to look at him at this time.

Marcel didn't expect this kind of reaction from his wife, but he could understand her emotions. *Maybe I shouldn't have started this confession in the first place*, he thought. But he continued to explain himself. "Of course I'm thinking of you…of everyone here. There's a war going on, and all of us have got to help if France will ever be free again."

Angelina looked up and said, "Marcel…you always do what you want anyway. I don't know why I'm surprised about this."

The children had their eyes wide open, not knowing what to make of this rare argument between their parents. They dared not interrupt. Babette didn't understand what was going on, but both of the boys found it very exciting that their father was in *La Résistance*.

"Well," Paul said, "I'm proud of you for getting involved, Marcel… wish I could do more myself."

"I agree," Paulette added. "Marcel…tell us more. This is fascinating!"

"Well, I got involved in the beginning, with the production of an underground newspaper that circulates throughout the Unoccupied Zone." Marcel took a sip of wine, and then walked around the table, putting his arm around Angelina, who just shook her head again. "I'm not involved with the paper any longer, but it called on all French people to do everything in their power to contribute to the overthrow of the *Vichy* regime, and the final defeat of Germany.

"Paulette, you said you wanted to do more? Well, maybe you can...you're in a perfect position to supply us with information, or false papers, when we need them."

Angelina looked up and gave him a questioning glance.

"Information? False papers? What else are you involved in, Marcel?" Paulette asked.

"Please tell me it's not the *Maquis*," Angelina said.

Marcel took both her hands in his and faced her. "If you must know...yes, I am with the *Marquis* now. I had no choice." He paused for a second, and then continued. "Several months ago, these three Gestapo agents interrogated me. They had strong suspicions that I was involved in some clandestine activities, but they didn't have conclusive evidence of that, and I denied everything."

"Were you involved, Marcel?" Elizabeth asked.

"That's beside the point, *Maman*. They let me go, but I knew that they were continuing to watch me, and I had to get out of Marseille. I'm sure that they would have brought me back for further interrogation and more severe punishment."

"What kind of punishment?" Angelina asked. "Oh, this is making me sick!" She put her hand up to her forehead and sat down.

Marcel looked at his three children and gestured with his hand toward them. "I don't know whether they should be listening to all of this."

"Please, Papa," J.P. said, "Raymond and I are big enough to know everything, too."

Marcel looked them over again and nodded his head. "OK, but I want you, Babette, to go in your room and play with your dolls for a little while…get them ready for their dinner."

Babette got out of her chair, and with her hands up high, came over to Marcel. He picked her up, kissed her, and held her tight. When he put her down, she happily skipped back to her room, and he continued.

"While they were interrogating me, they threatened to deport me to Germany to work in their factories, like many hundreds of others the *Vichy* already rounded up."

"But you're a dentist…" Elizabeth was starting to say.

Marcel interrupted her before she had a chance to ask anything further. "That's even worse…they could send me to their Eastern front as a medic, and force me to treat their wounded. Believe me, I've thought of everything and I didn't want to take a chance. The stories coming back from these so-called labor camps are horrible, and now the *Vichy* Peace Committee is randomly kidnapping young men and boys over 15 years old, and sending them. I wouldn't want this to ever happen to Raymond, or J.P." He paused, and then emphatically said, "And they're Frenchmen!"

"The *Vichy* swine are becoming no better than their Nazi masters," Paul said. "They have already started taking a percentage of our livestock and crops, and shipping them to Germany." He shook his hand in the air, with his fingertips together. "The nerve of those bastards!"

"Yeah, that's what I would say, if *Grandmere* would let me," J.P. said.

Marcel laughed, took another sip of his wine and looked around at the others. "You can't imagine how many young men are joining the *Maquis* now, just to avoid working in Germany."

"One thing I am curious about," Paul asked, "is what were those Germans doing in southern France in the first place? I thought they had signed an armistice to stay in the northern part of the country."

"Does it surprise you that Hitler wouldn't keep his word, Papa?" Marcel asked. "I was shocked, when they came to my office and took me to their headquarters."

"Were these the same *Gestapo* agents that were assassinated in Marseille?" Paulette asked. "We heard about it just now on the BBC."

"Yes, they were the same S.O.B's...*now*, they won't be able to torture any more people."

"Did you have anything to do it, Marcel?" Paul inquired. "And what about that German radio tower in Morieres?"

"I'm sorry, Papa...I can't comment on things like that. After the War, I'll tell you all some stories that you won't believe." Marcel could tell that he had everyone's attention, so he made one more important point. "I want everyone to understand...and that includes you two boys...that all the things that I've told you today, and anything I talk to you about in the future, is not to be discussed with anyone outside this house, or it could be dangerous to all of us. As far as you know, if anyone asks, is that I am still a dentist in Marseille, and nothing more...alright?" Everyone looked at him seriously, and then nodded their heads. "I'll sit down with Babette and make sure she knows where her Papa is. To be truthful, I shouldn't have even told you of my involvement, but it will explain a lot of things about my absence...and Angelina is right...we've always discussed things as a family, but in this case I don't want any danger to come to any of you, so the basics will have to suffice." He paused, and then reiterated, "The less you know, the better."

Angelina put her hand on Marcel's, and looked up at him. "Darling, may I ask when the Germans interrogated you, and how long has it been since you've been in your office?"

"It happened a couple days before we left for Elne." He paused for a second, "And I haven't been back to my office since I brought you all here."

"Is that why you were hurting so badly?" Angelina asked.

Marcel nodded his head. "Yes, but they'll never hurt anyone else again...and I may as well tell you, I went back once to check on our house, and it had been ransacked, either by the *Vichy*, or the *Gestapo*... probably looking for evidence against me, which I'm sure they didn't find."

"*Mon Dieu*," Angelina said in a sighing voice. "That's terrible...our house! Is there anything we can do? Should we go back to Marseille?"

"Definitely not go back to Marseille, and no, there is nothing we can do about it. What is damaged are things that can be replaced, so please, don't let this worry you."

Paul reached over and took his daughter's hand. "Fortunately, you were here with us when all this happened, my sweet Angelina. So you see, Marcel was right all along."

"Yes, I suppose you're right, Papa," Angelina said, "but it's such a shock."

"This whole day has been a shock, since Marcel arrived," Paulette said. "I think, that whatever you're doing with the *Maquis* is wonderful, and you know I'll do anything I can to help."

"And where have you been living all this time, *mon Cheri*?" Angelina asked.

Marcel massaged her neck as he talked to her, because he could tell that she was under a lot of stress. "We have to keep moving through the mountains and forests, and sometimes stay for a night, or two, in safe houses. It's not the most ideal way to live, but I'm managing nicely." He thought it best to change the subject.

"There is one area that you could be of great service, Paulette…and you too, Papa. Last night, on my way here to see you, I stopped at a friend's place that I had stayed before. He is also a member of *La Résistance*, and he has been doing something that I haven't been involved in yet, namely trying to speed up escapes for Jews, and other persons considered undesirable by the *Vichy* and the Nazis. This is going to increase in numbers tremendously very soon, because…and this is something that I also came to tell you…another shock for today…early this morning, from Tours and Dijon in the north, and at Bordeaux and Bayonne to the west of here, the Germans crossed over the borders into the Unoccupied Zone."

He paused for a second and let what he said sink in; then, he took another sip of wine. "They are probably headed for the southern coast of France. This is something that I told you months ago could happen."

"Do you know if we will be affected here, in Elne?" Paulette asked. "We haven't heard anything about the invasion on the BBC yet."

"I would venture to say, yes," Paul said. "Elne is both near the coast and is strategically located at the foot of the Pyrenees, so it wouldn't surprise me."

"I don't have any knowledge where they're going," Marcel added, "but I would say that there's a 50-50 chance that Papa is correct. We'll just have to wait and see."

"So," Paulette began, "what is it that you were starting to tell us, about your friend helping the Jews to escape?"

"Yes, some are being helped to slip across the border into Spain, and that is where you, Papa, can help me in figuring out where, and how, to get more of these people over the mountains. I don't think that there's anyone who knows this area better than you."

J.P. thought about this for a second, and debated whether, or not, to tell his father what he had learned about the tunnels up on the mountain. He had promised Sylviane's father that he would keep this a secret, unless it was necessary to use it for his family. *He would tell Papa and Grandpere when they were* alone.

"I'll be glad to help you, Marcel," Paul said. "I do know the way over to Spain, but it's pretty treacherous, and usually you can't go in the winter because there's no shelter."

Hearing this, J.P. couldn't wait any longer, and with enthusiasm, he blurted out what he knew. "Papa...*Grandpere*...I learned of a way to go from *Monsieur* Barton, when I went with them for *Les Feux de la Saint Jean*." He proceeded to tell them the whole story.

"That's excellent, J.P.," Paul said. "Marcel, I remember hearing of those railroad tunnels, but I never saw them."

"Do you think you can find these again, if you had to, J.P.?" Marcel asked.

Yes, Papa...I think so. I'm sure *Monsieur* Barton would help also."

"Is that Raphaël Barton, who owns the dairy farm?" Marcel asked.

"Yes, Marcel," Paulette said. "Have you met him?"

"We have met, and I'm sure he would be happy to help," Marcel replied, not telling them that Raphaël was also a formidable member of *La Résistance* in this Catalonia region. Marcel walked over to his younger son and ran his hand through his hair. "It was right of you to tell us this, J.P....it could save a lot of lives."

"Now we know you can keep a secret, J.P.," Elizabeth said. "If you could just watch what comes out of your mouth, you might turn out good after all."

The tension was broken, and everyone laughed at Elizabeth's remark. She could always be counted on to keep things in perspective.

"Now, getting back to you, Paulette," Marcel said, "for most of the refugees, we're trying to find safe havens in villages, all over southern France. Working in the position you're in at City Hall, I would think you'd have access to a lot of names, plus a lot of other information we could use, especially if the Germans do come here."

"Yes, I know of families here in Elne and other nearby villages, who could give shelter to these people," Paulette replied. "I'll speak to Monsignor Marois at the Cathedral, to see what he can do."

Marcel nodded, "That's wonderful, because as far as I know, we haven't placed anyone in this area yet. Of course, we'll need numerous documents for these refugees." He slowly counted them out on his fingers, "Identification and ration cards, and coupons for food, clothing and other necessities. And from time to time, *Résistance* agents will need to change their names, and will require the same type of identity cards."

Paulette put her hand on her chin and thought for a moment. "Hmm…All these forms come through my office, and…and I can easily get some of them." She paused for several seconds.

"The only thing I would need from you, is a photograph and description of each person---height, weight, age…you know. "I'll put the necessary seals on everything, so they'll be able to withstand any scrutiny."

"Whose names will you use on the certificates?" Marcel asked.

Paulette answered immediately, as if the wheels were already turning in her head, and the family could see that she was thoroughly enjoying this new challenge in her life. "That will depend on…who the person is, and where we'll be placing him. I could get names off of old death certificates, and use Perpignan as a birthplace, since the records were all destroyed in a fire at their City Hall, several years ago."

"Perfect…no way to trace the names, then," Marcel said.

"Exactly," Paulette replied.

"I knew that I could count on you, Paulette." Marcel walked back to Angelina, who had gotten out of her chair. He hugged her again, and said, "*Cherie*, do you feel a little better now that you know what's happening?"

"I feel better that you're here," Angelina replied, "but it makes me nervous to think that the Germans may be coming to Elne…we're just a big orchard, growing grapes and a few vegetables."

"Darling, you understand that I can't be absolutely certain," Marcel said, "but in addition to what Papa said, I'm guessing that the Germans are spread thin and can only occupy the larger towns…especially those along the main lines of communication." There was a thoughtful pause. "But we do have the bridge over the River Tech and the railroad coming through here, plus…"

Angelina interrupted him, "But I thought we'd be safe here…that's why we left Marseille."

"Trust me, you're a lot safer here," Paul said. "There's plenty of food for all of us, even though the bastards will be taking a lot of our crops and goods, and shipping them back to Germany for their war economy." He took a long swig of his wine. "Aah, that's good." He poured some more for everyone. "Another major factor, Marcel, is that being the highest village around, it's an ideal place for an observatory, at the top of our Cathedral."

"You understand it all, don't you Papa?" Marcel said.

"I fought in two wars, remember?" Paul replied. "Don't worry, I'll keep my eyes and ears open for you. The first chance we get, I'll take the boys and scout out those tunnels." Raymond was happy that he was going to be included, also.

Angelina still had her arms wrapped around Marcel. "How will we reach you, if we need you?"

Marcel thought for a moment, before speaking. "It won't be easy for me to come in and out of Elne, but do you remember that little ledge underneath the bridge, where we used to leave each other love notes when we were dating? That would be a perfect drop for messages."

Angelina was starting to relax more. "Yes. I could pretend I'm fishing on the bank, underneath the bridge…or painting…or something. I'll figure it out."

Marcel smiled at her. "Good. I, or one of my men, will try to check every week or two. If you must reach me immediately, take some of your red paint and draw…" He took a piece of paper and pencil that were laying on the table, and drew one long vertical line, crossed by two shorter horizontal lines. "…a large symbol of the two-bar Cross of Lorraine, at the entrance to the bridge, on the other side of the river. I'll be able to see it several kilometers away with my binoculars."

He paused for a moment, as Angelina looked at the drawing. "I have to warn you though, that it may become necessary to blow up the bridge, if it proves to be a strategic move against the Nazis. So stay away from there if you see any German troop movement."

"I understand, Marcel. I'll try to be careful." Angelina motioned to her mother with her hand. "Let's get dinner started, *Maman*."

"Well, good…that's enough about me," Marcel said, before he called out toward the first floor bedroom. "Babette…Babette, you can come back in here now."

Babette came out of her bedroom and sat down on one of the dining room chairs, while holding one of her dolls.

"Now, children," Marcel began, "tell me what you've been doing. I don't think I know the name of that doll, Babette."

"Yes you do, Papa," she said. "This is my favorite doll, Marie Joelle. Tell Papa about your three little pigs, Raymond."

"Three pigs?" Marcel asked. "Where did you get them, Raymond?"

197

"*Grandpere* bought them for me for my science project. I keep them in the cave, next to the secret cellar."

"*Grandpere* helped us name them," Babette said enthusiastically. "Tell Papa what we call them, J.P."

J.P. stepped away from his father and turned his back; he took a black comb out of his pocket and combed the front of his hair down and to the side of his forehead. As he turned back to face his father, he put the comb under his nose and gave the arm-extended, Nazi salute while saying, "Adolph One! Adolph Two!...*und* Adolph Three!"

Marcel laughed, and for a second, thought how lucky he was to see his wife and children again, after all he'd been through for the last few months. "That's a wonderful imitation, Jean-Pierre." He clapped his hands. "But, you've got to promise me you won't do that around any *Vichy*, or Germans. I believe they might take offense to it."

"OK, Papa," J.P. said. "Besides, *Grandpere* already told us not to mention the pigs because someone might try to take them from us."

"*Grandpere* is right," Marcel said. "If the Germans do come into our village, life here is going to change a lot. I'm counting on you boys to help *Maman* and *Grandmere* around the house and to look after your sisters...they can't do it alone, and neither can *Grandpere*."

"We'll help, Papa," Raymond replied, and then added, "We already do."

"And we'll take good care of Babette and Madeline," J.P. said. "I'll shoot any Germans that come near them."

"You're not going to shoot anybody, Jean-Pierre," Paul responded. "If those Krauts come into our village, I want you to stay away from them."

"Do you boys understand your grandfather?" Marcel asked.

"Yes, Papa," they responded in unison.

"Remember," Marcel looked at both of them, "*Grandpere* is in charge, so listen to him…and *Maman, Grandmere*, and *Tante* Paulette, too. This is not a game…this is very serious, and we don't want anyone to get hurt."

Marcel started walking toward Angelina's bedroom, and motioned for Paul, J.P., and Raymond to follow him. Once inside, he picked up the large rug lying on the floor, between the bed and window, and put it on the bed. There, in the middle of the floor was a trap door, which led down to the cellar. He pulled it up, and when it was fully opened, he peered down through the hole. "Hmm…Papa, in the next day or so, would you and the boys make sure the passageway is perfectly clear between the cellar staircase, the secret cave, and the barn? It may be necessary for me to get back in the house this way."

"Yes, of course, Marcel," Paul said.

Angelina opened the door and walked into her bedroom. "Is everything all right, *Cheri*? Why is the trap door open?" Elizabeth, Paulette, and Babette walked in to see what is going on. "I don't think we've used this since we were kids."

"No, not since I can remember," Elizabeth said. "Why did you open it…it must be filthy down there?"

Marcel pulled the trap door down and put the rug back over it. "Well, if I need to sneak back some evening, this would be the safest way to get into the house without being detected. Papa and the boys are going to clean the area out underneath." He picked up Babette, and she put her head on his shoulder, as Marcel continued to speak. "Let's decide on a signal, so you'll know it's me."

"Wow," Paulette said, "this is all so intriguing…it's almost like being in a spy novel." She shook her head. "I still can't believe that you're involved in all of this, Marcel."

Marcel laughed. "Ah, yes...stranger things have happened. But anyway, what I'll do is knock three times, so you'll know it's me. Open it up if the coast is clear; if not, give me a signal of two knocks. Does everyone understand?" They all nodded. "When the coast is clear, take the rug off and rap on the door three times, and I'll return the same signal."

Babette picked her head up and asked, "Can I open the door too, Papa?"

"No, sweetheart," Angelina said, "you come and get one of us to help you."

"And don't ever let anyone know about this secret door," Marcel said to her.

"OK, Papa," she answered, "That's because it's a secret."

Marcel looked outside and saw that the sun was going down. Still holding Babette, he walked back into the main room, as the sounds of the Cathedral's bells were heard in the distance. It rang six times, and immediately, Paul went to the radio and turned it on. At first there was some static, but then a voice came on in the middle of a sentence.

"...and without opposition from *Vichy's* army, and in violation of the terms of the armistice, Germany again has shown its true colors. General Charles de Gaulle has urged that all Frenchmen, in the once Unoccupied Zone, join with their brothers in the north to continue the fight. *Vive la France!*"

There was a short pause, and then the radio announcement continued. "The rain is falling on Bordeaux. Garrett loves Renée. All roads lead to Rome." There was a pause, and then, "The rain..." Paul turned off the radio.

"So...it's true," Angelina slowly said, "they're coming."

Paul pulled Marcel aside, and whispered, "Tell me, Marcel...are you 'Cavity'?"

"Who in the world is that, Papa?" Marcel winked at him. He put Babette down and then put his arm around his wife. "Angelina, darling, everything is going to be alright. If everyone acts just the way you always have and go about your normal routines, there won't be any problems. Remember, there's always the chance the Germans won't come to Elne, so let's pray that they don't."

"How long will you be able to stay, Marcel?" Elizabeth asked.

"I'm afraid that I'll have to be going soon, *Maman*. I'll stay for dinner, but it would be best if I left before it gets too late. I don't want to run into a German patrol on the road."

Before everyone sat down for dinner, Angelina and Marcel went into the bedroom and held each other tightly. "Oh, darling," Angelina said, "I was so hoping that we could spend the night together. I miss you so much."

"*Cherie*, I can't think of anything better than staying here and making love to you and then waking up in the morning and having breakfast with the children. I've really missed all that, and will probably be kicking myself the hour after I leave, but I can't take any more chances tonight. There's so much that has to be done and knowing that I have your support, will make things much more bearable for however long this war lasts."

After dinner, everyone said their goodbyes, and tears were shed. Marcel promised to return soon, and departed before it got any harder to leave his family. The Pontier's and Courty's had lived under *Vichy* control for more than two years. Now, they were about to enter "Phase Two" of *Le Combat* under the Nazi boot.

26

They had traveled all day through the small cities and towns of eastern France, staying primarily in the valleys skirting the Alps. Johann had even taken turns driving with Hermann, something highly irregular in the German army, but there was no way one person could do it by himself. Their orders were to arrive at their destination, a small place called Elne, at the southernmost point of France, by that evening. Seeing what their captain was doing, the other officers followed his lead and assisted in the driving also.

Johann was looking at a map with his flashlight. "It looks like we are entering the Roussillon area, Hermann. We should arrive in Elne within an hour or so, depending how long it takes to get through Perpignan." He let out a long sigh.

"What is it, *Hauptmann*?" Hermann asked. "You sound unhappy."

"Oh, I suppose I am just tired and not looking forward to another cold reception by the town's citizens. This is the first time that you and I have been occupiers of a foreign city. In Poland, at least, we were camping in the fields and not disrupting the lives of innocent people." There was a long silent pause. "What do you think, Hermann? Am I the odd-ball in the Third *Reich's* Army?"

"No, *Hauptmann*. I am sure that a lot of soldiers feel the same way, but would never express it." He laughed, "You realize, of course, that no one has a sympathetic sergeant that works for him, like me."

"That is right, Hermann. You are the only one left that I can really talk to. The whole country is so paranoid about what they say...it is stifling to have to live this way."

"Like I told you before, *Hauptmann*, I have a good feeling about coming here...you will see. So, please, try to put aside all the bad things of the past and take one day at a time. I do not want to see my friend suffering anymore."

"Thank you, Hermann. You are probably right...I need to relax more and get on with my life. My wife and Albert are always in the back of my mind, and I will never be able to forget them, but I can still be thankful that my parents are safe for now."

"Yes, that is the way I look at things...if my wife and girls are safe, then I have no worries." Hermann paused for a few seconds. "Of course, I am in the military as my career and have accepted everything that goes with it; though in your case, I can see where it would be much harder."

After they crossed through Perpignan, Major Von Klemper stopped the convoy and assembled all the officers. "Gentlemen, we are about to take over this small town and we must establish who is in control, from the very beginning. More than likely, we will be here for some time and want to avoid any problems with the population. We have an important job to do, possibly the most important in the defense of Europe.

"I have never said this to you before, but our battalion that will be building the pillboxes, entrenchments, wire, mines and installing the underwater obstacles, may be the only means to offset the Allied superiority and mobility. The field marshals believe that the battle here in the South could be decided at the water's edge, so our aim is to create a defensive belt around strategic points along the entire coast of France."

One of the officers raised his hand, and said, "Major, that is a lot of coastline for our small group to cover. Will we be using the local civilians as workers?"

"*Leutnant*," the major said, "first of all, there are not a lot of beaches large enough for an expeditionary force to land between here and Marseille, so it is not as enormous as you think. Secondly, I cannot foresee using any of these ballet-dancing 'Frogs' for a job like this. From what I have been told, they are mostly farmers in this area, and all they will be good for is to provide us with food." He paused, and then said, "*Hauptmann...*"

"Sir," Johann answered.

He handed Johann a piece of paper, and said, "I want you to call the Mayor of Elne, at this number, and tell him that we will be arriving shortly. I want him to assemble all the men living in the village, at some central point, so that I can talk to them when I arrive...from my map, it looks like there is a public square."

"Yes, Major, I will get right on it," Johann said, as he started walking toward the communications wagon.

"For you infantry officers, and the ones in my battalion," the major continued, "have your men placed around the square in the normal, military fashion. I want them off their trucks before we enter Elne, and marching in front of the convoy until we reach the square. I need the people to know that the German Army has arrived. Understood?"

They all nodded and returned to their cars and trucks. After a short briefing to their men, the convoy was on its way again.

Two hours after Marcel left, the children were getting ready for bed. The adults were downstairs listening to classical music on the radio. Everything was peaceful and serene; Paul was sitting in his chair, with a pipe in his hand, reading a book; Elizabeth and Angelina were sewing; and Paulette was working on reports spread in front of her on the dining room table.

Angelina broke the silence. "I do hope that Marcel is safely on his way to… who knows where. I still can't believe what he's involved in, and he probably only told us a fraction of that."

Paulette looked up from her work. "It doesn't surprise me that much, if you want to know the truth. He has always been very outspoken in his political convictions, and now he's simply taking action, instead of just talking about it."

"I suppose you're right," Angelina said, and then went back to her sewing. She looked at her watch. "It's almost 8:30, so perhaps we got lucky and the Germans *won't* be coming here. I hope so, for the children's sake."

"I think the boys understand a lot more than you would imagine," Elizabeth said. "They'll do just fine, no matter what happens."

"Yes, Maman…I think that's true," Angelina responded. "Did you notice how attentive they were to all of us after Marcel left?"

Paul put his book down and looked over his reading glasses. "Well, they should be…I need more help around here taking care of all you women."

"Oh, shush, you old goat!" Elizabeth said. "You're just lucky you have us around."

Paulette looked up and jokingly said, "Remember, Papa…*Grandmere* and *Grandpere* never wanted *Maman* to marry you, so you better be good."

Elizabeth nodded her head. "Believe me, he knows when he's well off…we're both well off. Even though I didn't have my parent's approval to marry Papa, I just couldn't resist. He looked so handsome and debonair in his uniform."

"Well," Paul began, "the best thing that happened…is we had two wonderful girls, and now four beautiful grandchildren. Now, we have to be strong for their sake, whatever the future brings." Then jokingly he said, "I did look rather dashing, didn't I, Elizabeth?"

They all laughed and went back to their sewing and reading, as the radio continued to play. At 9:00, Angelina got up and walked into her bedroom, carrying a few clothing items. After putting them into her dresser, she was about to go back to the main room, when she glanced out the bedroom window and did a double-take. "*Mon dieu!*" she shouted.

The others stopped what they were doing, and came into the bedroom. "What is it…what's wrong?" Paulette asked.

Angelina was standing at the window, and pointed her finger toward the outside. "Look at all those lights! I see at least twenty or thirty vehicles, in the distance, heading this way. It looks like they're on the road, across the river."

"Oh, my God!" Elizabeth put her hand to her mouth. "The Germans *are* coming! What should we do, Paul?"

"Nothing at this point," he said. "Let's all be calm and see what happens." He motioned for them to return to the main room. "Come, let's go back."

"Should we hide some things, Papa?" Paulette asked, "The Germans usually confiscate radios and guns…gold and silver, too."

"The Germans may be many things," he said, "but they're not stupid. Put away a few good things, but not everything, or they'll know we're trying to conceal something."

"What about the radio, Papa?" Paulette asked again. "We'd lose our contact with the outside world, without it."

Paul looked at the radio sitting on the credenza. "Well, first of all, it's too big to hide, so if they take it, that's fine. Remember, I have that smaller, short wave radio somewhere in the house."

"It's upstairs, in our bedroom closet," Elizabeth said. "What should I do with it, Paul?"

"Bring it down here...we'll keep it in the highboy, in Angelina's bedroom. There's a space behind the bottom drawer, where it should fit perfectly."

Raymond and J.P., completely dressed, came running down the stairs. Raymond was the first to speak. "*Maman*, J.P. and I saw the German trucks coming, so we got dressed in case we had to do anything."

"That's fine, boys...you did the right thing," Angelina said, as she looked down to see Babette standing next to her. "And, I see that my big girl is not asleep yet either."

"No, *Maman*...I heard all the noise, and got out of bed," Babette said, while clutching her favorite doll.

A high, screeching sound was heard outside from the loudspeakers set up in the square. The mayor's quivering voice began to speak. "Attention citizens of Elne! Attention citizens of Elne! This is Mayor Jean Astruc speaking."

Elizabeth, Angelina, and Paulette moved toward the window in the main room as Paul opened the door to the balcony. The children were at his side...all waiting in anticipation of what the mayor would be saying.

"As I'm sure everyone knows by now, the Germans are moving into the Unoccupied Zone. I've just received word that a small battalion of German troops will be camped in and around Elne."

There was a silent pause before the mayor continued. "These officers and enlisted men are part of the...326th Infantry Division of the *Wehrmacht*. They should be entering our village very shortly. Please... Please...do not show any type of force or *résistance*. Don't do anything that may bring harm to your families, or to your fellow citizens."

After a short pause, he continued. "I have also been told, that the German commander wants to meet with the male head of each household as soon as he arrives...so each of you, please report to the front of my office building immediately." He coughed, and said with a nervous edge on his voice, "Be strong...be valiant...keep your chins up...and act like Frenchmen."

The mayor then began singing *La Marseillaise* and, coming in on the second line, the French National Anthem could be heard throughout the village, including Paul and his family.

"Arise you children of our motherland,
  Oh now is here our glorious day!
  Over us the bloodstained banner
  Of tyranny holds sway! O tyranny holds sway!"

After the first verse, Paul wiped a tear from his eye. He walked back into the house and spoke to the others. "Yes...well, I'd best be going to Astruc's office." He walked over to his chair, took the sweater draped over the back and put it on, along with his beret that was hanging on the coat rack. He grabbed his cane and started walking across the room toward the door.

Paulette, meanwhile, had taken a peek through the window in the bedroom, and came out to tell everyone, "The trucks aren't more than a kilometer away."

Babette, sensing that everything was not alright, tugged at Paul's pants, and looked up at him angelically, asking, "Are they nice people that are coming in the trucks, *Grandpere*?"

He looked down at her, and patted her head. "I don't know yet...we shall see, my sweet." He turned around to face the others. "I'll be back soon."

Elizabeth came over to him and put her arms around his neck. "Please be careful, darling...and don't antagonize anyone," and then gave him a hug.

"Can I go with you, *Grandpere*?" J.P. asked. "If we have to, we'll fight them together."

"I'll come too, *Grandpere*," Raymond said. "We don't want you to go alone."

Paul gave the boys a friendly smile. "That's all right, boys. I'll be fine."

Angelina and Paulette kissed him on each cheek. Arm-in-arm, they walked him to the door. "Bye-bye, Papa," they said in unison. Everyone went out on the balcony to watch Paul walk out the door, from the first level. He made a right turn and went down the cobblestone street toward the square, being joined on the way by his neighbors, coming out of their houses. At the end of the block, Paul disappeared as he entered the square. Elizabeth went back into the house and the others followed.

Paulette was the first to speak, as everyone sat around the dining room table. "This is so surreal, isn't it? Who would have ever thought that we would be sitting here, three grown people, with four children, having to accept an enemy's occupational force, and not knowing what they have in store for us. I just hope that Papa won't be treated badly." She paused, and then said, "At least Marcel is doing something about it...I envy him."

"For the first time," Angelina said, "I think you're right about Marcel doing what he's doing. He's taking the bull by the horns and not letting these Nazis dictate his fate. I don't know why it surprised me so, when he revealed that he was working with the *Maquis*. Now...I could never picture him doing anything else. Isn't it funny that I never saw that until right this minute, and you had seen it immediately, Paulette?"

Paulette laughed. "I was always smarter than you...you know that."

"In your dreams, sister," Angelina kidded back.

"You two are still at it," Elizabeth said, "aren't you? All I know is, that you're still the only girls in Elne to ever graduate from college. So I think it's a draw, as to who is smarter." She paused for a moment, and then said, "I wish I knew why they needed all the men at the mayor's office? This is making me very nervous."

Emotionally, Raymond asked, "Do you think *Grandpere* is in any danger, *Maman*?"

Angelina shook her head, and replied, "Those German soldiers have done some dreadful things in the north." She stood, crossed herself, and with both hands, motioned for the children to come to her. She put her arms around the boys' shoulders and Babette held on to her leg, as they formed a little circle. She quivered, and said, "We're all together as a family, so everything's going to be alright. We've got to stay calm and just go about our normal...daily routine. OK?"

"Yes, *Maman*," the three said in unison.

As they could now hear the trucks in the distance, the tension in their home was increasing, making everyone, except for Babette, feel more nervous and unsure of what would happen that evening. For the children's sake, Angelina forced herself to put on a normal face, even though she was more anxious than anyone.

"We'll do whatever we can to help, *Grandmere*," Raymond said.

"And we'll protect you and the family, *Maman*...just like Papa would," J.P. added.

Angelina squeezed the boys' shoulders. "I know you two will, and we're very proud of you." She looked down at Babette, "OK, sweetie...let's get ready for bed. Raymond, J.P., you still have some homework to do."

Raymond and J.P. got their books that were sitting in the corner, and brought them to the table to finish doing their assignments. Madeline started to cry, just as Angelina walked Babette to her bedroom.

"I'll take care of the baby," Paulette volunteered. The crib was sitting across the room and Paulette got Madeline out of it. She patted her back softly, as the crying slowly declined, and then walked into Babette's bedroom.

"Can I stay up until *Grandpere* gets home?" Babette asked her mother.

"No, sweetheart…it's getting very late, and we don't know when *Grandpere* will be home."

"Oh please, *Maman*…just for a little while. I don't want Michelle and Marie Joelle to be scared of the trucks."

"After all, it is an historic night, Angelina," Paulette said. "This is something she'll be able to tell her own children about." *I wonder if I'll ever have children to tell*, she thought.

Angelina looked down at Babette out of the corner of her eye, and said, "All right then…just for a little while. We wouldn't want your dolls to be scared, and it is an important night."

Babette hugged her mother's leg, and then went to Paulette, who had just walked out to sit with the boys, and gave her a big hug around the neck. "Thank you *Tante* Paulette."

Elizabeth wiped off the last of the dishes, and then walked past everyone towards the stairs, saying, "I just remembered that Papa wanted me to bring down the short-wave radio…I'll be back in a minute."

Paulette put Madeline back in her crib, and then wandered out to the balcony. She called back into the house, "They're right at the entrance gate of the old city walls, and it appears that the soldiers are getting out of the trucks."

Everyone rushed out to the balcony for a perfect view of the spectacle unfolding before them. When Elizabeth came downstairs holding a flat, black box, she was surprised that no one was in the dining area, but then noticed everyone was outside. She continued to Angelina's bedroom, put the radio behind the bottom drawer of the highboy, and then joined the others.

Babette pointed her finger toward the troops. "Look, all those men have costumes on. Is this going to be like that circus we saw in Marseille?"

"No, silly," J.P. said, "they're soldiers and those are their uniforms." He put his hands on her shoulders. "See how they're all lining up in formation?"

Through the night air, they could hear commands being barked out in German.

"Achtung! Achtung! Hinfallen…Macht schnell!" The men fell in formation quickly in front of the convoy, as the next set of commands were given for a left face and forward march. *"Kompanie…links!"* The sound of boots turning could be heard by the family, and then, *"Vorwärts…marschieren*! They marched through the gates, made a sharp right turn, on the sergeant's command, and headed directly toward the square two blocks away. Their jackboots on the cobblestone street resonated throughout the village, giving the residents an eerie chill, exactly as it was designed to do.

"The bastards are marching right this way!" J.P. exclaimed.

Elizabeth gave him a light slap on the back of his head. "You just watch your mouth, young man, or I'll get the stick after you…do you understand?"

Not backing down, J.P. answers, "Yes, *Grandmere*…but that's what they are, a bunch of …"

Angelina interrupted him, in an admonishing tone. "Jean-Pierre! Behave, or I'll wash your mouth out with soap. You're beginning to sound just like your grandfather."

The soldiers were now directly below the balcony of their house, almost drowning out J.P. as he spoke. "That's OK...I want to be just like *Grandpere* and Papa, so that one day I'll be able to fight for France."

"Let's hope there aren't any more wars, and no one has to fight," Paulette said. "War is not a game, J.P."

"But there's nothing wrong with J.P. wanting to be a soldier," Raymond said. "He'd be good at it."

The soldiers were followed by the officer's cars, two APC's, and ten trucks. The noise was almost deafening as they all passed by, and finally the family could see part of the convoy assembling in the square, at the end of their block.

"Wow...look at them marching around the square," Raymond said. "It *is* like a circus parade, Babette. How many troops do you think there are, J.P.?"

"There's a lot of them...at least a hundred or so. Why do you think they're marching around the square?"

"Like I told you before," Paulette said, "they want us all to see how many there are, so we won't be tempted to try anything foolish against them."

Angelina pulled Paulette aside, out of earshot of the others. "Paulette, we must get word of all this to Marcel. I'm sure he will want to know their numbers and what their mission is here."

"I'll try to find out more at work tomorrow. We can't do anything for a few days, because I imagine they'll be watching us pretty closely at first."

"Yes...you're right, especially if I leave the village and go toward the bridge," Angelina said. "We must be discreet in gathering the intelligence that Marcel and *La Résistance* can use."

Paulette tilted her head, squinted her eyes, and then pulled her head back, as she looked directly at Angelina.

"What?" Angelina asked.

"You sound like a different person, now. Is this my sweet, non-political, big sister talking?"

Angelina shook her head and then sighed. "I just can't bear the sight of German soldiers on French soil. They've messed up our lives for more then two years now. I know we have it better than most, but still I'm here with the four children and Marcel is up in the hills with the *Maquis*." She paused, then said, "And now, seeing those Nazis… marching around the square! We should be at our children's music recitals…and soccer matches…and…"

Paul had been waiting in the square for almost thirty minutes with the other men from the village. The mayor reiterated that they should all remain calm, because there was no reason the Germans had to be abusive to them.

"But don't act like sheep, cowering to these bastards, either," Paul added. "Stand proud, like Frenchmen."

The noise by the troops, and the rest of the convoy, clearly made an impression on all the men assembled in the square. As the soldiers marched in, they formed six separate groups…one on each of the four entrances to the square, and two small groups facing the entrance to City Hall, where the mayor and villagers were standing. There was a space between the two groups, where Major von Klemper's four-door, Mercedes convertible parked. The other officer's cars were in a line across the square, directly behind the two small groups. The two APC's flanked the City Hall building, facing out into the square, and the rest of the trucks parked themselves at the back. There was clearly enough fire power here, to destroy Elne, ten times over.

Like the conquering hero, the major stood up in his car to survey what was going on around him. When he finally faced the assembled villagers, he stared at them for several moments, looking over each person individually, and then gave the command for some soldiers to stand behind these men, which was promptly done.

"*Wer ist der Buergermeister?*" the major asked the Frenchmen facing him. No one answered, but just looked at one another and shrugged. "*Verstehen Sie Deutsch?*" Still no reply.

On seeing this, Johann got out of his car and came over to von Klemper's. "May I be of some assistance, Major? I speak fluent French."

"Yes, please," the major said. "My French is a little rusty."

Johann took over from there, facing the mayor and his group. "*Bonsoir.* This is Major von Klemper, the commander of our group, and I am Captain Weller, the second in command. Obviously, no one here speaks German, but what the Major was asking, is who the Mayor of your village is?"

Astruc stepped forward and said, "I am Jean Astruc, the Mayor of Elne… *Bonsoir.*"

Johann proceeded to translate the remainder of the conversation between the major and mayor, in French. "This will be brief…we are very tired from our journey and wish to get some rest, so I do not want any questions tonight. You will begin to implement my directives immediately. Understood?"

"Yes, Major," Astruc replied, "we understand."

"Very well," Johann said, continuing to translate the directives, until he came to the one that concerned the crops grown by the farmers, at which point, Paul Courty raised his hand.

"I'd like to say something in regard to this point, that…"

Before he could finish his sentence, a soldier came up behind Paul, knocking him to the ground, and then kicking him in the ribs. He was about to kick him again, when Johann abruptly yelled out in German, "That is enough soldier…get back in your position!" The infantryman was not in Johann's engineering brigade, and for a moment just stood there, surprised at the reprimand. "Now!" Johann added, and the soldier stepped back against the building. Switching back to French, Johann asked the men around Paul to assist him to his feet, and make sure that he was alright.

After a couple more points were made by the major, Johann told the villagers that they could return to their homes. Mayor Astruc was asked to stay and assist with some logistics questions, and he announced to the officers that a short meeting would be held in the mayor's office in 10 minutes. This would give the officers some time to spend with their troops.

Johann went back to his car and spoke to Hermann. "Well, that went smooth enough, except for that unfortunate incident with that local man."

"It must have scared the town half to death, with all the noise," Hermann said. "I didn't recognize the soldier who hit him."

"Speaking of that soldier," Johann said, pointing toward the front group, "there he is standing with his buddies. Get him for me, Hermann."

Hermann walked over and spoke to the man for a moment, and then walked back to their car, with the soldier following him. "Here he is *Hauptmann.*"

The soldier snapped to attention, with his rifle at his side. "Sir, you wanted to see me?"

"Yes, I wanted to see you, corporal. I don't know what gave you the right to hit that elderly man the way you did, and I cannot remember hearing an order telling you to do so. We have an important mission to accomplish, and we're not here to humiliate, or harm the civilians. Is that understood?"

"Yes, sir…I am sorry for my actions, Hauptmann," the man answered.

"Well, you better be, because the next stupid thing you do will get you demoted to private, or worse. What you did could antagonize the whole population, and possibly compromise our entire mission. If you happen to see that man again in the village, I want you to apologize to him; and furthermore, you better pass on what I just said to your platoon. Now get out of here, before I demote you right now."

The soldier saluted and walked briskly back to his men, as Johann turned and headed to the Mayor's office.

Elizabeth came off the balcony, into the house. "I can't tell what's happening in the square. I'm just happy that the marching has stopped, and hopefully Papa will come home soon." She went to the credenza and poured three glasses of wine. "Come girls…let's have a glass of wine to settle our nerves."

They touch their glasses together. *"A votre sante! Vive la Republique!"*

"Do you know what really bothers me?" Paulette said. "Now we have this traitor regime collaborating with the enemy who are in our village."

"What is collaborating, *Maman?*" Raymond asked.

"Well, when a country like ours is occupied, those people who cooperate and aid the enemy are called collaborators," Angelina explained. "And, as *Tante* Paulette said, our *Vichy* government are traitors."

"I hope they shoot all of them after the War, for not being good Frenchmen," J.P. said.

"Yes, and then General de Gaulle will be the head of the government, and France will again be a great country," Raymond added.

Elizabeth took a long sip of her wine. "Boys, things will probably work out just like you say, because we're a strong people; but remember, these men have guns, and if all the stories are true, they can be brutal... just don't do anything foolish...especially you, Jean-Pierre."

J.P. got out of his chair and sat down on Elizabeth's lap. He put one arm around her neck, and tickled her under her chin with his other hand, as she shook her head. Jokingly, he said, "Ohhh, *Grandmere*...I'm so happy you're worried about your new favorite grandson...and here I thought it was Raymond you loved the best." He kissed her on both cheeks.

"Eh...you're such a naughty boy, J.P.," Elizabeth said, as she pushed him off her lap. "I don't know what's going to become of you."

Angelina stood and put her arm around J.P. "He's a very good boy, *Maman*...he's just a flirt, like his father, that's all."

Paulette sighed, "And bound to break a hundred hearts, no doubt."

Babette walked in from the bedroom and put her head in her mother's lap. "You're getting very tired, aren't you, darling?" Angelina asked.

"Ah, huh," Babette answered.

Remembering that Marcel didn't have a chance to talk to Babette privately, Angelina said, "Darling, listen to *Maman* for a minute." Babette raised her head. "I want you to do something for me, OK?"

"OK, *Maman*."

"If anyone asks you if you've seen Papa, you must tell them that you haven't seen him for a very long time. Just pretend that he wasn't here this evening...do you understand?"

"Yes, I understand. I haven't seen Papa for a very, very, long time."

At that moment, a noise was heard on the stairs leading up to the main floor. Babette ran to the door and looked down the stairs. Then, she turned around to speak to the others. "It's *Grandpere*...it looks like he's having trouble getting up the stairs. What's wrong with him?"

Raymond and J.P. jumped up from the table and rushed down the stairs to help Paul. When Paul walked into the house, his left arm was around Raymond's shoulder; his right hand was holding his cane, and J.P. was holding him under his right arm. He was obviously in pain and looked disheveled...he was not wearing his *beret*, his hair was messed up, and there was blood on his forehead, and on the side of his lip.

"Thank you boys," Paul said, as they released his arms. He began rubbing his neck and shoulder on the right side, and his limp was a little more noticeable.

Elizabeth went to him and put her arm around his waist. "What happened, *Cherie*?"

"Papa," Paulette exclaimed, "you have blood on your head!"

Paul winced. "This Nazi goon hit me from the back when I tried to ask a question. Before I knew it, I was on the ground, and then he kicked me in the ribs, the bastard. As I lay there, I saw that he was about to kick me again, when this officer, who was doing the translating, yelled at him to stop.

"I don't know what happened to my *beret*." He touched his forehead and then looked at the blood on his finger. "I must have gotten this when I fell."

"Paul, my darling...this is awful!" Elizabeth cried.

Angelina pulled out a chair at the table, and then grabbed Paul under his arm. "Come sit down, Papa. I'll get a cold washrag for your head."

Paul sat down slowly into the chair, wincing with pain when he did so. Babette came over and hugged his arm, then crawled under the table, sitting at his feet and holding one of her dolls. Elizabeth rubbed his neck and shoulders, trying to ease his pain. Angelina wet a rag, and then dabbed the blood off of his head.

Even in his pain, Paul tried to joke and minimize his injuries. "Thank you. I haven't had this much attention, since that horse kicked me a few years ago." They smiled, but he could see that they were all very much concerned, so he paused, before telling them what happened. "Well, the arrogant son-of-a-bitch…he expects all his demands to be met without question, and threatened to shoot anyone who causes problems."

"Who said this, Papa?" Angelina asked.

"Who? The *Commandant*…that's who. His name is Major von Klemper, and he means business."

"What do they want us to do, *Grandpere*?" Raymond asked.

"The first thing I was told we have to do, is house one of their officers."

Astonished, Elizabeth asked, "House one of the officers? You don't mean here in our home, do you?"

"Unfortunately, yes. The enlisted men will be taking over part of the school, the library, and some other public buildings and the officers will all be billeted with families around the area."

"I don't want any *Kraut* living with us, *Grandpere*," J.P. said. "Isn't there something we can do?"

Paulette shook her head. "J.P., don't you see what happened when *Grandpere* just tried to ask a question? Thank God, he's not hurt more than he is!"

Paul took a long swig of the wine which Elizabeth had handed him. "If anyone protested, they would throw you out of your house completely. So, no, there's nothing I could have done." He took a deep breath and held the side of his chest, as he let it out. "Somehow, we'll just have to make do."

There was a noticeable silence for several seconds, as everyone digested what seemed like a ton of bricks being thrown at them. Finally, Paulette spoke up, "Yes, Papa, we must be practical. Let's see," she thought for a moment, "why don't you give him my room upstairs? I'll move in with Angelina and the baby, down here."

Angelina nodded in agreement. "That sounds good…we can't give him my room, under any circumstances, with the trap door being there." She paused, and then said, "Boys, help Tante Paulette move her things down."

"OK," Raymond said, "let's go, J.P." The boys headed for the stairs, with Paulette following close behind.

Angelina pulled up a chair next to her father. "I just can't believe any of this is happening. What else did he tell you, Papa?"

"Well, to start with, all the adults will have to carry identification cards… and each family will get new ration coupons for fuel and other necessities. We can also expect to have our food storage inventoried, over the next few days…and it's our responsibility to help feed the troops here."

Elizabeth indignantly responded, "Our responsibility! How do they think we can do that? We only have vineyards for wine, and orchards for growing fruit, and we grow just enough vegetables to feed our family!"

"They apparently know all that, Elizabeth. We'll need coupons also, for any food that we don't raise or grow…a directive will be issued soon, obliging us to grow vegetables, instead of fruit."

Elizabeth was incensed with these directives. "They can just march in here, and in only a few minutes change our whole life? Our parents… our grandparents and their parents, have worked this land, and ran this village for two hundred years…and there's nothing we can do, or the mayor can do?"

"Elizabeth!" Paul exclaimed, "Get a hold of yourself!"

Paulette, Raymond, and J.P. came down the stairs carrying clothes and a couple small boxes. After putting Paulette's belongings in Angelina's bedroom, they joined the others.

Paul continued speaking to his wife, trying to calm her. "We're being occupied...do you understand? Occupied...they have the guns and the tanks and the bullets. No, there's nothing we, or the mayor, or anyone else can do at this point...we have to be patient." He paused. "Perhaps Marcel and the *Maquis* can harass these Germans...lower their morale, as they've been doing in the north. *La Résistance* is going to get more explosive...so there is hope...there is always hope."

"We'll all do everything we can to aid *La Résistance*," Paulette said, "because now, they speak and act for us; but, in the meantime...yes, we must be patient. With the Allies now having a foothold in North Africa, it won't be long before they invade Europe, and..."

There were three loud knocks on the door, downstairs. "Let me handle this," Paul said. "Remember...Silence! Try to avoid talking to him, unless you absolutely have to...and please, Angelina and Paulette, don't let him know you speak German." He pointed to Raymond, "Go downstairs and let him in, but come right back up here."

Raymond did as he is told, and immediately returned upstairs and closed the door behind him. The family waited in anticipation, as they heard two people coming up the stairs. There was another knock and Paul opened the door. A thirty-three year old, tall, slender, statuesque German officer, with sandy-brown hair, walked into the room. He had a high-brimmed hat tucked under his left arm, which was bent at the elbow. Attached to the thick, black, shiny belt around his waist was a holster carrying a German Luger.

He was followed by a pudgy, very jovial German soldier, carrying a canvas-like suitcase and a duffel bag. Both men were wearing the

Wehrmacht grey uniform with the insignias of a captain and sergeant respectively, and high, black, polished boots. The sergeant wore an enlisted man's cap.

The captain clicked his heels together and gave a quick bow of his head. "*Guten abend*, Herr Courty. *Ich heiss* Johann Weller." As if in shock, they just looked at him with blank faces, even though Angelina and Paulette knew exactly what he was saying. "*Spricht hier jemand Deutsch?*"

Again, no one responded to him, so he switched to French, with a mild German accent. "Ahh…I see. No one speaks German?"

"No, Captain," Paul said, "we only speak French here."

"Ah, I see," Johann said, as he noticed the cut on Paul's forehead. "By the way, were you not the gentleman that was knocked down in the square?" Paul nodded his head. "My apologies, *Monsieur* Courty…I have spoken to the soldier who did that, and it will never happen again."

Paul nodded his head again, and said, "Thank you, Captain."

"No thanks are necessary *Monsieur*…the incident should never have occurred in the first place." He gave a courtesy bow of his head. "Very well…let me begin again. My name is Johann Weller, and I am the engineering officer with the *Wehrmacht* division here. This…" he turned around and gestured with his hand, "… is my aide, Sergeant Hermann Koch." Hermann put down the bags, and bowed his head at the mention of his name. "Sergeant Koch speaks very little French, and would be most appreciative if the children could teach him from time-to-time."

Hermann looked at Raymond and J.P. and smiled. "Ah, *danke, danke*. My French not goot…I make better."

Babette crawled out from underneath the table, holding her doll, stood and looked up at Johann and Hermann. Angelina pointed her finger at her and emphatically said, "Babette!!" She moved forward and grabbed her hand.

Johann squatted to her level, and with a friendly smile said, "Well, what do we have here?"

"My name is Babette and this is my doll, Michelle."

"Michelle is very nice. Do you have any other dolls?" Johann asked, as he stood up.

"Yes, Marie Joelle. I'll show her to you tomorrow…she's sleeping now."

"That will be nice…I will look forward to it, Babette." Johann looked at his watch, and then leaned down to her again, with both hands on his knees. "It looks like you should be in bed by now, too."

"Maman let me stay up tonight, because *Tante* Paulette said that it was 'restoric'. Do you have any children, Johann?"

Before Johann could speak, Angelina looked down at Babette, and slowly said, "His name…is Captain Weller. And it's not restoric, darling, it's historic."

"*Nein*…that is alright, Johann smiled. "Please call me Johann…it is nice to hear my name again. And you are right, it is historic…something that we all will remember for a long time." He looked around at the others, and added, "In a nice way, I hope." He paused and then looked back at Babette. "No, I am not married, Babette…"

Paulette slowly let her gaze rise, until she was looking directly at Johann, and then removed her glasses. *He is good looking,* she thought, *and his manners are impeccable. But it's probably just a front to win us over.*

"…but Hermann has two daughters about your age…Marlena and Sigrid."

Hermann, hearing his daughters' names, pulled out a picture from his jacket pocket and showed it first to Paul, standing next to Babette, and then to everyone else standing across the table. "*Ja,* Marlena *und*

Sigrid." He kissed the picture and then put it next to his heart, before returning it to his coat pocket.

"Can they come and play with me?" Babette asked.

Johann whispered this to Hermann and Hermann whispered back for Johann to translate. "Hermann says that one day, when this terrible war is over, you can all be friends, and he will bring them to play with you…all right?"

"Yes…that would be nice. I know I would like Marlena and Sigrid."

"I am sure you would," Johann said, as he turned to face Hermann. "And now, Hermann…*das ist alles. Gute Nacht.*"

"*Gute Nacht, mein Hauptmann,*" Hermann said, as he turned to the others and nodded his head several times. "Goot night, goot night."

"Good night, Hermie," Babette said, making up a new name for him. He smiled and walked out the door and down the stairs.

Johann turned to Paul, and said, "So, I have not been introduced to the rest of your family, *Monsieur* Courty."

Paul coldly replied, "I…I don't think that's necessary."

Johann felt intrusive and nodded his head. "I understand, *Monsieur* Courty."

"We haven't seen Papa for a very, long time," Babette abruptly said.

Paulette jumped in anxiously, "I…I am Paulette Courty. I work in Mayor Astruc's office, as his administrative assistant."

Johann clicked his heels…they looked at each other for a moment, and then he nodded his head. "A pleasure, *Mademoiselle* Paulette."

Trying to avoid the subject of Marcel, Paulette continued the introductions. "This is my mother, Elizabeth…" Elizabeth looked away from Johann without acknowledging him, as did Angelina when she was introduced. "…my sister, Angelina Pointier and her children… Raymond, Jean-Pierre, the baby Madeline is sleeping over there in the crib, and you've met Babette."

"Ah yes, Babette…the diplomat." He looked at Angelina. "And your husband, *Madame* Pontier…where is he?"

Without expression, Angelina said, "My husband is a dentist, living in Marseille. He thought we would all be safer here, living with my parents." She paused and looked down at the floor. "Maybe he was wrong."

Johann could sense that enough had been spoken for one night and he should let them be by themselves. "Well now…I have had a very long journey over the last few days, and I am quite tired. If someone would be so kind as to show me my room…"

"You'll be taking my room upstairs, Captain," Paulette said. "I've already moved my things down here to Angelina and the baby's room." She turned to Raymond and J.P. "Boys, please show the captain which room he'll be staying in."

Raymond and J.P. walked toward the stairs, as Johann picked up his bag and followed. Before reaching the stairs, he turned and spoke directly to Elizabeth. "*Madame* Courty, you have a very warm, lovely home. I am sorry I have to intrude like this. I know it is an inconvenience for all of you, and I will try to be as inconspicuous as possible."

"We understand the circumstances of war, Captain," Paul said. "I hope you understand that we are loyal Frenchmen, and would never do anything voluntarily to aid or assist your cause, or your troops."

"I spent a great deal of time in France, before the War," Johann said, "and I would not have expected anything else. But as you said, *Monsieur*, I too am loyal to my country, and just a soldier following orders."

Elizabeth spoke up for the first time. "Captain, am I required to make you breakfast in the morning?"

"No, *merci*. I will be eating all my meals in the officer's mess. Well, again, goodnight." He and the boys proceeded up the stairs. They showed him his room overlooking the street, and the bathroom across the hall, with freshly laid out towels across the front of the bathtub. After the boys left, and went to their own rooms on the top floor, Johann hung his uniforms in the closet and put his clothes away in the small dresser. He got undressed, put on his robe, and went across the hall to fill the tub with water. He lay soaking for 30 minutes, and just relaxed all the muscles in his body that ached from the long journey. *Paulette seemed very nice*, he thought to himself, *but fraternizing with the enemy may not be a good idea*. Yet, he thought about her once again, as he lay in his bed and dozed off.

After the children were all asleep, the adults congregated again at the dining room table. Elizabeth poured them all tea, and then shrugged her shoulders and shook her head. "Just to think that we have a German officer sleeping in a room next to ours…it's like my worst nightmare."

"Let's try to make the best of it and accept things the way they are, Elizabeth," Paul said. "He is the one that helped me in the square, so it could be a lot worse."

"Excuse me, Papa," Paulette said, "Can you think of anything we should let Marcel know? I'll try to find out exactly how many men are here."

"Yes, he should know that, for sure," Paul replied. "Also, the Captain mentioned that he hadn't spoken French for quite awhile, and he had been traveling for a few days, which means…"

"…Which means that his unit came from somewhere other than Northern France," Angelina added.

Paulette thought for a moment. "Perhaps Belgium, or Germany itself? Marcel was right...they do expect an invasion coming from Africa."

"And did you hear what the Captain said...that he was an engineering officer?" Paul said. "Normally, when they have an engineering officer attached to a battalion, they're going to be building something. We'll have to find out what, because that alone could be critical."

"You know, Papa," Angelina said, "I think I better take Madeline for a nice, long stroll to the bridge in the next day or so, and not wait any longer than that. It's about time I started painting again, so I'll get all my supplies together in the morning."

Paul stood up, stretched out his arms, and rubbed his neck. "Just be careful...and warn Marcel that the Germans will probably have patrols all over the Delta, if he's planning to sneak back here." He paused, and then said, "Well, Elizabeth, I think it's time for bed. I feel a little sore...would you help me put a cold towel on my shoulder? Goodnight, girls."

Angelina and Paulette stood up and kissed their father and mother goodnight, something they didn't always do, but tonight had brought them even closer as a family. After Paul and Elizabeth walked up the stairs, Angelina and Paulette went into their bedroom. They both sat on the bed with their legs crossed, facing each other as they've done so many times in the past.

"Soooo...what do you think?" Angelina asked.

Paulette leaned back on her pillow. "What do I think about what?"

"The Captain, of course."

"Hmm," Paulette paused, "well, he's definitely not what we were expecting. But again, that might be just a ploy to win us over. I've read about their tactics in the underground newspapers." She sat up, stretched out her arms, and yawned. "The Germans feel they can mollify us by saying nice things about our country and our pleasing qualities. In reality, what they want is to be our protectors and control the labor force of Europe. France would keep all the cultural and attractive things to entertain our masters...you know, the ballet, our outdoor cafés, the Louvre, the *haute couture* that we're known for in Europe."

"Maybe so...Hitler is a terrible person, and it would be horrible having to live under a regime like his forever. I'm just glad that tonight, though, the Captain was polite to us and nice to the children...and he did help Papa in the square."

"You're a saint, Angelina. Even now, in the middle of all this chaos, you try to see some good in everyone and everything."

"I'm just trying to keep some normality in our lives, that's all. It's so hard without Marcel here." She reached over, grabbed one of the pillows next to Paulette's, and put it at the foot of the bed, where she laid her head back and stared at the ceiling. "Remember when we were little girls..." Paulette started to close her eyes. "...how perfect everything was? We would run through the fields and pick berries and grapes." Angelina moved around to get more comfortable on her pillow. "And then we would help Papa stomp on the grapes with our feet." She laughed. "We thought we were the best wine makers in the valley.

"And school was so much fun...*Maman* would have a hot lunch for us every day, and after school, when it was cold out, we'd come home and have hot cider with Papa, and read our books by the fire. I think most of the villagers were shocked when we went off to college, but *Maman* and Papa always encouraged us to further our education. I wouldn't have met Marcel, if I hadn't gone on to pharmacy school."

Angelina folded her hands and took a long sigh, before continuing. "I was so sad for you when Jacques was killed. I know you'll find someone else one day. You deserve to be as happy as Marcel and I." She paused for a few seconds. "Do you think about him much, Paulette?" There was no answer. "Paulette?"

Paulette stretched and yawned again. "Sometimes. He was a wonderful man and I think he would have gone on to become a noted professor, but lately, I try to keep focused on the present and not dwell on the past. It *is* sad when I think about him." She closed her eyes, and sleepily said, "God knows what's going to happen now from one day to the next."

Angelina sat up and saw that Paulette was trying to sleep. She took a coverlet that was draped over the foot of the bed and covered her sister. "Goodnight, dearest."

27

The next day, Paulette went to work as usual. Many of the offices were taken over by the German staff, but the mayor's two rooms were unaffected, and Paulette was thankful that she still had a job. On arriving, Mayor Astruc called her into his office, before she got to her own, which adjoined his.

"How is your father doing, Paulette," was the first thing he asked.

"He's still a little sore, especially in his back, but the place he hit his head when he fell, is swollen." She shook her head, and emphatically said, "Those idiots!"

The mayor held a finger to his lips, and in a whisper, he said, "Shh, you know how thin these walls are. Be careful what you say from now on, because the *Commandant's* office is right next to yours."

On hearing this, she thought *now I'll be able to pick up some valuable information for Marcel.* "Papa said that the Major didn't speak French, and that the captain, who is staying with us, was translating for him."

"He may not speak as well as Captain Weller, but he still may understand some French. In our meeting this morning, he seemed to know a little of what I was saying, but he only answered in German."

"You're right…we can't take any chances. So what did the Major have to say?"

"Well, he basically wants us to run the local government the same as we've done in the past, but with fewer people. It was sad that I had to let some of them go this morning." He paused. "Of course, we have to organize and report to him on the progress of the food production for his troops, and the distribution of food to our people through the ration coupons, which I'm sure your father told you last night."

"Who said, 'To the victor belongs the spoils'? Yes, Papa told us everything."

"I'm happy that he wasn't hurt that badly. It could have been much worse, had Captain Weller not stepped in. You said that he is the officer you're housing?"

"Yes, he is," Paulette said matter-of-factly.

"He stopped in here, before we went to see the Major, and I must say that he was most charming. I almost forgot who he was."

"Well, *Monsieur* Mayor, I wouldn't trust any of them. That might be just a ploy." She waited a few seconds before she asked, "How many soldiers do you think are in Elne?" She paused for a few seconds more, and then asked, "Do you have any idea what they're going to be doing here?"

"From what I saw last night, I would estimate anywhere from a hundred to one hundred and twenty-five…and…I don't know exactly what their mission is. But the Captain said that they would have to put certain areas, near the beach, off limits to civilians. He requested some maps of the area and said that he would be surveying it today."

"Do you want me to get them together for him, *Monsieur* Mayor?"

"Yes, that would be helpful, Paulette. You know more about where things are than I do." In a low voice, he said, "His office is across the hall from the major's, so why don't you do that first, and then we'll go over some of the other problems we've got to solve."

Paulette admired Mayor Astruc tremendously, because he always appeared so calm in any situation. Even in times like this, with the German occupation, his demeanor didn't seem to waver. He had a job to do and expected everyone to do their jobs accordingly.

Paulette left the mayor's office and walked down to the end of the hall. She opened the door to a long, narrow room which contained the filing cabinets. Her search took 45 minutes, and when she was through, she returned to her own office and sorted through the maps, arranging them in a sequence of their location. *One thing for sure, the Germans are going to be building something on the beach for the invasion,* she thought. One of the maps was a topography of the hills overlooking the beach, the drop-off down to the dunes, and the beach itself. *It would probably take weeks to do this survey,* she assumed, and then made a quick decision.

She got up from her desk, closed and locked her door, took the topography out of its cylinder, and cut it into four sections, carefully labeling each one on the back ...Top Left, Top Right, Bottom Left, and Bottom Right. She found her burlap shopping bag in her bottom desk drawer, took her sweater from the bag, and neatly placed the four sections at the bottom, with her sweater covering them. She smiled, *this will delay those bastards for awhile, and Marcel surely could use this information. Now, what do I do with this extra cylinder?* She remembered that one of the cylinders contained one large map and a smaller one. She took out the smaller one, put it in the extra cylinder, and then relabeled it.

Paulette unlocked her door, walked down the hall to Captain Weller's office, and knocked on his door.

"*Herein…Die Tür ist offen!*" he said, thinking it was someone on his staff.

Paulette opened the door, and sarcastically asked, "I take it, that that meant to come in?"

Johann was sitting at his desk, and on seeing Paulette, he stood up. "*Bonjour, Mademoiselle* Courty. *Oui*, by all means…please come in."

"*Bonjour*, Captain…please, call me Paulette. I have the maps that Mayor Astruc said you needed." She laid the cylinders on his desk, which was full of other official papers.

"Ah, yes…thank you, Paulette. I do need to get started on these right away." She was about to turn and leave, when he said, "Now, if I am to call you Paulette, I would kindly ask you to call me Johann."

"I'm sorry, Captain, but that wouldn't be the correct thing to do here in the office."

He smiled at her, and gave a short laugh. She almost gave him a little smile back, but caught herself in time. *He is rather charming, though*, she thought. *But, he's the German enemy, so forget it.*

"You are correct," he said, "but when we are outside the office, at your home, please try if you can, to call me by my Christian name. I would feel a lot more comfortable." He paused and looked at her gently. "But I do understand, if you feel that you cannot do that…I want you and your family to be comfortable, also. I realize that this is no easy thing for any of you."

"No, it's not, Captain." When she got to the door, she looked back at him, and in a gentler voice, said, "We shall see," and then walked back to her office.

Johann sat back down at his desk and began looking at the maps; but his concentration was not there, as it should be. For some reason, his thoughts were more of Paulette, and the short conversation they just had. *I am not sure, if I have ever met anyone quite like her.*

"Paulette," the Mayor said, "you don't seem to be into your work, today. Is there anything wrong?"

It was the afternoon of that same first day, and as much as Paulette tried, the thought of Johann in civilian clothes, kept coming back. *I wish that he didn't speak French so well…it would be a lot easier.* "No, there's nothing wrong, sir. The adjustment to all of this is a little harder than I thought it would be…that's all. I'll be fine."

That evening, and for the next few days after dinner, Paulette made a point of staying in her room, saying that she had tons of work to do and wanted to get to sleep early. She infrequently saw Johann at his City Hall office, because he was out in the field most of the day. The few times that they ran into each other, they both tried to keep it very professional, but cordial.

I think that Paulette despises me for what I represent, and is therefore keeping her distance, Johann thought. *It is really unfortunate that everyone thinks all Germans are a bunch of monsters.*

28

A few days after the Germans had come to Elne, Raymond and J.P were walking back from school, when Hermann met them in the square. In his broken French, he invited them to his office, which was in one of the Cathedral towers. Neither of them had ever been in the tower and both were surprised at how far they could see... almost the whole Roussillon valley was in view, and the Mediterranean seemed much closer than it actually was.

This tower was set up as an adjunct office for him and Captain Weller. There were drawing boards and sketches all over the room, none of which Raymond or J.P. understood. When they looked across at the other tower, they could see two soldiers, with binoculars, looking in different directions. In one of the windows, they spotted a machine gun pointing down into the square.

Hermann went to a small ice box on one of the tables, showed them a bottle of milk, and in his broken French, asked, "You want...*mit strudel*?" opening up a paper bag to show them that he had several pieces of that also.

"Sure, Hermie, that would be nice," Raymond said, as he nodded his head.

Hermann smiled, as they sat there eating their *strudel* and drinking their milk. When they were through, J.P. said, "Thank you Hermie… that was very good…and now, we'll teach you some French."

Hermann understood enough to say, "*Oui, oui…*I learn French. *Ja?*"

"And we," Raymond said, pointing to himself and J.P., "will learn some German from you," pointing to Hermann.

Hermann gave a big smile, "*Oui*, J.P. *und* Raymond learn *Deutsch*. Goot, goot." He rubbed the top of their heads and laughed.

Regardless of what they heard about the Germans, the boys couldn't help but like this very robust and funny man. Over the next hour, they taught him some simple phrases, and they in turn, learned the same ones in German. When they were about to leave, Johann walked in carrying some more rolled up papers. He was surprised to see them all together, having a good time. Raymond explained what they were doing and Johann genuinely seemed very pleased.

"Thank you very much for spending the time with Hermann," Johann said. "I know that he really appreciates it."

"You mean *danke schön*, don't you, Johann?" J.P. asked.

"We better be going, before it turns dark," Raymond said. "*Maman* will be worried. *Auf weidersehen* Hermie…*auf weidersehen Johann*."

Johann laughed. "Your pronunciations are excellent, boys."

"*Danke*, Johann," J.P. said.

"*Bonjour*, Raymond…*bonjour* Jean-Pierre," Hermann said in flawless French, as the two boys started walking down the steep stairs.

When they arrived home, they told everyone about their experience in the tower and how nice Hermie was.

"What about the captain?" Paulette wanted to know.

"Well," J.P. began, "he came in as we were getting ready to leave, so…"

"Johann seemed very friendly, too," Raymond said. "He was very pleased that we were teaching Hermie some French, and he did pick it up very quickly."

"Could you make out *anything* on those drawings?" Paulette asked, anxiously. "Did you see any buildings, or weapons, or anything like that?"

"No, it wasn't like anything I've ever seen before," J.P. said. "What do you think, Raymond?"

"I don't know what it was either...just a bunch of crossing wood and string between them. We really didn't have much time to look at the drawings, but what I saw was pretty weird looking. Why is it so important, *Tante* Paulette?" Raymond asked.

"It might be something that Papa would be interested in," Angelina said. "Did the sergeant ask you to come back again?"

"Yes, *Maman*," J.P. said. "We told Hermie that we would come back in a couple days. He's a lot of fun, and we can learn another language, too."

Raymond went over to Paulette and put his arm around her, and said, "Should we ask him about the drawings, *Tante* Paulette?"

"No, sweetheart, I wouldn't want you to do that. We don't want anyone to know that we're interested in what they have up in the tower." Paulette paused for a few seconds. "Just try to be more observant...and you know...casually look at them."

"OK, we'll see if we can make out anything."

"I've got all my paint brushes and a new canvas together," Angelina said, "so I'm planning on going to the bridge tomorrow with Madeline. I'll set up my easel and start painting, and when I'm sure no one is around, I'll leave a message for Marcel under the bridge. He'll be interested in everything that we've learned."

"*Maman*," J.P. said in such a way to get her attention, "when we were in the tower, we could see the bridge pretty clearly. I bet that the Germans, in the other tower, can see it much better with their binoculars, so they'll probably be watching the bridge."

"Yes, you're right J.P.," Angelina said. "I'll have to paint from the other side of the bridge, and if I get down low enough, they won't be able to see me. There's a little path that leads down to the River Tech, so Madeline's carriage won't be a problem…in fact, it's big enough to hold everything, too."

That night at dinner, Angelina wrote down everything she needed to tell Marcel, and then rewrote it later on a smaller piece of paper. She folded the paper small enough to fit into one of the cracks beneath the bridge.

The next morning, after the children had gone to school, Angelina got all her materials together and put them in a basket beneath the carriage, which she usually used for shopping…the easel fit nicely over this. She took the note that was neatly folded, and put it in her bra. With Madeline resting comfortably after her feeding, Angelina started out on her first covert mission. No sooner did she get through the city gates, than she came upon three German soldiers sitting in a truck. A machine gun was pointing right at her. One of the men got out of his truck; his rifle was slung over his shoulder, and he approached her. In understandable French that he must have learned for this occasion, he asked for her papers.

Angelina tried to stay as calm as possible. She got her purse out of the basket and fumbled through it looking for her identification papers. She hoped that he didn't see her hand trembling when she handed them to him. He took a minute to look it over, and then he stared at her, the baby and the materials underneath.

"Was ist das?" he asked, pointing to the narrow box of paints.

Pretending not to understand, Angelina shrugged and said, "This?" She pulled out the box and showed him the paints and brushes, and with her moving hand, she pretended to paint on the canvas.

The young soldier nodded his head, "I understand, but where are you going to paint?"

"I'm going down to the river, near the bridge."

The soldier, behind the machine gun, called out in German, "Why not ask if you can fuck her little French ass, Hans?" The three men laughed, not knowing that she spoke fluent German.

Angelina gripped the carriage handle as tight as she could and looked down at the ground. She felt a flush come over her, and she was sure that it showed. She remembered all the stories about the barbarians that ravished Europe and raped the women, and prayed this wouldn't be her. She was relieved when he handed back her papers and cocked his head to the side, indicating that she was free to go.

She quickly pushed the carriage down the road, even though she felt sick to her stomach, and could have just as easily turned around and gone back home. It was a 15 minute walk to the bridge, and by the time Angelina arrived, her nerves had calmed considerably. Madeline had slept through the whole incident, and was content by the rocking effect of the carriage and the fresh air. Angelina set up her easel on the opposite side of the bridge, and first began sketching a scene on the canvas with pencil. This would later be painted into a picture of the bridge and river, the countryside behind it, and on the horizon, the towers of Elne, with the Pyrenees barely seen in the distance.

The baby awoke 30 minutes after her mother had begun drawing. It wasn't quite time for her feeding, but Angelina felt that she had been out long enough not to look suspicious, and if anyone inquired, they could see the picture she had started. Knowing that someone in the tower may be watching her, she picked up Babette and walked her around, slowly making her way down the path, to the river. Angelina knew that she couldn't be seen, once she was behind the bridge. She took the slip of paper out of her bra, and easily slipped it into a familiar crack under the façade, at the beginning of the bridge…the same place that Marcel would leave love notes, while they were dating. She walked back up the hill to the carriage, laid Madeline down, packed up her easel and materials, and began the walk back to town. She dreaded having to walk past the soldiers at the gate, but when she arrived there, the same young soldier waved her through. There were a couple comments made by the other two, but Angelina pretended not to hear them, and walked with her head held high.

On arriving home, Angelina fed and changed Madeline, and then lay down in her bed, completely exhausted. When Elizabeth came back from the market and asked how everything went, Angelina didn't want to upset her, and said, "Oh, it was fine. I left the note without any problems, and Madeline seemed to enjoy the fresh, cool air."

Later that night, when Angelina and Paulette were alone, Angelina told Paulette what had happened. "You have no idea how scared I was…not only for myself, but for Madeline, also. I'm not sure if I can go out there again."

"Oh, that's terrible!" Paulette exclaimed. "I see Johann at work everyday… maybe I should tell him about it…he did help Papa, after all."

Angelina couldn't help but notice, that Paulette was now calling the captain by his first name. "I'm not sure if I would do that, because that might bring attention to my being at the bridge."

"You have every right to paint at the bridge, but your safety is more important than anything and he should know what his men are doing." She paused for a moment. "Besides, we really need to keep a line of communication open with Marcel. I can hear almost everything they're saying in the major's office, right next door to me; although, so far, there hasn't been much to pass on, but I'm sure there will be in the future."

"Yes, we can't pass up the opportunity to help *La Résistance*, and if we have to use the captain…well, so be it."

The next morning, Paulette walked into Johann's office, unannounced, and closed the door. "Captain, may I speak to you privately?"

He looked up from what he was doing. "Ah, what a pleasant surprise; and good morning to you too, Paulette."

"Good morning, Captain." She wanted to keep this as brief as possible. "I hate to bother you, but…"

He stood up. "Please, have a seat. It is a little chilly, so I am having some coffee…would you like some?"

She thought that she had better not, but it smelled so good from the pot that was brewing on a little stove in the corner, that she found herself saying, "Yes, that would be nice…thank you."

"Wonderful!" He walked over to the small pot and poured each of them a cup. He set her cup on the desk in front of her, and then sat down in his chair. He took a sip, and said, "We need this, to warm us up. How cold does it get here in Elne?"

She felt very relaxed with him, almost like talking to an old friend. "Well, it sometimes snows, but that's very rare. In the winter, it can vary from minus 5 Celsius to plus 15 degrees."

"Oh, that is not too bad. I was stationed in Poland last winter and you can not believe all the snowstorms, and how cold it was." He chuckled, "If I took a deep breath, I knew I would freeze my lungs. My long underwear became part of my body."

Paulette laughed and took a sip of her coffee. "Hmm, this is very good. I can't imagine living in a place that cold. We have a nice change of seasons, but nothing that extreme."

"Yes, it seems very pleasant here, so I know I will enjoy it." He smiled at her, and then took another sip of coffee. "So, how can I help you today?"

She began telling Johann what had happened to Angelina and how frightened it had made her. "She doesn't speak German, but sometimes, as a child, you pick up certain vulgar phrases in other languages, and believe me, this was extremely vulgar."

Johann stood up and paced around, holding his coffee cup. His expression had dramatically changed. He heaved a sigh, "You cannot believe how this disturbs me, Paulette. No woman should ever be talked to like that, or be afraid to walk around their own city. I will find the three men that were on duty yesterday, and strongly reprimand them." He put his cup down, took his cap off the clothing rack, opened the door, and said, "Please excuse me, but I am going to find those men right now. My deepest apologies to your sister."

Paulette stood up and said, "Thank you, Johann. My sister and I appreciate your doing this, but please don't mention this in our home, because my parents don't know that it happened."

He nodded, "You can be assured that this will not happen again." He walked down the hall and out of the building.

Paulette finished her coffee, then took both cups to the women's bathroom and washed them out, before returning them to his office. *Did I really call him Johann?* She had a stirring inside that she hadn't felt for a long time, and it bothered her. *I could have sat and had coffee with him all morning...what's wrong with me, he's German.*

243

29

After leaving Elne on the night of November 12th, Marcel got his car out of the woods and headed north, toward Perpignan. He went through the city without any problems and continued on the highway for another 5 kilometers, when he spotted the German convoy in the distance. He immediately turned his car around until he came to a country road that he knew would take him west, and then north again, until he eventually reached Carcassonne. It was a longer route, but much safer traveling through the towns of Quillan and Limoux.

Simon was anxious to hear if Marcel had found any new routes to get into Spain, and when Marcel told him about the old railroad tunnels, Simon was elated. "I would suggest that we do this within the next month, because the Nazis are starting to round up Jews in many of the major cities around Paris."

"How many people do you think will come with you?" Marcel asked again.

"Including my family...I would say about 15 all together are ready to go now." He paused, and then said, "Do you think that will be any problem?"

"Truthfully, Simon, I really don't know." Marcel thought for a moment. "Usually, the smaller the group, the better, but if that's what you have, we'll work with it." Marcel tried to sound encouraging, but knew that it wouldn't be easy.

"I'll go by your judgment, Marcel, and I want you to know that my own *Maquis* group can supply the manpower, instead of using an outside group like yours, which would have to travel too far."

"Simon, let me run this by the leaders at the meeting tomorrow. I'll get back with you as soon as possible, because it could be snowing in the mountains very shortly."

Marcel left the next morning for Montelimar. When the subject came up, he was surprised that three of the ten regional leaders, which were at the meeting, were opposed to any risky operations "just to save Jews." Anti-Semitism was by no means new to France, but nevertheless, Marcel was appalled.

"I can't believe that in these days of war, while we're fighting the most evil empire that ever lived, you would be opposed to saving loyal, French citizens, no matter what religious beliefs they have!" Marcel exclaimed.

Florette looked directly at the three men, and addressed them pointedly, "There are many *Résistance* and *Maquis* fighters that are Jews, and even though Marcel hasn't mentioned the names of the people he's talking about, one of the men that wants to get his family out of the country, is the leader of the *Maquis* group in that region…an exceptional leader, I might add."

"Getting these people over the Pyrenees," the Council Chairman added, "will be a major accomplishment for our organization. This is something that we should be doing on a regular basis, not just here

245

and there. What better mission for *La Résistance* than to save the lives of our citizens, or for that matter, any freedom-loving people? Our credo is not just to kill the enemy, but to preserve everyone's rights and liberties. This is what France has always stood for, and frankly, I too, am surprised at you gentlemen.

The three men were taken aback, and apologized for their remarks. It was agreed that Marcel should lead the operation, after getting all the logistics worked out. He said that he would report the progress to the group at a later meeting.

More discussions followed about other covert operations, especially disrupting communications and railway transportation. Marcel, and his unit, were commended more than once, for their heroic feats over the last few months.

After the meeting was adjourned, Marcel made his way back to his group in the *bories*, outside Gordes.

30

In the guise of a family and friend's picnic, Raphaël Barton and his family, and Marcel Pontier and his, minus Babette and Madeline, hiked up *Le Canigou*. It was a very brisk Saturday morning, but the sun was shining and there were no complaints. There was even some dusting of snow in the lower elevations, which reinforced Marcel's urgency with this matter.

The day after Marcel had been in Elne, Paul and J.P. had driven out to the Barton's dairy farm. Their horse-drawn wagon had several bushels full of vegetables to trade for milk, in case there were any Germans curious of their destination. They met with Raphaël, and told him about their concern for the Jews, who needed to get out of France.

Not having mentioned Marcel's name, Raphaël brought it up, himself. "I'm sure that Marcel is involved with this, isn't he?" Neither one of them responded, but merely looked at him curiously. "That's alright…I'm quite familiar with Marcel's activities. You see, I am also a member of *La Résistance*, and have met with him, on occasion, so please feel free to discuss anything you wish."

"I'm sorry I told a secret, *Monsieur* Barton," J.P. said, "but I thought it was important information my father should have."

Raphaël put his arm around J.P.'s shoulder. "You did the right thing…it is something that could help your father, and hopefully save some lives."

"We don't know exactly when Marcel will be coming back," Paul said, "but we wanted to get your help in setting this up. From what I've gathered from J.P., you obviously have been up that mountain many times, as I have, but I've never seen the tunnels." He paused and tapped his right knee. "To tell you the truth, Raphaël, I don't know if these old knees could make the hike anymore."

Raphaël agreed to help in any way that he could, and suggested the picnic idea, the next time Marcel was in town. He would be ready to go at a moment's notice. He invited Paul into the house for coffee and Gisele's freshly baked cookies, while J.P. and Sylviane played hide-and-go-seek around the barn.

Now it was three days later, and the group was having its picnic lunch on *Mont Canigou*. They took an alternate route to get here, two kilometers northwest, because there was a German patrol near the path Raphaël usually took. After lunch, while the children played in the fields, Raphaël showed Marcel the entrance to the tunnels, and this mental image of the layout was all Marcel needed to devise a plan.

Marcel had received Angelina's message, and surprised everyone by sneaking into Elne the night before, via an underground cistern, that led out to the River Tech. It was the first time in months that Marcel and Angelina had made love, and it was as passionate as either one could remember. That morning, Paul drove back out to the Barton's, and arranged the meeting for early that afternoon.

It was a relaxing day for everyone, especially Marcel, but to avoid running into Captain Weller, he departed shortly after coming down the mountain. He felt good about the shelter that the railroad tunnels would provide, and to help Simon would be personally gratifying to him. He now had to lay out his plans carefully, before presenting them to a special session of the Council. Florette would have to be notified immediately, in order to make the arrangements. Time was of the essence with winter coming.

31

It was late afternoon, in Major von Klemper's office. He, Johann, and the other officers were gathered around a conference table. Maps and topographies were covering the table, as Johann laid out the plans for the defensive measures to be taken on the beach. "By observing the tides along the coast, we know now that they can be extreme." He unrolled another drawing to emphasize his point. "So, in my opinion, we need to put the underwater barriers, and mines, at least another 50-100 feet further into the sea. I would not want our first two lines of defense to be sticking out of the water, for the enemy to see."

This was the first significant bit of information that Paulette had heard, listening behind the wall of her office, which was to the right of the major's. Fearing that someone might pass, she closed her door and stood next to her open file cabinets, and pretended to look through the files. What she heard only confirmed what *La Résistance* projected to be the German plan.

"But," the major said, "they would be able to spot the ones closer to shore, I presume."

"Yes, of course," Johann answered, "that is unavoidable if we have an ebb tide; although, from what I gathered in my meetings in Frankfurt, before coming to France, the High Command strategists assume that the Allies would never attack on an ebb tide and take the risk of getting bogged down in soft muck, further away from the shoreline." He looked over the drawing one more time, stretching it out on the table for everyone to see. He pointed back and forth across one of the sections. "Now in this area, between the shoreline and approximately 100 feet out, we will be laying a series of shallow-water mines, and, at a few key places along the coast, we will be placing a newly developed, special 70 kilogram concrete mine."

The junior officers all looked at each other, and then at Johann, with questioning stares. "Please explain this to them, *Hauptmann*," von Klemper said.

"Well, what I just mentioned is considered top secret, and only Major von Klemper and I were privy to it. Since all of you will be working on this project, this is on a need-to-know basis, but I stress that this is still a top secret development, and should anyone leak this out, even to the enlisted men under you, it would be considered a treasonable act. Does everyone understand this?"

They all nodded their heads, and responded, "*Ja, Hauptmann.*"

One of the young officers raised his hand, and asked, "*Hauptmann*, exactly how much more damage can one of these new mines do, compared to the ones we have been working with?"

"Good question, *Leutnant*." Johann coughed a few times before continuing. "Where our smaller mine can only destroy, or do considerable damage to the APC that hits it, the large concrete one will explode under water, and can take out potentially everything within 100 to 150 feet."

There were gasps around the room. Johann coughed even longer this time, and then sneezed twice, before someone said "Bless you".

Johann wiped his nose, and said, "Excuse me…I must be getting all worked up about these mines." Everyone laughed, including the major, who very seldom laughed anymore. "Unfortunately, from what I understand, they are so expensive and hard to transport, that there will only be about six of these for the entire Southern coast. They will be brought down to Marseille by open-car rail. Then each one will be put on a barge in the port and transported to the six locations. It will require our underwater divers to assist in this special operation. Somehow, these concrete mines have got to be anchored and stabilized on the ocean floor. *Leutnant…*" he coughed again for several seconds, and then looked at his junior officer, "*Leutnant* Schammel, do you think your group will be able to handle this, or do we have to get some extra divers?"

The young officer thought for a moment, shook his head, and then said, "To tell you the truth, *Hauptmann*, I do not think our divers will be able to handle it alone."

"Why not, Schammel?" the major asked.

"Well, sir, it took the four men we have just to put in each of the barriers that we tested back in Germany…and that was in a relatively, calm river. In the sea, it could get fairly rough, not to mention its size. To be on the safe side, Major, we need to double what we have, as far as divers are concerned, and I would recommend extra men on the barge, to help unload this into the water."

"What is your opinion, *Hauptmann*?" von Klemper asked. "I do not like asking for more people, unless it is absolutely necessary."

Johann thought for a moment, walked to the blackboard on the wall, and drew a picture of the concrete mine. "As you can see, the structure is in the shape of a pyramid, and, as Schammel has suggested…if we have eight divers, one of them could be on each side of the pyramid, and one on each corner. These have not been tested yet, but I would imagine that the eight divers should be able to keep this steady, and prevent it from toppling over…once it does that, it would be almost impossible to get it back upright."

He allowed what he was saying to sink in. "Unfortunately, we are not sure how to proceed, since we did not have the luxury of testing it like the other pieces. So the first one we place in the water will be *our* on-the-job training…and yes, I would have to agree with the *Leutnant* about the extra men, Major. Since we don't have all the knowledge, the lack of manpower should not be the reason to botch this job."

"Alright, I will request the extra men," the major said, "but, can you see any other potential problems with this?

Johann drew a circle around the pyramid and several lines coming down to a floating device. "The biggest problem that I can see is getting it from the barge into the water, without it sinking. What I would like to try, Major, is to see if we can get it to float. It may not happen, but to manage it better, it is worth a try."

"To float, *Hauptmann*?" the major asked skeptically. "How in the world could you accomplish that?"

"My idea is to cover it with life preservers and have it sit in a large raft."

"Is that what those lines are attached to, a raft?" Lieutenant Schammel asked. Before Johann could answer, he said, "And then we would slowly deflate the raft and guide it toward the ocean bottom?"

"Precisely, *Leutnant*," Johann replied. "You would gradually have to remove the life preservers also, as you were descending." Johann let the men, who were all engineers, talk among themselves for a minute. "Like I said…it may not work at all, and then again, it could make your job a lot easier, and safer."

It was decided to try Johann's suggestions when the time came, and after a few more technical items were discussed, the major broke up the meeting. Most of the officers walked away with a new found respect for *Hauptmann* Weller, including Paulette, who had heard every word behind the wall. They all knew he was smart, but his demeanor and sureness put everyone at ease, and he had proven to all that he was a leader they would follow, no matter what the conditions were.

Paulette couldn't wait to get home and tell the others what she had learned from the meeting in Major von Klemper's office. The children were still outside, playing in the square with their friends, when Paulette conveyed all the information to her parents and sister.

"This is more valuable than you can imagine, Paulette," Paul said. "In essence, we've learned the German's coastal strategy. It must be passed on immediately to Marcel, who will surely pass it on to Allied intelligence."

"I'll go to the bridge tomorrow," Angelina said, "but, I don't think that it would be a good idea to write all this down. If by chance it was intercepted, and fell into the German's hands, we could all be in danger."

"Yes, you're right," Paulette said. "I would suggest that you do as before… simply leave an anonymous note, such as 'need to see you at once'."

Elizabeth leaned forward on the table. "And what did Marcel say to do in an emergency…paint something in red, on the other side of the bridge?"

"Oh yes, I remember!" Angelina exclaimed, "…the two bar Cross of Lorraine. I'll do that also."

A little later, when Paulette was alone with Angelina, she said, "I hope you won't have any trouble with the guards at the gate. Johann never mentioned the incident again."

"You know," Angelina said, "I forgot to tell you, that the other day I took Madeline for a walk outside the city walls. The same soldiers were at the gate and were bending over backwards to be nice to me. I think the captain must have really chewed them out, and now I can walk through without any problems."

Paulette nodded her head. "Well, all I can say is that I think that it's lucky that he's living here, and not one of those other officers. You should have heard him conduct that meeting this afternoon…he was very articulate…very impressive."

"It sounds like you two have built up a very good rapport, Paulette."

"Yes, something like that. He is nice…it's just too bad he's German."

It was 7:30 that same evening, following dinner. Elizabeth and Angelina were washing and drying the dishes. Light, French music was playing on the radio. It was a quiet time in their home, especially tonight, knowing that Johann was upstairs in his room. At the dining room table, Raymond was doing his homework, and J.P. was working on a model airplane, with Paul standing over his shoulder.

In her bedroom, Paulette sat on the bed reading a book, with her legs up and a pillow behind her back. At the foot of the bed, Babette combed the hair of one of her dolls. It was a very tranquil time, only broken when Johann came down the stairs, wearing his army gray pants, a brownish-gray shirt, suspenders, and his black boots.

"*Bonsoir,*" Johann said as he entered the room.

Without enthusiasm, or looking up, everyone in the room answered, "*Bonsoir.*"

Johann walked over to Elizabeth and Angelina. "How is everyone this evening?"

Paulette, thinking she heard something, pulled off her glasses, and turned her head to one side. When her sister started to speak, she put her glasses back on and continued to read.

Angelina, wearing a blue dress and apron, turned around slightly, and said, "Fine, Captain...and you?"

"Oh, I have a bit of a cold, I believe. I came back to my room earlier than usual tonight, to rest."

"Can I fix you some hot water and thyme?" Elizabeth asked. "That might help."

On hearing this, Paul turned around and sneered at his wife.

"Yes...that would be nice," Johann replied. "Thank you. My mother always makes me drink that, whenever I have the sniffles." While Elizabeth got a cup and saucer and began to prepare the drink, Johann walked over to the table next to Paul, who shrugged away to sit in his chair. "Jean-Pierre, what kind of aircraft is that?"

Hearing Johann's voice, Paulette took off her glasses, put them with her reading material on the bed, and walked into the main room.

"It's supposed to be a *Mauran*...a French fighter plane," J.P. said, "but I don't have all the pieces."

"That is too bad...it is..."Johann paused when he saw Paulette. They looked at each other for several seconds, and then Johann turned back to J.P. and continued, stumbling over his words. "It is...it is, ah...very fine airplane." He looked back at Paulette. "Hello, Paulette."

Angelina felt some tension in the air, and turned around to observe.

Paulette, wearing a printed dress, walked across the table from Johann, and greeted him matter-of-factly. "Hello, Captain. Thank you for the supplies...I found them on my desk after lunch."

Elizabeth poured hot water into a cup, and handed it, with the saucer, to Johann. "This should make you feel better, Captain."

Johann took a sip. "Aah…that is good. Thank you, *Madame* Courty."

Paul looked over the top of his book, sneered, put his feet up on the ottoman, and continued reading, while shaking his head.

Elizabeth ignored Paul, observing Johann instead. "You must not have eaten…would you care for something?"

Paul threw his head back in disbelief. *What is with my wife?*

"I am really not hungry, but thank you anyway." Johann took another sip and then looked at Paulette. "Well…yes…it was good that I ran into you this morning…our shipment just arrived. Let me know if you need anything else for the office."

Today you've given me much more than you can imagine, Paulette thought. "Yes, I'll do that." She abruptly changed the subject, putting her hands on Raymond's shoulders. "So, Raymond…what are you studying?"

Raymond continued to look down and write. "Science and evolution." He paused, and then asked, "I still don't understand where God fits into all of this?"

Johann and Paulette both smiled, with Johann answering, "Aaah… that is a difficult question."

While still doing the dishes with Angelina, Elizabeth turned around and said, "All you have to know is that God created everything…and leave it at that."

"But…" Raymond held up his index finger, about to say something else, when Babette came into the room, wearing her flannel nightshirt and robe.

"I'm ready for bed now, *Maman*."

Angelina dried off a dish, put it on the counter, and took off her apron. "All right, darling…say goodnight to everyone. *Tante* Paulette and I will take you to bed." She glanced at Raymond and J.P. "Boys,

I want you to go upstairs in a little while and finish your homework before bed."

"Yes, *Maman*," they answer.

"I'll be coming upstairs, too," Elizabeth said. "It's been a long day."

Babette proceeded to hug Paul around the neck and Raymond on the arm. J.P. hugged her with both arms. Then she walked over to Johann and looked up at him. "Are Marlena and Sigrid going to come and play soon?"

Johann put his hand on her shoulder. "I wish they could, then all of this foolishness would be over; but, I am afraid it will be awhile yet."

"OK...goodnight, Johann." Babette hugged him around his leg.

Johann patted her on the head. "Goodnight...sweet dreams."

"Tell Hermie I said goodnight, too." Babette skipped toward her room, with Angelina and Paulette following.

"I will," Johann said, "and I will be sure to tell him you asked about Marlena and Sigrid." Before closing the door, Paulette smiled at him and he smiled back. He put his cup and saucer on the table next to a chessboard that was sitting there. He sat down, took a sip of his thyme, picked up a chess piece, and looked it over before putting it back in place. "Who has been playing chess?" he asked the boys.

Raymond looked up from his book. "*Grandpere* and I played before dinner. He made a lucky move and beat me."

J.P. laughed. "Oh, sure. *Grandpere* could beat you in his sleep."

"Oh, yeah? I've beaten *Grandpere* a few times...haven't I, *Grandpere*?"

Paul looked up from his book, over his glasses. "What's that... Yes...Yes you have...getting much better."

Johann looked on amused, as the two boys bantered with one another.

"Besides...I'd kill *you* in a game, anytime," Raymond says to J.P. "You can't concentrate for more than two seconds."

"Raymond…I don't even play chess. And if I did, I'd beat you, like I do at everything else."

"Well, that's because I've been sick and can't play outside as much."

With his voice slightly raised, Paul said, "Boys…boys…stop arguing all the time. There are better things to do."

"Raymond," Johann said, "would you like to play a game of chess with me? I am a little rusty, but I could give you a decent game."

"Thank you, but *Maman* wants us to come upstairs and finish our homework…and go to bed." Raymond stood up, gathered his books, and motioned to J.P. "C'mon…let's go." He looked at Johann. "Maybe when I have more time. Goodnight."

Johann nodded, as Raymond walked towards the stairs. "I will look forward to it. We will do it another time."

J.P. got up and left his stuff on the table. "Goodnight, *Grandpere*… Goodnight, Johann." He walked briskly toward the stairs.

"Goodnight," Johann said, "and thank you for helping Hermann with his French."

"Goodnight, boys," Paul called up after them with a louder voice. "I'm going to need your help with some things tomorrow."

There was an awkward, half minute silence, as Johann sipped his tea and played with the chess pieces. Paul squirmed in his chair, continued to read, then stopped, shook his head and body slightly as if it's uncomfortable to be sitting there, and went back to his reading.

Johann looked around the room and then back at the board. Finally, in a soft voice, said, "*Monsieur* Courty, could I interest you in a match?"

Paul didn't hide the fact that he was uneasy…squirming in his chair, sneering, and with a grunt, said, "Hmmp!"

Johann, in a rejected tone, said, "I understand perfectly, if you do not wish to play." There was silence for a few seconds. He took a sip of his drink, put down the cup and was starting to get up, when Paul gruffly spoke.

"Am I expected to lose?"

"*Monsieur*, I would not play if I thought that. If you cannot win with honor…"

Indignantly, Paul cut him off, "*Honor*? Since when have the Germans been honorable? They've broken every damn treaty they ever made!"

"Regardless of what you think about my government, most Germans are honorable people. I can not make excuses for what has happened over the last ten years." He looked away and softly said, "It is unfortunate and embarrassing."

Paul was silent for a few seconds, and then nodded his head back and forth. He got out of his chair, walked to the table, picked up a pawn off the chessboard, put it behind his back, and hid it in his right hand. He then put both hands out in front of him for Johann to see. Johann looked at Paul's hands, then at his face, then back at his hands. He pointed to Paul's left hand, but Paul opened his right hand to reveal the pawn, then sat down across from Johann, took a deep breath, and let it out.

"My move." As a general going into battle, Paul's expression was serious and confident as he moved: Pawn to D4. His expression was tense, as he folded his arms and watched his opponent.

Johann squared himself to the chessboard, looked at it for a couple seconds, and moved: Pawn to D5. He sat back, put his elbows on the table, folded his hands and stared at Paul, who stared back at him with his arms still folded.

The tension continued like this throughout the match, consisting of two more moves for each man…Paul: Bishop to F4…Johann: Pawn to G6…Paul: Queen to C3…Johann: Bishop to G7. Neither man spoke, but stared, squirmed, frowned, sighed, and fidgeted in their chairs.

Finally, Paul made his fourth move: Queen to C7, sat back, put both hands on the table, and declared in a victorious, drawn-out word, "Ch-eckkk!"

Expressionless, the two men looked at each other, stood up, shook hands, and retired upstairs for the night.

32

They met in Simon Cadeaux's upstairs apartment, each of the four men coming two hours apart to Carcassonne. It was four days after the *Maquis* meeting in Montelimar. First to arrive was Raphaël Barton, followed by Marcel, and two of Simon's *Maquis* group. Florette had come the night before, to make sure that everything was on schedule.

"Since Marcel has organized this from the beginning," Florette began, "I'll let him brief you on the details of the mission...Marcel."

"*Merci*, Florette. First, let me say that it was Raphaël's knowledge of the mountains, which will allow us to get Simon's family, and others, across the border into Spain. Just after dark tonight, we'll be taking down fifteen people in five cars, to three safe houses, which Raphaël has prearranged. The houses are very close to the path we'll be taking tomorrow morning to get us up *Le Canigou*, and eventually to these abandoned railroad tunnels that cut through the mountains. If all goes well, we'll be in Spain by late afternoon. Do you have anything to add, Raphaël?"

Raphaël looked at the two men from Simon's *Maquis* group, whom he had worked with before on a mission similar to this one. "The only thing I can add to what Marcel has already told you, is that the route we're taking is further north than the one we've used before the Germans came into Elne. We're hoping that they won't be watching the entrance to this area…at least they weren't when Marcel and I scouted it out recently. The tunnels, to my knowledge, have never been used for this type of mission; actually, they never needed to be, because we always went in warmer weather, and could take the lower route to cross the border."

"If we run into a snowstorm up there," Marcel said, "the tunnels will give us the maximum protection." He paused to collect his thoughts, and then said, "Simon, just make sure that all your people dress as warmly as possible, and take as little with them as they can. If we're stopped on the roads by the *Vichy*, or the German patrols, we don't want it to look like any more than a day's outing in the country."

"Yes, I thought as much so," Simon said, "and I've already informed them to bring picnic lunches, and plenty of wine. There's one question I don't think I've asked you. Is there going to be anyone on the other side to meet our group?"

Florette spoke up, for the first time. "We have sympathizers in Spain, who we've used before and…"

"The same ones that my *Maquis* met several months ago?" Simon asked.

"Those and three more," Florette answered. "We had one of our intelligence people slip back and forth across the border, in the last two days, and arranged everything. Once you're across, all of you will be taken to a small, Catalonian town near Lleida, in the western part of the region. There are farms there for everyone to live and work, until the War has ended."

Simon had tears in his eyes. "I can't thank all of you enough for what you're doing, and sacrificing for my family and the others."

"Simon," Florette began, "you have single-handedly done more for France, and the Maquis movement, than any of us here today. We could never repay you for that, nor would you even expect it. We're doing this only to help Frenchmen, who are in danger, get out of the country…just as you have done in the past for other Frenchmen."

"Personally," Marcel said, "you've become a good friend, and I hate to see you leave us."

"*Merci beaucoup*, my friends," Simon replied, "but, I have no intention to stay in Spain. I merely wanted to get the others across safely, so I won't have to worry about them." He shrugged his shoulders. "You see, by myself I'm in the same position as all of you, without the added weight of having a Jewish family. I am foremost a Frenchman… my family has lived here for hundreds of years, and now, I merely want to go into the hills with my *Maquis* fighters. I'll do everything I can to make those Nazi bastards' lives miserable." He looked at Florette. "You've had me working on planning and intelligence for the last two years, and only on occasion did I get out in the field." He chuckled for a moment. "Now, Florette, with the roundup of Jews all over France, you have no choice, because I surely can't stay here any more."

Florette gave him a big smile. "Simon, I am *so* happy that you're not leaving, that you can choose to do whatever you would like."

Simon's two men came over to him and each gave him an embrace. One of them said, "We need you with us in our camp. It will make it a lot easier for all of us with you right there."

"I'm thrilled that you're staying, Simon," Marcel said, "and I look forward to doing more missions with you." He walked over to shake Simon's hand, and putting his arm around his shoulder, he said, "Well, what do you say we all stagger out of here, in 15 minute intervals, pick up our people at the designated places, and be on our way? Everyone knows where to meet tomorrow morning, and if there is any enemy activity in the area, then return to your safe houses near there. Are there any further questions?" Everyone shook their heads. "OK, I'll lead off and Simon will be the last one to leave."

He started for the door, gave Florette a kiss on both cheeks, and proceeded down the stairs.

Using the back roads, the two hour journey to the South was unremarkable for all of the cars. Unbeknownst to them, had they used the main highway, they could have run into several German patrols, which were randomly stopping, and searching vehicles. Marcel had been designated to pick up two of Simon's cousins, who were from Paris, and had been living with Simon's family for the last six months. The stories they told him of the Nazi brutality in the North should not have astounded him, but they did, nevertheless. Here were two people, who had seen other members of their families taken away in trucks, to be deported to the East.

It made Marcel furious to hear reports like this, but at the same time, it strengthened his resolve for *Le Combat. Getting Frenchmen across the border, like these people who are in danger, should become a top priority for the Maquis,* he thought, *just as the Chairman had said.*

He and the couple from Paris spent the night at a farmhouse, and after having a hearty breakfast the next morning, the farmer took them to their meeting point, leaving Marcel's car parked at the farm. There were no signs of any patrols, and when they arrived at the path that would take them up the mountain, the others were waiting for them.

Raphaël led the way up a winding path and through the woods. Everyone had been briefed by a *Maquis* member, so there was no reason to linger any longer than need be. After 45 minutes, the trees started to thin out, and they soon came above the tree line, which would be like this until they reached Spain.

"I think that this would be a good resting place for about 20 minutes," Raphaël said to the group. "If you want to go to the bathroom and need some privacy, walk back into the woods a little ways." All the women and children headed in that direction, along with some of the men.

"Well, Raphaël, so far so good," Marcel said. "How do you think everyone is holding up, Simon?" he asked, as Simon approached them.

"They're a little bit out of breath, but no one is complaining," Simon replied, a little winded himself. "It looks like it's going to get much steeper up ahead, so I would request that you stop more often, Raphaël."

"Yes, of course. I'm glad you told me. Having lived here all my life, I'm used to hiking in the mountains and don't realize how the altitude affects different people."

After everyone had rested, Raphaël said, "Try to take short, even breaths, instead of real, deep ones that might make you hyperventilate, or give you altitude sickness. Also, drink a little bit of water every few minutes, so you won't dehydrate." He scanned the group, to make sure everyone was alright. "OK, let's move out...our next stop will be at the first tunnel, in about 20 minutes."

Most of the people couldn't keep up with Raphaël's pace and had to take more frequent breaks. Nearly 40 minutes later, the land flattened out into a mesa, and they could now see the tunnel. As they walked towards it, Marcel spotted a plane in the distance. It appeared to be coming in their direction, and he made a quick decision. He didn't think that they could all reach the tunnel, before the plane flew overhead, and didn't want to bring attention to a group of people running.

"All right, everyone...as quickly as you can, spread out your blankets and sit on the ground. There's a small plane headed our way, so let's pretend that we're just picnicking."

They did as they were told, and were sitting on their blankets much quicker than Marcel could have imagined. Ten seconds later, a single engine, *Messerschmitt* fighter plane, flew 300 feet directly over them. They could easily see the pilot's face.

"Where in the hell do you think he came from?" Simon asked, still looking up in the sky. "We had better sit here for awhile, to see if he circles back this way."

It was already mid-morning, and they needed to eat, so Marcel said, "Simon is right…it's better not to move too quickly from this spot, in case he does decide to come back…so bring out some of the food, and we'll have a snack now."

For the next half hour, the adults ate and talked among themselves, while the children played on the hilltop meadow. From the air, they looked like a big family having a picnic. The pilot, after patrolling the border further west, decided to take another sweep of *Mont Canigou* before returning to his base. He popped up quickly over the higher alps, and surprised everyone in Marcel's group. As he flew overhead again, the Iron Cross on his plane was so large, some thought that they could reach up and touch it. This only confirmed the pilot's first instinct, that this was a family enjoying themselves on a beautiful, Saturday morning. As a normal greeting, he rocked his wings back and forth as he flew by, heading northeast.

"I would guess that the Germans have taken over the airport in Perpignan for the *Luftwaffe*," Marcel said.

"That would seem like the most logical place," Raphaël replied. "They must have it under very tight security, but it's worth checking out, if for no other reason than to report it to intelligence."

"I concur," Simon said. "The Allies need to know where these airfields are located. When the invasion does occur, they'll be taken out quickly. I would recommend, Marcel, that you don't even consider any covert actions against the airfields, or the *Luftwaffe*, unless you have definite orders to do so…the risk factor is way too high."

"Now, why would you think that I would want to attack the *Luftwaffe*?"

"Because, I've gotten to know you too well, and I know the way your mind thinks." Simon laughed. "I could almost see the wheels turning in your head, when we started talking about it."

"You are becoming quite a legend, Marcel," Raphaël added. "We've been seeing a lot of J.P. lately, and I think he's going to turn out to be just like you."

"Poor boy," Marcel said. "Well, do you think we should get under way?"

They all gathered up the blankets and baskets of food and water, and followed Raphaël to the first tunnel, which turned out to be one kilometer long. When they emerged from it, they were higher up and there was snow on the ground. Putting on their extra, warmer clothes that were in their lunch baskets and tied around their waists, they hiked for another hour before they came to the second tunnel. There they warmed up and rested inside for an hour.

"I've got good news for you," Raphaël told everyone. "When we emerge from this tunnel, we'll be going downhill." Everyone clapped and cheered, as he continued. "So, the point we're at right now is the highest we'll have to go; but we still have a few more hours of hiking, and it can be hard on your knees, so try to lean backwards as we're walking." He paused for a few seconds. "The best of the good news is that we may technically be in Spain right this minute." More cheers.

As Raphaël had promised when they emerged from this tunnel, they were heading downhill, and 40 minutes later came to the third and last tunnel. Here they rested again for a short while, then walked through and were greeted by a picturesque, Spanish valley. Within minutes, four Spanish agents, working with the *Maquis*, were there to meet them with wine and snacks.

There were a lot of tearful goodbyes between Simon and his family, not knowing whether they would ever see each other again. No one in his family said anything about his staying with them in Spain. They knew that his mind was made up to stay in France and fight with the *Maquis*.

After 30 minutes had passed, Simon suggested that he and the other four men start back across the mountains. Marcel didn't want to tear Simon away, and was thankful that Simon had recommended that they leave. They took a couple baskets of food and drinks that were left over. Everyone said their thanks and farewells, and the men started hiking up the mountain, never looking back. It was now 3:30 in the afternoon.

"How far do you think we'll be able to go tonight?" Marcel asked Raphaël, after they had gone through the first tunnel.

Raphaël looked up in the sky, and thought for a moment. "It will probably get dark by 5:30, so we have almost two hours of good hiking to do before that. That should put us somewhere between the second and third tunnels. The questions are, how cold and tired we will be, and what kind of visibility will we have? There *is* a full moon tonight, so that's a plus, but if it gets too cold for anyone, then I would suggest we spend the night in the second tunnel and leave at daybreak."

Since no one had any problem keeping up, they were more than halfway between the second and third tunnels when the sun started to set. They continued on to the first tunnel, stopped to rest and eat, and even though the temperature had dropped 30 degrees, they agreed to try to make it down the mountain that night. At 7:00, they emerged from the tunnel, found the main trail that led down *Le Canigou*, and before long, they were approaching the woods.

They walked for 10 minutes more, when they first saw the flashlights spread out across the mountain, 150 meters below them. Raphaël halted everyone in their tracks, as they all stood there and listened for a moment. The voices coming through the woods were definitely German, and without hesitation they turned around and headed back up the mountain as fast as they could. Fortunately, Raphaël knew the way well enough to lead them off the main path, and back into the tunnel, where they huddled together for warmth.

They were all out of breath and freezing, but the tunnel at least gave them some protection. Marcel was the first to speak, and then it was in a whisper with his teeth chattering. "I think it would be better if we moved to the back of the tunnel, secure a position behind some rocks, or just find a hiding place outside if they find this place."

They moved to the back and waited. Simon's two men assembled their rifles, which were broken down in their backpacks...the other three took out their pistols.

"Try to keep as quiet as possible," Marcel whispered, as the men gathered around him.

"There's no way for them to see us from above," Raphaël added, "and the tunnel has all that growth in front of it, so you would really need to know where you were going at this time of night, to see the opening."

They huddled together for another ten minutes, before they heard voices above them, and to the right. They tensed when they saw lights going back and forth past the brush at the end of the tunnel, but that ceased very quickly, as the Germans made their way further up the mountain. Over the next few minutes, the voices became louder as the soldiers discussed their situation almost directly above Marcel and his men.

Simon held up a finger, like he was about to speak, but then thought better of it, and waved it off. They could tell that the soldiers had gone up further, but then heard them coming back again, and from their voices, definitely retreating down the mountain. It was then that Simon quietly spoke. "I was about to tell you what the Germans were saying, when they were overhead, but I thought I had better wait until they were gone." He paused. "Apparently, that pilot reported that he had seen a group of us picnicking on top of the mountain, earlier in the day, and the army obviously came here to check and see if anyone was trying to escape across the border. Well, it appears from what they were saying, it was too rugged to cross these mountains into Spain, and everyone would probably freeze to death at the higher altitudes."

"I'm happy they think that way," Marcel said, "and it does sound like they've moved down the mountain...which I think we ought to do, before we *do freeze* to death." He stood, and everyone else followed suit, as Marcel led them through the tunnel in the darkness. "Please no flashlights...we don't want to take a chance of being spotted."

"It's good that they haven't found out about the tunnel, yet," Simon said, as they walked. "Hopefully, we can continue to use it and bring a lot more people through."

"Yes," Marcel said, "this is an ideal situation that Raphaël found for us. It's best that we keep this to ourselves and not talk about it with anyone else...even our fellow *Maquis* members."

"You're right, Marcel," Simon said. "The fewer people that know about it, the safer our missions will be. I would also suggest that we monitor the flying schedules of the *Luftwaffe* in this area. That way, we'll know what times they'll be watching the coast, and can get our people up the mountain without being spotted."

271

"Excellent idea, Simon," Raphaël said. "Since this is more in my area, I'll have my men start logging their flights immediately, unless you have other ideas, Marcel?"

Marcel could now sense that the men were deferring to him more and more, and his leadership role was becoming greatly enlarged. He was comfortable in this position and thankful that he had very capable men working with him.

"Thank you Raphaël," Marcel said. "You know this area better than anyone else, so please go ahead and get this information as soon as you can. Either I or Florette will be in touch with you." Before they reached the end of the tunnel, Marcel asked, "Does anyone know of any other means of getting over the border?"

After a moment, Simon said, "You know, my family and I have been taking some of our holidays in Andorra over the last few years, and since it's a neutral principality, it might be worth looking into for a place for refugees. It's quite small, you know, only 20 kilometers or so across, but it may be a good alternative for a small number of these people...I'll discretely check it out, Marcel."

Marcel nodded his head. "That may work out, Simon. I never even thought of Andorra, and the border can't be more than what...three hours by car from Carcassonne?"

"That's about right," Simon agreed. "Andorra la Vella is a lovely city, and I do have some jewelry contacts there, if I'm still able to get through to them. But it's definitely not a good winter alternative for conducting our missions."

"Why is that?" Raphaël asked.

"Well, the main reason is that the altitude is much higher...you know, it's the largest ski resort in the Pyrenees and very cold in winter." He paused and thought for a moment. "But, now that I think about it, the altitude isn't that bad near the border...it's getting through the mountains after that I'm concerned about." He was silent for a moment, and then said, "The positive thing about the Andorran border is there are no major French cities or towns near there, and therefore, the Germans may not have thought this area worthy of their troops. Anyway, I will look into the feasibility of it."

They remained very quiet when they reached the opening of the tunnel. Without saying a word, Simon communicated to his two men with hand signals, and they very slowly moved out to check the immediate area and that above them. One of the men came back to tell the remaining three that the coast seemed clear. They had also spotted what looked like a troop truck heading back toward Elne. Because it was too far away, he couldn't be sure if a smaller vehicle stayed behind at the bottom of the mountain.

"We had planned to go back the same way we came up, anyway," Raphaël said, "so that shouldn't bother us, even if the Germans are watching the normal route. All we have to do is stay on the left side of this ridge and spread out before we reach the woods."

"That sounds like the plan," Marcel said. "Let's not get all clumped together like sitting ducks. Lead the way, Raphaël."

To be extra cautious, Raphaël led them even further west, and when they came through the woods, they were directly across from the house where their cars were parked. He made a mental note to *take future groups up the mountain on this route, even though it was a slightly harder climb.*

After thawing out in the safe house and having a hot meal, everyone fell asleep quickly from exhaustion. The mission was a success and laid the groundwork for many more like this to come.

33

Over the next month, the overall situation for the French people got considerably worse. Further rations and restrictions were put into effect, mainly to increase production of goods to be shipped back to Germany. The citizens of Elne were starting to feel the pressures of occupation, almost unknown to them before November 12th. The Courtys, like others who grew some crops, had it better than most. After giving a large percentage to the Administrator for the Occupational Forces, they still had an adequate amount to feed their family, plus exchange some for other things they didn't have, with their neighbors and friends.

Things were changing for Paulette and Johann also, as neither could suppress the feelings they were developing for each other. Even though they didn't show it openly, each thought about the other on a daily basis. They were quite friendly at the office, and the short times that Johann was in the house. She knew that he felt like an intruder into their home and tried to spend as little time there as possible, respecting their privacy. She liked him even more for that reason, but at the same time, she was still having guilt feelings for even thinking about him.

On Christmas Eve, December 24, 1942, Paulette felt bad that Johann had to spend the holiday by himself. *Yes, there were his men and the other officers, but it wasn't the same*, she thought. She couldn't bring herself to ask her parents if he could join them, even though her father was getting along better now with Johann. Their first chess game had apparently broken the ice, and now Paul was asking Johann to join him for tea and chess, on occasion.

After dinner, the family gathered in the main room near the fire place. It had gotten rather cold outside, and this was the coziest place in the house. The adults sat and watched the children decorate the nativity scene on the floor. They moved the figures around from one part of the scene to another, and for the first time in many weeks, there was a joyous mood in their home.

"These Christmas cookies are delicious, *Grandmere*," Raymond said, as he, J.P. and Babette ate the special treats that Elizabeth had made for the holiday.

"Well enjoy them now, children," Elizabeth replied, "because there's not enough flour left to make anything like this for a long time. Maybe we'll get…" She stopped speaking long enough for everyone to hear three raps coming from the bedroom.

Excitedly, Angelina said, "Marcel!"

Angelina and Paulette rushed into the bedroom, with the others following immediately. They picked up the rug and put it to the side. Angelina tapped three times and Marcel returned the signal, by tapping three times. Paul then reached down and pulled up the trap door, with Marcel slowly climbing up the ladder and coming into view of the others. He looked quite untidy, wearing dark wool pants, a plaid shirt and sweater vest, a black wool waist coat, and a blue beret. "It's Father Christmas," Marcel joked, as he stroked his beard. The children were all on the floor and Marcel hugged and kissed them all, before he finally climbed up.

"Oh, *mon Cheri*!" Angelina said, as she kissed and embraced Marcel. The children joined in, so that all five of them were intertwined. This was followed by hugs for Elizabeth, Paulette, and Paul. "Oh, darling… this is the best thing that you could have given us for Christmas. We've all missed you so much."

"I've missed all of you, more than you know," Marcel replied. "It's been terrible living in the hills. Some days, I can barely walk after sleeping on the ground all night."

"Let's all go sit down at the dining room table, and I'll fix you some Christmas dinner, Marcel," Elizabeth said. "You must be starved."

"Yes, I can surely use a nice, hot meal for a change, *Maman*." Angelina went to help her mother in the kitchen, as they all walked into the main room. Marcel put his arms around Raymond and J.P., while Babette hugged his leg. He noticed Paul quickly locking the door that led downstairs, before he sat down in his big chair. "So, where is your Nazi officer, Papa?"

Paulette winced at the way Marcel described Johann, but she understood his feelings.

"He won't be home for quite awhile…something about an officer's Christmas party, he told us this morning," Paul said. "I just want to be safe, in case he does come up the stairs."

"So tell me, Papa, how have you been getting along with him?" Marcel asked.

Paul thought about this for awhile, and to his surprise and everyone else's, he answered, "Well, to tell you the truth, and I never thought I'd be saying this, if it weren't for that uniform he's wearing, I think that even you would find him quite interesting, and humorous. He's very polite, to be sure."

"Hmm, really," Marcel said, as he turned to Paulette and asked, "And what are your feelings towards him?"

Paulette blushed, but in an as matter-of-fact tone as she could manage, she replied, "Oh, we get along fine at the office, and as Papa said, which surprises me to no end hearing it from him, Johann is really quite a nice person."

They could tell that Marcel wasn't very impressed, and he replied sarcastically, "Well, just remember that he *is* a German officer, working for a totalitarian regime, and would probably shoot you, if he found out that you were trying to sabotage their mission here."

Paul nodded his head, knowing that what Marcel was saying was probably true. Paulette simply ignored him, by sitting down at the table and thinking what she could do to change the subject. Fortunately for her, Elizabeth and Angelina came from the kitchen carrying the food that they had prepared for Marcel. He began eating heartedly, and said, "*Maman*, this is the best meal I've had in ages. It tastes like roast pig!"

"It is roast pig, darling," Angelina said. "We splurged tonight, because it's Christmas Eve.

"Really? It's wonderful...which one did you have to kill?"

J.P. jumped up enthusiastically and stood by his father. "Adolph number three, Papa. He was the largest and starting to make too much noise. I know the captain heard him once, and told us to try and keep him quiet. He said that he was afraid that his people in the commissary might ask us to give them the pig to feed the soldiers."

"Well, it's much better that we had him for dinner, right?"

"Yes, Papa," J.P. answered. "Raymond and I will try to save the other ones as long as we can."

"Good boys," Marcel said, continuing to eat until his plate was empty. He then looked over to his wife. "I got the two messages you left at the bridge, darling." He paused and then spoke to Paulette. "I was happy that my courier, here in Elne, relayed what you told him you heard about the German's mission on the beach, Paulette. I've passed this on to our intelligence, who were extremely impressed with this important information. By now, I'm sure it's in the hands of the Allies."

"I knew that you should get it as soon as possible, Marcel," Paulette said. "Your courier was very discrete when he approached me in the market, but I wasn't about to tell him anything, until he showed me the note from you. Will he be the same man that will contact me in the future...if you, or I need to pass on anything to each other, as we both did on this occasion?"

"Hopefully, but then again, in this business you never know. Just let Angelina continue to leave the messages at the bridge, and I'll have him contact you if I need something done here. By the way, you did a good job arranging to place the Rabbi from Lyon, in the Cloister."

"Oh, I'm glad," Paulette smiled. "I haven't heard how it's working out?"

Marcel began to laugh. "I just had a meeting with Monsignor Marois, and he said that Bernard Altman is now Father Maurice Duval, and is doing very well. The other priests look on him as their scholar-in-residence on the Old Testament." He paused and laughed again. "The other day, when Rabbi Altman was walking through the courtyard of the Monastery, two German soldiers stopped him...he was scared to death, but all they wanted was for him to hear their confessions. Well, since he speaks perfect German, he now has a list of other soldiers waiting to see him."

"So, what does the Monsignor say about all this?" Paulette asked.

"Oh, he's delighted. He taught the Rabbi all the right things to say...how to cross himself, what penance to dole out, the sacraments... the usual stuff priests do."

"I'm happy I was able to help…this may be a first for the Church. Heaven knows what the Vatican will say about all this." She was silent for a moment. "And what about the other refugees?"

"Well, thanks to all the documents you've gotten to us, Elne will become a major staging area to get them across the border to Spain. But there's no way to get anyone across the Pyrenees at this time of year, so we've been able to place people all over the countryside temporarily until spring. We had no choice with the Rabbi, but to bring him here." He paused. "So, what's happening, children?"

"It hasn't been too good for them," Angelina injected, before they could answer.

"They're only letting us go to school every other day, Papa," Raymond said.

"Why is that?" Marcel asked.

Paulette stood up to get a napkin, and spoke as she was doing so. "They're using some of the school, and the auditorium, to house the enlisted men. Plus the Germans have requisitioned the teachers to do a lot of the administrative work… I oversee most of this, so I'm able to pass you any information I feel is important."

"We have courier agents, like the one you met, linked throughout the countryside, so you'll be seeing him, or someone else from time to time to pick up this information," Marcel said. "We can't take a chance of passing this over the telephone, and the mail is all censored. The material that we've collected in all these small towns has really been helpful."

"It sounds like you're becoming more of a spy and intelligence officer, than anything else, Marcel," Paul said.

"You're right, Papa." Marcel stood and poured himself another glass of wine from the decanter sitting on the credenza. He took a sip and continued. "Most of my time…maybe 90%…is spent gathering information. The remaining 10% may get us involved in actually implementing this information, and possibly engaging, or disrupting the German's normal plans."

"Tell us some of the things you've done, Papa," J.P. said excitedly.

"Well J.P., I'm not at liberty to discuss certain things, but one thing I can tell you…we were unaware of a munitions factory near Bayonne that the Germans were getting their supplies from. After receiving *Tante* Paulette's message, we not only intercepted a convoy of munitions, but a few days later, the factory was blown up by a *Maquis* unit from the Bordeaux region." Marcel paused and then looked at Paulette. "You know, Paulette, most of *La Résistance* couriers are women."

Paulette was not surprised. "French women have always played a role in the defense of our country."

"A perfect decoy, using women," Paul said. "The Germans would never suspect a woman of being a 'terrorist', as they call them. They don't think they're capable of anything but cooking and raising children… I would never make an important decision about this farm without consulting Elizabeth."

Marcel laughed. "In Spain, they call that *Machismo*. Hell, we have women fighting alongside us now." Angelina gave him a questioning stare and he regretted saying that as soon as it came out of his mouth. He went over and embraced her, making light of what he said. "None as pretty as you, darling."

"I should hope not," Angelina said, backing away from him and ruffling his hair.

Marcel wanted to change the subject as quickly as possible. "Papa, how are we doing on time? I don't want to endanger any of you by being here."

"I'll go out on the balcony, so I can watch the Square," Paul said. "We don't want any surprises; even though I don't think he'll be home until much later."

"I think that's a wise thing to do, Papa," Paulette said. "We heard recently of a *Résistance* fighter who had his legs sawed off by the *Gestapo*…and his relatives were arrested, even though they had nothing to do with his actions."

"The Germans call that 'collective responsibility'. That's why I can't stay long," Marcel said. He could tell that the children were getting used to his comings and goings, because now they just gathered around him and didn't ask why he couldn't stay longer. He felt guilty about the short amounts of time he was spending with his family, and especially not seeing Madeline progress through her first few months. He assumed that she was sleeping now and he would take a peek at her before he left. Angelina walked over to Marcel and he asked her, "How are your supplies lasting?"

"We have shortages of everything…food, soap, heating fuels…the children need new clothes and shoes." Her voice quivered, as she was about to cry. "They're growing so fast, you know." Marcel put his arm around her, and she in turn put her head on his shoulder, as he comforted her. "I know I shouldn't complain, darling …you were right to bring us here. I'm sure the people in Marseille have it much worse."

"By the time milk reaches the cities, it's already sour and making the children sick," Marcel said.

"I wish I were a doctor, so I could help," Raymond said.

"Perhaps one day you will be, son," Marcel replied. "But what they really need now, is more food. They've just begun serving vegetable soup in the city schools to supplement the student's diets. Everyone is undernourished and many people are starving."

"I've heard that tuberculosis is on the rise," Paulette said.

Marcel picked up his glass of wine off the table and took a sip. "Yes, I've heard that too…almost twice the pre-war totals. Men and women in their twenties are in especially poor health, because the Nazis are working them to death in the factories. Yes, France is the most important supplier of raw materials and manufactured goods to the German economy."

"Marcel, what else do you hear from Marseille?" Angelina asked.

"I guess I didn't mention it, but I went back into Marseille for a meeting, just a few days ago. From what I've seen, the Jews really have it bad…the Marseille underworld has a license to loot their homes, and are being paid to round up men, women and children for deportation. One of my men told me he heard that the Germans have brought in some of their own *Einsatzkommandos*, who hunt and murder Jews anywhere they find them."

In the distance, they could hear soldiers marching from the direction of the Square. It got louder as they turned the corner and started coming down the Courty's street. When they almost approached the house, Paul called out, "Marcel, get in the bedroom. It's probably just their nightly patrol, but let's not take a chance. Boys, go in with your Papa, in case he has to go down into the cellar. We'll let you know when to come out, and be sure to put the rug back in its place."

Marcel, Raymond and J.P. went into the bedroom and shut the door. Paul was still on the balcony, and could see the patrol below him suddenly come to a complete stop. He couldn't understand what they were saying, but it looked like the sergeant in charge was pointing at his house. Paul went back inside, closed the door to the balcony, and went to the bedroom. As he entered, he saw that the rug had been removed and the trap door had been raised. He was about to tell Marcel what he had just seen, when they heard someone knocking at the front door.

"Marcel, get down the ladder, now, and stay in the loft," Paul said. "The soldiers are right outside our house. I'm going downstairs to see what they want, so boys, close the trap door when your Papa gets down the ladder...and be sure to put the rug back where it belongs."

The women and Babette were standing in the bedroom doorway, listening to what was being said. As Paul passed them, he said, "Stay busy with what you were doing before, in case they come up here...and put Babette to bed. I'll be back soon." With that said, he walked down the stairs and apprehensively opened the front door. He wasn't expecting what was awaiting him.

It was Sergeant Hermann Koch, Johann's aide, holding a big basket with a red ribbon on it. In almost perfect French, he said, "Merry Christmas, *Monsieur* Courty! Here is something that *Hauptmann* Weller and I would like to give for your lovely family, for being so nice to us as long as we have been here."

Paul was relieved, thinking what the consequences could have been if they were somehow looking for Marcel. He would have normally refused the gift, but he took it from Hermann and graciously said, "How nice of you to do this, Sergeant. It really wasn't necessary...thank you...and please thank the captain. *Bonsoir.*"

"*Bonsoir, Monsieur,*" Hermann smiled. He gave an order to the patrol and they began marching down the street.

Paul closed and locked the door behind him, and walked back up the stairs. He told the others what had happened, and there was a sigh of relief from everyone. The boys went back in the bedroom, took off the rug, opened the trap door, and called down to their father to come up.

Marcel was shocked to hear what had just transpired. "I was really getting concerned when you didn't come upstairs for awhile, Papa. I'll just have to be more careful with my visits, because that was too close for comfort."

Elizabeth came out of the kitchen holding a cloth sack, and gave it to Marcel. "I've prepared some food for you to take with you, and I put in some of your favorite almond paste with pistachios and melon jam."

"Thank you, *Maman*, but you didn't need to do all that." He took the food and put it in his knapsack. "But, this *will* save me the trouble of having to find some food in the morning."

"What else did you do in Marseille, besides your meeting, darling?" Angelina asked.

"It was quite close to our house, so I went by, and found out that none of the homes in our area are being occupied by the Germans," Marcel answered.

Babette was peeking out the door of her bedroom, listening to the conversation. "Did you bring us any of our things, Papa?"

Marcel put down his head and glared at her with one eye closed. "I thought I heard that *Grandpere* told you to go to bed?" He winked at her, and then jerked his head to one side, indicating for her to come to him. She ran to him and jumped up into his arms. "No, my sweet…I could only carry some valuables, which I hope *Grandpere* can sell, or trade for on the black market."

Marcel reached inside his undershirt and pulled up a money pouch, which was attached to a string around his neck. To everyone's astonishment, he opened the pouch and dumped the jewelry and coins on the table.

"Oh, *mon dieux*!" Angelina exclaimed. "These are the family heirlooms we had hidden away." She looked through the rest of the jewels, just shaking her head. "Here's your *Maman's* ring and your *Grandpere's* gold coins…I couldn't part with these!"

Marcel looked at her sternly. "Listen to me, Angelina…what's important, is keeping our family alive. If we had to sell everything in our house, it would be worth it."

"He's right," Paul said. "Now that my Army pension has been cut off, all we have to live on is what Paulette brings in, plus the little we make from the fruits and wine, and that has been cut back considerably." He looked over to Marcel, and said, "On the German's orders, I've had to hire someone to help us plow up three-quarters of our orchards and vineyards, and plant vegetables. The crop won't come in until late spring."

"I'm sure most of that will be sent directly to Germany," Marcel said. "Isn't that right, Paulette?"

"The majority of it, yes, and they'll pay us in Occupation Marks, which are so inflated, its ruining the economy of the area."

Marcel picked up some of the rings and coins on the table. "This is why these jewels and coins are so valuable."

"I understand, Marcel," Angelina said, as she went to the credenza and pulled out a satin pouch. She put all the jewelry and coins in the pouch, and without saying a word, handed it to Paul. "We have nothing left in our safety deposit box, do we?" she asked Marcel.

"No…fortunately I took everything out a year ago, except for some legal papers. The Nazis aren't respecting any personal ownership rights. Once you open your safety deposit box, one of their agents is there to confiscate all your securities and precious metals."

"The captain has been very nice to us, Papa," Babette said. "He's even brought us chocolates and other sweets."

"Oh, really?" Marcel said.

"Grandpere said it would be wrong to eat them, so we flushed them down the toilet," Raymond added. "J.P. gave some of his candy to his girlfriend, Sylviane."

"Sylviane Barton?" Marcel laughed. "So that's your girlfriend, huh?"

"She's not my girlfriend!" J.P. said emphatically. "She just helped me get milk for Madeline and Babette, so I gave her the chocolates as a gift."

"Actually," Angelina said, "the Barton's have been most generous in allowing us to trade some of our fruit and vegetables for fresh milk. They're one of the few farms that the Germans have allowed to keep their dairy cows…isn't that right, Paulette?"

"Most of the others have been confiscated for shipment back to *Deutschland*, or are being slaughtered here for the troops. The farmers get such a poor return on the sale of their fresh milk; they take half of it and turn it into cheese so it can be sold on the black market. The other half, like everything else, goes to the occupying troops."

"I don't blame the farmers…they've got to make a living for their families, too," Marcel said. "I'll have to thank Raphaël for the milk."

Madeline began crying, so Angelina went to the bedroom to get her up and change her. She brought her back into the dining room and handed her to Marcel. He held her close for quite awhile, and then put her in his lap where she held on to his fingers and cooed up at him. *I'm missing a lot, not being here with my family*, Marcel thought.

"Your children have been very helpful around the house, Marcel," Elizabeth said. "Babette has been folding clothes and watering the garden out back; and the boys are helping Paul plow under the orchards and planting the vegetables."

"That's wonderful that you are all helping out around the house and with *Grandpere*…"

"But, when will we be able to come with you and fight in the hills, Papa?" J.P. asked. "I want to know what you're doing, so when I get there, I'll be able to help you too."

Marcel looked at him sympathetically. "It's a very tough life, son… and you're much too young. We're never in one place for very long…we get the resources we need by constantly stealing equipment, clothing, or ration coupons." He paused long enough for this to sink in, and then continued. "As far as our mission goes, I can tell you that we're making life more difficult for the Germans, and we especially want to make it tough on anyone who collaborates with the enemy.

"We've attacked mayors' offices, banks, and tax offices, even in broad daylight. If bookstores, or newsstands, display German or *Vichy* magazines and newspapers, they're warned to remove them…if they don't, we break the windows as a further warning…and then blow up their businesses, or homes, if they continue."

"But, Marcel," Angelina said, "These are Frenchmen."

"They have a choice…just as the *Vichy* had a choice. Any Frenchman who helps the Germans in any way, except those trying to get information, is a traitor… and we have the names of every one of them. They can't make a move without our knowing about it. We have *Résistance* agents and sympathizers at every level of government."

"I guess that makes *Tante* Paulette an agent, doesn't it, Papa?" J.P. asked.

"Absolutely…she's given us some very valuable information." Marcel paused for a moment. "By the way, Paulette, do you think that anything has changed, as far as their thinking that the Allied invasion will come along the southern coast of France?"

"Not really…they believe it will come either there, or up the boot of Italy."

Angelina handed Marcel a bottle for Madeline. "I don't want you to forget how to feed the baby."

He took the bottle and put it in her mouth, while he continued their family discussion. "This aide of the Captain's, who brought the gift...what's his job?"

"Hermie is an observer in one of the towers of the cloister," Raymond said. "He and Johann talk back and forth on the radio all the time...I guess about the construction they're doing."

"We go up in the tower and visit him during the day," J.P. added. "We've been teaching him to speak French, and he's picking it up real well."

"He has two little girls, that are going to come and play with me one day," Babette said.

"We're learning a little German, too," Raymond said. "He and the captain are very nice...they must be the only good ones in Germany, huh, Papa?"

"There are a lot of nice people everywhere, son. It's these crazy dictators who want to conquer the world that mess everything up. They don't do the fighting, but have people like Johann and Hermie do it for them." He put Madeline on his shoulder and burped her. "Well, I haven't lost my touch, darling."

Three beeps from the radio are heard, and Paul signaled everyone with his hand, to be quiet. "It's the B.B.C.," he says.

"Good evening France. This is the B.B.C. The French speaking to the French. General Charles de Gaulle sends his wishes for a very happy Christmas to all of you. He knows of the atrocities committed by the Nazis, with arrests and hostage executions, and the suffering of many of you throughout France.

"Last month, Admiral Darlan appointed General Henri Giraud as commander-in-chief of the French Armed Forces in North Africa. Since then, French troops have been in action against the enemy in Tunisia, fighting by the side of American and British soldiers.

"On the Eastern Front, the Germans have given up the fight for Stalingrad, and are in partial retreat, as Russian troops take the offensive."

There was a five second pause; then slowly the B.B.C. announcer said, "This bulletin was just handed to me." He paused again. "I regret to inform you that French Admiral Darlan has been assassinated in Algiers."

There was a sad "Ohhh" from the adults, upon hearing the news.

"He was a true French hero," Paul said. "They should have killed Laval and Petain…they deserve to die."

The radio voice resumed. "General Giraud will now assume the duties of High Commissioner of French Africa.

"On this Christmas Eve, Prime Minister Winston Churchill sends his special wishes to *La Résistance* forces in France. You've managed to cause havoc within the German high command, and have helped demoralize their troops…Good show at Bayonne."

There was a long pause, followed by a message for the *Résistance*. "A stone rolls down the hill. Nesie and Jerome are in the wedding. Elaine gives a basket to Sam." The message was repeated and the announcer signed off. "Wishing you again, a very happy Christmas and peace in the New Year. *Vive la France!*"

In a low volume, Christmas music continued to play on the radio.

"You know," Marcel began, "I just realized that you still have the radio. I thought it would be confiscated by now. Doesn't the captain realize he could be court-martialed if he listens to any Swiss or British broadcasts?"

"He's never mentioned that," Paul replied. "He sometimes sits down here at night by himself, and listens to the music while he has his tea."

"He came home once while we were listening to the B.B.C.," Paulette said. "I went to turn it off, but he asked that I leave it on. He said that he wanted to listen to the 'real news'."

Paul looked at his watch. "Marcel, the curfew starts in half-an-hour. I think you'd better leave. Besides, Johann could come home any minute now."

"You're right, Papa. It was wonderful seeing all of you, and I know it's against everything we stand for, but keep working on the captain...it could be worth a world of information."

Paulette took a deep breath and sighed. *I'll be working on Johann, but it won't be easy*, she thought.

Babette hugged her father. "Please don't go, Papa."

Angelina bent over and kissed her. "Papa has got to go, because he's doing some very important things for our country. And remember, as before, we haven't seen him in a very long time. He wasn't here this evening, either...do you understand?"

"Yes, *Maman*...it's been a very, very, long time."

"As much as I hate to do this, I must say good-bye now. I love all of you, and it was wonderful spending Christmas Eve with my family." He kissed everyone, and with his arms around Angelina, they walked into the bedroom and embraced one more time, before he made his way down the ladder.

34

It was Christmas Eve, 23:00 hours, and the Courty family had all gone to bed. Marcel had left several hours before, and had made his way out of Elne without any problem. He would spend the remainder of the night in his car, which he parked in his usual spot in the woods, three kilometers away.

There were two knocks on the Courty's front door, but no response from inside the house. Angelina faintly heard something but fell back asleep. A few minutes later, there were two more knocks and Paulette sat up in bed, not sure if she had heard something.

Angelina, still half asleep, groaned, "Who could that be?"

"I don't know," Paulette said. "Maybe Papa forgot to unlock the door. It's probably the captain." She got up and put on her robe and slippers. "Go back to sleep, and I'll go see." She opened their bedroom door to the main room, walked out, and then closed it. She went to the lamp, next to Paul's chair, turned it on, and continued to walk out onto the balcony, where she peeked over the edge and asked, "Who is it?"

Hermann looked up and told her, "It's Hermann with *Hauptmann* Weller."

"OK, Hermie, I'll be right down." Paulette went down the stairs, unlocked the door, and let Johann and Hermann enter. Johann's uniform collar was unbuttoned, and his arm was around Hermann's shoulder.

Johann was obviously a little tipsy, but enjoying himself. "*Bonsoir* Paulette."

"*Mein Hauptmann* had a little too much French wine, *Mademoiselle*," Hermann reported. "I'll help him up the stairs." The two men climbed the stairs, with Paulette following close behind.

"Hermie," Paulette said, "I'm impressed! Your French is getting so good!"

"Ah, *merci, merci*," Hermann nodded his head. "Raymond *und* Jean-Pierre teach me much French…they very goot boys."

"The children liked your gifts very much," Paulette said. "Did you carve the birds, yourself?"

"*Oui*, it has been a hobby of mine for many years."

"Well, they're beautiful, and the German chocolate cake was wonderful." They came inside and Paulette pulled out a chair at the front of the dining room table. "Why don't you sit here, Captain, and I'll fix some hot, thyme tea for everyone." She walked toward the kitchen, to prepare the tea.

Johann sat down, smiled, and put his hat on the table. "Tea sounds wonderful. I don't normally drink that much wine…but with Christmas Eve, and no one to spend it with…you know…" he slightly slurred out his words.

Paulette felt bad for him being alone, but ignored this and called out from the kitchen, "You understand that we haven't had real tea for quite a while. So, we've been using *chicoree* or thyme. It will be ready in a minute." A few minutes later, she emerged with two cups of hot liquid. "Have a seat, Hermie."

"Thank you, no. I must go back to my men. Happy Christmas to all your wonderful family. Next year, I pray to be with *meiner Frau und* little girls."

"I'm sorry you won't join us, Hermie." Paulette put one cup down in front of Johann, and the other next to him, for herself.

Hermann straightened his uniform, stood at attention, clicked his heels, and bowed his head once. *"Gute nacht, Hauptmann.* Goot night, Paulette." He opened the door and walked down the stairs.

Johann took a sip of his tea, and said, "Ah, that is good. *Danke.*"

"Bitte," she replied in German.

"Ah! I caught you...you do speak German."

Very nonchalantly, she replied, "No, just a couple words I picked up from you and Hermie." Paulette changed the subject abruptly, "My father told me you live in Schwanndorf...isn't that near the Czech border, outside Munich?"

"Yes...how did you know that? Most Germans have never heard of Schwanndorf."

"A friend of mine and I traveled to Prague, about ten years ago. We went through there on the overnight train from Munich. I just happened to remember the name, because it sounded so funny to us," she laughed and put her hand to her mouth.

Johann laughed also. "Oh, really...how so?"

"Well, everything for the next week was, Schwanndorf this...and Schwanndorf that...How's your Schwanndorf?" They both found this quite amusing. "I'm sure some French words strike you as being funny."

"Well, to tell you the truth, I feel like I'm talking through my nose, half the time." They both laughed and he took a sip of tea. "But, I love the French language and culture, especially the art and music." He reflected for a moment, and then said, "Ah, Monet, Renoir, Manet…and Debussy and Ravel. I couldn't get enough of it while I was in Paris."

"When was that?"

"I was there several times with my parents." He paused and smiled. "My mother was a concert pianist, and played with orchestras all over Europe. Paris was also one of our favorite places on holiday."

"Your mother is not Hilda Weller, is she?"

Angelina couldn't go back to sleep, so she got out of bed and listened at the door to their conversation.

"Yes…you have heard of her?"

Emphatically, Paulette answered, "Heard of her! Why, I stood in line for over two hours to get a ticket to see her. She was performing with the London Symphony Orchestra at the *Salle Pleyel* in Paris." She shook her head and smiled. "Oh, that's amazing…and she was your mother?"

"She still is." They both laughed. "But, sadly, she and my father are not performing since the War started. He was the first violinist for the Symphony Orchestra of Munich." Johann stood and unbuttoned his coat completely. He felt a little lighted-headed, so he sat back down and rubbed the top of his head. *What a fool I was to get this drunk*, he thought. *I hope I am not slurring my words.*

"It's a shame they're not doing what they love the most," Paulette said, as sincerely as she could.

"Yes, it is sad. They actually had a chance to go to the United States, in 1934, a year after Hitler came to power. This booking agent from New York, Myron Lipshitz, had a tour arranged for her, if she would have come. And my father had an offer with the New York Philharmonic."

"Why didn't they go?"

"Well, for one thing, I was still in architectural school in Berlin… and they thought if they went to the States, they might not come back… which could be bad for me if I stayed in Germany. I encouraged them to go, because I could see things getting much worse for the intellectual and artistic communities.

"My father still thought things would work out, and the people would eventually overthrow *Herr* Hitler when they realized how bad he was; but, that was just a dream, because Hitler was so powerful by then. For the next two years, more and more of their friends were being harassed, and some just disappearing…many of them were Jews."

"Why didn't you just go with them?"

"I had two more years of graduate school, and I had already accepted a six month fellowship in Paris to study Gothic and Romanesque architecture, like you have here in Elne…which is magnificent, by the way." His head was starting to clear a bit, after drinking the tea. For the first time in months, he was relaxed. "It was too good an opportunity to give up. I felt at the time it would have been too difficult for me to start all over again in America…I was wrong."

"Couldn't they have left Germany in 1936, or '37? The War hadn't started yet."

"By that time it was too late. I was taken into the army as soon as I graduated and sent to officer's school. There was no way the government would have issued them an exit permit after that. I still feel guilty they stayed because of me, even though I know they could have left earlier."

"I spent a year at the *Sorbonne*, about the same time you must have been in Paris. It was the most wonderful year of my life."

"Mine too, I think. Where did you live?"

"Not too far from the school…a couple of blocks from the crossroads of St. Michelle and St. Germain, going towards the Luxembourg Gardens. I shared an apartment with three other girls I met at school."

"I had a small flat on the other side, also in the Latin Quarter, going toward the Seine." He smiled at Paulette. *I have not enjoyed myself with someone like her for a very long time*, he thought. He sighed, "Aahh…it was so nice to sit in the cafés, with all the other students…"

"And drink that horrible coffee." They both laughed. *We're so much alike, it's frightening, and now I'm completing his sentences*, she thought. "We'd sit there for hours and solve all the world's problems." *And now, how am I going to solve the problem of how I feel about Johann?*

"Yes…that was something I missed when I went back to Berlin. The students would gather at the coffee houses there also, except one had to be much more careful about what one said. You never knew who was a Nazi, and who was not."

She was surprised at how much he was opening up to her, and decided to push on. "And yet, you're able to serve in the army and fight for something you don't believe in? Isn't that hard?"

"Yes, it is hard, but it is still my country…and as a soldier, you do not question why. Unfortunately, after the War, people will judge all Germans by what the Nazis have done."

Angelina was starting to get sleepy again and went back to bed. She fluffed up her pillow against the headboard and leaned against it, thinking about the conversation she had been hearing, and wondering if her sister was getting more personally involved, than just gathering information. *They do make a nice couple*, she thought, *but this would be an impossible situation. So many things would be different, if it weren't for this damn war!*

Paulette felt that she had to reply to what Johann had just said, and felt comfortable in doing so. "But, Johann…" she shook her head and sounded more serious, "...this is the third time in seventy years that you Germans have turned France into a bloody battleground. How do you expect Frenchmen to distinguish between one kind of German and another?" She paused to let this sink in. "You're raping our country and humiliating our people, and under the Nazi boot we've lost our liberty, and that to Frenchmen is the unforgivable outrage."

Johann sighed and nodded his head. "Believe me, I understand fully. If I myself could change things, then I would. In the long run, *Deutschland* is going to suffer more than France. *Monsieur* Roosevelt has no intention of stopping at the Rhine River...my country will be reduced to rubble once the Allies get a foothold in Europe."

They sat, drank their tea, and looked at each other for almost a minute without saying anything. There were some sensitive subjects that they had touched on, and neither wanted to alienate the other.

Changing the subject, Paulette matter-of-factly asked, "Where do you think the invasion will begin?"

"I would conceive initially in Sicily, or the lower boot of Italy, because the Allies are already in Africa and would not have that far to go. But, the main invasion has got to be somewhere here in France... Italy would not be a good base of operations."

"Well, no matter what happens, it would be awful if Paris is destroyed. The thought of not seeing the *Louvre* again, or walking along the Seine..."

"...Or strolling along the *Rue de la Paix*." Johann took another sip of tea and they looked at each other for a few moments, before Paulette looked away and took a sip of her tea. "It is nice that you got to go to Prague. That is also another favorite city of mine."

"Mine too!" she replied enthusiastically.

"I can remember the many hours I spent on the Charles Bridge, watching an ensemble playing Mozart or Wagner, and talking to the many artists."

"And didn't you just love the Old Town Square? The vendors were so colorful."

"How long did you spend there?"

"Only a week...I wish I could have stayed a month. Every night, you had a choice of an opera, or concert, or ballet...it was wonderful."

"Yes, Prague was one of the leading cultural centers of Europe, before the War. Fortunately, British Prime Minister Chamberlain just handed Czechoslovakia over to Hitler, so there wasn't any destruction of the city."

Paulette pursed her lips together, and although she was trying to hold her feelings in check, she shook her head and sarcastically said, "No, not physically... but you destroyed one of the true democracies in Europe."

Johann closed his eyes, looked up at the ceiling for a few moments, and then nodded his head. He couldn't fault her for what she was saying, things that he tried to suppress in his mind. Paulette was sorry that she had again said something to upset Johann. She picked up his hat and fumbled with it awkwardly, turning it over and running her finger around the inside brim. There was a long pause, and while looking at the inside of the hat, she saw his initials.

"J...I...W? Johann...What?...Weller." She put the hat back on the table towards Johann, but kept her hand on his hat.

"The 'I' is for Ilich, the middle name of Tchaikovsky, my mother's favorite composer. 'Johann' is for Johann Sebastian Bach."

"Did you play the piano?"

"I tried...that and the violin. It did not take long to see that my musical talents were very limited. However, I did enjoy art tremendously, and began drawing at a very early age…" He reached his hand over and put it on hers. "…my mother says before I could walk."

They both laughed and look at each other again for a few moments. Nothing had to be spoken, but they both knew that they were enjoying each other's company tremendously. Paulette finally withdrew her hand and stood up. She picked up her cup, and then picked up his. "Here, let me get us some fresh tea." She walked to the kettle near the hearth, and poured some tea in each cup; then, she resumed her place at the table and handed Johann his cup.

"Thank you…this is very good, Paulette."

"You're welcome, Johann, but not exactly what I would have pictured myself doing late at night, in the middle of a war."

Johann sat upright in his chair and laughed. "What do you mean?"

"Well, I think it's a little ironic, don't you? We're sitting here talking like old friends, about the exciting places we've been, and all the wonderful times. It's very confusing for me, because I find myself forgetting that you're a German officer…the enemy."

"I am happy that for a while at least, you forgot that I *was* the enemy. I thought about the chances of this happening, for some time now. You do not know how nice it is to be able to sit and talk about subjects that bring back fond memories, because lately, I have had this terrible feeling that I may never experience those things again."

This time it was Paulette that reached across the table, for just a moment, and put her hand on top of Johann's. "Sure you will, Johann. When the war is over, there'll be plenty of time to get your life and career back in order. It seems safe enough here in Elne, so I wouldn't be too concerned."

"But who knows how long I will be here? When my work is finished, I could be sent anywhere…even to the Eastern front, and I am sure you have heard how bad things are there. Some troops have already started to move out of Elne."

She sounded surprised, but not inquisitive. "Oh, really?"

"I think eventually, the only troops that will be left, are the ones taking care of the food supplies that are shipped to Germany, and of course the fighting units that defend the coast."

This is great information, she thought. *But I feel that I'm being pulled in two directions, by gathering this information from someone I'm getting quite fond of. My country comes first, so I've got to keep pursuing this.* She took a sip of her tea and nonchalantly said, "Oh, I don't think I've seen that many troops around here …there's got to be a lot of them."

"Not really…maybe a couple hundred. Most of them are staying at small farms outside Elne. They have taken over some mansion, several kilometers away, as their command post." He paused and pushed his index finger to the top of his forehead. "I cannot recall the name right now."

Paulette jumped right in with the answer to that one. "That must be the *Mas d' Avall*. It's the only place around here that would be considered a mansion."

"Yes, that is the place. You would think that we would have more troops, if the military command really thought the invasion was going to take place here." He took a sip of tea and thought about this for a moment. "But then again, it could be another year or two before the Americans and their allies have the fighting power to mount an invasion like that."

"I just hate to see the war drag out. So many innocent people will be killed… families will be split apart…it's just chaotic, Johann…and for what? You said yourself, that Germany has practically no chance of winning; so why don't they call a truce and end this thing? It's so barbaric and futile!"

"I think the Nazis still have visions of world domination. They will probably fight to the bitter end for Aryan supremacy. There has been dissension for years between the *Wehrmacht* and the SS, but Hitler's early victories have more or less silenced the Regular Army Command. If the little corporal stays in power, he will drag the whole country down with him." He watched as Paulette just shrugged her shoulders and shook her head. He didn't want to get her upset, so he asked, "What is it, Paulette? Did I say something that troubled you?"

"No, not troubling me, just surprising and funny, because I never would have imagined a German officer saying these things." She reached over the table and he took her hand in his. "From the newsreels and magazines that I've seen over the years about Germany, I always thought that the *Füehrer* was a beloved man among his people. Are there very many people in Germany that think the way you do?"

He held her hand tight and they could both feel the energy between them. He noticed that she didn't pull away, as he spoke. "You would be surprised. I would guess a pretty good percentage. People are so afraid to talk about these things. So what you were led to believe, is exactly what the Propaganda Minister wanted you, and the rest of the world, to see and hear." With his free hand, he took another sip of tea and continued. "There is no political debate in the *Vaterland*. If you express any views, other than the Nazi doctrine, you could find yourself shipped to a concentration camp. That is why I fear for my parents, with their being part of the more liberal community."

Paulette gently pulled her hand away, stood up, and then sat back down in a more relaxed, cross-legged position. "The *Vichy* have been attacking our intellectual and social life for over two years now, just hoping to imitate their Nazi masters. They've tried to encourage women and girls to be nothing more than concubines." She shrugged and flexed her wrist in an animated motion, "Forget the Latin and mathematics… have more babies and raise more farmers."

Johann chuckled. "That is the old German adage applied to women… '*Kinder, Küche, und Kirche*'…'Children, Kitchen, and Church'. My mother thinks it is a bunch of rubbish, just as you do. You and she would get along marvelously, and I hope one day you will be able to meet her."

Paulette looked over her teacup, as she took a sip. "Do you think that could ever happen? Realistically?"

"Of course! You are so sure that I will make it through the War, so I can at least hope that one day you will meet my mother and father. After all, I have met your parents…who are lovely people. I understand their reserve; they did not have to treat me as well as they have. I have heard many of my fellow officers say how tense it was here, and how cold the people are to them."

He looked at her for a few moments, and then continued, "And wherever they turn, they see these butterfly stickers with anti-German slogans. Most of the families they are living with have maintained almost a complete silence toward them, which I imagine is the proper thing to do, because we are the occupiers, nevertheless." He expected an immediate reaction from her, but when it didn't come, he said, "But it does get to you after awhile."

Paulette thought about this before she spoke. "I know, Johann, but don't expect us to feel sorry for you, or have compassion for the German army."

"Believe me, I realize that and truly appreciate you, and your family, even more." He rubbed his fingers across his lips, began to speak, but then stopped, knowing what he wanted to tell her was important. Finally, he said in a very sincere tone, "Sure I would like more…want more."

"What's that...some miracle to end the War tomorrow?" she asked.

"No, nothing as complicated as that, although that would be nice. If I had a wish, it would simply be to take you for a walk down to the bridge, and out into the countryside...and hold your hand, while we had a nice picnic on the side of a meadow, or up on *Le Canigou*, which I understand is popular for picnics."

She blushed and looked down at the floor. *Little does he know that the Maquis took five groups of people, pretending to be picnickers, across the border last month, she thought. Raphaël Barton had it down to almost a science, knowing when the patrols on the ground, and in the air, would be a danger.* "We really shouldn't be talking about things like this." Slowly, she looked at him, and in a teasing sort-of-way, she said, "Perhaps I should be more like my neighbors, and not speak to you at all."

He smiled. "I hoped you would not do anything like that. If you do not mind my asking, is there a man in your life somewhere?"

She paused for a few moments, looked up at the ceiling and then down at her feet. "Yes, there was someone. He was killed two years ago in northern France. He was serving his reserve duty in the army when the War broke out. Jacques was a gentle man...all he ever wanted was to teach classic French literature to college students. He would have finished his doctoral thesis in another year." She paused and slowly looked back at Johann. "We went together for five years and planned to be married after he presented his papers to the University."

He looked at her sadly for a moment, and then down at the floor. "That is too bad, Paulette...I am sorry."

No one said anything for quite a long time. Finally, Paulette wanted to break the gloom that was in the air, and said, "And what about you, Johann? I'm sure there's some *fräulein* waiting for you back home?"

"There was..." After a moment of reflection, he continued. "Actually, it was my wife. She was carrying our first child, when she died of tuberculosis eighteen months ago. She could not get into a hospital to be treated, because they were overflowing with wounded troops shipped back from the East. My parents did everything they could."

Now it was Paulette's turn for compassion. She put her hand back on his. "I'm so sorry, Johann. It must have been very hard on you."

"It still is…every time I think about it. You are the first woman I have had any interest in speaking to, since Anna died." He looked back down at the floor. "I will remember this evening for a very long time."

"I will too, Johann, no matter what happens in the future." She withdrew her hand again, and felt terrible that she had touched an obviously painful nerve.

Johann broke the silence. "I know that you do not want to hear certain things, but one day after the War, maybe we *can* see each other."

This made her feel more relaxed and changed her tone to a lighter mood. "Perhaps. You never know…maybe we'll run into each other at one of the great art museums."

Bells from the church were beginning to ring, and they both stood up. "It must be midnight," Paulette said. "Happy Christmas, Johann."

"Happy Christmas, Paulette. I should be getting upstairs and going to bed. Father Maurice is conducting an early Christmas mass, in German, for the soldiers." He took both of her hands in his and kissed them. "It's been a wonderful evening. *Bonne nuit.*" He slowly released her hands and turned to go upstairs.

"*Gute Nacht,*" Paulette called after him.

Johann turned on the landing of the stairs, smiled at Paulette, and then continued up to his room. Paulette straightened up the dining room area, went to her bedroom, and opened the door. With her back to the bed, she gently closed the door, only to be startled when Angelina turned on the lamp next to the bed.

"Oh…you scared me. What are you still doing up?" Paulette asked.

Angelina yawned, "I couldn't go back to sleep."

Paulette walked quickly over to the night stand and picked up a notepad and pen, and began writing.

"What are you doing?" Angelina asked. "Come over here and tell me everything."

"I've got to write down some of the things that Johann said." She looked around the room three different times and wrote down her thoughts. After a minute, she tore the paper from the notepad, folded it a couple of times, and handed it to her sister. "You've got to get this to the bridge the day after Christmas. Some points definitely need to be analyzed as soon as possible, and I don't want to wait for one of Marcel's agents to contact me. Just stick it in one of the crevices like you always do. Draw a two-barred Cross of Lorraine on the other side of the bridge entrance, so Marcel will know that it's an urgent message." Angelina nodded. "And use red paint to draw the cross large enough to be seen several kilometers away."

"I know all this, Paulette. But don't you think the Germans will be more suspicious, seeing the Cross of Lorraine?"

"No, they're getting used to seeing anti-German slogans. The French symbols and colors are displayed everywhere. After talking to Johann, it sounds like all of these things *are* having a demoralizing effect on their troops."

"Good. I hope they get so demoralized, they pack and go back to Germany." They both laughed. "So, tell me what went on. It sounded like you two were engaged in quite a conversation…he likes you, doesn't he?"

"I suppose. But I made it clear, that as a French woman, I had no desire to be involved with a German officer." She got up, took off her robe, and sat on the bed facing Angelina, with her knees up to her chest and arms folded around them. "Frankly, I still don't completely trust him…seeing him in that uniform…I just don't know."

Paulette looked down at the bed for a few seconds and then looked back at her sister. "It's amazing though, that we have so many of the same interests. We've never thought of Germans as being anything but large bears, behind big cannons."

"I suppose that's what stereotyping is all about, Paulette. And after the War, what then?"

"Who knows? A million things could happen between now and then. Why even bother to think about something so uncertain…and with someone so unlikely to ever come back into my life." She was silent, then looked directly at her sister, and said, "You know as well as I do that even though I'm very fond of Johann, I shouldn't even be thinking about anyone like him…it's just not right."

"A lot of things in this world aren't right. You and Johann wouldn't be the strangest couple to ever get together." She fluffed up her pillows again, and sat upright. "Well, I'm still waiting to hear what else happened tonight."

"Oh, Angelina," she giggled, "the funniest thing…the Rabbi from Lyon, who is now Father Maurice, is conducting mass for the Aryan soldiers in the morning…"

Paulette and Angelina laughed, and never stopped talking for another two hours, as the bells continued to ring, welcoming in Christmas Day.

35

They had been busy for the last four hours, digging small trenches and laying the dynamite between the train tracks; then, they ran the wires from the dynamite to four different detonation boxes and connected them. Direct orders had come to the *Maquis* leadership from the top, namely General de Gaulle, that this was a top priority. Dr. Marcel Pontier was designated to coordinate the mission. He could choose the team, or teams, he felt were necessary to accomplish their goal, namely to blow up the train headed for Marseille that was carrying the new deep water obstacles and mines. Marcel chose to use all of his group, plus Simon's old group…fifteen fighters in all.

It had been more than a month since Marcel had first reported what he had learned from Paulette; subsequently, Allied intelligence was able to pinpoint the shipment date. January 13, 1943. Marcel and Simon had found the ideal spot to ambush the train…it was 100 kilometers south of Lyon, the station that was used for a rest stop, after coming in from Germany. When the train reached their position, it would have to go through a ravine, with wooded hills on both sides of it. It gave the men and women in the *Maquis* group a distinct advantage of their elevated and entrenched positions. It was also ideally suited, because it was in the middle of nowhere, 25 kilometers from the nearest town. Both Marcel and Simon felt that the two days they spent looking for a place like this was well worth the effort.

When the preparations were complete, everyone took their assigned positions up the hills, on both sides of the ravine. It was now 3:00 A.M., and the train was estimated to pass through between 3:30 and 4:00...plenty of time for them to escape while it was still dark, and avoid the *Luftwaffe* being called in that early.

Claudine and Marcel shared the same foxhole they had dug. When the train was far enough into the ravine, they would set off the first explosion. This would be followed in sequence by the people manning the other three detonation boxes. If everything worked out as planned, they had enough dynamite laid on the tracks to blow up fifteen railroad cars. If all else failed, they had removed two sets of steel railroad tracks, and the attached wooden crossties, 100 meters past the furthest point from where the dynamite was laid. Now was the hardest part--the anticipation and waiting for the locomotive to reach them.

As they sat in their foxhole facing each other, Marcel thought about the night after Christmas, when he returned to the *bories* from Elne. He had been surprised to see Claudine, but as she told him, she wasn't able to get back to visit her family in Lyon, because the whole city was crawling with German troops. Denis and Olivia weren't expected back until the following day. Simon, who sometimes stayed in their camp for special assignments, was now staying more with his former group outside of Carcassonne. They embraced when they saw each other, and after dinner they made love all night, until they fell asleep in each other's arms. Without anyone else in their camp, they felt freer to try new things and Claudine was more than willing to experiment, even showing Marcel some positions he had never thought about.

As good as the love making was with Claudine, who he was very fond of, he knew that *it was just plain sex and nothing more.* She felt the same way, that it was merely an animal attraction for each other, and could never go any further. It was mutually convenient for both of them, and when the chance arose, which wasn't very frequently, they made the best of it. Even though he thought it was hypocritical, Marcel missed Angelina and the children more than ever, and couldn't wait for the Allied invasion to end the War.

The group became alert when the sounds of the train in the distance broke the night silence. It was now 3:50 A.M., so their time prediction was right on target. Everyone made sure that their weapons were in a firing mode, and off the safety position. They were using two of the machine guns that they had acquired from the raid, months before, of the German relay station in Morieres. Nearly everyone was carrying a new submachine gun of their own, a spare rifle, or pistol, and some grenades. As of late, the Allies had been parachute dropping food supplies, and an assortment of military equipment, to the *Maquis.* To date, this was their biggest encounter with the enemy since November 12, 1942, when the Germans took over Southern France.

When the train was one kilometer away, Marcel whistled to give the signal to raise the levers of the four detonators. Claudine raised the lever in their foxhole and heard the "click", indicating that it was manned. Each of the others whistled back that theirs were manned also. As the locomotive approached, Marcel could see that there were apparently more than fifteen separate boxcars, or flatbeds, being pulled, and as the locomotive was even with them, he gave the signal to Claudine to push the lever down.

The explosion was huge, sending the locomotive cabin, and the coal car it was pulling, flying into the air and tumbling end over end down the tracks. The other cars were still coming forward, some crashing into the first two, while others were exploding or being propelled up the sides of the ravine and then tumbling back down, as the second, third and forth detonators were ignited. It was a domino effect that created a heap of metal, concrete, and bodies below them. Before long, fires broke out from the wood being ignited, which rapidly spread down the tracks.

The last two boxcars on the train, which were the least damaged, contained German soldiers, and those least injured jumped off with their rifles drawn, only to be shot from above by the *Maquis*. After five minutes, smoke filled the air from the ever-growing fire and no one was moving below them. Only cries for help and moaning could be heard from the last two cars.

Marcel yelled across to Simon, on the opposite side of the ravine, "Number Two, can you hear me?"

"I can hear you fine," Simon replied.

"I'm sending a few men down to assess and neutralize the situation. Why don't you send a couple also?"

"They're on their way," Simon called back. "Number One, let's not linger here too long. Those explosions were heard many miles from here, so let's get out as soon as possible."

"We hear you Number Two. Good luck."

The men, on both sides, slowly made their way down the ravine, in and around railroad cars that were lying on the sides of the hills. They started at the beginning of the train, and worked their way back. If there was any sign of life, they shot it. When they reached the last two boxcars, they came under fire from the remaining soldiers inside, and retreated back for cover. Everything was clearly visible from above, and Marcel gave the signal to commence firing. The machine guns opened up from both sides of the ravine, riddling the two cars with bullets.

"Aristide," Marcel called down to his man on the ground, who was approaching the boxcars with two grenades, "be careful, there may be some of them still alive." François and Lucien were 10 paces behind Aristide, backing him up.

Aristide gave a thumbs up, indicating that he understood. He slowly came around the debris and approached the first boxcar. With his teeth, he pulled the plug of the grenade, stood up, threw it inside, and immediately jumped down for cover. Three seconds later, it exploded inside the boxcar, causing wood to be thrown in all directions and the top of the car to implode. Two of Simon's men came up from the other side, and raked what was left with their submachine guns.

François yelled out, "Cease firing…we're moving toward the next railroad car."

The firing stopped, allowing Marcel's men to move forward in a crouching position. Unseen by anyone from above, or on the ground, was a wounded soldier lying between two large boulders, his rifle pointing through the opening. When Aristide got close enough to throw the second grenade, he pulled the clip, put his left arm back, and was almost standing when the shot rang out, hitting him squarely in the left side of the chest. François and Lucien dropped out of their crouch to the ground, as the grenade left Aristide's hand and rolled under the boxcar. The resulting explosion was not as loud, or dramatic as the first one, leaving some of the soldiers still alive and crying out in pain.

Marcel heard the shot and saw Aristide go down, but couldn't tell if he was dead or simply wounded. He apparently couldn't have been shot from anywhere except from in front, and Marcel didn't want to risk any more of his men getting injured. "Stay down, François, until we can neutralize this situation," he shouted. François and Lucien looked up at him and nodded. Then Lucien yelled over to Simon's men, who were on the other side of the tracks, to do the same.

Marcel motioned Denis to follow him and the two men went laterally to their left along the ridge of the hill. They didn't drop down until they were 50 meters past the last car of the train. They gradually made their way through the woods and almost down the hill, when to their surprise, there were four soldiers 30 meters to their right, and slightly up the hill. Two of them were manning a machine gun pointing in the direction of the train. Denis slipped on a rock when he caught sight of them, and fell on the ground. One of the soldiers heard the noise and swung around with his rifle, but not in time to get off a shot. Marcel opened up his submachine gun with a burst of fire.

The soldier was killed instantly, but his three compatriots immediately turned around, set up their machine gun, and began firing. A bullet grazed by Marcel's temple, as he fell on the ground. He rolled down the remainder of the hill, off a small, steep drop-off near the tracks. When he reached the bottom of the ravine, the right side of his head felt warm. He reached up and touched it, feeling the blood oozing through his fingers. He didn't have time to worry about this now, because the soldier who had shot Aristide had seen what just happened, left his position, and was now coming towards him. He heard shots being fired from behind him, and the soldier went down.

Marcel looked around and saw Denis firing from a kneeling position. He apparently slid down the hill behind Marcel and saw the soldier before Marcel had. The men with the machine gun were still up the hill, and out of sight because of the drop-off, preventing them from firing down on them. Denis rushed up to Marcel and examined his bleeding head.

"Looks like you got a flesh wound on the right side of your scalp," Denis said. He took out a fresh handkerchief and wrapped it around Marcel's head. "It also looks like they got the upper part of your ear."

"My ear?" Marcel asked, as he reached up and felt how sore it was. "It does feel like something there is missing. I'm sure that's not going to look very pretty."

"Marcel, you're just lucky that one of those bullets didn't hit you a half-inch to the right. You wouldn't even be here to talk about it. We'll have to bandage your head a little better when we get out of here."

"Before we can go anywhere, we better let the others know what's happening down here." Standing up, Marcel felt a little woozy, but didn't see any Germans in sight. He yelled toward the back of the train, where François and Lucien had been pinned down, "François, can you hear me?" Nothing happened, and he yelled again, adding, "The soldier that shot Aristide has been taken care of."

This time, the reply came back, "Yes, we can hear you. Shall we start forward to the last boxcar?"

"No...definitely not!" Marcel shouted. "Denis and I are pinned down inside the ravine, on the same level as you are. There are three Krauts with a machine gun on the hill above us, about 20 meters. They can see the last boxcar perfectly, so don't make a move until we can get rid of them. Do you understand?"

"Yes, we understand," came back the reply from Lucien. "I'll relay this to Leon and Georges and see if they can out-flank them." There was a long pause before he added, "Do you agree?"

Just then, a spurt of machine gun fire came over the heads of Marcel and Denis, and hit the embankment on the other side of the ravine. Marcel waited ten seconds before he yelled back, "Yes, I agree...have them try that."

François and Lucien retreated back toward the front of the train and yelled instructions up to Leon and Georges, who then began moving laterally to their left to see if they could get above the three Germans, and take out their machine gun. Claudine and Olivia remained at their positions, keeping guard from above.

After a few minutes, Georges came back to speak to Olivia. "We can see the three Krauts, but there are too many trees between us to throw grenades, or get off a clean shot. Do you think you'd be able to pick them off at 30-40 meters with that rifle of yours? I'm sure that Leon and I aren't as good a shot as an Olympian, and we must hit them fast, or they'll turn that machine gun on us."

Without hesitation, Olivia got up enthusiastically holding her single bolt-action rifle. "Nothing would please me more than to kill a few more Krauts today. At that distance, it will be like shooting fish in a barrel. I'll pick them off faster than they can say *eins, zwei, drei.*"

"Great, let's go," Georges said.

Olivia grabbed Georges arm. "There's no point in both of us going. Stay here and man my position. I'll be just fine with Leon." With that, she took off across the ridge, keeping her head down until she was next to Leon. At this point, they were both in a prone position, with their heads facing straight down the hill.

Until Leon pointed them out, Olivia couldn't see the three Germans through the heavily wooded area. Once she saw them, she needed no instructions on what to do. She got into a comfortable shooting position and fired the first shot at the soldier manning the machine gun. It was a clean shot in the back of the neck, and within a second, she had re-bolted her rifle. The other two soldiers were confused where the shot had come from, but it didn't matter...within five seconds all three were dead.

Leon yelled the news down to Marcel shortly after confirming this, and Marcel wasted no time in informing the other men in the ravine. They moved in quickly, throwing grenades into the last two boxcars and raking them with bullets. When Marcel, Denis, Lucien, and François reached Aristide, they turned him over and Denis felt for a pulse in his neck...there was none, and he knew that he had been killed instantly when the bullet had ripped open his chest and penetrated his heart. They picked up the dead body and carried him up the hill.

Simon, on the other side of the rubble, expressed his deep sorrow, and waved goodbye to Marcel. With his own fighters, he disappeared up the other side of the ravine. There was nothing more to be said or done. Everyone knew that they had to get out of there quickly and go their separate ways. The place would soon be swarming with German troops.

They made their way back to the road, where the four cars were parked, and put Aristide's body in Marcel's trunk, wrapping it in an old rug. Denis took some bandages out of his car, cleaned Marcel's wound with an antiseptic solution, and wrapped his head the best he could. In two minute intervals, they each left, taking the back roads. Marcel and Claudine would be spending the night with Philippe Lambert, at *Le Clos des Saumanes*, in Châteauneuf de Gadagne. Philippe would be expecting them.

Marcel drove for almost an hour before his head started pounding. Claudine asked if he wanted her to drive, but he declined, saying he was alright. The sun was starting to come up and they were making good time, avoiding the larger towns as they had planned. They had gotten as far as the outskirts of Sederon, a small town where four roads came together; then they spotted a roadblock 75 meters up ahead.

There was no way to turn around now, because they were the only car on the road. Surely they must have been seen by the three soldiers standing behind their motorcycles, and the makeshift, barbed wire crossties. Marcel slowed the car and pulled over to the side of the road. "Claudine," he calmly said, "get out of the car, open the hood, and pretend you're looking at something around the engine. It will give me a chance to get our rifles out of the back seat without being seen."

She did what Marcel said, as he retrieved and armed the guns. The soldiers started shouting in their direction. When Claudine finally turned around, they motioned for them to approach the roadblock.

She first shrugged, and then nodded, like she understood what they were saying. She closed the hood and got back in the car, taking her automatic rifle from Marcel.

"I'm going to speed up when I get close to them, so be prepared to fire at whoever is on your side, and I'll do the same." He started the engine, put the car into first gear, cradled the rifle barrel in his left elbow, and slowly moved forward, until he was halfway to the partial barricade. Then he shifted into second gear and floored the accelerator, heading directly at the small opening between the barbed wire.

The soldiers barely got their weapons raised, when Marcel and Claudine began firing. There was one man on Claudine's side, which she promptly riddled with bullets, and Marcel shot the first of the soldiers on his side, at the same time. The remaining soldier, to the left of him, was ten feet further back, and before Marcel shot him, he was able to fire one shot through the window of the car. In the excitement, Marcel didn't realize what had happened, and continued speeding down the road looking straight ahead.

He began speaking to Claudine, "That was absolutely unbelievable. I don't know how we got through there, but we had better get to Philippe's soon, or we might run into more roadblocks...and I'm running out of gas. That's about all the excitement I can handle for one day." He let out a sigh, as he took a quick glance over to Claudine, and then looked again, seeing her slumped against the car door. He slowed the car, "Claudine, Claudine...are you alright?" When she didn't answer, he reached over and grabbed her left shoulder, straightening her back against the seat. Her head fell towards him and he saw that she had been hit squarely in the center of the forehead. Her beautiful eyes were still open and he closed them gently with his two fingers.

Marcel felt sick to his stomach. It was as if someone had knocked the wind out of him. First it was Aristide, a good friend, and now

Claudine, his mistress that he cared for dearly. It was more than he could take. He pulled the car over to the side of the road, got out, and puked until he didn't have anything left. He was feeling dizzy, when he got back into his car. He looked in the rearview mirror, saw his ashen face staring back at him, and a stream of blood running down the side. It was another half-hour before he would reach Philippe's, and he drove there not caring if he would be stopped again, or not. On reaching *Le Clos des Saumanes*, he collapsed at Philippe's front door.

36

Inevitably, had Marcel followed the back roads after the encounter at the roadblock, he would have run into two more patrols before reaching Philippe's. Because of his head wound, and the trauma of losing Aristide and Claudine, he wasn't thinking clearly and took a more direct route.

Minutes after the *Maquis* blew up the train, the Vichy mayor of Hauterives was on the phone trying to reach the nearest German outpost. He had been awakened by the first blast, and had gone out to his balcony to witness the last two, he estimated at 20 kilometers away. It took him thirty minutes before he finally reached someone in Lyon. By that time, the *Maquis* had already fled the scene. It didn't take long, though, for the alert to go out from Paris to Marseille, and from the eastern part of France to the western.

German troops were swarming all over the countryside within an hour, trying to find anyone connected with this terrorist sabotage. Roadblocks were set up, suspected *Résistance* members, their families, or sympathizers were taken from their homes, questioned, and some were shot on the spot after their houses were searched.

Once an investigative team reached the disaster area, they estimated that at least seventy-eight soldiers had been killed and three more seriously wounded. The equipment that they had been transporting had been completely destroyed. The German High Command in Paris was furious, and made it clear to their officers throughout the country, "that they shouldn't rest until these culprits were found and executed". Additional *Gestapo* agents would be sent to the major cities, to begin more thorough investigations of present and past suspects.

Although two of the *Maquis* fighters had been killed, the mission had been judged as an overwhelming success. They had expected a major German response to their actions, and planned accordingly to go into a long-term hiding mode. Only Simon and Marcel knew where to find each pair in their respective group, and when to make contact again…it could be weeks, or possibly months.

Their previous missions, including the destruction of the relay station, were dim and minute, compared to this operation. They had destroyed a potential German defensive measure, approved in Berlin, which was designed to stop the ultimate invasion of Europe by the Allied Forces. With this success by the *Maquis*, the Germans would be set back months in rebuilding these underwater obstacles.

It was Beth, Philippe's wife, who had found Marcel on her front doorstep. She had been in the kitchen, about to prepare breakfast for her and Philippe, when she heard a car pull into their walled-in compound. She couldn't imagine who it was at this hour of the morning, and continued to gather the necessary ingredients for their apple pancakes. When she didn't hear anyone knock on the door, she went there herself and opened it.

"*Mon Dieux!*" she exclaimed, seeing a strange man lying there with his head bleeding. She closed the door quickly and caught her breath. "Oh, this is terrible," she said out loud, before she called upstairs to her husband. "Philippe, come down here quickly. There's a man lying on our front step."

Philippe, still in his pajamas, leaned over the stair railing, and asked, "Darling, did you call me for something?"

Beth, holding her chest and panting, looked up at him. "Come down here quick, Philippe. There's a man that's lying at our front door and bleeding. Hurry!"

Philippe ran in to their bedroom, got dressed quickly, and came down the stairs. When he saw Marcel on the ground, he told Beth who he was, and they both carried him to the back bedroom on the first floor. Beth put towels on the pillow, before they put him on the bed.

"I'll call Dr. Chambord and have him come over," Philippe said.

Beth stayed in the room, washing Marcel's wound, and tried to make him comfortable. Philippe had spoken many times about his new friend, but Beth had been away visiting her ill mother, and had never met Marcel. She knew that he had become one of the most active leaders in *La Résistance* movement, and Philippe thought very highly of him. After a few minutes, she heard the front door open, and then close. *It couldn't be Dr. Chambord already*, she thought.

Then she heard a car starting, which didn't sound like theirs, and saw Philippe driving past the window and into the barn. Several minutes later, he came back into the house and told her what he found in Marcel's front seat and trunk, not to mention that there was a large bullet hole through the windshield, which now looked like a spider web. She was shocked to hear about the two dead bodies, but Philippe calmly explained that they would have to bury the man and woman sometime that day, and not to mention this to Dr. Chambord, even though they both knew he was a *Résistance* sympathizer. "The less people that know, the better," he said.

Dr. Chambord, a jovial, rotund man of 67, came twenty minutes later to examine Marcel. He said that he was in fine physical health, and sewed the side of his head up with ten stitches. "You've lost a lot of blood...not to mention part of your ear," he laughed. "I hope you realize how lucky you are, young man. I want you to stay in bed and rest for at least four or five days...you're suffering from shock and exhaustion. It won't do you any good to try to get up and move around." He paused and stared at Marcel. "Understood?"

Marcel was half awake. "Yes, I understand, Doctor. Thank you very much for your help. I'll try to pay you as soon as I am able."

"You don't owe me anything," the doctor said, as he walked to the bedroom door and opened it. He looked back at Marcel. "Great job today," he winked and walked out of the room.

Philippe and Beth buried the bodies of Aristide and Claudine in their private family plot. This was also was the gravesite for the former Bishop of Avignon, from whose ancestors they had bought the villa. They covered the graves with sod, dug up from the end of their property, so that it wouldn't look like a fresh grave.

Marcel recovered nicely, and after getting a new windshield from a mechanic friend of Philippe, he left one week later. There was a prearranged meeting with Florette and Simon, and he couldn't miss it. From now on, he would have to be more careful than ever.

37

The German dragnet for suspects was in full force for the next three weeks. Even though Georges, who worked at the *Vichy* headquarters in Marseille had purged Marcel's file after the killing of the three Gestapo agents, the name of Dr. Marcel Pontier had somehow surfaced again. The new *Gestapo* agents had been ordered to interrogate the *Vichy* under them for any possible *Résistance* members that they might have missed, and a police officer had given them Marcel's name. "No stone was to be left unturned in rounding up these terrorists."

Marcel's office and home were searched again, and the fact that they were unoccupied, further proved his guilt. Margo and Annette, his secretary and dental assistant, were found, arrested and tortured. Neither they nor anyone else living near the Pontier's could give information on his whereabouts. He and his family had vanished into thin air. The *Gestapo* agent now in charge in Marseille had put Marcel on their "Most Wanted List", which would be circulated throughout France.

On the day of the train attack, the BBC had reported on the tremendous *Maquis* victory, which would ultimately save the lives of Allied soldiers. Winston Churchill, himself, made a few comments about the bravery of these *Résistance* fighters, and how some had sacrificed their lives in this encounter. Angelina, and her family in Elne, were on pins and needles after hearing this, not knowing if Marcel was actually a part of this mission. Paulette had no doubt that he was, but she didn't say so out loud; after all, she was the one who passed on the information about the water mines to Marcel. It had been weeks now since they had heard from him, and it was beginning to worry Paulette more than she let on.

After receiving word of the train disaster, Major von Klemper was furious. He called a meeting of his staff to tell them the bad news. Little did he realize that listening in the office next to his, at this very minute, was the person who informed the terrorists about the new equipment.

"We will continue to install the small barriers that we brought with us, until Berlin can manufacture the ones that were destroyed," the major said. "All of us must be on the lookout for anyone who could be the least bit suspicious, and report it to *Hauptmann* Weller immediately." He looked at Johann, and said, "I want you to check the teletype for names of known terrorists who might be in our area. The *Gestapo* will be sending out bulletins daily."

"Yes, Major, I will do that," Johann replied. "Is there any indication how long it will take to build more of these new obstacles?"

"They have not told me that, *Hauptmann*," the major curtly replied, "but once you finish laying the smaller ones, you may have to build some more of them. Russian labor should be on the way shortly to assist you and your men."

Paulette winced on hearing this. *Russian labor, coming here to Elne?*, she thought. *I'll have to start checking the teletype, before anyone else sees it.* She was hoping that Marcel's name would never appear, because that could mean serious consequences for all of her family, especially her sister and the children.

After the meeting concluded, Paulette went back to her desk quickly and began looking over some papers that Mayor Astruc had told her to reply to, or act on. Most of them were from the regional *Vichy* office, which received them most likely from the Germans in charge. The *Vichy* did very little on their own. Now that Germany had invaded the former Southern Unoccupied Zone, they were nothing but puppets. Most of the edicts, inevitably, would take more and more away from the French citizens of the Roussillon area…their money, their crops, and the labor of their young men and women…the noose was getting tighter, squeezing what little the people had left.

"Come in," Paulette said, hearing a knock on her office door.

Johann opened it, walked into the room, and then closed the door. She pretended to be engrossed in her work and didn't look up at first. When she did, he was walking towards her and then around her desk. She stood up, and for the first time he put his arms around her waist, and she instinctively put hers around his neck. They stared at each other, for what seemed like a long time, and then came together for an embrace, her head resting on his shoulder. After awhile, they broke apart and kissed on the lips. When they heard someone walking in the hall, they separated, and Johann took a step back, still holding both her hands. They just looked at each again and nodded, knowing that what had just transpired said everything they wanted to say. Johann squeezed her hands, then let go and walked out of the office. Not a word had been spoken between them.

Paulette had to catch her breath, her heart was pounding so hard. She had to sit down, to think of the conflict she had gotten herself into. She was being pulled in two different directions, and one had to take precedence over the other. She knew that she would never compromise her country, and would continue to gather information for *La Résistance*, no matter what her relationship turned out to be with Johann.

She tried hard not to admit it to herself, but she had missed him terribly over the last few weeks. He had had to leave suddenly for Marseille, the day after Christmas, and had not returned until late last night. This was the first she had seen him, and it was quite obvious how they felt about each other. *There is no way that we could ever be alone, except here in the office, and late at night in my dining room, she thought, and that could never be intimate.* She cursed *the damn War* under her breath, and reconciled herself to the realization that everything was on hold until after *Le Combat.*

The door opened again, and Paulette almost jumped out of her chair. It was Mayor Astruc, who laughed and said, "I didn't mean to frighten you. You must have been deeply engrossed in your work, huh?"

If he only knew what I was engrossed in, she thought. "What can I do for you, *Monsieur* Mayor?"

"You can help me make a chart for the crop distribution," he answered.

38

Paulette began coming to work earlier than usual every morning, in order to check the teletype machine. It was in a little room directly off the hall. If there was a *Gestapo* report, it was always the number one, or two, item on the page, followed by directives from German High Command Headquarters in Paris, or Berlin. Lastly, were orders from the local *Vichy* office in Perpignan, for Elne's Mayor.

For the first ten days after the railroad attack, there were no names listed by the *Gestapo* which Paulette could recognize. On the eleventh day, a Saturday, Paulette needed to come into the office for a few hours to finish some paper work that had piled up. There was no one else in the building at that hour of the morning except for two German soldiers at the entrance. She was in her office for a short time, when she heard the clanking of the teletype. She went across the hall and watched, as the *Gestapo* report was coming in. Nothing seemed to be of interest until the "Most Wanted List" came up. Marcel's name was on the top, along with this statement:

> DR. MARCEL PONTIER... BELIEVED TO BE LEADER OF MAQUIS
> CELL... EXTREMELY IMPORTANT THAT HE IS LOCATED AND
> ARRESTED IMMEDIATELY. CONTACT GH IN MARSEILLE.

Paulette's heart sank and she felt nauseated. She waited until the entire Gestapo report came through, and ripped off that section before the next teletype started. She went back to her office, cut out the part about Marcel, folded it into a small piece of paper, and stuck it in her purse. She took the remaining part of the sheet to the fireplace and burned it. There was more coming in over the machine, and when she checked it, there was a second Gestapo report, but no "wanted" list, so she decided to leave it the way it was. No one would suspect that anything was missing.

After she finished her work, she went back home and told Angelina to go to the bridge, leave an urgent message, and paint the Red Cross as before. There was no need to alarm her at this time because it would only be upsetting, and there was nothing Angelina could do about it.

When Angelina had left the house with Madeline, Paulette told her father what was transpiring. He appeared to her as very philosophical about the whole thing.

"I knew, at some point, that this was going to happen," Paul said. "It was only a matter of time; so now, we have to make some plans of escape." He took Paulette's hand. "Let's just keep this between us and no one else…Okay?"

"Yes, Papa, I agree. It's safer not to alarm everyone. I just hope that Marcel is still alive and gets this message as soon as possible." This was the first time that anyone in the family had ever broached the fact that Marcel may have been killed.

39

The prearranged meeting between Marcel, Florette, and Simon would take place in Berre l'Etang, a little village north of Marseille. There was a small, summer cottage on a beautiful lake, which was deserted at this time of year, and owned by a friend of Marcel's. On the day he left Philippe and Beth Lambert, Marcel made his way carefully to Berre, and found the long dirt road that led to the cottage. He spent most of the afternoon tidying it up, and then decided to go into Marseille. He knew how dangerous that was now, but then again, he knew the city like the back of his hand, and didn't feel that it was much of a risk.

Florette and Simon would not arrive until the next day and this might be the closest he would come to Marseille for awhile. He had to make contact with François, to make sure his other men got back safely from the train attack. He felt surprisingly well, considering the stitches in his head and the loss of a lot of blood. His rest at the Lambert's was what he needed, and there were no more bandages.

It was 5:00 P.M., when he arrived a few blocks from François's butcher shop. He parked his car on a quiet street. This was a busy time of day…people were getting off from work and doing their shopping, that is if they could find anything to buy with all the shortages. He blended into the crowd, as he walked across the street from the shop, and as he neared it, he saw a large crowd gathered in front. He couldn't believe his eyes at what he saw. There, hanging in the front entrance on a large meat hook through his back, was François. He was completely naked, with his eyes open and bulging. A sign hung around his neck that read, in large letters: *Résistance Saboteur.* There was also a flyer posted in the window of the butcher shop, urging people to turn over to the police all traitors known to have committed terrorist acts. A reward of more food rations was promised, for being good citizens.

Marcel felt so dizzy, and sick to his stomach, that he had to lean against a building for support. A woman came up to him and asked if she could be of some help, but he waved her off and said that he was just a little tired. When he felt a little more stable, he turned around and walked back toward his car. He only got halfway there, before he had to stop at a curb and throw up everything in his belly. He had never, in his lifetime, witnessed anything so grotesque.

He sat in his car crying and shaking for a few minutes. His nerves were shot, and he felt very alone. He needed to get back to Elne with his family, as soon as he felt it was safe enough to go. *First it was Aristide, then Claudine, and now François. Who was left*, he thought? He made a quick decision to find Georges, before he got off work at the *Vichy* Headquarters.

He got down to the Vieux Port area and waited in a sidewalk café. If Georges hadn't left his office, then he would have to pass by here. It was getting dark, almost 6:00, and Marcel had almost given up hope of seeing him, when he spotted a man a block away that looked like Georges, and was coming toward him. When Georges saw him, Marcel, with a cock of his head, told him to keep walking.

Marcel knew where Georges was heading…they had met there several times. He continued to sit in the café, drink his *demitasse*,

329

and look for anyone who seemed suspicious that might be following Georges. Seeing no one of this description, Marcel paid for his drink and nonchalantly walked out of the café. He made his way to an alley several blocks from the waterfront, came to the third garage on the left, made sure that no one was following him, and opened the back door.

Georges came over and gave him a friendly hug. "Marcel, you were the last person I expected to see today." He looked at Marcel's head, and said, "So, how are you feeling? I see that you've had some stitches, but they're not that noticeable with your hair growing over it."

"I was fortunate to be taken care of for a week."

Georges pulled up a couple chairs, and offered one to Marcel. "Here, sit down…I've got some bad news for you about François."

"Yes, that's why I'm here. I just came from his shop and saw him…it was horrible."

Georges stood up in amazement, as if he had seen a ghost. "I don't understand? What do you mean, you saw him? He's dead…the *Gestapo* tortured him."

"You mean you don't know what they did with his body?"

Georges shook his head and sat back down staring at Marcel, almost afraid to ask. After Marcel described what he had seen, the color left Georges' face, and he rested his head in his hands. "*Mon dieux*…those Nazi bastards! It wasn't enough to just beat him to death, they had to do this?" He paused for a few seconds, and stopped Marcel, who was about to speak. "Listen, before you say anything more, I've got to tell you that the *Gestapo* knows about you, and now there's a price on your head. Teletype bulletins have gone out all over the country, with your name and description. Apparently, someone knew you were previously a suspect, and then told the *Gestapo*. You really shouldn't be here in Marseille."

"You're right…I had no idea," Marcel said with alarm. "I just wanted to make sure that all of you had gotten back safely. Now, I have to worry about my own family getting involved in all of this." He let out a sigh. "I'm almost afraid to ask, but how are Lucien and Leon?"

"Leon and I got back without a problem, but from what I can gather at the office, Lucien, the one they called the 'other terrorist', escaped when he and François had a run-in with a German patrol and François was captured …this was shortly after we all dispersed from the train that day. I haven't heard from him, and have no idea where he could be. You're the only one that knows where he lives, Marcel, but like I said before, I wouldn't advise you to stay around here."

"Yes, I must go to my family and see what arrangements I can make for them. Perhaps, when you see Leon, ask if he can make contact with Lucien." He took out a piece of paper, and wrote out an address. "Give this to him, and tell him that he'll be my new liaison with you and Lucien, if he can find him."

"And how is Claudine doing…you haven't told me about her?"

Marcel put his hand to his head, and rubbed it. "I'm sorry…I got caught up talking about these other things." He let out a long sigh and put his hand on George's shoulder. "On the way to our safe house that day, we ran into a German patrol, also. We made a dash at them, firing our automatics all the way at the three men manning the roadblock." He stopped again to collect his thoughts, and in a low, troubled voice said, "One of the Germans got off a shot through the windshield, before I shot him. Claudine is dead…she was buried next to Aristide."

Georges was speechless. The two men sat there for several minutes, each to his own thoughts. After a short hug, they said their goodbyes, and Marcel made his way to his car.

When Marcel arrived back at the cottage in Berre l'Etang, he was exhausted. He had done too much for one day, and needed to rest. He ate the food that Beth had prepared for him, took a hot bath, and went to bed, not waking up until 9:30 the next morning.

Simon arrived at 11:00, followed by Florette at 11:30. Marcel filled them in on what had transpired since the attack, and Simon did the same from his end. One of his men had fallen down the hill and broken his leg. Another had been shot in the shoulder while fleeing from a German patrol, but neither had been captured.

"As sad as it is to loose these three brave people, the mission was a crushing defeat for the enemy," Florette said. "Both of you have got to be commended for it. The Germans are pulling their hair out over this...all the way up to Berlin. Unfortunately, the Nazis aren't the *Vichy*, and won't rest until a great deal of people pay the price."

"And most of those will be innocent people," Simon added, "but, that's war and shouldn't deter us from what we've been doing."

"Exactly," Florette said. "We've got to keep up the pressure." She looked at Marcel, and said, "You're awfully quiet; is everything alright? Are you not feeling well?"

Marcel sat back in his chair and put his hands behind his neck. "Well, to tell you the truth, I am a little exhausted, physically and mentally. I think this head wound of mine, is taking a longer recovery time than I expected."

"That could very well be, Marcel," Florette said, "and you should lie low, until you feel better. But what else is bothering you?"

"I neglected to tell you that Georges found out that I'm on the *Gestapo's* 'Most Wanted' list. My picture is all over the country. What worries me the most is that my family could easily become involved in this, and I've got to find a way to get them out of France...soon!"

"Spain is out of the question right now, because of the weather," Simon replied. "But there is a possibility with Andorra, so let's see what we can do."

They discussed this, and other matters, for the next few hours. Florette and Simon left separately later that afternoon. Marcel, though, recuperated in the cottage for another two days, until he felt well enough to travel again. At this point, he knew that his problem was more psychological, than physical. The deaths of his friends haunted him when he tried to sleep. The only way for him to keep his sanity, was to focus on avenging their deaths by killing more Germans.

It wasn't like they didn't know what the risks were, or what they were getting themselves into, he thought, *but now they had paid the ultimate price and are true patriots of France. God bless their souls.*

40

It became routine for Paulette to check out the teletypes early every morning, including the weekends. After all, that's how she discovered the first one regarding Marcel. If his name came up, they would surely question her sister. With the name of Pontier, someone would know that she lived in the village with her children. *What would Johann do if he read the teletype*, she wondered?

The feelings between Paulette and Johann grew each day, and at night they would sit for hours in the dining room, talking about what could be in the future. They held hands and embraced when the feeling was there. They were now totally at ease with one another, but frustrated that they couldn't be completely alone, even for a walk in the country, or a picnic on the mountain. It wasn't worth the risk, especially for Paulette, and she wouldn't want to hurt her parents, although she felt that they knew there were feelings between her and Johann. The only person she could talk to about the situation was Angelina, who found it quite romantic, but wrong and quite dangerous...*If it was meant to be, then it would have to wait until after the War.*

At this moment, Marcel was in grave danger, and keeping everyone alive in her family was Paulette's most important consideration. Realistically, her personal life would have to be put on hold, as Angelina so appropriately suggested, and Johann was more than understanding and patient. Most of all, it was Johann that didn't want to put Paulette in a compromising situation, and for this reason, she felt that she loved him.

On a Saturday, two weeks after the first teletype, Paulette found Marcel's name on the *Gestapo's* report again. While she was reading it, she froze as she heard footsteps coming down the hall toward her. She hadn't had a chance to tear off the damaging part of the communiqué, so she dropped it back in its carriage on the machine, picked up some envelopes on a shelf above, and started walking towards the door. She opened it, just as Major von Klemper was about to come in.

Shocked to see him, she tried to stay poised, and said, "Good morning, Major. How are you?"

"I do fine," he replied in his broken French, a little surprised to see her. "But, why you here on Saturday morning?"

She held up the envelopes to show him. "I have a little work to catch up on, and needed to get some letters out for Mayor Astruc."

He walked by her, toward the teletype, and she continued across the hall and into her office. Her hands were shaking when she sat down. She could see the Major reading the messages, and then tear off the whole thing. She looked down at her desk and pretended to look over some correspondence, as she heard him entering his own office next to hers. She would actually have to do some work for awhile, because it would be too suspicious if she left now.

Paulette could only hope and pray that Major von Klemper didn't recognize the Pontier name. There was always the chance that he might hand this over to his security police. She stayed in the office for another hour, finding work to do that she could have done the next week. She walked out of her office and down the hall, holding the letters in her left hand. When she passed the major's door, it was opened and she waved with her left hand. "*Bonjour*, Major. Have a nice weekend."

"*Bonjour*," he replied, matter-of-factly, and barely looking up from what he was doing. She continued down the hall for a few steps, when she heard him calling her. "*Mademoiselle*, come back here for a moment."

Paulette's heart skipped a beat and she took a deep breath. *Maybe I should start running, but that would be foolish. He probably hasn't found anything in the teletype, and needs to know something else*, she thought. She walked back into his office and forced a smile. "Yes, Major…what can I do for you?" She was shocked, when she saw that he was looking at the teletype, and she was expecting the worse.

He tore the top quarter of the page off first, and then the lower half, leaving a quarter of a page that he handed to her. He looked at her quizzically for a moment, before he spoke. "You do not speak German, do you?"

"No, Major, I don't…if you're asking me to translate something."

"*Nein*, I want that you take the paper *und* see if you know any of the people on it. They are just some not important people we need to talk to. If there is no one on the paper that you know, then throw it away. That is all, *Mademoiselle*."

"Very well, Major. I'll let you know. *Bonjour*." She walked out of the building in a normal pace, and met an old girlfriend on the street that she started talking to. A car drove by, and in the reflection from its door window, she could see the front of her office building and the major looking down on her from his second floor office. *Did he really know something about that list of names, and is he testing me?* She finished her conversation, kissed her friend on both cheeks, and walked down the block towards her house. When she got inside, she went to her bedroom and flopped down on the bed, completely drained of energy.

After the Saturday market, Sylviane asked J.P and Raymond if they wanted to come back to the farm to play and have lunch. Angelina agreed, and Raphaël took them with him in his truck, promising to bring them back to Elne in a few hours.

Since there wasn't much to buy or sell at their booth, Elizabeth, Babette, and Angelina came home a little early, only to find Paulette asleep. It seemed a little unusual, and not wanting to disturb her, they went about their business of cleaning the house and making lunch. Paul was out in his vineyard and wouldn't be home for another hour.

"It looks like a nice, relaxing day for everyone," Elizabeth said.

"I hope so, *Maman*," Angelina replied. "But I'm still worried that we haven't heard from Marcel, or one of his men. It's been quite a while since I left that message and cross, at the bridge. I hope that he wasn't involved in that train affair, but knowing Marcel's position, I'm sure he was."

"Don't worry, darling," Elizabeth said comfortingly, "you'll hear from him."

It was fun for the children on the Barton's farm. Since this was Raymond's first time here, Sylviane and J.P. tried to show him all the things that they had done several times before...milking cows, riding horses around the enclosed pasture area, and jumping off the hayloft into a pile of soft hay. Raymond skipped the latter one because of his fear of heights.

At 1:00, Gisele Barton prepared them a full-course lunch of chicken, vegetables, milk, and pudding. Because of the shortages of food, especially meat and chicken, Raymond and J.P. rarely had such a sumptuous meal. They ate heartily, thanked *Madame* Barton, and went outside to play hide-and-seek around the barn. This was exhilarating for Raymond, because he never ran around as much as his brother, but preferred to stay at home and read, or work on one of his projects.

The three children were in the middle of their game, when two German supply trucks came roaring up the driveway. They watched, as Raphaël came out to talk to them. Then he and the four soldiers walked toward the cold storage building, near the barn. Sylviane didn't seem upset by any of this, but on seeing the expression on the boys' faces, she said, "Oh, this happens every Saturday afternoon when they come to collect all their milk and cheese. Next, you'll see them going over to the chicken coop to get the eggs, and probably some chickens…they always take some chickens with them."

"Those bastards," J.P. said. "*Grandpere* has to give them vegetables and wine, but not as much as this."

"Papa says that there is nothing we can do about it," Sylviane said. "We do the best we can, with what we have left to sell, or feed us, and it could be a lot worse."

"They'll pay the price one day, Sylvie," Raymond added. "It won't be long before the Allies come and push them back to Germany, where they belong."

After loading the dairy products on one truck, the soldiers got bushels full of eggs, and as Sylviane predicted, took six chickens, which they put into the second truck.

"Now, they'll go to two other farms like ours, and get more stuff to feed their army," Sylviane said, adding, "the pigs."

After the Germans left, Raphaël drove the boys back to Elne. J.P. was still mad about what he saw, and before getting out of the truck, said, "*Monsieur* Barton, we'll get even with them…don't worry."

"Boys," Raphaël said, "just be careful and don't do anything stupid."

It was 4:00 in the afternoon, when Paulette was awakened by a rapping on the trap door in her bedroom. She opened the bedroom door and called to the others to come. After the signals, she and Angelina took off the rug and pulled up the trap door. At first, they didn't think it was Marcel, because all they could see was a straw hat climbing up the stairs. But then, Marcel emerged wearing a farmer's outfit of overalls, gray shirt, and a working jacket.

He greeted everyone, and there were tears in Angelina's eyes as she embraced him. "Marcel, we've been worried sick about you! I don't know how much more of this I can take!"

Marcel took off his straw hat and threw it on the bed. He held her tight and then kissed her hard. "Darling, I'm fine now," he said, holding her at arm's length, and then wiping away the tears.

"What does *now* mean, Marcel?" she asked, as she caught a glimpse of something on the side of his head, under his hair. She moved his hair aside and saw the scar. "*Mon dieux*, what is that? You *were* involved in blowing up that train, weren't you?"

"Yes, but I was luckier than two others in my group, who didn't make it, and one that was killed later. I figured that you would assume I was involved in this mission, but I couldn't get back until now. I'm sorry I made you worry, but we have to fight on if France is to be free one day. The little bit that we do in *La Résistance* helps the war effort more than you can imagine."

Marcel told them about the train attack and what followed with his recuperation. It wasn't necessary to mention any names, but felt that it was important enough to let them know what a success the mission turned out to be. "Paulette, your information was invaluable to us, and

I wish it could go on longer. But, I have some disturbing news, and that's the reason I came here today."

"Before you tell us that, Marcel," Paul said, "how did you get through the German patrol lines in broad daylight?"

"I got here at midnight, last night, and stayed in the Cloister. Then I waited until the quietest time of the day, and made my way over here. The Monsignor loaned me some farmer's clothes, and also," he pointed down the steps, "that fruit cart, that I pushed over here."

"I also have some news, that couldn't be any worse," Paulette said, as she looked over at Marcel and Angelina. "Only Papa knows about it, because we didn't want to worry anyone. Thank God that you've finally made it home, so we can decide what to do about this."

"About what?" Elizabeth and Angelina asked simultaneously.

"Well, *Maman*," Marcel said, "it's probably the same reason I risked coming here at this time. Why don't you tell us what you know, Paulette?"

Paulette walked over to her dresser drawer, and pulled out the latest teletype. She handed it to Marcel and told them what had transpired today with Major von Klemper, and the briefing of the German officers following the train explosion. "Luckily, I intercepted the first teletype, with your name on the top of the list of the 'Most Wanted'. I haven't been able to sleep since all this started, and now I'm not sure if the major is suspicious."

"We're all in danger now, aren't we Marcel?" Angelina asked.

"Yes, I'm afraid so. That *is* the reason I came back, but after hearing Paulette's story, it's more acute than I thought."

"We've got to make some escape plans, son," Paul said to Marcel.

"Yes, Papa," Marcel said. "That's exactly why I'm here. The plans are already in the discussion stage, between me and two of my colleagues in the *Maquis*, one of whom has helped me get other people across the border."

"Darling, is this going to happen immediately?" Angelina asked. She seemed very calm about this latest announcement, unlike her outbursts when they had to leave Marseille.

"I really wish it could be. We have to assume that a few German officers, other than your captain, possibly know our name, plus other people in the village. Unfortunately, our biggest holdup right now, is the weather."

"Marcel, I assume that you're thinking of taking us across the Pyrenees, into Spain?" Paul asked. "You'd freeze to death at this time of year."

"Exactly, Papa…that's one of our options, and problems. The other options are better not mentioned at this time, but I can tell you, that we've definitely ruled out Switzerland. The Alps are just too high."

They were all silent for awhile, before Elizabeth spoke up. "Paul, did I hear you correctly when you said 'us'? I can understand why Angelina and the children would have to go, but why would you and I have to leave also?"

Everyone looked at Paul, who was contemplating the question. He stroked his chin a few times, and then said, "Let me preface my answer by saying that Marcel, and the *Maquis*, have been doing the right things at a great risk to themselves. We should all be proud of this…and we are, Marcel." Marcel nodded his thanks, and then Paul looked directly at his wife, and said, "But now, Elizabeth, his whole family is involved, because of the damned Nazi idea of collective guilt. And that especially includes us, because we've been harboring, and in their view, hiding his family; furthermore, Paulette could be implicated as a spy. I knew that it would eventually come to this, so I'm not the least bit surprised that we've got to think about escaping."

"I knew the risks, Papa, and I would do it all over again, if I had to," Paulette said.

"I'm sorry about that *Maman*...Papa...Paulette," Marcel said. "I never wanted any one of you to be involved in this...but now that you are, let's be practical and talk about some of the things I want you all to do in order to get prepared to leave."

After thirty minutes, just as the discussion ended, there was a loud sound of soldiers marching from the square, down their street. "That's odd for this time of day," Paul said. He opened the door to the balcony, and walked out to see what was happening. After a short while, he came back inside.

"What is it, Papa?" Angelina asked.

Paul looked astounded, as he said, "I don't know what has happened, but I saw Captain Weller dragging Raymond and J.P. up the street, by the collar, and six or seven soldiers marching with their rifles pointing straight ahead at them." He shook his head in frustration, and then looked at Marcel. "You better go back into the bedroom and close the trap door...put the rug over it too, and don't come out!"

Marcel went into the bedroom, closed the door, and stood behind it with his pistol drawn. He didn't go down the stairs of the trap door, but listened to what was happening in the other room. Paulette, meanwhile, went out onto the balcony, in time to see Johann approach their house with the boys. It appeared that he was jerking them around and they seemed to be in pain.

"*Komm, du kleiner Schwein!*" Johann said to Raymond and J.P., and then rapped on the downstairs door.

Paulette left the balcony, ran downstairs as fast as she could, and opened the door.

Johann dragged the boys inside the small entrance by the back of their shirts, and said, "*Komm herein, du laus buben.*" He threw them forward and they fell on the floor. He turned around, facing his troops, and motioned them to leave. "*Das ist alles*," he said, and they began marching back toward the square.

Paulette clenched her fist and began screaming at Johann. "You bastard! What are you doing to these boys? You're just like the rest of them!"

Johann held up his hands, and said, "Can we go upstairs and let me explain? It is not what you think."

The boys got up off the floor, and walked up the stairs, where Angelina was waiting with Paul and Elizabeth. Paulette, cursing under her breath, followed, with Johann behind her. When Johann reached the main room, Paul came over and got directly in his face. Johann backed off, holding his hands out in front of him.

In a loud voice, Paul said, "You don't care who you hurt, do you... treating these boys like they committed some kind of crime?"

Raymond spoke up first, "We did, *Grandpere*...don't yell at the captain."

"What!" Paul said.

"What do you mean, Raymond?" Paulette continued.

Raymond looked down at the ground, and sheepishly said, "We got caught letting the air out of the tires...on some of the German trucks..."

"And putting sand in their gas tanks," J.P. added. "I think the soldiers were about to shoot us..."

"Yeah...it was lucky Johann was there...he saved us." Raymond paused for a moment, and then looked up. "When he dragged us back here, he told us to act like we were in pain."

Marcel, listening behind the door, could hear everything. He looked up at the ceiling and shook his head. *I don't need any more tumult right now*, he thought.

Calming down, Paul looked at Johann, and said softly, "Is this true?"

Johann found the mood changing, and replied, "Yes…I just happened to be walking back to the tower to meet Hermann, when I saw the soldiers and the boys on the street leading out of the village."

"They had already hit us with their rifles and knocked us to the ground," J.P. injected.

Angelina put her arm around J.P., "Where did you get hit?"

J.P. put his hand on his right shoulder and rubbed it. "Right here," he told his mother.

Johann looked at Angelina and shrugged. "I do not know if they would have shot them, but it is possible. Two teen-aged boys, in Perpignan, were executed last week for marking up a staff vehicle with paint. He paused for a second, "This is the first I have heard about the sand in the gas tanks!" He shook his finger at Raymond and J.P. "Raymond…Jean Pierre…you realize that this is a very serious thing. I have taken a big risk by telling the men to keep this quiet, and that I would handle the punishment. I hope they will do what I ask…if this gets back to Major von Klemper, we are all in trouble."

"I think we owe you an apology, Captain," Paul said.

"Yes…I'm sorry too, Johann, but you all acted out your parts out too well," Paulette said.

"I can't thank you enough for rescuing my sons," Angelina said sincerely.

"No thanks, or apology is necessary," Johann said. "I just hope they learn a lesson from this and are more careful in the future. This *Commandant* is not a man of compassion, especially for the French."

Angelina ushered Raymond and J.P. to stand in front of Johann, and said, "Boys…do you have anything to say to the Captain?"

Raymond spoke up first. "We're sorry. It won't happen again."

"J.P.?" Paulette asked for a reply.

J.P. smirked and shook his head, before reluctantly saying, "Yeah… thanks." He paused for second, "But, I'm only sorry that we got caught."

"Jean-Pierre, what is wrong with you?" Elizabeth asked.

Johann half smiled, saying, "He is a tough one." He put his hands on knees and bent over to speak to J.P. "I may not be there to help you the next time, J.P., so you better think of the consequences of your actions. You are still not out of the woods on this one, and if I *am* called up by Major von Klemper, the only excuse I can make is that it was just a childish prank…and as punishment, I restricted you to your house for a week. I want you to do this until all this cools down…do you understand?"

Raymond and J.P. answered together, "Yes, Captain."

Just then Babette came up the stairs and opened the door. She skipped into the room. "Hello, Johann," she said.

"Hello, Babette," Johann answered. "How have you been?"

"Good," she answered. "I was just playing at my friend's house." She turned abruptly, and started skipping toward her mother's bedroom.

As she was about to open the door, Paulette called out, "Babette, where are you going?"

"I'm going to play with my dolls that I left in here," she answered.

Paulette was about to object, but Babette had already opened the door. She walked toward her dolls, which were lying on the floor, picked up one of them, put it on the bed and fluffed up its clothes, still unaware of Marcel behind the open door.

Trying to seem nonchalant, Paulette opened the front door, and began to speak in a friendly tone to Johann. The others were anticipating the worst, if Babette should turn around and discover her father in the room with her. "Johann, I'm sure you have work to do, and we don't want to detain you any longer. I hope you'll find a way to get that sand out of the gas tanks."

At the same time Paulette and Johann were speaking, Babette looked up and saw her father behind the door. Marcel reacted immediately by putting his left index finger up to his mouth, telling her to be silent. He motioned for her to come over to him, and he whispered in her ear. She nodded her head, walked back into the main room carrying her doll, and closed the door of the bedroom.

Johann put his hat on and went to where Paulette was standing. "You are right...I should check on the men and try to find someone from the motor pool who knows what they are doing." Babette walked up to him and he looked down at what she was carrying. "Well, I see that you have Marie Joelle today."

"Yes," Babette replies. "She and I are going to help *Grandmere* prepare lunch." She looked down at her doll, and then back up at Johann. "I haven't seen my Papa for a very long time," causing all the adults to cringe when she said it.

"Oh, that is too bad," Johann said, sincerely. "Well, I should best be on my way. Just remember what I told you, boys." He walked down the steps and Paulette locked the door, giving a big sigh of relief.

"Marcel!" Angelina exclaimed, as she went to the bedroom and opened the door. Everyone else was right behind her, but they didn't see Marcel, until he stepped out from behind the door, holding his pistol pointing in the air. "It's all right, Marcel, he's gone."

Marcel put the gun in his jacket pocket, sat down on the bed, and then greeted the children. "That was a little too close for comfort. Your captain seems like a pretty decent guy, from what I could hear."

"He saved us just in the nick of time, Papa," Raymond said.

Elizabeth, walking behind Raymond and J.P., snatched them by their shirts and turned them around to face her. "What were you two thinking of? Are you trying to win the War by yourselves? If I wasn't so happy you're both alive, I'd kill you myself. Now give your *Grandmere* a big hug." The boys did just that.

"You boys were lucky," Marcel said. "Just don't try anything foolish like that again. I don't want any dead sons." He grabbed them and started wrestling with them on the bed. Babette jumped on top of all of them, and it was like old times.

After the boys went back to their rooms, and Babette to hers, the adults talked some more about the eventual escape, which Marcel said could come at any time, and therefore, they had to be prepared and ready to go. It was now late in the afternoon, and Marcel said he needed to rest. He lay on the bed and fell asleep for two hours, with Angelina by his side. Shortly after dark, everyone said their goodbyes, and Marcel made his way out of the village. He knew that it was getting even more dangerous for his family to remain here, and that he must plan something as soon as possible.

41

Paulette was dreading going back to work on Monday, for fear that she would be questioned by Major von Klemper about the list he gave her. She arrived early at her office, checked the teletype, and was happy that nothing of importance was on it. She was at her desk, when the door opened, and Johann walked in carrying two cups of coffee. She was relieved it wasn't the major, and smiled when she saw him.

He sat across the desk from her, and they chatted for several minutes, before she said, "You seem very relaxed today. Don't you have any meetings with the major?"

"No, he had to leave early this morning for a big staff meeting in Strasbourg, and will probably be gone for a few days. Apparently, a lot of the top brass from Berlin will be there, and he has to give a report of our progress here." Johann paused, as he drank his coffee and stared at Paulette. "So, I am now in charge here, *Mademoiselle*, and I say that we have a long, picnic lunch down by the River Tech."

"That sounds wonderful, Captain," Paulette said in a flirting kind of way, "but you know that I couldn't do that."

He laughed, "Ah, but you are wrong. I have already cleared it with Mayor Astruc, and I will have the lunch all prepared for us."

"Cleared it with the mayor!" she exclaimed. "What in the world did you tell him?"

"I told him the truth…Hermann is very busy along the Sea, and I need someone familiar with the Tech, to help me survey the river and take notes. There did not seem to be any problem, as far as he was concerned. What do you say, Paulette? It could be one of our rare opportunities to be together."

"As much as I want us to be alone, I really shouldn't be seen with you driving out of town together. It wouldn't look right."

"Then, take your Citroën, and wait for me on that small road before the bridge. I'll follow you from there." He stood up, looked down at her, and asked in a pleading way, "Please?"

She looked up, stared at him for a few seconds, her heart racing, and nodded. "Alright, I'll see you there around noon." She smiled, and added, "for our business lunch."

Johann reached across the desk and squeezed her hand, before he went back to his own office.

Paulette left the office at 11:30, walked home, and told her father that she was taking the car for some business which she had to attend to. There were no questions from him, or her mother. She drove out of the village and headed for the river, arriving at the dirt road right on time. It wasn't long before Johann drove up and stopped his small, military truck behind her. He got out and opened her door.

"I am glad that you decided to come," he said. "I really do need you to help me survey the river, on both sides of the bridge…then we can have our lunch."

Paulette laughed, "So, this definitely is a legitimate request you made of the mayor, huh?"

"Of course," he smiled, and added, "The lunch idea was my own way of not going crazy. This could give us a little time alone, which I think we deserve. So, for a change, the hell with what the whole world thinks."

She sighed, "Oh, if life was just that simple." She paused. "OK, let's get to work."

Johann carried his surveying tools, and gave Paulette some rolled up topographies to carry. When they got to the river, he placed her near the bank, holding a measured pole. He crossed over the bridge to do the surveying, having her move in several different directions. As he called instructions to her, she wrote down the coordinates and other measurements. When he came back to her side, he opened his small, portable writing table, and flattened the topographies on it. He quickly wrote down the figures on various parts of the map, which Paulette had taken, connecting the dots with a ruler. The whole process took 30 minutes.

"*Das ist alles*," Johann said. They started walking back to his truck to load the equipment. "Do you know of a nice place down this road for a picnic?"

"Yes, I know a perfect spot," Paulette replied.

"Good...then I will follow you."

Paulette got in her car and drove one kilometer, with Johann closely behind her. They got out of their vehicles, and she led him through an opening in the bushes, down to a grassy knoll. It was a beautiful view of the river, the open fields across it, and the snow capped mountains in the distance. They both felt the excitement of just being there, and after Johann put the lunch basket down and spread an army, grey blanket on the ground, he took her in his arms and they kissed passionately.

There was a chill in the air, but they never felt it. Their bodies were close together, and holding each other as if it would be the last time.

Neither said a word, as they lowered themselves down to the blanket, lying facing each other. Johann let his fingers rub along Paulette's face and cheek, as they looked into each other's eyes. Finally, he kissed her gently on her forehead, then her eyes, her nose, and lips. In almost a whisper, he said, "I believe I am falling in love with you, Paulette." Her whole face was luminous on hearing this. "This is only the second time in my life that I have felt this way, so I know that it is true."

Paulette pulled his head forward, kissed him, and then held him tight. "I feel the same way, Johann," she whispered in his ear. "Oh, I so hope that we can make it through this damn War, and have a chance to be together." She sat up with her knees to her side and leaned against him; he put one hand behind her head stroking her hair, and the other on her hip. "We've both lost someone very dear to us, and now, I don't know whether I could stand to go through that again."

"*Liebschen*, I know that you are going to be just fine here in Elne," Johann said. "As for me, there are no guarantees when you are a soldier. But, now that I know you will be here waiting, I will do my best to come back alive."

Now I feel terrible, that I can't tell him that I may have to escape soon, she thought. "We have to think positive, *Cherie*, and just hope for the best." She paused, and then laughed out loud.

"What *is* so funny?" Johann asked, giving her a big smile.

"I was just thinking of being together in Paris, and how much fun it would be. I'd love to share Paris with you."

"Hmm," he closed his eyes, "that would be nice." He kissed her again, and said, "I might consider living in Paris, after the War; that is, if the Parisians would even consider hiring a German architect. I would not blame them, if they did not."

A cold breeze suddenly swept through the knoll, and Paulette shivered. She never thought about bringing a jacket, because the weather was fairly mild for this time of year. Johann gently brought her down towards him and held her tightly. She was at ease being in his arms, and when she felt his hand coming under the back of her sweater, she sighed and then kissed him. She leaned slightly on to her side, letting his hand come forward and caress her breast. They stayed in this embrace for quite awhile, until his knee came between her thighs, and she could feel his hardness. She didn't want Johann to stop, as her body got hot all over, moving with Johann in a rhythm together.

Another breeze, colder and heavier than the first, whipped across the river. It caused them both to stop and just look at each other. It was Paulette who spoke first, "I love you, Johann, and want you to make love to me, but this is the wrong place, and…"

"…and time," Johann said, finishing her sentence. "Yes, I love you too, and it *would* be wrong for us to continue going any further, at this time. It can wait until after the War, because now it gives us something to look forward to."

She got off from on top of him and sat on her knees, holding out her hands to help him up. He gave her a quick kiss, and playfully said, "Well, since we have already had dessert, how about lunch?"

She smiled quickly, and smacked his arm. "I doubt if anything you have in that basket of yours will be as good as the dessert."

They both laughed and joked back and forth, as Johann served the cold, boiled chicken and German potato salad, and Paulette poured them each a glass of wine from her father's vineyard. The weather was starting to get colder, and Johann took off his jacket and put it around her. Even as close as she felt to Johann now, Paulette was very uncomfortable wearing his uniform, but waited until they were finished with lunch, to give it back to him.

It was an exciting and memorable day for both of them, and when they arrived back at their offices, neither one could concentrate on anything to do with work. The future looked bright, and both Paulette and Johann were very optimistic that they would eventually be together to share their lives.

42

It was four days later, and that morning, Paulette had intercepted another teletype with Marcel's name on it. She was dreading having to face Major von Klemper, who was due to return from Strasbourg later that afternoon. She was hoping that she could avoid seeing him for as long as possible.

Paulette and Johann were able to have several quiet moments together every day in the office, and later in the evening when everyone had gone to bed. Her biggest dilemma was how to tell him that she might be leaving. For obvious reasons, she couldn't reveal why she and her family had to go, but if she just disappeared without any explanation, he may never try to come back after the War. Paulette would have to tell Johann that night, *that there were some personal things, which she couldn't talk about, and no matter what happened in the near future, she loved him and he had to trust her.*

Paulette heard the major arrive in his office at 4:30, which was 30 minutes before she could leave. Her door was open, and five minutes before the hour, the major went to check the teletype across from her office. Seeing nothing of importance, he turned around and saw

Paulette sitting at her desk. He started to walk back to his own office, stopped, and then came back to Paulette's. He stood in the entrance for a moment, before she looked up, and said in the calmest voice she could, "Oh, Major, welcome back. I hope you had a nice journey?"

"*Oui*, it was very nice retreat for a few days," he said. "By the way, do you remember the teletype I gave you, with many names on it?"

"*Oui*, Major." She felt limp. "There was no one's name on that list from this area that I could recognize."

"Are you *positive, Mademoiselle* Courty?" he said in an inquisitive manner. "The consequences for lying, you would not like. Do you understand?"

"I understand perfectly, Major." She could feel her legs shaking under her desk, and her face turning white. "There is no reason for me to lie."

"Very well, then…carry on with your work." He gave her a wave from the back of his hand, and went down the hall to his own office.

She sat there for several minutes taking deep breaths before she got her purse, and left for the weekend. It was Friday, and she hoped that Marcel had arranged to get her family out of Elne, as soon as possible.

Getting them off in a corner, so as not to alarm the children, Paulette told her parents and Angelina what the major had said. They could see how shaken and upset she was, and Elizabeth told her to lie down before dinner. She did so for an hour, and felt better when she awoke.

Paulette and Angelina helped their mother set the table and serve the dinner, consisting of three different vegetables from their garden. They hadn't had meat, or chicken, for over a week, and were learning to live on smaller amounts of food. No one complained, because they were more fortunate than most of their friends.

After dinner, the children took over the dining room table. Angelina had given each of them some large paper to draw on, and said to them, "Now remember, try to draw the bridge, and everything around it, exactly as you picture it in your mind. This will help me with the painting that I'm doing." She winked at her parents and Paulette, who were standing watching their progress, also. "You're all doing very nicely. I know you'll be good artists when you're older."

"I like to draw people the best," J.P. said.

"Naked ladies, you mean," Raymond added, and Paul laughed.

"Naked ladies?" Elizabeth was astounded. "Jean-Pierre, how do you know about...?" She stopped in the middle of her question, seeing Johann and Hermann walk in the room. No one apparently had even heard them coming up the stairs.

"*Bonsoir,*" both men said. Hermann was carrying a black tote bag, which he put on the floor next to Johann.

"*Bonsoir,*" everyone answered. Babette got out of her chair, ran over to Hermann, and gave him a hug.

"Babette," Hermann said, as he opened his arms to her, "how is *mein schönes fräulein* doing this evening?"

"Fine," Babette answered. "Am I really a beautiful girl? I haven't seen you for a few days, Hermie."

"Yes, you are a beautiful girl," Hermann said, "and you are understanding German very *gut*. I just get letter from *meiner Frau und kinder*. They all send greetings to you *und* your family."

Johann put the tote bag on the other end of the table from where the boys were drawing, opened it, and began to look inside.

"How is your family doing, Hermie?" Paulette asked.

Hermann shook his head, and very sadly said, "Mein Frau not feel vell lately. There is much shortages everyvere…but they manage."

"Are your girls in school now, Hermie?" Babette asked.

"*Ja*," he replied. "Marlena says that she vants to learn French to speak, so she can come play *mit* you." He paused for a moment and gave Babette another hug. "I see her soon, so I begin to teach her, as you and boys teach me."

Angelina looked surprised, and asked, "You're not leaving …are you, Hermie?"

Johann, still looking in his bag, answered, "We have just received orders tonight, when the major returned from his trip. My small group of engineers, and an equal amount of enlisted aides, will be pulling out in the morning…It seems that they need us elsewhere. The rest of the division will be staying in Elne to finish the job here, along with Major von Klemper."

Trying to avoid looking at Paulette, who was standing straight with a rigid expression, Johann pulled out two one pound bags, and put them on the table. "After going back to Frankfurt for a few days, we have been given a short furlough …so, Hermann and I will be going home for a week, before being redeployed."

"So, you won't be coming back here?" Paulette slowly asked, with feeling.

His eyes met with Paulette's and they looked at each other for a few seconds. "No. Apparently our designing job is through, and they do not need us for the remaining construction work." He paused, as they continued to stare at each other, and then his mood became lighter. "Well, I have brought some parting gifts for all of you. It is not much, but I hope you will accept them. Please think of these as coming from a friend, not a German officer. I have not had many friends, over the years, as nice as you."

357

Paul started to speak, "I don't..."

He was interrupted by Paulette, "Thank you, Johann. That was very thoughtful of you." Paul nodded his head.

"It does not compare to the kindness you have shown to Hermann and me. We will always be grateful." He paused and picked up the two bags. "So...first for you, *Madame* Courty...some sugar."

He handed her the two bags, but she put up her hand and backed away slightly, saying, "I'm not sure if I can accept this...it wouldn't be right."

He ignored her and reached into his tote, pulling out two more bags, and placed it next to the sugar. "Also, here are two bags of flour, which I know you can use."

"But, Captain..." Elizabeth started to say.

Insistently, but in a light sort of way, Johann continued, "Please, you can bake some of your wonderful cookies, and share them with some of the less fortunate at the church. I know that Father Duval would help you distribute them."

They all looked down at the floor, and bit their lips to keep from laughing about the Jewish rabbi, who was still at the monastery.

Elizabeth said, "Very well then...thank you. The flour and sugar will go to good use."

"Good. Now," Johann said with a smile on his face, "Monsieur Courty... before you object," he held up his hand, "I know how you feel, because you have made that abundantly clear to me." He reached into his bag and pulled out a velvet pouch, with strings coming out of the opening, tying it together. "But I still like you in spite of that."

Johann opened the pouch and pulled out a German pipe, which bent straight down and then came up at the bowl. He held it out in front of him and looked it over. "My father gave me this when I graduated from officer's school...and since I have no intention of smoking, I would like to present this to you as the winner of our chess series." Everyone clapped, as if it were a real award given. "Besides, it is called an *Umm-Paul*, or Uncle Paul pipe…so it fits you to a tee." He handed it to Paul, with the pouch, and shook his hand.

"Very well…if you put it like that, how can I refuse," Paul said. Then he shook his finger at Johann, saying, "But, you know it's not right."

"What in the world *is* right today, *Monsieur?*" Johann thought for a moment. "If it makes you feel any better, do not smoke it until after the War."

Angelina smiled. "What do you say, Papa?"

"Thank you, Johann. I'm honored that you gave me a gift from your father."

"You are quite welcome." Johann paused, and then, "Ah, Angelina…" he walked back to his bag and pulled out a flat metal case, "and this is for you."

She opened the case to find different colored tubes lying in slots, putting her hand up to her cheek in astonishment. "Oh my…oil paints! Thank you, Johann. It will definitely be put to good use. How were you able to find these?"

Johann looked around, and in a low voice said, "Well, to tell the truth…I confiscated this from our propaganda graphics department." The adults all laughed. "At any rate, I am happy that you can use them, Angelina."

Johann looked in his bag again, and then at Paulette, "I have your gift upstairs, Paulette, so I will get my things together and pack my bags. I will be down in a little while."

Somewhat disappointed, Paulette asked, "You're not leaving now, are you?"

"Yes…I have to spend the night at the enlisted men's barrack, and…" he looked at his watch, "we are due back at 19:30 hours…less than an hour from now. We leave very early in the morning, so the *Commandant* wants everyone together." He paused, and then glanced at his sergeant, "Hermann...why don't you give the children the things we brought them? I will go upstairs and be down shortly."

"*Ja, Hauptmann*," Hermann answered. "Come children, and I will show you your gifts." Babette jumped into his lap, while the boys sat at his feet.

Johann started to walk toward the stairs and stopped when he heard Paulette call his name. "Johann...I'll come with you and help." Their eyes met and an affectionate look came over their faces, which Angelina and Elizabeth couldn't mistake.

When they got to Johann's bedroom, they closed the door and were in each other's arms immediately. No one said a word for a few minutes, as they grasped and clung to one another. Johann tried to make light of the situation, and said, "Well, I finally got you in my bedroom."

"It's my bedroom, remember?" Paulette smiled.

"There were many nights that I thought of you, while I was lying there. Do you think that they would know if we made love right now?"

"I would imagine so, Johann." Her smile turned into a sad expression, when she gazed into his eyes. "I knew that it would come to this eventually, but it's still shocking when it happens." *The only good thing, she thought, is now I don't have to tell him that I would be leaving.* "I suppose that it's better this way...I don't know?"

"When I found out this evening, I hated the thought of coming here and telling you." He brushed his hand across her face and through her hair. "It is never easy, when you have to part with someone you love, and I have had to do it too many times in the last couple years." He paused, and pulled out a small, wooden box from his drawer. He placed it in her hands and said, "I want you to have this...it will keep you safe until I return." She held the box and he opened it, revealing a silver chain with a small, round, silver medallion attached to it.

"Oh, Johann," Paulette gasped, "A St. Christopher medal…it's beautiful. "I'll wear it until we meet again." They kissed hard and then separated. Paulette looked at her watch, and said, "Let's get you packed. You only have twenty minutes to get to your barracks, and you don't want to keep the major waiting."

"That is one person I am not going to miss," Johann said.

If he only knew what was going on between the major and me, she thought. "Yes, I know what you mean."

They packed all his clothes and belongings, and walked downstairs. The children were playing with their gifts, while Hermann, Angelina, and her parents were in a conversation. When Angelina saw Paulette and Johann come down the stairs, she went over to the children and motioned Babette to come to her.

"Babette, darling…it's time for bed," Angelina said. "Say goodbye to Hermie and the captain. You won't be seeing them for quite awhile."

"You will come back with Marlena and Sigrid, won't you?" Babette asked. She ran over and gave him a big hug.

"*Ja*…like I promise you," Hermann said, as he wiped a tear from his eye. "I will miss you, Babette," he paused, and added, "and you boys, too."

Babette walked over to Johann and put her arms up. He picked her up and they hugged. "Goodbye, Johann. I'll miss you. Will you come back with Hermie to see us?"

"I would very much like to do that." Johann looked at Paul, and then the rest of the adults, saying, "Without this uniform, of course. You all have been very kind, and if some good can be said about the War, it was meeting your family." He gave Babette a kiss and put her down. She picked up her dolls and went to her bedroom.

"Well, Captain," Elizabeth began, "all I can say, is if we had to have a German officer living with us, we're glad it was you."

Johann bowed his head with a slight tilt. *"Merci, Madame...*that means a lot to me." He looked at Hermann, and asked, "Did you give the children their gifts?" Hermann nodded, too choked up to speak. "It is getting late...we must be going." Hermann walked around the room, saying goodbye to everyone, while Johann talked to Raymond and J.P. "Remember, boys...stay out of trouble, especially you, J.P. War is not as glamorous as you think. Your grandfather will agree with me."

Paul stood up, walked over to Johann, and nodded his head. "I've never really told you how bad it was, boys." Paul paused. "It's the most horrible experience you can imagine. Johann is right...men are bleeding to death all around you," he motioned with his arms. "Arms and legs are flying everywhere."

"No, it is not a pleasant sight," Johann said. "It is just plain stupid why men have to kill each other. Do you understand?"

The boys nodded their heads, and then shook hands with him and Hermann. Paul reached out his hand and Johann shook it warmly. "Take care of yourself, Captain." Johann nodded, his lips tight, unable to speak.

"Goodbye, Captain," Elizabeth said. "We hope your parents are safe."

"Thank you, *Madame*...you have been most kind." He turned to Angelina, shook her hand, and said, "Angelina, it has been a pleasure meeting you. You have a wonderful family, and I am only sorry that I did not get a chance to meet your husband...some day perhaps."

"Thank you Johann, and again, I appreciate what you did for the boys. I pray that you get home safely to your loved ones."

Hermann picked up Johann's suitcase and duffel bag, started for the door, and then down the stairs. Johann said his final goodbye and looked at Paulette, not able to say anything. She smiled, and then spoke up, "Come, Johann…I'll walk you to the door." She picked up his hat, which was sitting on the table, and carried it as they walked together. Everyone was looking at them, as they faced each other standing in the open doorway. They engaged in quiet conversation for thirty seconds, and finally he shook her hand with both of his. They looked at each other again without speaking, and then simultaneously hugged for several seconds.

After Paulette handed him his hat, Johann put it on, and looked at the others. With his thumb and forefinger of his right hand, he adjusted the visor as a salute to them. He walked down a couple steps, as Paulette stood on the threshold. He turned around and reached out for her hand, which he squeezed for the last time. Paulette stood there for several seconds, watching him continue down the stairs, and then closed the door. She saw the others watching her, sighed, and headed directly for her bedroom upstairs.

"Where are you going," her mother asked.

Paulette turned halfway around to face her, "I need to straighten up his room, so that I can move back tomorrow."

"So, what was in the box that he gave you?" Angelina asked.

Paulette wanted to get away from everyone for awhile, and seeming a bit irritated, answered, "Later, Angelina…later. I'll show you some other time." She remembered, as she walked up the stairs, that she didn't ask Johann to write, but that would have been impossible, and impractical, due to Nazi censorship of mail. *Everything would have to be put on hold, until after the War.*

43

Again, they met at their safe-house hideaway, in Montelimar, north of the Provence area. The house was owned by Dr. Gabriel Panzian, a physician who had come to France from Armenia when he was a young boy. Marcel, Florette, and Simon were among ten *Maquis* leaders in attendance. The topics of discussion were mainly on future missions, and long-term strategy in dealing with the increasing repressiveness of the occupying German forces. Marcel, of course, brought up his impending need to get his family out of France, and Simon's group was again assigned to assist Marcel and his group.

For this reason, both groups were nearby in the hills outside of Montelimar. There was too little time to round everyone up for this mission, and on leaving Elne, Marcel had contacted both Simon, in Carcassonne, and Leon in Marseille. Leon, who had taken over François's job, had in turn contacted Lucien, Georges, Olivia, and Denis, all of whom were there, except for Georges who would arrive Friday, that evening. Leon and Lucien had already decided that it was becoming too dangerous to stay in Marseille any longer, and would remain in the hills with the rest of Marcel's group, from this time forward.

Each night, Marcel and Simon would meet with their groups. Logistics had to be worked out on getting Marcel's family over the border, along with four more people that Simon had been in contact with. That would be a total of twelve people they were smuggling out, plus an equal amount of Maquis to accompany them. For security reasons, no one, except for Marcel and Simon, knew the exact location where this large entourage would be crossing. That would not be revealed until they were near the Pyrenees. They had learned at their meeting, in Montelimar, that the Germans and *Vichy* had been able to infiltrate spies into the ranks of *La Résistance* throughout France, so no one was above suspicion.

When Georges arrived at the camp, he told Marcel, and the others, that he too had decided to live in the hills. "I think that the *Gestapo* might be on to me."

"How do you know that, Georges?" Marcel asked.

"Well, at first, I thought that I was just becoming paranoid…people seemed to be watching my activities around the office…you know, a lot of little things. Then the other day, one of the *Gestapo* agents saw me looking at a teletype coming across the machine, which I'll tell you about in a minute. He asked why I was so interested in this message from Berlin."

"So, what did you tell him?" Leon asked.

"I said that I was looking for a communication from Paris that the CO had been waiting for, which was actually true. He didn't buy it, and continued asking me more questions…"

"Like…?" Marcel wanted to know.

"Well, like, did I know anything about the train ambush, and where was I when that happened? And, was I friends with François, or any *Maquis* members?"

"And, what did you tell him?" Leon asked.

"I denied knowing anything, or anyone." Georges paused for a moment. "I tried to stay cool, but I had the feeling that he didn't believe me. Today, the same agent heard that I was leaving for the weekend, and asked me where I was going."

"How did he know that you were leaving?" Marcel asked.

"There is obviously someone reporting back to him who works with me. Yesterday, a few of the guys said they were getting together tonight at one of the local beer halls, and wanted to know if I would join them. I quickly made up a story that I was going skiing, and packed my car accordingly today. This is what I told the agent...as soon as I was through with work, I would be driving up to Villard de-Lans, near Grenoble. Then he, and another agent, followed me outside at 5:00, and began searching my car. When they didn't find anything but my skis, boots, and poles, and a suitcase of après-ski clothes, they said I could go, but the *Gestapo* chief wanted to see me Monday morning on another matter." Georges paused and shook his head. "There's no way in hell I'm going back there."

"Are you sure you weren't followed here?" Leon asked.

"I'm positive. I took extra precautions to make sure."

"What did you see in that teletype?" Marcel inquired.

Georges thought for a moment, and rubbed his chin, "I just glanced at the major information, enough to see that there will be three small convoys of soldiers leaving from different parts of southern France. They'll be passing west of here, and heading north sometime tomorrow. They'll be crossing the border into Germany, near Colmar."

"Colmar!" Simon spoke up, "why that's all the way up in the northeast, a little south of Strasbourg. Georges, do you have any idea where, or when, they will be near Montelimar?"

"Sometime late tomorrow afternoon. One of them will bivouac for the night at the medieval fortress called Rochemaure. I've been there before, so I know that it's not far." He paused, and then said, "I didn't get a chance to see where the other two groups would stop, or what time they would be passing by here."

"Well," Marcel said, "I know Rochemaure, also. It's across the Rhone River and a little bit north, maybe 15-20 kilometers from here." He thought for a minute, and then asked, "A small convoy would be what...less than twenty-five soldiers?"

"It could be up to thirty, and as little as fifteen," Georges replied. "Usually, there isn't any heavy armament with a group of this size... tanks, APC's, or heavy machine guns."

"Where are they coming from...Marseille?" Simon asked.

"I really don't know," Georges replied. "What I told you, is all I saw. But I doubt it is coming from Marseille, because the teletype came into our office; although, it might be Marseille, if it was a directive from Berlin, or Paris. I wish I could have spent another minute reading it."

"Regardless, that was good work, Georges," Marcel said. "I'll run this information by the committee in the morning and see if they want to pursue it." He paused, and spoke to Simon, "Let's get everyone together and go over the plans for the Southern operation." The meeting lasted late into the night.

44

With the two Maquis groups already in the area, plus another one close by, the committee unanimously suggested that they hit the convoy, at the fortress.

"This is how I would suggest we handle this mission," Marcel said to Simon and the others. They all stood looking at a map over Marcel's shoulder. Six men from the Montelimar area had arrived and knew that they would be under the leadership of Marcel and Simon. "The first thing we need to do is send one person in a car down to this road," he pointed on the map, "that passes by Avignon, on the west side of the Rhone, heading due north. And, another person here," he pointed again, "where these other two highways coming out of Marseille cross near Orange, on the east side. It seems logical that they would have to take one of these roads, and it's quite possible that you'll see them on your way down.

"So, as soon as either scout spots the convoy, and assesses how many vehicles and troops it's carrying, come back as quickly as you can," he pointed again to the map, "to this juncture on the west side of the river, where you'll see a Romanesque church. Someone will be there to escort each of you up to the ambush site, or wherever the group will be congregated. We need this information to make our final plans. If it turns out to be much larger than we thought, then we may have to scrub the mission." He turned around and faced the group. "Are there any questions?" Seeing none, Marcel pointed to Olivia, "I want you to do this for our group, so get started right now, and be careful."

Olivia held up her hand, "Marcel, what if I'm on the wrong highway, and don't see the convoy…how long should I wait?"

"Not more than two hours, once you get there," Marcel said. "Understood?" She nodded, and was on her way.

Simon did the same with a woman in his group. After she left, Simon said, "I think they'll be less obvious than the men, and draw the least amount of attention." He turned back to the map, and said to Marcel, "I think that you and I ought to scout out Rochemaure, and decide on the best plan of attack. We don't want a large group of people there at one time."

"You're right, Simon," Marcel said, as he pointed to the map, "but we do need to get across the river, make camp for a couple hours, and then proceed up to the fortress. Any ideas?"

One of the men from Montelimar spoke up. "In back of that church would be ideal, because it's like a forest, with a dirt road leading up through it."

"Well," Simon said, "you know this area better than we do."

The man proceeded to show everyone the route to follow, and they left in their cars in 15 minute intervals. One hour later, everyone was on their way, across the Rhone River, toward the church and forest. The first to arrive in the forest were the men from Montelimar, who had found a dense area of bushes to hide all the cars. Within two hours, the last car with Marcel, Lucien, Leon, and Denis pulled in.

"Good work," Marcel complemented the man from Montelimar. "This is perfect." It was one kilometer off the main road, and completely hidden from view. Marcel and Simon stayed for two hours, and then left to survey the fortress.

Built in the 12th century, Rochemaure was an impressive site, although in need of work in some places. They saw a sign outside the entrance indicating that the fortress would be open until 3:00 P.M. They found the caretaker, an elderly gentleman with combat medals on his suit coat, to be very accommodating. When asked if he locks up at that time, he said, "No, we just expect everyone to abide by the rules. I leave and shut the front gate...never had any problems... nothing to really steal here."

Marcel and Simon wandered around the place like tourists, and then left after half-an-hour. In the car ride back to their camp, Marcel said, "We're going to have to get our people in place as soon after 3:00 as possible. I assume that the Germans will park their vehicles outside, and then come inside to eat and sleep."

"That's probably what they'll do," Simon agreed, "but, we'll have to cover both the outside and the inside, and try to hit them, hopefully, while they're getting out of their vehicles. We can't let them get set up anywhere, and this is when they'll be the most vulnerable."

"I agree, Simon...hit them quick and fast, before they have time to react." Marcel drove for a little while longer, and then said, "I figure that we need about six to ten men on the interior of the second floor cannon level: a few covering the courtyard from across the balcony, and the rest looking down on the German vehicles themselves from the second floor. If some of the Nazis wander into the fortress before the fighting starts, we'll have them boxed in." He paused. "Did you notice those two large openings above the entrance? It gives us a definite advantage, to be firing down on those bastards."

"Let's use a two-tier system across the road," Simon said. "Some men set up in the ditch, behind those bushes, and some in the woods a little higher up."

"Alright, but we better get our best marksmen over there, because it's a much greater distance. I'll make sure that Olivia is there…she's probably the best shot of any of us."

When they arrived back in the holding camp, the scouts had already returned. They both spotted the German convoy about the same time, much further north than they expected. The convoy was moving very slowly on the west side of the Rhone, the road that Olivia was driving south on, and 29 kilometers north of Avignon. Simon's scout was driving south, on a road parallel to the one Olivia was on, but on the east side of the river. If she had deviated toward Orange any sooner, she would have missed seeing the convoy completely.

"I turned onto a side road, when I saw the convoy coming around a bend in the river," Olivia said. "I waited until they had passed, so I could count the number of vehicles. There were three small military cars with a total of ten men, plus three small covered trucks. I could see four men per truck, two in the front cabin and two at the rear. They appeared to be carrying cargo, but I can't be certain if there were any more troops inside, because of the canvas over the rear cabin."

Simon's scout could only confirm the number of vehicles and nothing more.

"That was a good job on both your parts," Marcel said, and then thought for a moment. "So, we can estimate at least twenty-two men in the convoy."

"I think that's manageable," Simon replied, "so why don't you go over the plan we've come up with, Marcel."

Marcel drew out the layout of the fortress, and its surroundings, and assigned the groups to cover each area. When he was through, he said, "As you know, it's a little unusual to be taking on an assignment like this on such short notice, but this type of opportunity doesn't fall in our laps very often. We haven't had a rehearsal, so stay extra alert, and be careful." He looked at his watch, and saw that it was 2:30...*just enough time to get to Rochemaure and set up.* "O.K., let's get going...five minute intervals...you know where to get rid of your cars, past the fortress...good luck."

Marcel was the first to go with his group, and as he was passing Rochemaure, he saw the caretaker pull the gate shut and get in his car. Marcel continued on for another quarter-kilometer, and ditched his car in the forest. They made their way back through the woods, and then across the road to enter the fortress. They could see, from their second floor vantage point, the others passing by in a five minute sequence. Within thirty minutes, everyone was in place. Marcel was glad that he couldn't make out the Montelimar group, hidden in the ditch behind the bushes. He could barely see some of Simon's men, along with Olivia and Denis, up the hill in the forest. He saw they were digging small individual trenches to lie in, to give them more cover and stability when firing their rifles and machine guns.

Simon, and three of his men, were positioned to the left of Marcel, Lucien, Leon, and Georges, and when he heard Marcel give a soft chuckle, he walked over from his side of the cannon level, and said, "Are you thinking the same thing I am, Marcel?"

"I don't know what you're thinking, Simon, but probably so. Seeing how our men and women adapt so easily, and work like a well-oiled machine, you'd think that we've been doing this all our lives." Marcel paused, as he continued to gaze across the road. "Is that what you were thinking, also?"

"Exactly," Simon replied. "It's amazing, isn't it? I just hope that we don't get careless, and lose our focus on what's important…like getting your family out of France tomorrow."

"They don't even know that tomorrow they are leaving," Marcel replied, "but I'm sure they're prepared to go. Things have gotten very dangerous for them in Elne." Marcel realized that this was the first time he had actually mentioned Elne to anybody, *but if I can't trust these men, who are willing to die with me, then who can I trust*, he thought?

"Well, you know that we're there to help, Marcel," Simon said, "just as you helped my family."

"I know I can count on you," Marcel said. He waved his hand toward the others, "and all the men, for that matter. If anything good comes out of this filthy war, it's the good, brave people you meet who are putting their lives on the line for their country. When all else fails, honor and integrity are the major virtues any Frenchman would be proud of."

It was 4:30, the sun was getting low in the horizon, and still there was no sign of the German convoy. The last thing Marcel wanted to do was to engage in a battle while it was dark. "It could be chaotic, and too many of us could get killed," he said to Simon.

Simon agreed. "We have the advantage now, but it could get out of hand, and besides, we have your family to think of."

"You're right," Marcel said. "It's not worth it…I'm going to pull the plug now, while we still have time to get out of here." He was starting to get his white handkerchief out of his pocket to signal his fighters across the road, when they heard the rumble of several vehicles approaching. He, instead, signaled for everyone to get down in their places. "Well, we have no choice now," he said to no one in particular. "We're in it, for better or worse."

With two of the military cars leading the way, they pulled in quickly to the parking lot and turned around facing the road. They were now parked 50 yards from the front entrance of the fortress. The three trucks were still several hundred yards back on the road, with the last military car bringing up the rear.

Marcel could hear voices below him and peeked around the corner of the large window. He saw an officer and an enlisted man get out of their car first, followed by four other officers getting out of the second car. They all stood in front of their vehicles, waiting for the trucks to pull in, and when they did, the officer in charge directed them to form a semi-circle in front of the three cars. It appeared to Marcel like a western movie he had seen several years before, where the wagons circled to fight off the Indians. This would make it more difficult for his people across the road to see their targets, and get off clean shots. He was counting on them to somehow improvise, when they saw the configuration of all the vehicles.

For fear of being seen, Marcel stepped away from the window, and was about to step back and initiate the firing through it, when he heard the entrance door being opened. He quickly signaled his three men, on the balcony across the indoor courtyard. They acknowledged that they were ready, should any soldiers come through the opening of the walled-in staircase, into the courtyard below.

Marcel quickly moved near the staircase, and listened. It sounded like the same officer and his aide, talking in the entrance foyer. When he heard them start walking up the steps, he nodded in Simon's direction to get ready; then, Marcel stepped out quickly to confront the Germans.

On seeing an armed man on the stairs above them, the two Germans momentarily froze, but then went for their Lugers. Before they could even get them out of their holsters, Marcel began firing his automatic rifle, cutting down the aide with three bullets to the chest, and the officer with one clean shot to head. They both fell back in a heap, lying at the bottom of the staircase.

Immediately, Simon and the other men stood up and began firing over the wall, and through the two large window openings, at the troops below. The Germans were caught completely off guard. A few of the soldiers had been killed instantly, and the rest took cover behind their cars and trucks, and began firing their weapons toward the second floor of the fortress.

This was a perfect opportunity for those Maquis, across the road, to open fire on the twelve soldiers hiding behind their trucks. There was no place for these Germans to go, and one by one, they were picked off like flies; however, the *Maquis* inside the fortress couldn't see this from above, and had to hold their positions, unless signaled otherwise.

After 10 minutes into the engagement, two of the officers, holding grenades, rushed towards the entrance and continued through into the center of the court-yard. They turned around, poised to throw their armed grenades towards Marcel's side of the cannon level, when the three men Marcel had placed on the opposite side of that level, rose up on their knees and shot the two officers in the back. Their grenades dropped behind them, as they fell face down onto the concrete. Two seconds later, the grenades went off in a loud explosion, sending shrapnel and debris flying in all directions. Two *Maquis* fighters, one on each side of the courtyard, were hit in the back and the side of their temples, but neither one critically. The explosion did put a large hole in the front wall of the fortress, and the wall of the staircase.

Marcel put his index finger across his throat, giving the sign to everyone to cease firing. He was hoping that the Germans, who remained in the parking lot, would become more imbued into thinking that the grenades silenced everyone in the fortress, and then make some stupid move. It wasn't long before Marcel heard them talking back and forth, so he started moaning, as if he were injured, and a few of his men followed suit. Then, he peeked around the corner and saw the remaining four officers scampering to get into their cars, and then driving away.

Their escape was short lived, as a barrage of rifle, and machine gun fire, opened up from across the road. Olivia could see her shot hit squarely through the windshield of the lead car, and appeared to take off part of the driver's head. The car spun around and then flipped over, exploding into flames. The second car was out of control, with the driver slumped over the steering wheel, and eventually crashed into a tree, sending both passengers flying through the glass windshield.

"C'mon, let's get this thing mopped up," Marcel said, as he started walking toward the staircase. He then called out to the three men on the opposite of the courtyard, "Let's go…it's all over." He waited until all the men had walked down ahead of him. When he got to the bottom of the stairs, he picked up the officer's hat that was laying behind the two bodies, and the Luger that had fallen out of its holster. *These will make good souvenirs for the boys*, he thought. He took a quick glance at the two men he had just killed, and for a split second, not knowing why, had a slight empathy for them. This quickly passed, as he walked outside, and said out loud, "Eh, just two less Nazis in the world."

His men had made sure that all the soldiers were dead, and took what armaments they thought they could use. Coming from the north, they could hear sirens in the distance, and quickly made their escape south at first, and then split up with the majority of the group heading west, and the rest going east over the river, back to Montelimar. The sun had set, making it harder for the Germans to track them. By tomorrow morning, Marcel and Simon's groups would be near the Pyrenees.

45

Taking a long, gratuitous route by himself back to Elne, Marcel spent the night in the Cloister of the Cathedral, as he had before. The bells woke him at 7:00, enough time to take a hot shower and change into the new clothes that Monsignor Marois had laid out for him. People from the town began arriving for the Mass at 7:45. Standing near the side entrance of the Cathedral that led into the Cloister, Marcel could observe the people entering the large sanctuary.

When his whole family arrived, they sat in their usual seats near the middle. Not wanting to alarm them, Marcel sat in the back, near the side entrance. He had left his knapsack in the small room he had slept in, but kept a pistol in the back of his pants…something he normally would not do in a place of worship.

Marcel found the service relaxing, and smiled when he saw that the Rabbi from Lyon was standing on the side of the alter, observing the routine. *I'm sure he already knows it by heart*, he thought. Near the end of the Mass, when the congregants started taking communion, Marcel slipped out of the side entrance. He went back to his room, got his knapsack, and waited in the gardens of the Cloister until he could see the people flowing out the Cathedral. He opened a gate that led him on a path directly to the square, and in no time found his family. As he walked toward them, he held up his forefinger to his lips, a signal that even Babette understood. No one made a scene, but politely, he kissed everyone.

Almost in silence, they walked through the square together, around the corner, and down their cobblestone street. Before they reached their house, Marcel quietly said to Angelina, "Is there any chance of the captain being home now?"

"Of course not, darling. I wouldn't have let you come this far, if he had been here."

"Well, when do you expect him?"

"He won't be coming back at all. His unit left yesterday for Germany, and we have no one staying with us now."

"Oh, really…that's wonderful news!"

They went upstairs to the main level, and everyone was able to greet Marcel much more warmly. "That smells like fresh, baked cookies, *Maman*," Marcel said. "The last time I was here, you never baked any."

"That's because we haven't had any sugar," Elizabeth said. "The captain was nice enough to get us sugar and flour, before he pulled out yesterday. We objected, but he said that he wasn't taking it back." She walked into the kitchen to get a pot of hot water ready for their thyme tea.

"He probably knew that we wouldn't accept it, otherwise," Paul said. "I must admit, that for a German, he was a very nice young man."

"Johann and Hermie were our friends, Papa," Raymond said.

"Yes," Marcel said, "I saw how he saved you two boys."

"I hope that Hermie gets to see his two daughters soon," Paulette said. "He missed them terribly."

Elizabeth brought in a plateful of cookies. "I'll get the tea ready," she said.

Marcel held up his hand. "Listen everyone, we've got to hurry, so have a cookie and some tea, and we'll get going as soon as possible."

The adults knew exactly what he was talking about, but the children did not. "Where are we going, Papa?" J.P. asked.

"Papa can't answer a lot of questions right now," Angelina said. "It's a surprise, and when we're almost there, we'll let you know." She sighed, and waited for them to finish their cookie. "Alright now, I want you to get dressed as warmly as you can…I've got everything laid out for you in a bag in your closets…wear your heavy, wool socks, and bring your warm hat. I'll help you get dressed, Babette."

The boys went up to their rooms, and Marcel followed them with his knapsack. When they all got to the bedroom floor, Marcel continued to walk up the steps to the next level. "Why are you going up to the attic, Papa?" J.P. asked.

Marcel looked over his shoulder, and said, "I've got a couple souvenirs to give you boys, after the Germans are gone, and I'm going to find a safe place to store them."

"What are they, Papa?" Raymond asked. "Can we see them?"

"Not now, boys. When I'm ready to show you, I will, but not before." Marcel motioned with his hand that they should go back in their room. Not to get them too excited, or overwhelmed, he wouldn't reveal that they were trying to make their escape today. "Hurry up and get dressed, as your mother told you." He continued up the stairs to a door that led into the attic. It always amazed him how nice it smelled in this huge room made of cedar, and how much light came through the two, gabled windows. He sat down in an old rocking chair and put his knapsack on the floor, looking around for something to put the hat and Luger in. He spotted a zippered, plastic bag on the shelf, just the right size, and put in his two treasures. He knew just the place to hide it…behind a loose, wooden plank on the far wall, next to the window.

This is where he hid Angelina's engagement ring for a month before he proposed, and sometimes where he hid small Christmas gifts for the children when they spent the holiday in Elne. With just a little nudge to the side, the plank moved and he slid in the plastic bag.

When Marcel came downstairs, Elizabeth had prepared two picnic baskets full of food, water, and wine. They all were dressed warmly, "for a family picnic on the mountain," as Marcel had instructed. The only one missing was Paulette. "Is Paulette still getting dressed?" Marcel inquired.

"No, darling," Angelina said, as she motioned him off to the side, and in a whisper, said, "she'll be back in a few minutes. She thought that it was important to tell Mayor Astruc that she had to leave on an emergency, a sick aunt in Bordeaux, and that she may not be back for awhile. The people in her office, especially the Germans, would be suspicious, if she just disappeared without a word."

"That sounds reasonable," Marcel whispered back. "I hope she gets back..." He didn't finish his sentence, as he heard Paulette coming up the stairs.

"Everything is just fine with the mayor," Paulette said, coming in the door.

"That's good," Marcel said. "I just need to go over a couple more things with you, Papa, and Angelina." He looked at Elizabeth, and said, "*Maman*, why don't you give the children another cookie?"

"Come in the kitchen, children," Elizabeth said to them. The three of them rushed in to get their special treat, while Marcel, Angelina, Paul and Paulette went into the bedroom and closed the door.

Marcel took command and went over the plan, much the same as he would have done if he were talking to his *Maquis* fighters. "Since we all can't go in one car, we'll have to split up into two groups." He paused, put his arm around his wife, and then continued. "*Cherie*, I want you to leave now with Madeline, in her stroller, walk to the bridge like you normally do every day, and take the three other children with you. I'll pick all of you up in my car, or should I say Papa's car that I'm using, on the other side of the bridge. Keep walking, until you go around the curve past the bridge…that way no one can see you from here."

"Should I take my paints and brushes?" Angelina asked.

"No, that won't be necessary," Marcel said. "Have one of the boys carry a picnic basket, in case you're asked what you're doing. I'll be there as quickly as I can sneak out of Elne, and get to my car." He kissed her and she hurried out of the bedroom to get the children.

"Don't you think the six of you would be more comfortable in your car, which is here in the barn, Marcel?" Paul asked.

"Probably, Papa," Marcel said, "but we're only going as far as Foix, three and a half hours away, and we can't take a chance of switching cars now."

"Foix?" Paulette asked, looking surprised. "Why are we going to Foix? I thought we were going across the Pyrenees, near Mount Canigou?"

"I'll be as brief as I can, so I can get the three of you going," Marcel began. "Escaping across the Pyrenees, into Spain, has been relatively easy…up to now; but the Germans, according to our intelligence, have recently been sealing off the southern frontier with Spain. They've declared that the first 30 kilometers, north of the border, a 'Prohibitive Zone', and the next 30 kilometers, a 'Restricted Zone'. Anyone caught in the former, is going to be arrested and more than likely imprisoned. Even those suspicious persons caught in the Restricted Zone, come under very severe questioning, and usually with the same result."

Paul nodded. "Since we live in the Prohibitive Zone already, they're not going to arrest us; but, we still can't go across the mountains from here because of the weather, correct?"

"Exactly, Papa," Marcel said, "and to answer your question, Paulette, we're going to Foix as a jumping-off point, because it is just north of the Restricted Zone…65 kilometers north of the Andorran border…that's where we're going to cross, into the neutral Principality of Andorra."

"Andorra!?" Paul said alarmingly. "I've been there, and that's an awful rugged country to get into from the north. The mountains are the highest in the Pyrenees…as high as 3050 meters, and the passes are almost 2500 meters."

"Do the Nazis also have this 'Prohibited Zone' north of Andorra?" Paulette asked.

"The zone does stretch across France, at the major exits on its southern border…Andorra included," Marcel said, "but, of course there are gaps, which we've used, before it got so cold. Now, to…"

"It's even colder at that altitude, Marcel," Paul said. We'd freeze to death if we tried to cross now."

Marcel was getting a little irritated, because he wanted to pick up his family, but he knew they were legitimate questions. "I was about to tell you that, Papa, so please let me finish what I have to say. We need to get on our way as soon as possible." Paul and Paulette both nodded, and Marcel continued. "First of all, there is no way that we could walk over the mountains at this time of year. Even in the summer, it would be an arduous task.

"Fortunately, my friend Simon went to Andorra recently, and made contact with a British expatriate, Hugh Garner, who now acts as the quasi-liaison for his country. He in turn introduced Simon to a guide named Quim Baldrich, who has brought many people across the border, including several U.S. and British airmen that had been shot down over France. Quim will be meeting us in Foix and showing us his plan for getting all of us into Andorra. I can tell you that once we do cross the border, there will be vehicles to pick us up, shortly thereafter."

Marcel drew a paper out of his jacket and laid it on the bed. "I know that you've been to Foix before, but I want you to take the same route that we're taking, on the back roads. Here's a map to the farmhouse that we'll be staying at tonight. Before we get there, though, we'll be making a stop for lunch at a little campground near Montségur." He pointed to the site on the map. "It's a perfect spot, because many people go there on Sunday for picnics at the base of the old military fortress. So, we won't even be noticed, if the Germans are patrolling the area. We're also going to meet the owner of the farmhouse there, a *Monsieur* Leo Montal. He will let us know if the coast is clear, and give us any last minute instructions."

"I wonder if it's the same Leo Montal that I knew in the last war?" Paul asked.

"Simon set this whole thing up, so I wouldn't know," Marcel replied. "I understand, though, that he is a member of *La Résistance*, and his farm has been used before to hide refugees." He paused, and then asked, "Are there any questions before we get started?"

Elizabeth walked into the room. "Are there any questions about what?"

"We'll explain everything to you in the car, Elizabeth," Paul said, and then looked at Marcel. "I don't have any questions...do you Paulette?" She shook her head.

"Good," Marcel said, "then we should leave now. If we do see each other on the road, let's try to keep a good distance between us."

They said their goodbyes, with Marcel leaving first. Ten minutes later, at 10:00 A.M., the Courtys locked up their home, got in their car, and drove out of the old entrance to Elne, not knowing whether they would ever return to their family village.

46

Sunday was the only morning that the bells from the Cathedral were allowed to be rung. It was also, the only time that there were no German observers in the two towers. Major von Klemper cursed every time he heard the bells, because Sunday was the one day he had to sleep late. He had fallen back to sleep when the 7:00 bells rang, but was awakened again at 8:00. The home he was staying in was the closest one to the church. Several times he had thought about moving to another house further away, but his office was more convenient at this one, being directly across the street.

The officer's morning mess would be over by the time he dressed, so he went downstairs and made himself breakfast, as he had done several times before. The family, with whom he lived, refused to speak to him unless it was a question that needed to be answered. On the very first night he moved in, the lady of the house assigned him a space in the ice box, and a part of one kitchen cabinet for his use. It didn't bother him that he was given the silent treatment, because he detested the French and wanted nothing to do with them.

He yearned for the day when the War would be over, and he could return to his beloved Germany. He could go to his favorite *bierhalle* and have the lager that he always drank, along with *Bauernschmaus*, sauerkraut garnished with boiled bacon, smoked pork, sausages, dumplings and potatoes; and then, for the *Nachspeise*, the dessert, he would order *Apfelstrudel mit Schokoladen*, apple strudel with chocolate ice-cream. *That is real food, food that makes you strong and smart...not this dainty French food for weaklings*, he thought.

On this morning, he made himself some toast, eggs and German coffee, which he had brought with him from the *Vaterland*. As he was drinking his coffee, he longed for a *Berliner*, a jam doughnut, but had to settle for another piece of toast. He looked at his watch and saw that it was approaching 9:00. He rinsed off his plate and frying pan, dried them, and put them away. He went back to his room and finished dressing, when the bells went off again. The family would be home soon, and he wanted to leave before they arrived. He couldn't stomach the thought of being near them for more than a few seconds.

There were several things the major had to accomplish before Monday, most being the reassigning of duties which had been handled by *Hauptmann* Johann Weller and his men. He felt that he had an adequate number of officers remaining to supervise what was left of the mining of the potential Mediterranean landing areas. All the design work, and testing, had been accomplished by Johann's group. Yesterday, Johann had been recalled to Germany to be given his next assignment, one that Major von Klemper surmised to be the northwestern coast of France, Normandy. It was one of the areas, where the High Command thought the Allied invasion of Europe would begin, although they put it low on their list of landing sites, because of its rugged cliffs. Nevertheless, work had already begun there with shoreline defenses, such as pillboxes, and concrete trenches. What was needed now was *Hauptmann* Weller's expertise in underwater barriers and mines.

The major worked at his desk, going through paperwork and charts, until 10:30, when he heard the sound of the teletype down the hall. A corporal with the Wehrmacht, who had been assigned to him yesterday as a typist, came out of his cubbyhole, tore off the communication, and brought it to his new boss. Von Klemper glanced at it, while the young, teen-aged corporal waited, and then dismissed him. As he was walking out the door, the major called him back and asked, as he pointed to the communication, "Do you see this list of the 'most wanted terrorists'?"

"Yes, Major," he said.

"Well, apparently there was another convoy ambushed yesterday, up north somewhere, and now the *Gestapo* is circulating a list of possible French suspects. These people need to be found and shot before they kill any more of our troops. I want you to post that list on all the bulletin boards in this building and in the barracks."

"Yes, sir, I will do this immediately." The corporal took the list from the major and went back to his desk, where he put a fresh sheet of paper in his typewriter. He typed out a heading, and an informative statement, at the top of the page, and then started typing the names and descriptions of the wanted men. When he came to the third name, he stopped to think where he had heard it before. After a few seconds, it came to him. "Of course," he said out loud. He went back to the major's office and knocked on the door.

"*Kommen Sie*," the major said.

"Excuse me, Major, but I recognize one of these last names." He pointed to the one on the list. "Here, this one...Pontier."

"Marcel Pontier? Hmm, how do you know this person?"

"Well, sir, I don't know that person, but I do know a *Madame* Pontier, who lives here in Elne with her children."

Interested, the major asked, "How did you come to know her?"

"Before I was reassigned to your office, yesterday, I was on guard duty at the front gate, and questioned her on my first day there. She was pushing her baby in a carriage, and said she was going out to the bridge to paint. While I was giving a thorough search of her belongings, which were just paint and a canvas, the two soldiers behind me, in the APC, made some nasty remarks at her...which I am sure were understandable in any language...and then she left and walked to the bridge.

"Well, the next morning, we got a visit from *Hauptmann* Weller, who rightfully so, chewed us out and gave us extra duty. He said that any time *Madame* Pontier wanted to take a walk with her children, we should let her pass without any questions."

The major looked over the description again, and said, "Hmm, it seems that Pontier was a dentist in Marseille, who disappeared with his wife and four children over four months ago, and has not been seen anywhere. Apparently, he is considered to be high up in *La Résistance* organization, and suspected to be involved in several major sabotage ventures against the *Reich*...Have you ever seen her husband?"

The corporal thought for a moment, and then said, "No, Major...I do not think so, but then again, I would not know him if I did see him. I have never seen her with any man when she takes her walks."

"Hmm," the major mused. "You said that *Madame* Pontier lives here with her children, but this communication says that Dr. Pontier is from Marseille, so it is quite possible that it is just the same name, and there is no connection whatsoever."

"But sir," the corporal began, "from what I understand, she and her children, four of them to be exact, live here with her parents and sister."

"Parents and sister!?" the major exclaimed. "And what is their name?"

"I do not know, Major, but it is in the same house that *Hauptmann* Weller was staying in. That is how he came to reprimand us."

Von Klemper stood up in a rage and banged on his desk. His face turned red, as he shouted out, "Courty...Paulette Courty! That bitch! I knew she was lying to me when she looked over this list." He paced up and down his office, and then pointed at the door. "Go and get me the head of the guard patrol immediately, and tell him to have ready, six or eight, armed men. Have him to report to me here in this office. When you get back, send a teletype to the *Gestapo* in Marseille, saying that we have located the family of Pontier. *Mach schnell!*"

Ten minutes later, the NCO in charge of the guard patrol was in the major's office. Von Klemper made it clear that he was to arrest all of the Courty's and Pontier's, including the children. "I am going to set an example that no Frenchman in this area will ever forget. The penalty for aiding these terrorists is death. By the time the *Gestapo* gets through interrogating them, they will all pray to die."

The patrol went to the Courty's house, and when there was no answer to the knocking, they broke down the door. They searched the house, on the major's orders, for anything that might be of importance, but there was nothing. Neighbors were questioned, but no one had seen them since the Mass that morning. The mayor was summoned, and he told the major that Paulette had come to him that morning, saying that she had to leave for a few days, because of a sick aunt in Bordeaux. At the front gate, the guards said that *Madame* Pontier had come through there about an hour and a half before, like she had many times, taking a walk with her two sons and daughter, who was pushing the baby carriage. The only people passing through with a car, was an elderly couple, with a young woman sitting in the back seat, with a picnic basket next to her.

"I want these people picked up immediately and brought back here," von Klemper barked. "Send out as many motor patrols as you have to search this entire area. The Pontier's should be easy to find…they are probably down at the bridge, having a Sunday picnic. The Courty's may have joined them, but if not, we have a description of their car and know they are heading for Bordeaux. Wire all our stations, between here and Bordeaux, to be on the lookout," he said to his corporal. "They could not have gotten far and, mark my words, we will find them." He was now two hours too late, and heading in the wrong direction.

47

As planned, Marcel picked up his family 250 meters past the bridge over the River Tech. It was quite crowded in his father-in-law's small car, and as they were trying to get settled in, Marcel saw Paul approaching them in the *Citroën*. He flagged him down; they switched cars, and then proceeded on their way with Marcel taking a ½ kilometer lead.

Two hours later, as they were coming closer to the campground at Montségur, a German motorcycle with a sidecar, and a patrol car full of soldiers passed them on the back road they were taking. This seemed a little odd to Marcel, but he realized that he must have infringed on the "Restricted Zone". He kept looking in his rearview mirror, but the Germans never turned around; nevertheless, he slipped off his pistol and holster strap, which was under his jacket, and pushed it as far under his front seat as possible. If they were stopped, he would never endanger his family and attempt to shoot it out with the Germans. Just then, it occurred to him that he had forgotten to remove his automatic rifle from Paul's car. It was hidden in a compartment under the back seat, where Paulette was now sitting; he slowed down until he could see them catching up to him.

They drove for another ten minutes, when Marcel spotted the fortress and campground coming up on his left. He reduced his speed to survey the area, and saw nothing suspicious. As Simon said, there would be a lot of cars and families having their Sunday picnics. He found a parking space near a stream. Angelina took the children to look for a bathroom, while Marcel spread out the large blanket and put the picnic basket on top of it. Paul pulled in a few minutes later and parked nearby. Marcel hadn't spotted Simon, or any of his men, but knew that somehow they would locate him.

It didn't take the boys long to find a soccer game, in a large, open field below the fortress. Babette played with her doll, as the women laid out the plates on the blanket, and the men walked along the stream for awhile. Marcel looked at his watch…it was exactly 12:00, right on time. Paulette went to find the boys and brought them back to eat. Elizabeth had taken all the food that would spoil, if it were left in her icebox, plus all the bread and cookies, so the family enjoyed a very heartfelt picnic. They didn't know if, or when, they would do this again.

Shortly after lunch, Marcel heard a familiar, bird-like whistle coming from the woods, and inconspicuously, he and Paul walked toward the sound. It wasn't long, before Simon and another man, with wavy grey hair and medium build, walked toward them. Paul knew Leo Montal as soon as he saw him, even though they hadn't seen each other for almost twenty-five years. They embraced like old war buddies would, and then Paul introduced Leo to Marcel, and Marcel introduced Paul to Simon.

"When Simon told me that a Paul Courty was coming," Leo said, "I knew it had to be you." He was a warm-hearted man, and with his arm around Paul, he told Simon and Marcel that, "this man saved my life more than one time, while we were fighting in Alsace and Lorraine. Ah, it's so good to see you my friend."

"It's good to see you too, Leo," Paul replied. "We have a lot of catching up to do."

"I'm sure you'll have plenty of time for that, over the next day or so," Simon said. "Right now, let me bring you up to date, and then, we'll make our way out of here." He took a map he had drawn out of his pocket, and showed it to Marcel and Paul. "This is similar to the one I gave you, Marcel, except for one change."

"What is that?" Marcel asked.

"We can't have you driving your own cars to Leo's farm and leaving them there...they would be too conspicuous; therefore, I've arranged for a couple of my men to meet us at this rest stop," Simon pointed at a place on the map. "It's about 2 kilometers from here. They'll take your two cars to a safe place north of here, and store them until you need them again. We'll then take all of you to the farm in Leo's truck, and my car. It will be much safer this way, because the Nazis are patrolling all over the area."

"Yes," Paul said, "we saw them on the road before we drove in."

"It must have been the same patrol that drove around the campground," Leo said, and then looked at Simon. "I think it would be wise to get going now. We will see you in about ten minutes."

Simon and Leo walked away, in the opposite direction of Marcel and Paul. After they had packed up their things and loaded the two cars, the rest of the family was told briefly, while they were driving to the rest stop, what the change of plans were. "We're going on an adventure and staying at a friend's farmhouse tonight," Marcel told the children. He felt that the boys were old enough to know everything, and would tell them as things progressed, but didn't want a lot of questions right now, and it wasn't something Babette needed to hear. Marcel knew that the next few days were going to be very hard on everyone and wanted to take things one step at a time.

The Montal farmhouse sat on 100 acres of land. It was considered large in this part of France. The main, three-storied house had six bedrooms, which easily accommodated Leo and his wife Helaine, and all of the Courty and Pontier family. There were three separate small cottages on the back part of the property, which usually housed the temporary workers during the harvest season, and now would be sleeping quarters for Simon, his men, and Marcel's group, who had all arrived that morning. The guide from Andorra, Quim Baldrich, had been expected to arrive later that afternoon, but didn't come till early that evening.

Quim was a jovial Spaniard, of Catalan nationality, with flaming red hair and a thick mustache to match. He was only 5'7", but at 160 pounds, he was as strong as an Ox. He found his way into Andorra during the Spanish Civil War, in 1939, after the Republican side lost to Franco's, fascist Nationalists. He loved the country so much, and the rugged mountains surrounding it, that he decided to stay. He could do anything with his hands, so he set up a woodworking and carpentry shop.

Soon thereafter, Quim also became a mountain guide, for there were many sporting Europeans fond of hiking. When the War broke out, he wanted to do everything possible to defeat Hitler and Mussolini, the Nazi and Fascist dictators that he despised. He made contact with *La Résistance* in France, letting them know that he was available to help get refugees and downed airmen across the border, into Andorra. He wasn't the least bit hesitant to kill Germans, if it would help him accomplish his mission. One of his new contacts, in southern France, was Simon. Simon had heard of Quim through other *Maquis* members, and after being introduced in Andorra by Hugh Garner, Quim personally took Simon out of the country, where they then made plans for future crossings.

Getting the Pontier and Courty families across the Andorran border was the first operation that Simon had arranged with Quim, and everyone was anxious to hear the plan, including the boys, who Marcel told about the escape. They gathered in the large living room, after Babette had been put to bed. Also present were both *Maquis* groups.

Speaking four languages fluently, Quim began by saying in perfect French, "First let me assure you, that all of you are in the best of hands," he held up his two palms, "mine." Everyone laughed, and then he continued. "This is not to say it won't be a difficult task, because things are getting worse every day. There is no way to escape along any of the few roads that lead southwards toward the border of Andorra. There are many fixed and flying checkpoints, so the only alternative is a roundabout way…through the hills in the countryside, and then through the mountains themselves, as we get closer to the border.

"Many refugees have tried it on their own, but with not much success. Others have found themselves in the hands of one of the escape lines, going from one *Passeur*, or guide, to the next, which took more time, but was more successful. What we are going to do is rather unique, wherein I will act as the sole *Passeur* and have the assistance of your *Maquis*." He paused for a minute, and then, in a very serious tone, said, "As I mentioned to my friend, Simon, I will be in complete charge and make any final decisions along the way." He looked around the room for any reaction, and seeing none, added, "Of course, I'll be consulting Simon and Marcel if we run into any problems with the Germans, but," he paused and looked directly at Marcel, "even then, I'll have the final say on what actions will be taken."

Marcel nodded. "Like you said, Quim, we're in your hands and will follow your lead. We wouldn't be here, if we didn't trust you."

"Good," Quim said, "then let me tell you how we're going to proceed." He took out a map from his jacket pocket, and laid it on a coffee table. Everyone gathered around to get a better view. Raymond and J.P were fascinated by the intrigue of this entire night, and got on their knees, next to the table, so they would understand everything that was said. "Here we are, a little north of Foix, and we'll be going on foot through both the Restricted and Prohibited Zones, but in a zigzag pattern…possibly covering only five to ten kilometers south per day. When we get down here to Tarascon, the going will be even slower."

"Why is that?" Raymond asked.

"Because, that is when we hit the foothills of the Pyrenees, which can be physically exhausting." He stopped for a few seconds, and looked at Elizabeth and Paul, and then directed his next statement toward them. "I don't want to be presumptuous, or tell you what to do, but are you two up for this? It can be grueling once we get up into those mountains."

Elizabeth looked at her husband, shrugged, and then answered Quim. "We've lived near the mountains all our lives, and used to do a lot of hiking, but from what you're saying, I'm not sure Paul would be up for it…not with his knees being the way they are."

"This time you're right, Elizabeth," Paul said. "I don't think they could take all the walking you're talking about, Quim, and I surely don't want to hold everyone up. I never realized that we wouldn't be going by car all the way."

"It's almost impossible to attempt driving," Quim said, "especially with all the patrols along the roads and in the air. When we get into the zones, especially the Prohibited one, there are curfews on any traveling after sunset."

"Maybe the best thing for us to do, Elizabeth," Paul said, "is for you and I to go back to Elne, and take our chances."

"You're right, *Cherie*," Elizabeth replied, and then looked at the rest of their family. "All of you are in more danger than we are, and there's no question that you must get out of France. Yes, Papa and I will go back to Elne in the morning."

Paulette came over and put her arm around her parents. "Then, I'll come back also. I can't let you go alone."

"Paulette!" Marcel exclaimed, "You can't go back now. Eventually, they're going to find out about our connection, and you could be shot for treason."

Leo held up his hands, and said, "Hold on...hold on. There is no way anyone is going back to Elne. The damn Nazis would line you all up against a wall and shoot you, just to set an example." He paused, and then looked at Paul, "My friend, I insist that you and Elizabeth stay with us until the War is over. As you can see, we have plenty of room, plus Helaine and I would enjoy the company. I'll even put you to work in the vineyard, if you'd like to help."

"Oh, I don't know if we could impose on you like that, Leo," Paul said.

"Nonsense," Leo said, "it's settled, and I don't want to hear another word about it. Paulette, you're welcome to stay here, but it sounds as if you had better go with your sister and children, also."

"Leo, Helaine," Elizabeth said, "your offer is the smartest idea we've heard so far, and we accept. Paulette, you must leave with Angelina... Papa and I will be able to manage just fine."

"Leo," Angelina said, "we can't thank you enough. This will work out well for everyone. We'd be worried sick if *Maman* and Papa had to face all the uncertainties of going back home...we know they'll be safe with you."

"We're all family here," Leo said, "and I know that they would do the same for us." He paused. "Quim, please continue with your plan."

"Alright, where were we?" Quim asked, as he looked at the map he had drawn. "Ah, yes...Tarascon. From there we will be following the mountains above Vicdessos and Ussat, which is extremely rough country…many people have died from physical exhaustion on this part." He let this sink in, before he said, "*Madame* and *Monsieur* Courty, it was a wise decision on your part not to go any further." Then he spoke directly to Marcel, asking, "Is there anyone in your family with any respiratory problems, such as asthma, or bronchitis?"

"No," Marcel answered, "and I'm sure that there will be enough of us to help carry Babette, if necessary. As far as the baby is concerned, I've rigged up a contraption to carry her on my back, which will also keep her warm. So, no, there aren't any physical problems, and I thank you for being so up-front with us."

"You can't be too cautious in these situations, *Señor*," Quim said, as he unconsciously switched to his native Spanish. "Now, from Ussat, we'll have to climb up over the pass called Port de Rat, which will lead us into Andorra. If the weather is too cold, or the winds become unbearable, which they can be in the pass, there are several caves where we can find refuge and warm ourselves."

Hearing no comments, or questions from the group, Quim continued. "Once we cross the border and find our way to a road, there will be someone to meet and take us down the Ordino Valley, by cars or trucks. When we get to Ordino, I'm sure that Hugh Garner will be there, and let you know where your family will be staying. Are there any questions?"

Marcel spoke up first. "Only one…when do we leave?"

"I think the best time would be tomorrow, after dark," Quim said. "This will give Leo and Simon time to set up the safe-houses in the areas we'll be traveling through, at least for the first couple days. You, and your men, will continue doing this as we move further south." He paused, and then spoke to them directly. "I'll go over this with you tonight in more detail; because you will have to find two or three houses in each area…I'll furnish you with names and locations that I've used in the past, also. It's always possible that we may have to change our direction, or get slowed down by unforeseen circumstances, and we'll need alternate housing."

Leo and Simon nodded their heads in approval. "It sounds like a wonderful plan, Quim," Simon said. "I feel that we'll be able to handle this without too much of a problem, since we're both familiar with this area."

Marcel was impressed with the way all of this was going down, and said, "Quim, I can't say enough about how thorough your planning has been, and with Simon and Leo assisting you, I know my family is in good hands."

"*Muchas gracias*, Marcel," Quim replied. "Coming from you, that is a real complement." He laughed out loud. "I have heard of some of your exploits also, and I'm counting on your helping me, should I ever need it."

"Any time, Quim," Marcel said, and then added in Spanish, "*Mi casa, su casa*."

48

Simon and Leo, along with three of the men, returned from their scouting expedition at 2:00 the next afternoon. As Quim had suggested, they had lined up four houses, two for each of the next couple days of travel. Everyone tried to get some rest during the day, and at 6:00 P.M., they bid farewell to Paul and Elizabeth. They began by hiking south through the forests and farms, and avoiding any roads. There were fourteen people in all: Marcel's family, Paulette, Simon, plus three of his men, and three of Marcel's men, Lucien, Leon, and Denis. Georges and Olivia headed back into hiding at the *bories*, near Gordes. The four people that Simon had been expecting to take with them, never arrived at the farm in time and would have to wait for the next crossing; therefore, eight *Maquis* members, including Marcel, seemed sufficient.

It was a very tearful goodbye, because there was a chance that neither Elizabeth and Paul, nor the Pontier's and Paulette, would ever see each other again. They were both at risk...one group escaping, and the other staying behind in occupied territory. It was a dilemma that tens of thousands of families faced during the War, and the odds were never favorable.

Quim led the way and the others followed. The weather was mild for the first three nights, and for the most part, everyone kept up with the pace, save for Babette who got tired by the middle of the night, and had to be carried until they reached their safe-house. It became a routine, sleeping all day in the houses and barns, and hiking from sunset till almost sunrise. Simon and his three men got less sleep than the others, because they spent a few hours each morning scouting out their next safe-house, and looking for any unusual German activity that would be in their southern path.

By the forth night, the weather had turned unusually cold, forcing Quim to scrub that night's hike. He felt that the group could use an extra day to rest, because the hard part was approaching...Vicdessos and Ussat. If their legs were tired once they reached the mountains, it would make the crossing twice as hard. Quim was happy with the progress they had made so far...everything had run according to plan, and no one was holding them up. Fortunately, they hadn't seen any Germans, but once they started climbing the mountains, they would be more exposed, especially to small surveillance planes.

The Pontier family appreciated the extra day's rest, for they were all more exhausted than they thought. "We must have been running on adrenalin," Marcel said. It also gave Angelina and Paulette a chance to wash some clothes and diapers, plus Angelina and Marcel were able to spend some needed time together. The farmers, at every stop they made, were very hospitable...feeding them while they were in their homes, and giving them provisions to take with them when they left.

When the time came to leave on the fifth night, the weather had become a little milder; however, as soon as they reached the foothills, and began climbing, they felt the 10 degree, and then 20 degree drops in temperature. Quim wanted to reach the mountain above Vicdessos before sunrise. As they got higher, and looked down into the valley, he was dismayed to see military trucks patrolling the roads leading into the town. Some appeared to be coming up the mountain in the direction they were headed. It was unusual seeing patrols at night, and he had to make a quick decision.

Quim conferred with Marcel and Simon, telling them the situation. "We have a choice to make...either we continue our present course, toward the same road the Germans are using, or we can zigzag along our same height, going further west of here...about 5 kilometers...and then coming back east along a steeper trail to reach Ussat. All together, it's about 10 kilometers out of our way. At sometime, though, we have to cross that road to get to the pass, which is above Ussat."

"Quim," Marcel asked, "if we do go the alternate route, do you know if there are any caves along the way?"

"Yes, there are a few caves, but not quite as big, and not as sheltered, as on this side of the mountain. It definitely wouldn't be as comfortable to spend the day." Quim paused a moment, as the three of them observed the German movement across the valley. Finally, he spoke again, as he rubbed his chin. "You know, if it were only just the men, and even the women, for that matter...I would say that we could probably find an opening in that road ahead of us, where we could cross in staggered, small groups; but, with the children along, especially the baby, who might start crying, or whatever, it would be too risky and could easily jeopardize the whole plan." He turned around, and said, "We've got to go the alternate way." He started walking west, without another word said.

Even though the distance that night was less than half the actual kilometers traveled on previous nights, it was much more grueling. The terrain was rugged, and the cold was stinging, because of the wind.

As they hiked, the children hung on to their parents and Paulette for warmth. It was no trouble for Madeline, who seemed very content in the baby-carrier Marcel had rigged up. When it became evident that Babette couldn't keep up, Lucien put her on his back, with her arms around his neck and her legs wrapped around his abs. Being a dock worker, he was used to carrying objects three-to-four times heavier than her.

Quim didn't want to push them too hard on this, their first night in the mountains, but he had no choice. He didn't stop, even after passing two of the caves, because he needed to get his party back to the other side, the west side, so they wouldn't freeze to death. They stopped every half hour, huddled as close together on the ground as possible, for warmth. Quim insisted that they nibble on a little food, to give them strength, and drink a cup of water each, to avoid getting hypothermia. No one argued. No one complained. They had put their trust in Quim, and prayed that he would get them through this night.

When it seemed that all in the group were ready to drop, they came to a long, S-shape curve on the trail, which followed the shape of the mountain and the valley below. Quim was now leading them perpendicular to the path they had been on, but instead of continuing to follow the curve of the mountain, he kept going straight for ⅔ kilometer, crossed over a ridge, and then went 75 meters down. It was as if they had been transposed to a different place in time. It was warmer, with no wind.

"We made it," Quim announced. "We'll be spending the night, and tomorrow, in a shelter just a little ways ahead."

There was a general sigh of relief. Within 15 minutes, they had entered a huge cave, sitting behind a mound of shrubs. Quim turned on his flashlight and led the group to a room, off the main part of the cave. There was a small circle of rocks on the ground, with ashes from a previous fire, lying in a small pit. He asked a few of the men to gather some wood and twigs from outside, and when they had returned with an ample supply, they started a fire.

Even though the cave was warmer, and able to give complete shelter from the wind, everyone was still quite cold. The fire gave them the warmth they needed. Marcel looked up and saw the smoke exiting through a small opening, thirty feet above. "Quim, do you think that the smoke will be visible from below?"

Quim glanced up, and said, "Not at this time of night, with the wind coming from the north. We will have to put the fire out before dawn, in case there are any spotter planes flying up there, so get as comfortable as you can. If anyone needs to relieve themselves, you'll have to go outside…but, stay within the bushes area so you won't be seen, and of course no flashlights." He paused, and then added, "Try to keep as quiet as possible, in case there are any Germans patrolling this area, and under no circumstance should anyone wander beyond the mouth of the cave, except for toilet purposes."

"Are you listening to what *Monsieur* Baldrich is saying?" Angelina asked the children. "We must keep very, very quiet and never, ever go outside. If you have to go to the bathroom, tell Papa or me, and we'll take you. Do you all understand?"

They all said that they did, at which point Babette said, "I have to go right now, *Maman*."

After having something to eat and drink, everyone, except for Quim, formed a circle around the fire, found a comfortable position, and slept for the remainder of the night. Quim stayed on guard at the front entrance to the cave, and came back to the fire, only to warm himself sporadically. "I'll have plenty of time to sleep tomorrow," he told them, "and all of you need your rest more than I do at this altitude."

Just before dawn, he quietly smothered the fire with dirt, and then woke up everyone. They had slept for four hours, which he thought was sufficient. "I don't want you sleeping for too long," he told them. "I'd rather have you tired until after lunch, and then let you take a nap until dusk. We've got a big night's hike ahead of us."

Marcel and Simon both admired the way Quim took charge. He was the expert in these mountains, and scrutinized every little detail to the best interest of the group. He told them when to eat, sleep and pee, and no one even thought of questioning him. If there was anyone that was indispensable on this mission, it was definitely Quim Baldrich.

49

At precisely the end of dusk, Quim led the group along the path that would take them above Ussat. This was the jumping off place to Port de Rat, the pass that would lead them into Andorra. This pass would be the hardest part of their journey, but first, they would have to circumvent the many German checkpoints and patrols in the Ussat area. This worried Quim more than anything else, because it was an unknown factor...the Germans could suddenly appear from out of nowhere, and although the children had been virtually no problem up to now, having them along was an added risk. At lunch that day, he discussed his concerns with all the adults. He advised them to be especially alert, and for Marcel and Angelina to keep the children close by them.

It was starting to snow as the group moved at a crisp pace. Having had a good night and day's rest, everyone was anxious to get this ordeal over with, and it was obvious that they were adjusting to the altitude. As an added precaution because of the light snow, Quim assigned the last man on the trail to attach a rope around his waist, which was connected at both ends to a pole that he pulled behind his back, to cover their tracks. He knew that a spotter plane could easily see their footprints and report it. While they were in the cave, they had heard several small planes flying overhead that day, and didn't want to take any chances.

It took two hours before they saw the lights of Ussat, and as if this was a signal to Quim, he turned due south and headed toward the top of the ridge of the mountain they were on. This took another hour to reach the peak, and once on top the full moon came out, enabling them to see for miles ahead of them. Quim pointed to a rugged-looking set of peaks to the south, and said, "That is the Port de Rat. On the other side is Andorra. From here, we'll be going down this mountain, before we begin our climb up and over the pass."

He pointed again, but this time down the mountain. "Can you see the road down there? I told you that we would have to cross it eventually, so that's where we're headed now. If we spot any German vehicles along the road, everyone needs to get down on the ground for cover, until they pass. If we do have to engage the enemy, it would be best to use silencers on your rifles or pistols, if you have them. Sound travels a long way in these mountains, and we don't want the whole Nazi army on top of us."

"How many men have silencers for their rifles?" Marcel asked. Three of the men raised their hands...two were Simon's men and the other was Lucien. Marcel knew that all were good shooters and assigned them to begin any confrontation, if it became necessary.

Listening to the banter, back and forth between the men, was a little startling to Angelina and Paulette. The men spoke of killing as if it were their everyday job; the sisters realized now just how much Marcel had been involved over the last year. Raymond and J.P. were in awe of the whole thing, thinking of their father now as some type of general. As for Babette, she still thought that this was a marvelous adventure, just like the fairy tales her mother always read her. If they survived the next couple days, it *would* be an adventure that no one in the family would ever forget.

Leaving Ussat in the valley behind them, they moved down the other side of the mountain toward the road…and the looming Port de Rat, 2349 meters (7704 feet) high. The road led directly to the border, and into the main highway of Andorra; however, over the pass was their only option, and with all the accumulated winter snow, it wasn't going to be easy. Quim was happy that he had instructed Simon, at their first meeting, to have snowshoes for every person on this mission, including the children. Now everyone, except for Marcel and Babette, was carrying a pair attached to their backpacks. Theirs were being carried by two of the men.

They had come almost two-thirds of the way down the mountain, when J.P. ran up to Quim, and said, "*Monsieur* Baldrich, I think I saw lights coming this way from the valley, to the left."

Everyone turned to look, but could see nothing. There were some boulders sitting not far in front of them, and Quim said, "To be safe, let's get down there in a hurry and hide behind those large rocks…on your stomachs…and I want the women and children to stay near the back. The patrol may be around a few of those turns, and we can't see them yet." He never once questioned what J.P. saw, but patted him on the head, saying, "Good work, Jean-Pierre."

Once they were safely behind the boulders, the men had their backpacks off, with their rifles ready to fire. They spotted a transport truck, two curves down the hill, using search lights on both sides of the road. Marcel quickly crawled back 5 meters, to where his family was hiding. "I wanted to make sure everyone's O.K., and give you this, just in case you need it." He pulled a pistol from his back holster, handed it to Paulette, and then crawled back behind his boulder, which he shared with Lucien and Quim. Denis and Leon were behind a bolder on the same level, and parallel to his, 3½ meters to his right. Simon and his three men were to Marcel's left and further down the hill.

As everyone waited for the patrol to approach them, Paulette couldn't help but think of how Johann was doing, and if he was able to see his parents. She looked at the revolver in her hand, and thought of the possibility of her having to kill a German soldier with it. *Would he be a young man and have parents waiting for him to return home, also?* Her heart was pounding, as she let out a large breath. *I'd kill anyone to protect Angelina and the children.*

The truck had made its last turn and would soon be just below their hiding places. They could already see the lights shining above them, and to their left, coming closer and closer as the truck made its way up the hill. Quim knew all the checkpoint stations leading up to the border, and had observed the schedule of the German patrols. He assumed that the truck was heading up the hill to the first station, in order to change the guards. It was 1½ kilometers from where they were now, and the patrol would continue for another 15 kilometers, stopping at other checkpoints that were closer to the border. He, and everyone else, was surprised when, for some reason, the patrol truck stopped 25 meters just below them. The searchlights had gone off in their direction, giving Quim, Marcel and Simon an opportunity to get a quick peek down the hill.

They saw two men getting off the back of the truck, and taking a leak in the snow, and could distinctly hear the voices of several soldiers. Quim understood from their conversation, that they "hated this duty, because every night they froze their asses off." The officer, sitting in the passenger side of the front seat, leaned out his window and told the two that they "could walk up to their station, and that the fresh air would do them good." There was a lot of laughter from the men in the back of the truck, and then it pulled away, leaving the two peeing in the snow.

When they were through, they each lit up a cigarette and stood there for a few minutes talking.

After lying on the snowy ground for 15 minutes, everyone in Quim's group was starting to get cold. They were relieved when the soldiers finished their cigarettes, and started walking up the road; however, they hadn't gotten far, when Madeline began crying. Angelina grabbed a bottle out of her knapsack, as quickly as she could, and gave it to the baby, but by then it was too late. The soldiers heard the cry immediately, turned around and flashed their lights up the hill.

One of them shouted, "*Wer ist da*? Who is it?" No one made another sound, as the soldiers began walking up the hill.

"*Wo sind Sie*? Where are you?" the other soldier yelled, as they passed far right of Simon's boulder, but continued on a strait path between Lucien and Denis. The baby, all of a sudden, pushed the bottle away and began crying again, which caused the soldiers to head directly toward the sound coming from behind the top boulder. Swiftly, and without hesitation, Lucien and Denis sprung out from behind their hiding places, each grabbing a soldier from the back, in a choke hold around the neck, and stabbing them in the chest. There was barely a gasp from either of the Germans. They fell to the ground in a heap on top of each other. To make sure they were dead, Denis felt for a pulse, but both were killed instantly.

Marcel ran up to his family to keep them from seeing the dead men, and as calmly as he could, said, "Everything is fine now, so just stay down for a little while longer until we get rid of these two bodies. Fortunately, they never got a chance to fire their weapons, so sit up and rest for a few minutes, have something to eat and drink if you like, because we'll be leaving shortly."

"Have something to eat!" exclaimed Angelina. "I've never been so scared in my life...I feel like throwing up. I can't believe that this has become your life, and you're so calm about it all." She started sobbing, with her face in her hands.

Marcel got on the ground and put his arms around her. "Darling, just try to relax. Those two soldiers would have killed us if they had the chance. We did what we had to do, and I don't expect you to take it calmly. You aren't used to these types of situations, and to tell you the truth, I did throw up after my first *Maquis* mission. But all of you did just fine, and it was no one's fault that Madeline started crying. We knew the risks of taking the children, but sometimes in war, as in life, you have to make tough decisions."

"I know, Cherie," Angelina said. "I'm sorry I got so upset...it was just so frightening hearing those soldiers coming up the hill."

"Can we see the bodies now, Papa?" Raymond asked.

"No, Raymond," Paulette said, "you don't need to see any bodies." She turned the pistol around, and handed it to Marcel. "Here...let me give this back to you. I'm just glad I didn't need to use it; although, I would have if those men came around the corner."

"Thank you, Paulette," Marcel said. "I'm glad you didn't have to use it either. It's not easy taking someone else's life, even if it is a German's."

How would Johann ever fit into this family? Paulette thought. *When the War is over, maybe things will be different.*

Simon came walking up to Marcel and his family, and asked, "Is everything alright?"

"Yes," Marcel answered, "everyone is fine. Have the men taken care of the German soldiers?"

"Everything has been taken care of," Simon said. "It will be spring before they'll ever find them." He paused. "We're ready to go, if you're all set."

The group followed Quim down the hill, across the road, and along a zigzag path up the foothills, that was barely visible. It had started snowing harder than before, and the moon could no longer be seen. Thirty minutes later, when they had gotten to a flatter area, Quim told everyone to put on their snowshoes. "I don't want anyone's feet getting wet, because the temperature will start dropping, and there's a greater chance of frostbite. We can expect the snow, from here on, to get deeper. For those of you who have never worn snowshoes, the easiest way to do it, is to walk like a duck." He demonstrated, and after a few minutes, everyone got the hang of it.

They made their normal rest stops for the next four hours, and when they started hiking again, the moon came back out. It was only then that they realized they were now surrounded by mountains. They hiked for another hour, when Quim led them to one of his hidden caves. It didn't come too soon, because everyone was sweating from exhaustion. The men built a fire, and then the entire group began taking off some of their layered clothes to dry.

Quim took the first guard duty, and let the others sleep. If he were by himself, he would have hiked until dawn…another three hours. He kept thinking about the two soldiers who were killed, and hoped that they would not be found for some time. The men had put them under a pile of fallen trees that were completely covered by snow, and then covered their tracks well. By morning, though, they would be reported missing and the search for them would begin. If the dogs were brought in, then there was a possibility of the bodies being found, and a border escape would be suspected…at which time, the Germans would send in both air and snow patrols into the mountains. *I have to assume the worst case scenario*, he thought, *and not take any chances of the patrols catching up with us.*

There were two more hours of darkness, and even though Quim knew his group was exhausted, he woke everyone for another march to the next cave. They all had at least an hour's sleep, and would have all day to rest. "The farther we keep ahead of the Nazis, the better," he told them. No one quibbled.

Even though it was only an hour's rest, it was enough to give the group the energy they needed to continue upwards toward the Port de Rat. They reached the next cave, just as the early light of day appeared in the horizon. This was the smallest lair they had been in, and Quim wasted no time in letting them know it wouldn't be as comfortable. "If you need to go to the bathroom, there are a couple small boulders back there," he pointed with his flashlight to the left side of the cave, "which will give you a *little* privacy. After you're through with your toilet, please cover up whatever you do with the sand on the ground." He paused for a moment, and then said, "Under no circumstances can anyone go outside, for any reason…we're just too exposed up here. Being out in the open, we could easily be spotted from the air, or by the snow patrols. Are there any questions?"

No one raised their hand, but finally Marcel spoke up. "Quim, I can't tell you what a marvelous job you've done in getting us this far." Everyone applauded, as Marcel continued to say, "So, whatever you say goes, because we all have confidence in your abilities to get us over the border."

"Thank you, Marcel," Quim said. "I'm trying my best, and I want to thank all of you for being so cooperative. If that were not the case, this whole exercise would be much more difficult. Tonight, we should cross over the pass and be in Andorra by tomorrow morning, so get some rest and stay as alert as before. Being so close, we don't want to make any unnecessary mistakes, because there's always a chance that there will be more German patrols along the border."

Quim barely got through with his sentence, when a plane flew directly overhead, causing the noise from its engines to vibrate loudly through the cave. Quim looked at his watch, and then remarked, "I see that the Krauts are right on time. One thing about them, they are consistent and that works to our advantage."

He paused for a minute, until everyone found a spot for themselves on the ground. "Before you get too comfortable, *señors*, let me show you the two lookout areas over here." He walked back toward the front wall of the cave with the men following him, and pointed out two holes, one low, and one higher. He stepped up on a medium-size flat rock and looked through the higher hole. "From here, you can see across the valley toward the mountains on the other side." He jumped down, got on his knees, and looked through the lower opening, saying, "And from here, you can see down in the valley itself. So, I think that it would be best to have not one, but two people on watch at each shift. Marcel, will you and Simon be so good as to assign the shifts?" They both nodded. "I would take the first watch, but I don't think I can keep my eyes open any longer."

"I do have one question, Quim," Simon said. "Is there any way to see to the left of us, where we hiked up that trail, without having to go outside?"

"Good point, Simon. As a matter of fact, there is, but it will take a very small, skinny person to stand in there." Quim walked further to his right and pointed out a small, narrow area. "If you stick your head around this corner, and look to your left, there is a sliver of an opening that gives you a view down the trail; however, it would be difficult to stay in that position for very long."

"I bet we could fit in there," Raymond said, excitedly.

"Yeah, we're old enough to help," J.P. added. "Let us help, Papa."

413

Raymond climbed in the opening and leaned his back against the wall. "I can see perfectly down the trail, *Señor* Baldrich."

"Let me take a look, Raymond," J.P. said. Raymond got out and J.P. climbed in. "Wow! I can't believe how high up we are."

"O.K., boys," Marcel said, "I'll let you alternate every two hours, and if you see anything, let one of the men on duty know, alright?" The boys agreed, and then Marcel added, "But whatever you do, don't yell...we've go to keep as quiet as possible."

Raymond sighed. "We understand, Papa...we're not stupid."

Marcel just chuckled and nodded his head, as Quim said, "You know it was J.P. who spotted the German trucks, so I think they're perfect for the job." J.P. beamed.

Marcel and Simon assembled their men and assigned a watch schedule for the day. It wasn't long before everyone else went to sleep. By mid-afternoon, almost the whole group was having their daily meal, and trying to keep warm. Fortunately, they had listened to Quim about layering their clothing and drinking plenty of water. They were running a little low on food and tried to conserve what little they had, for they would need some nourishment on the trail that evening.

Things were very quiet until Raymond said, "Psssst."

Leon, who was one of the men on watch, went over and peeked around the corner of Raymond's observation point. Quim, Marcel, and all the other men that were awake, got up when Leon motioned them to come over to where he was. "There's a snow patrol 150 meters on that ridge behind us. They're just standing there, looking around with their binoculars."

Marcel turned around abruptly and said to Angelina, "Give the baby her milk." Angelina started to say something, but Marcel held up his hand, and emphatically said, "*NOW!*"

Quim took a peek, and said, "There's a slope over that ridge, which goes down to the valley. Let's hope they decide to put on their skis and head below. It leads to one of the border stations." He paused, took another peek, and whispered, "One of those Krauts is looking right at us now, so get your weapons ready, just in case they come this way."

After a few minutes passed, Marcel took a look. "There are five of them, each carrying an automatic rifle. If they do come over here, we'll be able to take them, but the noise would echo all over these mountains, so make sure the silencers are on your guns." He kept looking, and then reported, "One of the men is cranking up a field phone that's on one of the other's backs. Now he's speaking......"

A deafening noise came on top of them, as another spotter plane flew over the cave. It occurred so fast, that Marcel flinched, and hit the back of his head on the small opening. He held his head and backed out slowly. The palm of his hand was a little moist, and when he looked down at it, he could see the blood on his palm. He felt a little dizzy, and sat down on the ground.

"Are you alright, Papa?" J.P. asked, as he looked at his father's head. When Marcel didn't speak, J.P. walked over to his mother, got a diaper, wet it, and then walked back and put it on his father's head.

"Thank you, J.P.," Marcel said, "I'm OK...just a little dazed. It will be fine."

Quim took Marcel's place at the small opening, and soon reported that three of the soldiers had put on their skis, climbed to the top of the ridge overlooking the downward slope, and finally went over the edge. The last two kept scanning the area with their binoculars. Quim was wishing out loud, "Go with the others. Go with the others, you sons of bitches." He was silent for almost 20 seconds, and then in a loud whisper, "They're coming this way, and one of them has a long, German grenade in his hand. It looks like he may throw it in this direction, so everyone get down and stay quiet." Everyone huddled in the back part of their lair, except for Quim, who got face-down on the ground with Marcel, Simon, and Leon.

Indeed, the two soldiers were walking in their snowshoes up the middle of the mountain, towards the trail that led to the cave. When they were within 20 meters, the soldier threw his grenade. It landed a few meters to the left of the opening, causing a huge blast, but very little damage inside the cave itself. Everyone in the group waited with baited breath, guns at the ready. Ten seconds passed, when they heard a metal object hit the roof of the cave, and then a blast that felt like it shook the whole mountain. Rocks, and other debris, came flying into their sanctuary. The smoke and dust were so thick, that it was hard to breathe, or see anything more than a foot ahead.

Babette started to whimper, but Paulette grabbed her and held her tight to her chest. People began to cough, but it apparently wasn't loud enough to be heard, at the distance the German soldiers were from the cave. Leon, who was lying next to Marcel, started to get up, but Marcel pulled him back, and asked, "Where are you going?"

"I'm going to try to pick off those two guys, before they throw another grenade," he replied.

"No," Marcel said, "they have a field radio with them, and obviously are reporting to someone on a regular basis. If they don't check in, then we'll have a slew of troops surrounding the area, and probably our *Luftwaffe* friend dropping an early Christmas present on us." The smoke and dust were starting to settle, as Marcel said to Leon, "Take a look and see what they're up to now. If they're coming to check the cave, then we *will* have to take them out."

Leon went to the narrow opening, and whispered, "They're just standing there looking right at us, and appear to be joking with one another. Now, one of them is drinking from a flask and passing it on to his friend." A minute passed before Leon spoke again. "They're starting to move up toward us...wait a minute, they've stopped and are facing across the hill...now they're taking the skis off their backs and getting out of their snowshoes. They have their skis on now and packing their snowshoes away...and yes, they're skiing back down...and over the ridge."

They all let out a sigh of relief. Marcel walked around to make sure everyone was alright. Angelina was shaking, but still holding Madeline with the bottle in her mouth. He put his arm around his wife, assuring her that everything was going to be OK. Then he led her and the other children to the opening of the cave for them to get some fresh air. It seemed almost surreal to Marcel that everyone was in a rather jovial mood, considering what they had just gone through. Except for a few minor bruises, no one was injured.

"There's a couple more hours of daylight, and then we'll get moving," Quim said. "I believe that we've seen the end of the Germans for the day, but I still don't want to take the chance of leaving until the sun goes down. With all the thrills we've just had, I hope you'll still be able to get a little rest before we leave."

It was a hard climb for the first three hours, but at 9:00 P.M., they almost reached the top of the Port de Rat. There was a small cave-like shelter in the mountain, where they had some relief from the wind and light snow. Quim told them to wait here and rest, while he, and a few of Simon's men, checked out the border area that they were heading towards.

An hour passed, before Quim and the men came back. "It looks clear ahead," he told the rest of the group. He smiled, and said, "Come on, let's get across the border."

They went up a little further, and then over the top of the pass. The hike down was considerably easier than what they had been used to lately. At exactly 12:00 midnight, while they were standing in an open field, Quim had everyone gather around him for an announcement. "Well, we made it…welcome to Andorra."

A big applause went up from the group, and everyone was hugging each other. With her arm around Quim, Paulette was the first to speak. "Oh, this is marvelous…I can't believe we're here! This is an adventure that all of us will remember for the rest of our lives. And we have you to thank, Quim…I don't know how we would have made it without you." She gave him a big kiss on his cheek, and everyone applauded again. "By the way, where exactly are we in Andorra?"

"We're standing at the top of the Ordino Valley, about a kilometer from the border of France. If you're not familiar with our little principality, it's one of the smallest countries in Europe…only 24 kilometers across and a total of 468 square miles, but it is the largest and finest ski area in the Pyrenees, and for that matter, one of the best in Europe. That's one reason why I plan on staying here, to ski and hike."

"Don't they speak Catalan here?" Raymond asked.

"That's very good, Raymond," Quim said. "It's one of the few countries that still speak a form of Latin, although it has generated into a mixture of Spanish, French, Italian and Portuguese, so I think your family will pick it up very quickly, indeed."

"I, too, would like to say," Marcel began, "that we appreciate the professional way you handled every aspect of this journey, Quim. My family and I cannot thank you enough." He shook Quim's hand and they embraced each other warmly.

"Thank you all for the memories you've given me from this experience," Quim said. He waved his hand back and forth, paused,

and then said, "Some of them I could have done without, but......"
Everyone laughed. "Nevertheless, we made it together. It was a good
team effort, and the children were wonderful."

"You were very brave to take us," Angelina said, "and I hope we'll
get to see you many times while we're staying here."

"You don't need to worry, Angelina," Quim said, "I'll be checking
on you and Paulette quite often, to make sure things are going smoothly.
It's the least I can do while Marcel and Simon, and all you men of *La
Résistance*, are fighting to rid us of those Nazi bastards. It was my honor
to be with all of you." He was silent for a moment, and then said, "We
have a little more walking to do, before we get to Ordino, where the
road begins. We'll be passing through some tiny hamlets on the way,
but there is no reason to stop until we get to the road. There will be
vehicles waiting for us."

They hiked for another 3 kilometers, passing El Serrat, Llorts, La
Corinada, and Sornas, and finally reached Ordino. As Quim had
promised, to no one's surprise, there were three small trucks waiting for
them, along with the British expatriate, Hugh Garner. He welcomed
everyone also, and said that he had found Marcel's family a place to
stay, in the tiny village of Arinsal. The men would be staying at another
village nearby, for a week, and then with Marcel and Simon, led back
to France by Quim.

When Hugh asked the Pontier's to get into the covered truck,
Paulette quipped, "And miss our evening hike?" It was a good laugh for
everyone, and then she followed up with, "This is too much of a luxury
for us, Hugh." Everyone said their farewells and got into their respective
trucks. Paulette was feeling very relaxed, for the first time since they
had left Elne. On their drive to Arinsal, her thoughts drifted to Johann,
and wished that he was here with her. She missed him terribly, and

knew now that she really did love him. *Somehow, we'll find each other after the War*, she thought.

It was almost daybreak when they arrived in the village, which was tucked peacefully in the valley below the tallest mountain in Andorra, Coma Pedrosa. They would be staying with the Marti family in an old, stone house called Cal Martinet. The owners greeted them very warmly, in French, and within a short time, they became fast friends with Martina, and her husband Francesc. They learned very quickly from the Marti's, that times here were desperately hard. To earn their keep, Angelina and Paulette would be put to work with the rest of the people in the village, including themselves, in traditional, mountain farming activities. Raymond and Jean-Pierre would be allowed to go to school until noon, have their lunch, and then work in the fields for the rest of the afternoon; Babette would stay in school, until Angelina picked her up at the end of the day.

"We're not afraid of hard work," Angelina told them, "and we expect to do our fair share. You're very kind to have us here, and we'll do everything we can to help you. And, yes, is there someone I can leave the baby with during the day?"

"That won't be a problem," Martina said. "My mother, who lives with us, will be happy to take care of her. In fact, you will probably have to fight with her to get Madeline back."

Marcel was relieved that things were settling in so well for his family, and when he left a week later with his *Maquis* group, he knew now that Angelina, Paulette, and the children *were* truly safe.

When he got back to France, he checked in immediately with his in-laws, Paul and Elizabeth Courty, and told them of their experiences in crossing into Andorra. They were comforted to hear that everyone was fine and safe, and they too felt more relaxed than they had in weeks. Leo and Helaine had been wonderful to them, and Paul had been able to start a small vineyard on the Montal property, something that Leo had always wanted to do.

Before Marcel returned to the *bories* to rejoin his Maquis fighters, he attended a scheduled meeting in Provence, at *Le Clos des Saumanes*. It was good to see his old friend Philippe again, as well as Florette. The other regional Maquis leaders were there, and they sat in fascination as Marcel related his adventures with the mountain man, Quim Baldrich, who now was scheduled to take at least one group a month across the border. When he finished, he made a recommendation that Quim be honored after the War with some type of commendation, preferably the French Legion of Honor. Everyone approved, and his name and recommendations would now be forwarded to General Charles de Gaulle.

Business was as usual, discussing past missions, results, and future plans against the occupying German forces. After the meeting, Marcel made his way back to the *bories*, near Gordes, and rejoined what was left of his group---Lucien, Leon, Georges, who had now left Marseille's *Vichy* Headquarters for good, Olivia, and Denis. Sitting around their campfire at dinner that night, they made a toast to their fallen companions---Estephan, François, Aristide, and Claudine. Marcel didn't let them dwell on this for long, and wasted no time in briefing them on their most important, future missions.

It was now March, 1943, and for the next 17 months, Marcel and his *Maquis* unit would continue to wreak havoc and disrupt the Nazi war machine. They had to move their base to three different locations in order to avoid detection, and by sheer cunning and good luck, no one else in the group was killed, or injured.

Angelina, Paulette, and the children fared well in Arinsal, even though food was scarce and the work seemed never-ending. Marcel was able to visit them three times while they were there, and stayed a week on each visit. They enjoyed these visits tremendously, because they were seeing more of him now than they had while they were living in Elne. They all longed for the day when the War would be over, and they could return home together.

50

On August 15, 1944, Lt. General Alexander Patch's U.S. Seventh Army, and General Jean de Lattre de Tassigny's French First Army, made an amphibious landing near Cannes, in southern France. It was called "Operation Anvil", and within a week, the Mediterranean coastal areas of France were free of German troops. It was on the morning of August 19, 1944, that the last German soldier left Elne. There was music and dancing in the streets, and in the square, that lasted throughout the day and night. Six days later, August 25th, Paris was liberated by French soldiers and the American First Army.

On the day that Paris was liberated, Marcel arrived in Andorra with his Citroën, making it the first time that he had actually driven into the country. He was there to finally take his family home. They would stop in Elne for a few days to drop off Paulette, and visit Paul and Elizabeth, who had come back a few days before. Then they would proceed back to Marseille, and start their lives over again. It had been two years since they had left, and they were looking forward to a new beginning.

Paulette was anxious to get back to Elne and see her parents. She had never been away from them for this long, and felt an obligation to take care of them in their older age. She was hoping also, that by chance, she might have received a message from Johann, which could have been delivered to her old office, or to Mayor Astruc. It was highly unlikely that this would happen, but she thought about it constantly while she was in Andorra.

The family's first night together was the most relaxing that any of them could remember. A great weight had been lifted off their shoulders. For the adults, there were no longer the worries of the War, or of Marcel's *Maquis* activities. For the children, it was more than just a marvelous adventure…it was history that they had been part of. Now the boys, especially, wanted to know more details about the whole experience they lived through.

"J.P. and I talk about it all the time, Papa," Raymond said, as they were half-way through dinner, "but we keep getting our dates, and people all mixed up."

"Yeah, we know all about when France was invaded," J.P. added, "but we want you to tell us what happened after Pearl Harbor, and how the Allies got in to this."

"How did Normandy come about?" Raymond asked.

Marcel thought for a minute, had another sip of wine, and then tried to enlighten his sons. "Well briefly, in December 1941, Roosevelt and Churchill had their first wartime meeting and adopted a "Defeat Germany First" strategy. The Allies considered an assault across the English Channel as early as 1942, and the preparations for this invasion of the Normandy coast began early in 1943. Then the British, Canadians, and Americans assembled almost 3 million men, and stored 16 million tons of supplies in Britain for the greatest invasion in history. From what I hear, the Allies had 5,000 large ships, 4,000 smaller landing craft, and more than 11,000 aircraft.

"Months before the invasion, Allied bombers pounded the Normandy coast to prevent the Germans from building up their military strength, and the French *Résistance* aided in assessing the damage, and then reporting the results back to Britain. On D-Day, June 6, 1944, just a couple months ago, General Dwight David Eisenhower told his forces, 'You are about to embark upon a great crusade,' and at 6:30 A.M., the first wave of infantry and armored troops were on the beaches of Normandy. The invasion should have taken place the day before, but was canceled because of bad storms in the Channel. The paratroopers *were* dropped behind the German lines on June 5th, in order to blow up the bridges, cut railroad lines, and seize the landing fields. Gliders were also used to bring in men, jeeps, small tanks, and light artillery, and *La Résistance* was there again to assist the Allies. So, D-Day marked the beginning of the end of the Third Reich." Marcel paused, and was happy that his sons had a look of awe on their faces. He got two more glasses, and poured each of the boys a small amount of wine. "And that, in a nutshell, is what happened." The three of them clinked their glasses together and toasted "Victory."

The night before they left for France, Hugh Garner threw the family a going- away party at La Borda, one of the few restaurants that was still open in La Vella, the capital city of Andorra. Martina and Francesc were there, along with Quim Baldrich and a few other friends that Angelina and Paulette had made, during their year and a half stay.

With tears in their eyes, Angelina and Paulette both thanked everyone for being so kind and gracious to them and to the children, who now spoke Catalan perfectly. Even two year-old Madeline was using Catalan as her first language. The boys, Raymond and J.P., thanked Quim for teaching them to ski. Raymond was all smiles, when he noted that, "This is the first sport that I can do better than my brother."

There were many toasts to the Allies, the French Army, to Marcel and *La Résistance*, and many bottles of wine were consumed. Marcel stood, raised his glass, and said, "Here's to all of you that helped get us here and took us in as family …Quim, Hugh, Martina and Francesc… we're forever grateful. *SANTÉ!*"

"*SANTÉ!*" everyone replied, and then took a sip of their wine.

With his glass still held high, Marcel said, "And this is a special toast to the love of my life, Angelina, who has put up with my absence for the last two years, and has raised our four children, a job much harder than the one I had." He paused for a moment, and then emotionally said, "I love you, *Cherie*." He and Angelina touched glasses, kissed and everyone clapped. Then Marcel continued, "I speak for my whole family, when I say that this is truly the best night we've had in many years. We'll never forget this, and all of you. *SANTÉ!*"

As they were crossing the border, Paulette said, "This sure is easier than the way we came in. It's hard to believe that we were here for so long."

"Yes," Angelina replied, "it went by so quickly, and it's sort of sad to be leaving. They were such nice people."

"We'll go back and visit one day," Marcel said. "It's only a couple hours drive from Elne. When we come to see your parents, it will be nothing to drive into Andorra from there."

"Can we come back and go skiing, Papa?" Raymond asked.

"Well, since this is the first sport you've ever been interested in, how can I say 'no'? Of course we can do that…and we can teach Babette to ski, too."

"I'd like that, Papa," Babette said. "They said that I wasn't old enough this time, and too little…by winter I'll be much bigger."

"It won't be long before I get better than you, Raymond," J.P. said, as he leaned over Paulette to tease his brother.

"That won't happen in our lifetime, J.P." Raymond quipped. "I'm already parallel skiing and you'll still be snow-plowing, like you're doing now. You better get used to skiing behind me, and tasting snow in your mouth."

"Yeah, you wish, smarty pants," J.P. said. "I'll ski right over you someday."

Marcel glanced over at Angelina, and raised his eyebrows. "Some things never change, do they? Those two are still at it."

"They've really gotten better, Marcel," Angelina replied. "They've become much closer through this whole experience, and I'm sure that they'll always be teasing each other."

It was a beautiful morning, as they drove through the French countryside, the Pyrenees to the south of them. There were no German or *Vichy* patrols to worry about, and everyone was enjoying the splendor of the day, especially their regained freedom.

"I haven't felt this good in years," Marcel commented. "I've had enough excitement to last me a lifetime."

"Well, I hope you won't find it too dull back in Marseille," Angelina quipped. "You've got to go back to work and make some money for the family. All these children have got to go to college one day."

"Darling, I can't wait to start my dental practice again, and get back into a routine," Marcel said. "It will be a piece of cake, after what we've had to endure these last few years." He paused, and then asked, "And you, Paulette...what are you planning to do?"

Paulette thought for a moment, and then sighed. "Oh, I just want to help *Maman* and Papa get settled again, and then relax myself for awhile. This is all happening so fast, I don't want to make too many decisions right now." She would have liked to tell them her feelings about Johann, and the plans they had talked about after the War ended, but thought better of it. Angelina knew that her sister was still very fond of Johann, but was never able to get her to say much. "I think that one day, I might want to go back to teaching, maybe at the University in Perpignan. I don't know yet, and I'm really in no hurry to do anything at this point." *I'd like nothing more than to be in Johann's arms right now.*

It wasn't long before they crossed the bridge to Elne over the River Tech, and were driving through the ancient, Roman gates of the village. As they approached the Courty's home, they could see Elizabeth and Paul sitting on the balcony, and then getting out of their seats and waving, as they saw Marcel's car coming down the cobblestone street. They had their arms around each other and never looked happier.

Marcel parked in front of the house, whereby everyone jumped out and ran up the stairs. It had been a year-and-a-half since the family was together, and other than a few messages passed by Marcel, they had not heard, or spoken to each other. Elizabeth and Paul had a lot of long embraces with their daughters and grandchildren, as well as Marcel, and quite a few tears were shed in the process.

The grandparents were astonished by Madeline, who was no longer the baby they remembered. She now had curly, blonde hair...something unusual for their family, and much different from Babette's, whose hair was now dark and straight.

Elizabeth bent down toward Madeline, and said, "You are absolutely gorgeous, just like your sister." Then she looked up at the other children. "The thing I missed the most, is seeing all of you growing up." She wiped a tear away.

Madeline replied in Catalan, "Thank you Grandmother...my mother has told me all about you and Grandfather. I am very happy to meet you."

"Darling," Angelina began, "you must tell them that in French, because they don't understand that language."

In perfect French, Madeline repeated what she had said. Elizabeth and Paul were astonished at her vocabulary, and Paul commented to Angelina and Marcel, "I think that you have a little genius on your hands."

"You may be right, Papa," Paulette said. "It was amazing to see how quickly she picked up everything. She was walking, and speaking in phrases, before she turned one."

"I think it helped having an older sister and two brothers, who have absolutely doted on her," Angelina said. "She kept us all focused, and it made the time in Andorra pass much more quickly." She looked down at Madeline, and said, "I think that *Grandmere* and *Grandpere* would like a big hug and kiss now."

Madeline ran to them, as she opened her arms. Paul and Elizabeth were thrilled, and spent the next few minutes holding and talking to her. Finally, Elizabeth said to everyone, "Why don't we make lunch…then we can all sit and talk? We want to hear everything from the beginning, even though Marcel has kept us posted."

"And we want to know how it was in Foix, with the Montals'," Paulette said.

"Leo and Helaine were absolutely wonderful," Elizabeth said. "There is no way we could ever repay them for all they did for us."

"The nicest part of it," Paul added, "is that they would never want to be repaid. They were just happy to help…that's the kind of people they are."

They all talked for hours about their experiences, and the children never left the table, because they too had a lot to say. "Someday, someone aught to write a book about all of this," J.P. said. "No one would believe everything we've done."

"Papa, you haven't told us if you've been back to Marseille recently?" Raymond asked.

Marcel shook his head, and let out a deep breath. "Well…I went back a few months ago…not to our house…it was just for a few hours."

Angelina could see that he was upset, and asked, "What happened, *Cherie?*"

Marcel hesitated, and then said, "It was terrible. The city was crawling with Nazi *SS*. I was near the railroad station and saw hundreds of Jews…men, women, and children, being herded into cattle cars. The guards were beating them with long sticks, and those that fell down, were kicked repeatedly. I saw a German officer shoot a young boy in the back, when he tried to run. The boy couldn't have been any older than Raymond, or J.P. I've heard that about four thousand Marseille Jews have been deported."

"Where were they taking them, Papa?" J.P. asked.

"To concentration camps in Poland." Marcel paused. "As hard as it may seem, our intelligence says that there is more and more evidence now that these are actually death camps! A place called Auschwitz may be killing thousands a day."

Paulette felt sick to her stomach. *Why did I have to fall in love with a man from Germany?*

"How is that possible?" Paul asked. "It may be an exaggeration… they can't be that barbaric!"

"The reports we're getting," Marcel replied, "are that the Nazis are gassing these people en masse, and then burning their bodies in large ovens." He paused for this to sink in. "Our sources are pretty reliable."

"Do you think Guy and Ira Rothschild were also taken, Papa?" Raymond asked. "They were our best friends."

"I don't know, son," Marcel shrugged. "It doesn't look good for any Jews that lived in Marseille, or for that matter, for anyone who spoke out against the Nazis, including the clergy."

"Hitler is a madman!" Paulette exclaimed. "Johann said that he was dragging the whole country down with him."

Marcel raised his eyebrows, looked at Paulette, and said, "That may be true, but he didn't come to power without the support of those people. They wanted to believe that all their problems...the depression itself...was being caused by outside forces, and their scapegoats were the Jews. They embraced Hitler as their savior. Now they've got to live with it...so don't start feeling sorry for any Germans." He leaned back in his chair and stretched his legs. "I hope that they all burn in hell."

"Yeah," J.P. said, "I wish I could have killed a few of them. Guy and Ira never did anything to harm them...those bastards."

Elizabeth looked at J.P., who was sitting next to her, but said nothing. *There were a lot worse things he could have said. They are bastards for what they've done to our country, and to our citizens*, she thought. She put her arm around him, mussed his hair, and gave him a kiss. She marveled at how much the three children had grown, especially J.P., who was now several inches taller than Raymond.

The room was somber for quite awhile, when a thought came to Marcel. He stood up quickly, clapped his hands, and said, "I just remembered that I left some things for you boys up in the attic, on the same day we all left for Foix."

"What did you bring us, Papa?" Raymond asked.

"I'll show you in a minute...just wait right here, and I'll go get it." Marcel ran up the stairs to the top floor, and a few minutes later came back down carrying a cloth bag. He sat down and put the bag on the floor, next to his chair. He reached down, pulled out a German officer's, high-brimmed hat, and laid it on the table. "A little souvenir from the War," he said, smiling.

Paulette stood up, as everyone looked intently at the hat, a symbol of the German occupation of Elne. She felt queasiness in her chest, and let out a deep breath. *I know that this can't be Johann's*, she told herself, but just seeing it reminded her of him.

J.P. picked it up, and then handed it to Raymond. "This is really neat. Where did you get this, Papa?"

"We raided a convoy that was going north...the day before we all left Elne."

Paulette felt lightheaded, and sat back down. She could feel the blood draining from her face. She put her elbows on the table, and rested her forehead on her fingertips. Elizabeth glanced over, and said, "Dear, are you feeling alright? You look so pale."

"I'll be O.K.," she replied, without looking up.

Raymond put the hat on his head, and then asked, "What other souvenirs did you get, Papa?"

"Well," Marcel took out a paper bag, and let the contents fall onto the table, "I have a bunch of these military insignias and medals...you children can make a whole scrapbook of these, when we get back to Marseille." He waited until the children had a chance to siphon through all the things on the table, and then said, "I've saved the best two things for last." First he brought out a medium size, red, Nazi flag, with a black *swastika* enclosed in a circle, in its center. "I got this from an officer's car, after it crashed into a tree." He reached down again, for the last time, and brought out a shiny, black holster, with a *Luger* inside. "And this is the prize of them all, which I got off that same captain...the one with the hat."

"Wow, this is great, Papa," Raymond and J.P. said in unison.

The children were laughing, and all excited, but Paulette didn't hear them. The last words she could hear, were "the captain", that Marcel seemed so proud of. She tried to take deep breaths, because she started feeling faint. In the distance, she vaguely heard a band playing a French march. The others heard it too, got up and walked out onto the balcony. As Raymond passed Paulette, he took the hat off, and put it on the table in front of her.

Paulette stared at the hat for several seconds, and then picked it up. She ran her forefinger around the top brim, and slowly turned it over. Her heart was beating as fast as she could remember. She finally forced herself to look inside. She gasped, as her left hand went up to her mouth. His initials were there, like that first night she had seen them...J.I.W. She looked down and closed her eyes. After a few minutes, she reached in the pocket of her dress, and pulled out a silver chain and medallion. *Oh, Johann! I remember that last night in your room, when you gave me this St. Christopher medal...to keep me safe, you said. How I wish now that you had kept it. I only knew you for a short time, hated everything your country stood for, but that night, when you first came to Elne, I could sense that you were different.*

Paulette examined the medal, kissed it, and then put it around her neck. *I never showed this to anyone...even Angelina. I'll wear it for myself now...it doesn't matter anymore. One day I'll join you in heaven, my love.* She sat there for several more minutes listening to the band playing, as it marched past her house toward the square. When she heard them begin to play "*La Marseillaise*", she stood up, walked onto the balcony towards her parents, put her arms around their shoulders, and with the whole family, joined in the singing of their French National Anthem.

EPILOGUE

On May 7, 1945, in the fortified city of Reims, in northern France, Col. General Alfred Jodl, of the German High Command, formally surrendered to the Allies. Lt. General Walter B. Smith, Eisenhower's chief of staff, accepted the unconditional surrender.

Four months later, September 2, 1945, aboard the battleship *Missouri* in Tokyo Bay, General Yoshijiro Umeza of the Japanese army, formally surrendered to General of the Army Douglas MacArthur, thus ending World War II and one of the bloodiest periods in history.

Marshall Henri Phillippe Petain stood trial in France, in 1945, for his role as head of the *Vichy* government, and for treason. He was found guilty, deprived of all his honors, and was sentenced to death. Charles de Gaulle commuted the sentence to life imprisonment, and he died on the island *Ile d' Yeu* at the age of 95.

Pierre Laval was found in Spain at the end of the War, and brought back to France to stand trial for treason. He was found guilty of collaboration with the enemy and plotting against his fellow Frenchmen. He was sentenced to death, in 1945, and on the day of his execution, swallowed poison in a suicide attempt, but was revived and shot by a firing squad.

After the War, Paul, Elizabeth, and Paulette Courty remained in Elne. Elizabeth lived to be 72 years old and died in 1958. Paul lived to be 82 years old and died in 1960.

Paulette helped her parents until their deaths, and remained in the same house she had always lived in, until she died in August, 2003, at the age of 94. This author had the privilege of visiting this lovely lady, in October, 1997, in Elne. She was surrounded by the antiques she had collected over a lifetime. She never married.

The Pontier family moved back to Marseille, where Marcel resumed his dental practice and Angelina worked for a short time as a pharmacist. In June 1998, Angelina passed away at the age of 92. Marcel died six months later, in January, 1999...he was 99 years old. Elizabeth, Paul, Angelina, Marcel, and Paulette, are all buried at the oldest cemetery in the village of Elne.

Raymond Pontier lives in Marseille with his wife, France, and their three children. He is an emergency room physician.

Jean-Pierre Pontier lives in Florida with his wife, Sylviane. He is an orthodontist, and was a professor at the University of Pittsburg School of Dentistry. As a young man, he served in the French Foreign Legion.

Babette (Pontier) Mairet is a widow and lives in Marseille. She and her husband, Christian, had one son. She teaches elementary school.

Madeline (Pontier) Bourdeaux lives in Marseille with her husband, Jacques, and has two children. With a PhD in physics, she teaches at the University of Marseille Medical School.

ACKNOWLEDGEMENTS

A book of this magnitude would not have been possible if I hadn't received the input, encouragement, and technical help from a number of people, including my Miami Beach High School English teacher, Mr. L. Brian Byrd. A special thanks to Jean-Pierre Pontier, for providing me with all the information I requested, in order to write about his family, and to his wife Sylviane, who was my French translation expert.

I could rely on Suzanne Fleuchaus, who grew up in Stuttgart, for any questions relating to Germany, and the language itself.

Bruce Thompson, a former agent with the Office of Special Investigations (OSI), while serving in the United States Air Force for 24 years, was my expert on German amphibian war tactics.

Computers seem to have a mind of their own, and when mine gave me problems, I could always call on my computer guru, John Nero, to get me back on track. I wrote my first play longhand, and then typed it on an electric typewriter. Today, I couldn't fathom going back to that system again, so thanks John for putting up with my computer ineptness.

Two good friends, Sam Cromartie, an author of three novels, and Anne Lichtigman, a former writer and editor for McGraw-Hill's "Medical World News", were kind enough to critique this work for me. Thank you for your expertise, all the hours you put into reading it, and on making those wonderful suggestions for my manuscript.

Thanks also to Joseph Bringe, the mayor of Elne, who answered all my questions concerning the Nazi occupation, from 1942-1944. Without his help, I would not have had the necessary information to accurately portray the events of the time, in this beautiful village of Elne.

For steering us in the right directions, while visiting your lovely villa in Provence, thank you Elizabeth and Philippe Lambert. It opened a whole new world for me to write about.

Thank you, Hugh Garner, for furnishing me with the historical and personal information I needed, on the Principality of Andorra. For one of the smallest countries in Europe, it surely did its part in saving countless lives during the scourge of Nazism.

I'm much obliged to Taylor Marois, stepping up at the last minute, for helping transfer my unskilled art ideas, for the cover of this book, to paper. This gave the Production Team at AuthorHouse the start that they needed to design the final product.

To all these people listed above, my sincere gratitude and appreciation for your contributions.

THE AUTHOR

A retired optometric physician, Indianer grew up in Miami Beach, Florida and attended the University of Alabama and Southern College of Optometry. He served as an Air Force Bio-Medical Services Officer for three years, before opening his practice in Daytona Beach, Florida. A long time lecturer on eye-related subjects, he has also lectured on International Terrorism for the past 15 years. An avid golfer, skier, and tennis player, he has traveled world-wide with his family and friends enjoying his other hobby, photography. He has written two plays, ∑AMMY, and the drama *A BRIDGE TO ELNE*, on which this novel is based. He and his wife have two daughters and four grandchildren.

Printed in the United Kingdom
by Lightning Source UK Ltd.
124384UK00001B/202/A